Praise for *The Personal Assistant*

"*The Personal Assistant* shows the consequences of living in an online world where nothing is as it seems, turning the glamour of an Insta-worthy life into a nightmare. Unputdownable and impossible to forget."

—Julie Clark, *New York Times* **bestselling author of** *The Last Flight*

"I never knew who to trust. A masterful novel that I read in an afternoon. I will be recommending to everyone."

—Sally Hepworth, *New York Times* **bestselling author of** *The Younger Wife*

"Master storyteller Kimberly Belle weaves an unforgettable tale of subterfuge and betrayal that will leave you wanting more. I loved it!"

—Liv Constantine, bestselling author of *The Last Mrs. Parrish*

"A missing assistant to an Instagram influencer, a mysterious dead body, and a nesting box of family secrets drive this cat-and-mouse thriller to a deliciously unexpected finale. A great page-turning read!"

—Wendy Walker, bestselling author of *Don't Look for Me*

"A gripping, propulsive page-turner packed with never-saw-that-coming shocks and surprises, with a plot that asks, *How much is too much to give away about ourselves?*"

—Kate White, *New York Times* **bestselling author of** *The Second Husband*

"*The Personal Assistant* is Belle at her best. A chilling, fast-paced read. I loved it!"

—Kaira Rouda, *USA TODAY* **bestselling author of** *The Next Wife*

"Smart, timely, and humming with suspense—you won't be able to stop reading this killer novel until you reach the final jaw-dropping page."

—Heather Gudenkauf, *New York Times* **bestselling author of** *The Overnight Guest*

Also by Kimberly Belle

The Last Breath

The Ones We Trust

The Marriage Lie

Three Days Missing

Dear Wife

Stranger in the Lake

My Darling Husband

THE PERSONAL ASSISTANT

KIMBERLY BELLE

PARK
ROW
BOOKS

PARK™
ROW
BOOKS™

ISBN-13: 978-0-7783-3394-4

The Personal Assistant

First published in 2022. This edition published in 2022.
Copyright © 2022 by Kimberly S. Belle Books, LLC

Park Row Books
22 Adelaide St. West, 41st Floor
Toronto, Ontario M5H 4E3, Canada
ParkRowBooks.com
BookClubbish.com

Printed in U.S.A.

For Claudia, my absolute favorite aunt.

THE PERSONAL ASSISTANT

PROLOGUE

This is how it begins, flying down a country road. Windows down, music blaring. An old Journey classic, one she knew by heart. She belted the lyrics into the warm wind.

The road she was flying down was like all the others in this godforsaken chunk of southern Georgia, two faded lanes slicing through endless pecan fields, and she took the curves faster than she should. Running with the devil, her father would say if he were here, but it was the perfect fall day and her hair was flying and the guitar riff made her think of her brother, who she missed like crazy. She wondered if he was even alive out there on the west coast, and, if so, how a Southern boy like him could survive in all that constant rain and gloomy green.

Up ahead, a truck lurched out of the field, lugging a belly piled high with nuts on the way to the factory. It turned her way, engine puffing up twin clouds of exhaust as it lumbered straight at her, its wide girth eating up the asphalt. She gripped the wheel, her right tires hugging the shoulder. This country road wasn't big enough for them both.

The truck driver didn't slow. Didn't move over, either, though he lifted a hand in a friendly wave. There wasn't much she agreed about with her father these days, but he was right about the pecan farmers. They already owned enough of this county, the least they could do was share the damn road.

Suddenly, they were side by side. The trash bag she'd taped over the busted back window flapped and pulled, then blew off entirely when the truck missed her by a hair, flooding the car with stinky exhaust. He blew past and she blew out a big breath, her fingers relaxing on the wheel just long enough for the back tire to slip off the asphalt. It spun in the shoulder for a second or two, then exploded with a spectacular pop.

The Honda lurched to a messy stop, dumping yesterday's Big Gulp into her lap. She ignored the mess because she had bigger problems. She didn't need to look to know her back tire lay in tattered ribbons across the road, or that the truck was long gone. The air reeked of burnt rubber and pecans.

Well, hell.

She couldn't afford a new tire. She couldn't even afford an old junky one from Wade up at the dump, who she still owed fifty bucks to for her last tire. The hotel where she worked was a good five miles from here, and it's not like her asshole boss offered sick days. You don't work, you don't get paid, it was as simple as that.

She rested her forehead on the wheel and thought through her options, but she didn't like any of them. Her father was no help. The last time she asked him for a loan, he called her a whore and a devil child, and she wasn't looking for a repeat scolding. She couldn't hitchhike, not in this getup—an up-to-there dress that could do double duty as a costume for slutty maid. Hitch-hiking was how girls like her got in trouble.

So…walk, then?

She groaned, lifting her feet from the floorboard where a slice of toe peeked through the sole of her battered flats. "So far I really, really hate this day."

She didn't hear the car sidle up alongside her until it was already there, motor purring in her ear. She lifted her head, looking into a window as black and smooth as a mirror. Her own face staring back.

With a whirr, it lowered to reveal a man. Dark hair, square chin, sharp cheekbones under shiny shades. Her very own knight in shining armor.

He whipped off the sunglasses and tossed them on the console. "Looks like you could use some help."

ONE

ALEX

I know the second I crack an eye that the day is going to be brutal. Hot and muggy, the kind of heat that gathers into thick clouds that turn violent later in the afternoon. I feel it before I am fully awake, the low pressure clanging in my temples.

Then again, that's probably just the tequila.

Pictures flash through my head, stop-start images from last night.

Me disco-dancing around the kitchen... AC pouring shot after shot... My husband, Patrick, watching with a grin.

Oh, God. AC. My social media assistant and operations assistant and every other assistant role you can imagine, my work wife and right-hand gal. Remorse creeps in as I roll to my side, breathing through a wave of nausea. I'm supposed to be the responsible one, the older and wiser boss who sets an example, not her drinking buddy. That last shot was a mistake.

No. The mistake was the half dozen that came before it, and the way I tossed them back one after the other, *boom boom boom*, like a sorority sister on a mission. I should have stopped after the first one, well before AC's face started turning fuzzy around the edges.

On the nightstand, two white Excedrin flank a sweaty bottle of water. Patrick, my hero. With a grateful groan, I drop them on my tongue and turn the bottle up, but at the movement or the sudden surge of liquid, my stomach flips and rolls. For a few hairy seconds, I wonder if I will keep them down.

I stare at the ceiling and talk my stomach off the ledge, consoling myself with the reason I was celebrating in the first place.

One million followers.

Even serious, stoic Patrick had to blink twice when I shoved my phone in his face. His eyes bulged at the digits atop my Instagram page, a number that after so many months refusing to budge finally flipped into surreal territory.

The thought sets off a chirrup in my chest, a familiar fizzle and pop behind my breastbone.

One million freaking followers, and they're following *me*. @ UnapologeticallyAlex.

"I don't get it," Patrick said the first time my fame eclipsed his, when a fan handed him her phone and asked for a picture with *me*. "What are you selling? Some mantra about staying positive in a house with two hormonal girl-monsters? A motivational meme you pilfered from the internet and slapped your logo on? Don't take this the wrong way, but why is that woman grinning like she just met Beyonce?"

Patrick doesn't understand the charm of Unapologetically Alex because he's a numbers guy, a self-made moneyman who dishes financial strategies on the nightly news. He covers topics like how to become a millionaire before the age of twenty-two. How to cultivate real wealth and lifelong financial freedom. How to never work for anyone but yourself ever again. For all my husband's brilliance, the world of Insta-influencers is as real to him as the tooth fairy. It's like trying to explain the appeal of cats to a dog person.

The only thing Patrick understands about my job is the financials. How for every ten thousand followers I have, I can demand a higher price for sponsored content; how when those followers are engaged—watching my videos, liking my posts and commenting—I can demand even more. And I'm not going to lie. After years of raising two girls on my own, without a penny or pat on the back from their father, the money is the best part.

But that night in the restaurant after my fangirl left, I did my best to explain the rest.

"She's grinning because I'm *not* a rock star. I am her cheerleader, the person who believes more in her than she believes in herself. I am the woman she could be if she just learned to *live unapologetically*." It's my slogan, the one I close out every post and video with. "*That's* why she's so excited, because she's me. I'm her. We are the same person."

"She's you." Patrick looked over and sure enough there she was, typing away happily on her phone, uploading the picture he'd just taken of us. "She doesn't look anything like you."

"It's not about looks but how I make her feel. She and all the millions of women just like her are sick of scrolling Instagram and feeling shitty about themselves as a result. Why do women insist on comparing ourselves to people we don't know and will likely never meet? When did external validation become a prerequisite for our inner peace? Doubts, stresses, anxieties, expectations, comparisons. Let all that shit go. Live your own life, be your own person. Show the world your authentic, badass self and the rest will come. You are perfect as you are."

It's the speech I've used many times on panels and interviews to explain the success of Unapologetically Alex—a persona I fell into almost by chance. It all started with a silly post that went viral, but in the comments and DMs I noticed a theme: a very loud, very vocal tribe of women who are sick of stuffing themselves into the mold other people created for them. The perfect mother, the perfect housewife, the perfect hostess and friend and lover. What even are those things, anyway? And why would we let anyone else define how we want to live our own lives? But for whatever reason, they latched on to that post and appointed me their de facto leader. After that, all I had to do was hang on to that crown.

A billion users. A hundred million images uploaded a day. After that first, viral post, I wanted a piece of the Instagram pie.

But cranking out a constant stream of content is exhausting, and followers and likes don't necessarily equal money in the bank. It's why I hired AC, to take over some of my day-to-day tasks and free up my time so I can translate my platform into actual cash. A podcast series, sponsorships that pay with checks instead of boxes of merchandise that clog up my garage, a kick-ass book proposal that's about to go to auction—these are just a few of the projects in the pipeline.

As if my thoughts have conjured him, Patrick appears in the bedroom, a steaming mug and a plate in his hands. "Morning, sunshine." He flashes a smile. "I figured you might be having a rough go of it."

I groan and push myself to a sit. "Why didn't you stop me after the second shot? You know how tequila makes me crotchety."

"Woman, I tried. I told you about that time in Tulum when you drove your bike into the ocean and spent the entire next day hanging over an eco-toilet. Or when you fell headfirst into the bushes outside Lasky Steakhouse, and I had to drag you out by your ankles. I even poured the bottle down the sink, but you made AC go out and get another. You seriously don't remember any of this?"

I wince, shaking my head, and it thuds in response. "Please tell me I was passed out by the time she came back."

"Uh, no, you were not passed out. You were screaming about belly shots."

"You're lying."

He hands me the mug, then reaches past me for a button on the wall. The motor hums and tugs the shades upward, filling the bedroom with bright light.

"Sadly, no. There were no belly shots, but not for lack of trying. Though I will say, that image of you draped across the kitchen island in your underwear, screaming for AC to—and I quote—'pour the freakin' tequila in my belly button so my smokin' hot husband can suck it out' will stay with me until the end of time." He lifts my white tank to reveal my stomach, where the skin is still sticky. "Very little liquid actually made it into your belly button. AC was laughing too hard."

I plunk the mug on the nightstand and cover my face with both hands, discovering the remnants of yesterday's mascara in tiny beads smeared down my cheeks. "No. No no no no no. Tell me I did not do that. And tell me the girls didn't hear."

My twins from my first marriage, Gigi and Penelope, whose rooms are at the top of the stairs, are twelve going on twenty-five. An age where they are all raging hormones and shitty attitudes and mortified by my very existence. They tell me this with slamming doors and rolling eyeballs, because otherwise they would have to actually talk to me, their mother, who is too loud, too silly and weird and embarrassing—mostly the last one. There's nothing quite as savage as a preteen's ridicule. It leaves a mark, one that lingers for a very long time.

Patrick sinks onto the edge of the bed, sliding the plate onto my outstretched legs. He picks up a triangle of toast and presses it to my lips. "Here. The bread will soak up some of the booze."

"The girls, Patrick."

He dips a meaningful gaze to my plate—a bite for an answer. Good God, I love this man. Solid and stable and endlessly good-natured, an excellent protector and stepfather to my two girls. The kind of man who is the polar opposite of their dead-beat father.

And Patrick has always been so generous, sharing this house and his bank account with me and the twins, never treating it as *his* money but *ours*. His financial advice segment at WXBA is another way he gives back, his contribution to the city in the form of investment tips and money tricks in language anybody can understand. Atlanta's very own money guru.

I nibble off a corner of the bread, and it's gone soggy in the middle from the butter, but he used the good kind, the organic one with sea salt. When my stomach doesn't revolt, I follow it up with another.

"This is delicious, thank you."

"You're welcome. And judging by the side-eyes the girls gave me this morning, I'm guessing they heard most of it, though I did give them a stern talking-to in the car on the dangers of binge drinking. I've never seen them so excited to get to school."

The thought of that awkward twenty-three-minute drive un-ravels something in my chest. Patrick adores taking the girls to school. It's one of the few times he gets them all to himself, and they tell their stepfather things they would never in a million years tell me, their own mother. It's good for him to get some special time with them, eye rolls and all.

My phone buzzes on the nightstand, and we both ignore it.

"Thank you for being the responsible one, and for taking such good care of me. But mostly, thank you for not fussing." I reach up to cup his cheek with my free hand.

"Last night you told me if I fussed, I could forget about get-ting another blow job. Ever. For the rest of my life. No way I'm risking that."

I laugh. "Even when drunk off my ass, I know what makes Patrick Hutchinson tick, and guess what? It's not money."

"Don't tell anyone. The truth would ruin me."

"Your secret's safe with me."

We are quiet for the span of three breaths, a shared moment of complicity.

His hand skims up my leg, making the skin of my thigh tingle. "How's the head?"

I test it with a little shake. "Better."

"The stomach?"

I drop the last bite of toast onto the plate, and Patrick moves it to the nightstand, his gaze never leaving mine. The fingertips of his other hand hit the fabric of my pajama shorts and keep going. Six years with this man, and he can still do this to me—melt me with a look, heal my hangovers with a kiss. I wrap my arm around his neck and pull his face to mine, so handsome it makes my heart ache.

On the nightstand, my phone buzzes again and again, a solid stream of messages and notifications, reminding me of the million things on the agenda for today, the meetings and the strategizing and the twins' late-afternoon soccer game halfway to Tennessee. I let all that shit go and feel my husband's warm, willing body on top of mine. His strong hands, having their way with me.

His lips freeze halfway across my collarbone, and he glances at the screen, lit up with an avalanche of incoming notifications. Patrick spends a lot of time in a newsroom. He witnesses every crazy storm and school shooting. Of *course* he has to look.

"Oh." He lifts my phone from the nightstand. *"Oh."*

"Oh, what?"

"Just some trolls." He shakes his head, replaces the phone. "Really angry ones."

Last week a few trolls were after me because of the casual mention of the fact I have a house cleaner, and the week before that the jeans I was wearing weren't earth-friendly enough, and before that an eagle-eyed follower identified the champagne I was sipping as Ruinart instead of some cheap prosecco. I've been in this business long enough to have learned to ignore the haters. And I do. Mostly.

I think about what they could possibly be objecting to this time, posts and comments I've made in the past few days. I shuffle through them in my mind, but it could be any one of a million things. Trolls, internet warriors, keyboard crusaders, whatever you want to call them—they're *always* angry about something.

I pick up the phone, and the notifications roll by faster than I can read them, an endless stream of vitriol.

Also, these aren't trolls. These are handles I recognize, ones I interact with all the time. I know the emojis they favor and the superlatives they throw around in my comment sections. *Amazing. Obsessed. Thank youuuuu.* These are women normally gushing with gratitude, who share my posts and DM me like we're old friends. Now they have nothing but ugliness, pummeling me with hateful words that sear themselves onto my skin like a cattle brand.

I push Patrick off and lurch to a sit, trying to make sense of the storm rolling across my cell phone screen.

And that's when it happens—the toast making a reappearance, the tequila returning for revenge. I toss my phone and the covers and sprint to the bathroom.

> **@Patriciainpa** Ummm @rachel76 did you see this latest post? Am I the only one who feels hoodwinked?

> **@rachel76** I see it, and no, you're not the only one. WTF is wrong with this woman? Unfollowing.

> **@Patriciainpa** I'm still following but only to see what horrible things come out of her mouth next. If nothing else this thing with @unapologeticallyalex is gonna be hella entertaining.

@misterfluffles @rachel76 @patriciainpa I've been telling you all along this bitch is not what she seems, and neither for that matter is her husband. Do y'all believe me now?

TWO

I'm brushing my teeth when Patrick comes into the bathroom, my cell phone clutched in a fist.

"Did you find it?" I say around a mouthful of foam. All the phones in this house have the same passcode—a rule Patrick and I insisted on when the twins got theirs—and I assume that's what he's been doing in the bedroom all this time, searching for the source of the blast. The post that sometime during my tequila-infused slumber turned into ground zero.

"Found it." Patrick's gaze flits to mine in the glass. His shirt hangs loose from where I pulled it out of his pants, his hair still mussed from my fingers. But the look on his face sets off a sinking sensation in my gut. "It's the one you uploaded last night."

I flip on the water, spit into the stream, use it to rinse out my mouth. "I didn't post anything last night."

The words come automatically, because it's another rule. I

don't upload anything before AC double-and triple-checks for typos, and I definitely don't post when I'm drinking. An iffy word choice, a misinterpreted sentiment—you never know what people will latch on to and blow up big enough to knock you off your perch. That's the thing about internet pedestals, they're shaky. I've seen too many other influencers crash and burn.

"I didn't post." I say the words, but my skin goes hot with foreboding.

"According to the fifteen thousand notifications and counting, you posted."

My molars snap shut because fifteen thousand. It's a number that any other morning would make me merry as a rat, whacking away at the endorphin lever. Fifteen thousand is a *lot*.

I stare at him in the mirror, trying not to notice how his mouth looks pinched. "How many likes?" Ratio is important. When the comments outnumber the likes, it means there could be a problem.

"Only a couple hundred." Patrick winces, because he knows what it means, too. "Not all the comments are bad, FYI. Some of your followers are actually sticking up for you."

It's easier for someone like Patrick, whose entire brand is built around teaching people how to find financial freedom. The trolls generally leave Patrick alone. What person in their right mind could possibly object to having more money?

"Oh my God, just tell me!"

"Okay, so you know that actress in that show the girls are always talking about, the one about some boarding school for rich kids in France?" Patrick steps closer, reaching past me to turn off the water. "Dark hair, big lips, fake British accent?"

Something screeches through my mind like a bad memory, one that flicks away before I can grab hold.

"Krissie Kelly, the one I can't stand? That one?"

While it's true I'm not a fan, I didn't post about Krissie. And even if I did—which I definitely *didn't*—I'd know better than to say what I *really* think.

But my heart taps double time because I was talking about her just yesterday. Penelope and I got into an argument about it, because she worships Krissie Kelly.

He slides a thumb up my phone screen. "Apparently, she posted a video from some friend's birthday party and—"

"It wasn't just some friend, it was her *best* friend, who also happens to be a porn star, and that video was like an episode of *Girls Gone Wild*. Booze everywhere, which, okay, fine, I'm one to talk, I get that. But she also didn't bother to hide the powder and pills on every horizontal surface or the threesome taking place in the corner. This is not someone we want our daughters to be looking up to, Patrick. She's a bad influence."

He blinks at me in surprise. "That's pretty much word for word what you said when you reposted it."

"I reposted her video?" He nods, and the knot between my shoulder blades loosens, just a tad. "Okay. I can spin that. I'm a mother. I'm speaking up for impressionable children everywhere. That'll work, right?"

"Maybe, but it's the words in your caption that people seem to be latching on to. Three very long paragraphs calling her an attention-seeking slut—"

"I called her a *slut*?"

He makes a face. "It gets worse. You also said—and I quote—'Somebody please tell me what's so great about Krissie Kelly. She can't act, she's ass-ugly and she's got the brains of a dodo bird, and the only talent that is even remotely relevant is her willingness to hang her bare ass out for all the world to see. Somebody get that girl a GED and some self-esteem, and while you're at it maybe a nose job because the one she's got isn't doing her any favors. Can we please stop worshipping this talentless train wreck? Eyes wide open, people. Krissie Kelly is—'"

"*No.*"

"'—a two-bit whore.'"

For a long moment, I can't speak. I don't know what to say. Krissie Kelly *is* a train wreck, which I might not find so offensive if my girls weren't so obsessed with the former Disney star, and though I may have said those words in the privacy of my own home—I've thought them plenty of times—there's not enough tequila in the world to make me upload a post that damning.

"Oh my God. Oh my *God*." I toss my toothbrush into the sink and whirl around, snatching my phone from my husband's fingers and navigating to my profile, and there it is. The reposted video with the scathing caption, just like Patrick reported. It's as awful as he said. I tap the link for insights—likes, comments, shares and reach—and my fingers clamp around the phone. "A hundred and seventy-five *thousand* views?"

I stare at my screen in disbelief. A hundred and seventy-five thousand people saw my post, and almost half of them aren't even following me. "Oh, no. No no no no no. This can't be happening."

Patrick doesn't respond, because he knows that sometime in the middle of the night, while I was sleeping off the tequila, I went and did that thing millions of people spend countless hours brainstorming and concocting and scheming to do but almost no one ever achieves. A feat as elusive as a unicorn, as magical as pixie dust and fairy wings.

I've gone viral.

At the top of my screen, the notifications scroll by at a blinding pace, but I catch enough to get the gist. People are pissed. Their comments are brutal. If there was anything left in my stomach, I'd throw it up.

"This is bad, Patrick. This is really, really bad."

"So take it down."

I tap the three dots at the top right of the post for the pull-down menu, but my finger hovers over Delete. "Julia Saccone took her post down, the one where she skewered the recipes in another food blogger's cookbook, and it blew up in her face. The trolls got ahold of it and posted the video to YouTube. There were screenshots and memes. There were Facebook groups plotting her demise. It turned into this whole big thing."

"For what was essentially a book review? That's so stupid."

"I agree, but that's not the point. The point is if the trolls get there first, if they slap a target on your back, rationality no longer applies."

"Just take it down. You can worry about the cleanup later."

He's right. I delete the post, then lift the phone to my face. "Hey, Siri, call AC."

Any other morning, I'd have heard her tires rolling through the pea gravel by now, or caught a glimpse of her dark head bobbing through the bathroom bay window as she navigates the stepping-stones to the carriage house at the end of the backyard. I press the phone to my ear and will her to appear, but except for a couple of squirrels nicking the birdseed from the feeder, the backyard is empty. After four rings, the call flips me to voice mail.

"Mayday, mayday. Call me the second you get this, will you? All hell is breaking loose, and I need you."

I do *need* her, despite what Patrick thinks of my personal assistant. He's never been a big fan of AC, though he also can't ever seem to explain why, at least not in concrete terms. She's too weird, too nosy, in the house far too often, no matter how many times I explain to him that it's because she works *in our house*. Secretly, I think it's not her but the job that he doesn't love, the way it keeps me constantly connected to my phone, the way I'm constantly whipping it out to document every second of our private lives.

I follow up my voice mail with a text, all caps and excessive punctuation: SOS CALL ME ASAP!!!!!!

I wait for the message to land on her phone, for the typing bubbles to appear right before a text ordering me to sit tight, take a breath and not do a thing until she gets here. I picture her battling rush-hour traffic in her ancient Honda when the text dings her phone, wedged in the cup holder with our morning Starbucks, and I will her to look at the damn screen. The internet moves at warp speed, which means I need her here yesterday.

Patrick checks his watch, his expression reminding me that he's late to work. He came home after dropping off the girls to check on me, and now he's running more than an hour behind and on a Thursday—the day of his weekly segment.

I wave a hand in his direction. "I love you for looking after me, but go. You're already way late."

"Just…don't do anything rash, okay? And maybe be careful what you say. The last thing we need is some angry idiot to show up here, looking for a fight."

It's one of the stickier points between me and my husband, that Unapologetically Alex isn't just about me, but our whole family. Patrick and the twins have starring roles in my posts, too, as does our home. The 1926 stone-and-stucco rambler that Patrick owned when we met, with original wood floors and carved crown molding and a kitchen that was once featured on the cover of *Southern Living*. Any crazy person with Google and a gun could find the place with very little effort.

But this is a worry for later, because it's coming up on eight thirty and I'm running out of time. I push up on my tippy-toes and give my husband a lightning kiss. "Love you. Mean it."

And then I'm off before he can say it back, racing through the bedroom for the stairs.

In my carriage house office, I collapse on the chair at the vintage farm table AC and I use as a desk. Lemon-tinged light filters through the windows behind me, drenching the room with sunlight that won't last long. Already the air outside is turning thick and soupy, heavy with the scent of cut grass and the coming rain. I peel open my laptop and wake the screen with a fingertip.

I sit in stunned silence while the numbers on the dock icons climb and climb. I watch them tick up up up, and my skin goes hot and clammy. How? The post went up after midnight, an hour when normal people would have been asleep. Are my followers insomniacs? Are they vampires? How can there already be so many?

My email app maxes out in the four figures, which is bad news because it means the drama isn't confined to Instagram. It means people are so fired up that they went to the trouble to surf my website, dig around until they found my email address in the tiny letters at the bottom of the contact form and pound out their frustrations in lengthy, shouty paragraphs.

I leave the in-box for later and click on my browser instead, cruising through the social tabs pinned to the top. Instagram, Facebook, Twitter, Pinterest.

My eyes bulge at the volume of notifications…more than I could respond to in a month, rolling in faster than I can scrub them from my screen. Even my stodgy old LinkedIn is getting slammed. Too many offensive comments to delete, the threats too specific and tangible to ignore. I would need an army of interns to scroll through them all.

I pick up my phone and pound out another text to AC.

Are you on your way? Bc help hurry mayday!!

It lands on her phone, delivered but unread. I stare at the letters and will them to change, willing my phone to buzz in my fingers. AC calling back, telling me she knows just what to do. It's one of the reasons I hired her, because she's a millennial and when it comes to social media she *always* knows what to do. I could have never reached a million followers without her help.

My cell phone screen goes dark, then black. I drop it on the desk and turn back to my laptop with a groan.

Already there are screenshots of my post blanketing every social media platform. Instagram, Twitter, Facebook. I see them, and my skin itches with a déjà vu type of tingling, because every word feels familiar. I have no memory of posting them, but then again, my memory of last night has more than a few black holes.

Surely, *surely* I didn't.

A gust of hot wind rattles the windowpanes, followed by shoes crunching on the gravel outside, and I pop to my feet, thinking, *AC. That must be AC.*

I rush down the stairs, pulling up short at the threshold because it's not AC but Shannon Tuttle, the neighbor's nanny and my former intern. Shannon is a junior at Georgia State, majoring in digital marketing. She says TikTok, not Instagram, is where it's at—but then again, she's also twenty, and not exactly my demographic.

I toss her a wave but she's too busy scrolling on her phone to see.

The constant ding-ding-dinging from my laptop drags me back up the stairs, where I do another scroll through the comments clogging my screen. I tell myself trolls do this. They come to my page for a kind of drive-by entertainment, hurling vile threats they would never dream of saying out loud. That the veil of anonymity makes them brave, gives them an excuse to let their meanest impulses out to play.

@deaconsmom386 stfu you stupid bitch the only train wreck here is you

@sarahb34 wtf, this is so cringey. Why do you think you're better than everybody else bc your not fyi. Krissie is sixteen your the one who needs therapy.

@emmabugg99 What happened to positivity? To everybody being worthy the way they are? Way to be tone deaf and come across like the judgmental, righteous-sounding bully you are. Unfollowed.

@alvisdtl Yikes, girl, that's some serious shade 🙁 I used to love your Instagram but now you're so icky. I'm embarrassed I ever followed you.

@halfmoonyogi3 I can't stand women like you. Your entire platform is about being positive and now look. Slut shaming a young girl because she's not afraid of her sexuality, making fun of her appearance. Look in the mirror, lady. Your no prize

@misterfluffles I hated this bitch before it was cool 😄 It's about time people are finding out she's full of shit

@readerroger_1 if I meet you in an alley you will definitely get fukked 😈😈😈😈😈

@margswithsalt tell the twins I'm bringing them a rope so they can hang themselves for having such an awful mother

And with that, I slam my laptop closed.

THREE

"Hey, Alex?" Shannon's voice fills the carriage house air. "Don't panic, but I think you were hacked."

Hacked. That's it, maybe I've been *hacked*. What a relief it would be to think that, if only those words about Krissie didn't sound suspiciously like my own. I've said them all at some point, maybe not in that exact order, maybe not quite that frank, but there's nothing there I haven't secretly thought. How awesome would it be to honestly say I've been hacked.

Shannon clomps up the carriage house steps, and I sit motionless at the desk, palms pressed flat to my closed laptop, a steady drumline beating in my chest hard enough to rattle my ribs. *Tell the twins I'm bringing them a rope so they can hang themselves.* That comment crossed a line, and it's not the only one. There were dozens and dozens more just like it.

"Alex, did you hear me?" Shannon's head pokes through the

metal railing, her phone clutched in a fist. "Somebody tore into Krissie Kelly on your page. You know Krissie, the former Disney star turned—"

"—talentless train wreck, I know."

"I was going to say reality show wannabe, but okay. I take it you've seen your Instagram."

I nod. "Yes, along with everybody else on the planet."

She winces, Converse squeaking on the hardwood. She stops at the console on the far wall, flipping the switch on my Nespresso machine. "You seem awfully calm about it. Are you in shock? Are you on Xanax?"

Shannon is in her typical nanny attire—denim cutoffs under a roomy button-down, smeared with whatever she fed the kids for breakfast, something sticky and purple like grape jelly. Her hair is pulled back in a messy ponytail, all but a few well-placed tendrils that curl over her unlined forehead. She's young and effortlessly adorable; meanwhile, I'm still in the clothes I slept in, my face smeared with last night's makeup.

I look down at the tank top and stretchy shorts I don't remember putting on and think about what else I might have missed in my tequila-induced fog. How did I go from happy-dancing around the kitchen to venting about a girl I don't know and will likely never meet? What happened to make me lash out?

"I'm not calm. I'm the opposite of calm. Have you seen what they're saying in the comment threads?"

Shannon nods, handing me the first cup even though caffeine is the last thing I need, then punches the button for another. "I saw. The trolls are being way harsh as usual."

"Honestly I… I don't know what happened. I hit a million followers last night, so AC and I whipped out the tequila. This morning I woke up to a five-alarm fire."

"Like I said, you were hacked."

"That's just it, Shannon. That post is pretty much word for word of what's come out of my mouth at some point. I don't know how it couldn't have come from me. Krissie *is* a train wreck. She *doesn't* have any discernible talent to justify her level of fame, unless you count lifting her shirt for every camera pointed her way. And she's so young. Like, where are her parents? It's infuriating because the twins worship her. Penelope wants to be just like her one day."

"What—famous and slutty?"

I laugh despite myself, my hungover cheeks stiff from dehydration, but this conversation is getting me all worked up again, that same indignant fury, like a bitter pill on my tongue. All those filters my girls use to make themselves look like cartoon porn stars, all the booty shorts and crop tops they beg for at the mall. Krissie is not the only bad influence out there, but she's one of the bigger ones. I can't be the only mother saying these things.

But Penelope wasn't having it. When I laid in on her favorite celebrity during dinner, she called me old-fashioned and out of touch. She said I didn't understand her entire generation, and that if I believed even half the stuff I post on my feed, I wouldn't be so judgmental. I can read between the lines. My daughter might not have actually used the word, but she was calling me a hypocrite.

Shannon swipes her cup from the machine and sinks onto AC's chair. "For what it's worth, I still have a hard time believing drunk you would make that kind of fumble. You're too good at this. Even plastered off your ass, you'd know what a post like that would do to you."

I groan, scrubbing my eyes with both hands. "Ugh, I love that you believe that."

She peels open AC's laptop, sitting on the desk in front of her. "I hope you're reporting these trolls."

Before AC came along, it was Shannon's laptop, Shannon's spot at the desk. She sat in that chair for much of last semester, interviewing me for her junior project, a deep dive into how social media influencers are transforming the market. She's smart and she's funny, and I would have offered her the job of personal assistant in a heartbeat if I thought for a second she would have accepted. School and her nanny position aside, Shannon doesn't have the time or the desire to be second in command. She's gunning for my job.

"It's like a game of Whack-a-Mole out there. And you haven't even seen the half of it. There's also my other socials, my inbox, the hundreds of DMs I haven't even looked at yet because it's like sticking my head into a live volcano."

"Yeah, but you can't ignore them, either. What if one of those nutbags shows up at your front door?"

Now she sounds like Patrick.

And maybe it's a false sense of security, but I've always felt safe here. We live in a gated community. The carriage house is tucked at the very back of our fenced-in lot, surrounded on all sides by private yards. It features windows almost as big as the walls. From where I sit, I can see the entire backyard, a straight shot between me and the house. I never bother locking the doors because I'd see anyone coming from a mile away.

"Can you please report the worst of them? I can't bear to look." I drop my face in my hands with a groan. "Tequila is the devil."

Shannon laughs, then spends a few minutes clicking around. "Correct me if I'm wrong, but shouldn't your personal assistant be doing this?"

I check the messages on my cell, searching for a response from AC. Still nothing, though plenty of others are checking in. Friends, neighbors, a few other influencers, my literary agent. I turn off the screen without reading any of them. That bitter pill, the one that was sitting on my tongue earlier, turns into a soggy lump that trickles down my throat.

"Still sleeping off her hangover, I guess. She hasn't checked in."

She glances up with a frown. "Don't you find that strange?"

"Find what strange?"

"That AC is MIA right now, the morning after all hell breaks loose on your page."

AC. It's not the first time her name comes spinning through my head, especially since it's eleven a.m. and she's still a no-show. The laptops, my phone and hers, those are the only devices that can post to my socials. AC has all my log-ins. No one else, not even Patrick, has access.

"You're just saying that because you don't like her," I say.

"That's because she's weird as shit. Always watching, always taking everything in. It's creepy."

"So she's observant. That's what makes her good at her job."

"It's more than just observant. It's like… I don't know, like she's trying to memorize everything about you so she can copy it. The way you dress, the way you talk and walk. Last week I caught her in the backyard, reciting one of your Reels. I thought it was you at first, her voice was so similar."

"Okay, that's…that *is* weird. But AC adores this job. She told me that. She used that word—*adores*—even though the hours are long and the salary is trash and she could earn more pretty much anywhere else. Why blow up a job that she loves?"

"Maybe something happened to change her mind."

"Something like what?"

Shannon shrugs and goes back to her laptop, and I think through last night's timeline in my head. That magical moment when I hit a million followers, the giddiness that had me popping bottle after bottle. Things get fuzzy sometime after dinner, after the girls disappeared to their rooms, and it occurs to me I have no idea what time AC left. I don't even remember going upstairs.

I shoot Patrick a quick text asking him about when AC left last night, then drop my cell back on the desk, thinking. Even if it was AC who posted, even if I *was* hacked, that doesn't erase those awful words or save me from the trolls currently piling on all of my socials.

I feel it then, the heavy, dark weight of this train, and my helplessness to stop it.

When I look up, Shannon is watching me. "Look, just… maybe talk to your husband."

"About?"

"About AC. Because he might have some insight, you know, into her motivations." She winces, closing the laptop. "Okay. I wasn't going to say anything, but I saw them last week when I was walking Wolf."

Wolf is the neighbors' family dog, a miniature Chihuahua whose tiny legs give out before he makes it to the end of the driveway. Shannon's boss, Danica, uses one of those ridiculous dog strollers for her weekend loop around the golf course, but Shannon would rather deal with his constant whining to be carried than be caught dead with a dog stroller.

But it's the words that came before the dog I'm focused on. "Saw them doing what?"

"Arguing. In the front yard, in the middle of the afternoon. They were standing by the big bushes near the gate, and Patrick was obviously pissed. I couldn't hear them, but they didn't even look over when Wolf started losing his shit. You know how he gets when he wants up."

"What day was this?"

"I don't know. Friday, maybe?"

I frown. It's odd that Patrick came home in the middle of a workday. He was here, and he didn't come to the carriage house to say hi. Clearly because he was too busy arguing with my personal assistant about something so momentous he didn't even notice a barking dog.

I think of his face in the kitchen last night, the parts of it I can remember. Patrick was quiet; he always goes quiet when AC is around. He hates the way she's always there when he gets home from work, how she knows things, personal things about us and the twins.

And sure, okay. He gets pissed when she leaves her empty dishes lying around or takes the last water bottle from the fridge, but this isn't that.

This was a screaming match in the middle of the day.

And neither of them mentioned it to me.

Shannon sighs. "Look, I'm sure it's nothing. I mean, so your husband's not a fan of your personal assistant, big deal. Not many people are. But if whatever they were arguing about upset her enough to... I don't know, do something harmful to you, then I thought you should know."

A surge of affection for this girl warms my frosty skin. "Thank you, Shannon. I really appreciate it."

"Good. And like I said, I'm sure it's nothing." She swipes her cup from the desk and carries it into the bathroom. She leaves the door open, but her back is to me as she flips on the water at the sink. "Oh my God, though, you should have seen your husband's face. I've never seen him look at anybody like that."

She laughs, but the sound has a forced casualness, like her words don't hold that much meaning even though we both know that they do.

My heart gives a heavy thud. "Like how?"

When she finds my gaze in the mirror, her smile has gone stiff. "Like he wanted to kill her."

When Patrick and I first met, no one thought we were right for each other, least of all me.

First of all, there was his age. He's older than me by a good seven years, pushing forty at the time, and had never been married, which my girlfriends and I agreed was never a good sign. Neither was his reputation for dating busty Brazilians, animated model types with a penchant for mink lashes and wrapping themselves in tiny strips of bright silk they thought qualified as a dress. He was the eternal bachelor while I was a struggling single mom of twin six-year-olds whose father hadn't paid a cent of alimony since they were two. We had literally nothing in common.

But he was a gentleman, I had to give him that. He saw me hustling from a restaurant to the valet stand and let me jump the line. "After you," he said, stepping aside.

I knew who he was, of course. I'd seen him plenty on the news and local magazine covers, but he was even more handsome in person. Taller, too. I had to tip my head all the way back just to look him in the eye.

"Oh, no. You were here first."

"Please don't take this the wrong way, but it looks like you need your car more."

I laughed, because he was right. We were in the middle of a moody fall, and what started out as an unseasonably warm day had taken a nosedive halfway through my salade Niçoise. All of a sudden, it was forty degrees and pouring icy rain, and my hair and sleeveless top had gotten drenched from the mad, twenty-yard dash. I hadn't thought to bring a coat or an umbrella, and my arms were crossed against a chest that for *sure* had sprouted headlights.

"Thanks." I handed my ticket to the valet with shivering fingers.

"I'm Patrick Hutchinson."

"I know," I said. "Your face is plastered on billboards all over town." Patrick standing between his fellow anchors, toothy smiles high above the downtown connector. Hard-hitting news and money advice, every weeknight at six p.m.

"Part of the job, unfortunately." He unwrapped the scarf from his neck and hung it around mine. When I protested, he said, "Just until he gets back with your car."

I thanked him through chattering teeth. "Alex... Statler."

My hesitation wasn't from the cold, but because I still wasn't used to saying my maiden name. The divorce papers had been signed for more than a year, but I'd never gotten around to changing my name back, not until my ex up and disappeared. After six months of radio silence, I started filling out the forms. Fury is an excellent motivator.

"Very nice to meet you, Alex… Statler." He said it just like I had, pause and all, and I laughed again. Even more charming was his smile in return, nothing like the one he used on TV. Warmer. Wider. More genuine. "Do you live in town?"

"Born and raised."

"Me, too. I grew up in Marietta."

I already knew this about him, along with the fact that up until his mother's death last year she lived in the rickety two-bedroom doublewide he'd grown up in, even though he kept threatening to drag it down to the city, closer to him and the hospital where she went for treatment. "My Patrick is so generous," she'd told the *AJC*, her words beaming with pride. "But that's *his* money, not mine, and I love my home. What do I need a new one for? Not while this one's still standing."

It barely was, according to the picture that accompanied the article, but that's why people in this town love Patrick Hutchinson. He has humble roots, ones he didn't try to hide. I'm not the only one who found his rising star so dazzling.

He asked me about myself, where I lived and how I made my living, and I told him about the post that had just gone viral, an unexpected surge of attention I was trying to transform into a business. He asked all the right questions, said all the right things, and he was so damn charming. His scarf smelled good, like spice and expensive leather. When the valet slid up with my car, neither one of us even noticed.

"Ma'am?" he said, tapping me on the shoulder. His other hand held my key.

"Oh. Just a sec." I pulled out my wallet at the same time I realized I'd forgotten to swing by the ATM. I riffled through it, hoping for an old, wrinkled dollar or two, but there was nothing there but business cards and receipts.

Before I could apologize, Patrick handed him a twenty. "This is for both of us."

"You really are a knight in shining armor, aren't you? Thank you. Again."

I took the key from the valet, forked over his scarf and dropped into my car, trying not to let on how flustered and embarrassed I was. On the way home, I made a pit stop at an ATM, dropping one of the tens into an envelope. No note, no return address, just the cash. I figured he'd know who it was from, and I told myself an eternal bachelor like him would never be interested in a harried single mom like me, one who didn't have time to think about tips let alone to date.

I was shoving the envelope in my mailbox when he called.

FOUR

ANNA CLAIRE

Anna Claire looked at the man who'd pulled up next to her, took in his fancy clothes and car. In the rearview, her tire lay in tatters across the road.

"Not *some* help. *All* the help. I need all of it."

Her words made him smile, and she had to admit, for an older man, it was a nice one. All crinkly eyes and straight white teeth, the kind of smile you'd see on a television screen. Almost as nice as his car, sporty and low to the ground, and his clothes when he climbed out, white shirt over dark pants, with a crease as sharp as a knife. Suddenly, she wished she'd thought to put on some lip gloss.

He leaned into her open window, and she caught a whiff of expensive aftershave. "Pop the trunk."

"What for?"

"For the spare. I'll put it on for you."

Her gaze dropped to his shirt, the fabric so fine it was almost see-through, to his big gold watch with diamonds where the numbers should be. To his bare left hand, draped across the windowsill. No ring, but she also knew rings could be dropped into pockets and ashtrays.

"You'll get all dirty."

This time he was the one who laughed. "So? That's what dry cleaners are for."

She didn't own a single piece of clothing that was dry cleaning only, but she wasn't about to admit that out loud. Instead, she pointed to chunks of rubber scattered across the asphalt behind her. "That back there? That's my spare."

He straightened, squinting down the road at the remnants of her tire. "You're joking."

AC shook her head even though he wasn't looking her way.

"Triple A would be very disappointed, you know." He looked back with another smile. "They'd lecture you on driver safety and the importance of being prepared."

"Yeah, well, unless Triple A is coming with a free spare, they can suck it. I'm about to be late for work."

"You need a ride?"

"What I need is a new set of tires, and while we're at it a decent car."

She cranked the window up on the passenger's seat, then did the same with her own and grabbed her bag from the floorboard. She reached for the door handle, but he beat her to it, pulling it wide and offering her a hand.

She ignored it and climbed out.

This was when he noticed the pink shirt that her skeevy boss called a dress, with too few buttons and a hem that made it impossible to make a bed without showing the world her ass. His gaze dipped lower and lower still, stopping on the Pepsi stain, which had glued the bottom half of her dress to her thighs.

"This isn't some stripper costume, FYI. I work at the motor lodge. I'm a maid."

"A noble profession."

She rolled her eyes. "It's a disgusting profession. You wouldn't believe what people do in those rooms. In the bathrooms."

"I hope they at least tip you well."

"Clearly you've never been to the Starlux."

"Clearly not." He smiled, finally lifting his eyes to hers. "Because I definitely would have remembered you."

She let his words hang in the air for a moment, taking in his tanned skin, his height. He was a good head taller than her father, than her brother, even. AC had a thing for tall men, but this one was too old, maybe twenty years older than herself, though he didn't seem to mind. She knew that look on his face right now. She'd only been getting it all her life.

"Okay, well, nice meeting you." She hoisted her bag onto her shoulder and turned to go.

He stopped her with a hand, a feather touch of his fingers to her elbow. "Wait. Where are you going?"

"To work. It's only a mile or two up the road."

More like five, but until she could earn enough to pay for a new tire, she'd be walking a lot. She might as well get used to it.

"What about your car?"

She looked at it, ticking off the low points in her mind. Busted tire. Rusted-out frame. Fickle engine on the best of days. Missing back window and squealing, ancient brakes. Not even the chop shop would take it, not even for free.

"What, you really think somebody's going to steal that old thing?"

"At least let me give you a ride," the man said, and there it was, the reason she was still talking to him in this sticky dress on the side of this dusty road. Because the sun was hot and she was late, and his car was nice and cool. She could feel the air-conditioning from here.

Still, she shook her head. "I don't know if that's such a good idea."

The truth was, AC wasn't used to people doing her favors. That wasn't the world she lived in, where people did things for her just because. In her world, favors came with strings attached, especially when they came from men. What were this man's strings?

"Why not?"

Because you're old enough to be my father. Because you're the type of man who needs to hear no now and then. The type who tosses aside anything that comes too easy.

"Because I don't know you," she said instead. "What if you're some serial killer? How do I know you're not thinking of dragging me into that pecan field over there and leaving me for dead?"

He laughed. "If I was planning to do any of those things, I certainly wouldn't be above denying it to get you in my car."

She didn't find it nearly as funny as he did. She stared him down with a straight face, and the smile slid off his cheeks. "I don't want to kill you, Anna Claire."

She frowned, and then she remembered her name tag. She covered it with a hand. "It's AC. Nobody calls me Anna Claire but my father, and even then it's only to fuss."

"AC, then. I don't want to kill you, AC." He gave her that look again, and to her surprise, something fluttered deep in her belly. "What I want to do is take you to dinner."

FIVE

PATRICK

I'm so screwed.

That's the first thing—hell, it's the *only* thing—I can think when my boss, Rachel, raps a knuckle on my office door. It's the day of my weekly segment, and I'm seated behind my desk at the studio, breathing through a cold wave spreading under my skin, a familiar dread sliding down my torso and tingling the tips of every finger and toe. Even after all this time, I'm still not used to the sensation.

I slap a stupid smile on my face. "Hey, Rach. What's up?"

As usual, her expression gives nothing away. Rachel is second in command at WXBA, the first woman to hold the position of technical director and editor, and her poker face is practically an Olympic sport. She's legendary, as is her ability to make grown men cry. I wonder if today is my day.

"I'd like a quick huddle in the conference room if you don't mind."

The way she words it, a request masquerading as a favor, tells me two things. First, that the huddle isn't optional, and no way in hell is it going to be quick.

But I owe this woman my television career, even if I don't particularly like her all that much. Rachel is the one who discovered me at a mutual friend's dinner party. Over rosemary potatoes and roast leg of lamb, I told her my story. First million by twenty-two, five more by the time I was thirty, coupled with an investment philosophy that promotes wealth not as having money but the financial flexibility to live your best life, however you want to define it. For me it meant never working for anyone else but me, a job I could do from anywhere—the study at home, the deck of a rental house on the shore, my phone while hiking up the Appalachian Trail. By the time dessert was served, she'd offered me a weekly segment and the use of every WXBA resource to keep growing my own pot of money, as long as I shared my strategies with the viewers.

So no, I don't need this job for the money. But now that I've been on television for almost a decade, I have a reputation to uphold. There's only one thing people in this town love more than a local celebrity, and that's watching that celebrity crash and burn.

"Can it wait? I had to shuffle some things around and I'm kind of in a time crunch." Not exactly the truth, but there are a million other things I need to be doing, a million problems that need solving, and it's probably better not to mention I haven't even thought about tonight's segment.

She puffs a sigh heavy with disappointment or impatience, it's hard to tell which. It stirs the silk flower pinned to her lapel, sending over a whiff of expensive perfume. A citrusy floral that reminds me of a gelato Alex and I once ate in Rome. I think of my wife, and my stomach twists.

"See you in there." Rachel whirls around without waiting for confirmation, because there's not a soul in this building that would dare refuse one of her orders. I watch her through the glass as she barrels into the bullpen, the sunken area smack in the middle of the building where research assistants and lower-level reporters spend twelve-plus hours a day, shouting into their phones or to each other over their laptop screens. They see her coming and clear a path, scurrying like cockroaches back to their desks.

A message pings my phone, but it's from an insurance provider, a resource for an upcoming segment, and his words weave together in a blurry dance. I can't think of anything but AC. What she's doing here, how she found me, how to get rid of her when she's attached herself to my wife like a barnacle.

I look up, and Rachel is on the opposite side of the bullpen, glaring at me through the glass. She lifts her palms to the ceiling—a WTF gesture if I've ever seen one—then gives a pointed look at her watch.

With a sigh I heave myself to a stand, dropping my phone in my pants pocket on the way out the door.

The conference room is on the northern end of the building, a dark, rectangular space with a view of a nine-foot wall decorated with ivy. I pause to read the room through the glass, and see Rachel, grim as ever, sitting shoulder to shoulder at the head of the table with an executive in a slick suit—Jake Somebody from the legal department. Next to him sits Simon, an IT nerd who I grab the occasional beer with, but it's the fourth person, a Black woman in a complicated denim dress, that gets my blood moving. I can't remember her name, but I know she runs the station's social media.

"Somebody want to tell me what's going on?"

"Close the door, please," Rachel says as I step inside.

Behind me, the door falls shut with a soft whoosh, snuffing

the clamor from the bullpen to a dull monotone. I remind my-self I don't need this job for the money. If it fell away tomorrow, the missed paycheck would barely make a blip. I tell myself I have the negotiating power here.

She folds her hands atop the shiny black desk. "Have you taken a look at your socials this morning?"

"I've been too busy working on tonight's segment." A lie. I sink onto the closest chair, an empty one to the right of Simon. "Why? What's up?"

"Apparently, one of your wife's more recent posts has gone viral, and the response has been…not great."

My chest starts heating up again, but I manage a nod. "Yeah, that's why I was late getting here this morning, because Alex woke up to a social media pile-on. When I left she was han-dling things."

"How? How was she handling things? Because from what we can tell, she just took the post down a couple hours ago, after it being live for ten hours. She also hasn't apologized. She hasn't addressed the incident at all, not even in the comments section. As far as I can tell, your wife hasn't handled a thing."

I try not to be insulted by the judgment in Rachel's tone, while also swallowing down the instinct to defend my wife. Now's not the time to mention the tequila or my hunch it wasn't Alex who penned that post, because then they would ask *why*. Why would somebody put a target on your wife's back? Why would they torpedo her page? I definitely don't want to get into the *why*s.

I mumble something like, "I'm sure the whole thing will blow over soon."

The social media manager sees this as her cue. She plants a forearm on the table and twists on her chair to face me. "I've spent much of the morning scrolling through your wife's Ins-tagram, and even with the post gone, people don't seem any-where near ready to let this go. There are screenshots popping up everywhere, and her silence has created a vacuum that she needs to step in and address, and quickly. In the absence of a response, the comments and shares will only keep increasing, not the other way around."

She stares at me, this woman half my age whose name I can never remember, and funny enough, I don't disagree. Alex should be responding to the issue, not going silent. But I haven't spoken to Alex since this morning, when she ran out of the bedroom. I have no idea what she's been doing in the meantime.

"Is that why you called me in here, to talk about my wife's crisis management strategies?"

"We called you in here to discuss her *lack* of a strategy," Rachel says, "as well as ours moving forward. Nelly?"

Nelly—the barely-out-of-grad-school social media manager.

She taps the screen of an iPad in front of her, and the flatscreen on the wall flickers to life, lighting up with the station's Facebook page. Everyone swivels in their chairs to get a better look, leather and metal squeaking.

"On a typical Monday, one of our posts will get a few dozen comments or shares over the course of the workday." She flashes a glance at Rachel. "I realize that seems rather low, but it's comparable to the other Atlanta networks and something my team and I are working on improving. Our followers are much quicker when it comes to clicking the emotive icons—the likes, the wows, angry faces, etc. A post usually gets anywhere from two hundred to four hundred of those."

My phone buzzes in my pants pocket, and I slide it out to check the screen. Three texts from Alex. I click the side button without reading any of them and settle my phone facedown on the desk.

Nelly scrolls to a post about the upcoming jazz festival. "As you can see, this morning's post is up to four *thousand* emotive icons, and the majority of them are negative. Ditto for the comments, a good ten times our usual numbers for such a post, and they don't show any sign of stopping. Very few have anything to do with the actual festival."

Nelly clicks to expand the comment thread and scrolls slowly through, even though they're all the same. *Alex Alex Alex.* Her drama has bled onto the station's page. The trolls have made the connection to me, to WXBA.

She stops on a comment from a person named @MisterFluffles.

> Listen, I can't be the only one who thinks Alex Hutchinson is full of crap. First she spews off all this bullshit about being this evolved human filled with inner peace and acceptance, then she goes off on an underage girl, slut shaming her in the most offensive terms. Patrick, blink twice if you need saving.
>
> 57 likes 123 replies

I sit up straighter on my chair, pulse quickening.

"Whoever he is, this Mister Fluffles is very vocal." Nelly flips the display to a spreadsheet listing all of Mister Fluffles's forty comments, dated and timed and pasted word for word.

> Alex's voice is so unbelievably irritating, like nails on a chalkboard. Never mind that she's a bully.
>
> She took down the post, but where the hell is her apology? Sorry, but at this point I just don't believe a word she says.
>
> Terrible choice Patrick made picking this one. She gives the word loser new meaning.
>
> She's so famethirsty but she'll never be a celebrity on merit alone. Patrick has probably paid for his following too.

"I didn't pay for my followers," I say, my voice louder than I intended. "Not a single one."

"He said probably," Jake points out, not helpfully. "And Mister Fluffles is stating his opinion, which in this country is a God-given right even if they are crude and filled with typos. Until he says something, either explicitly or implicitly, that's a provably false statement of fact, we have no grounds to stand on to deactivate his account." Jake leans back, seesawing a hundred-dollar pen between two slim fingers.

"Can you block him?" I say, turning to Simon.

But it's Nelly who answers. "Our Facebook page is public, meaning anyone can access it. Mister Fluffles could easily return under a new name, and he's probably already working under multiple handles, anyway. Trolls often do."

"He's all over Alex's pages, too," Nelly says. "It would be helpful if she reports any inflammatory comment to the corresponding social. Is she doing that? Has she been monitoring the conversations?"

I lift both hands from the table. "I don't know. I haven't talked to her since this morning."

Nelly's mouth twists in frustration, in judgment.

Rachel slaps her palms to the table and pushes to a stand. "Nelly, you monitor the conversations online and maybe advise Alex on next steps. Simon, see how far you can get with tracing this Mister Fluffles person. Jake, you're on standby in case we get sued or need to sue, whichever comes first. And, Patrick, the sooner this is in Alex's rearview, the sooner it's in ours, too."

Translation: *Fix your wife's shit. Now.*

"Daily updates from everyone, please and thank you." And with that, Rachel breezes out the door. Meeting adjourned.

All around me, people start packing up their things, swiping notepads and iPads and phones from the table, while I sift back through what I know—sharp and fast. AC inserting herself in my life. That post that came out of nowhere, incendiary and so out of character for my wife. The pile-on on her socials leaking over to the station's, stoked by an anonymous account named Mister Fluffles.

This is just the beginning. That's the one thing I know for sure.

"There are also some less legal options if you're willing to shell out some cash," Simon says, hanging back after everyone's gone. "I know a guy who knows a guy, a somewhat sketchy one. It'll take him about five seconds to track the IP to an actual person, but you didn't hear that from me."

I thank him, and we head back to our desks. Less than four hours until showtime, and I still have no fucking clue what I'm going to say.

I'm halfway across the bullpen when it hits my phone—the more I knew was coming. It arrives in the form of a text from Alex, seven little words announcing my own personal hell.

The police were just here. Call me!!

SIX

Somehow, by the grace of the news gods, I make it through the segment without flubbing or stumbling over my words. The camera light flips to green and I turn up the Patrick Hutchinson charm, grinning like an idiot while debating the merits of cryptocurrency like I give a flying shit. Afterward, I have no idea what I actually said, and the cameraman's expression when he gives me the all clear says he doesn't give much of a shit, either. I thank the team, pitch my notes in the trash and hustle out of the studio.

Normally, the moments after the segment are my favorite part of the day, when the pressure is off but the adrenaline still zings through my veins, my body wound tight with pride. Normally, this is when I strut out of the studio and into the sea of wannabe reporters and starry-eyed assistants, all of them overly effusive with praise.

But not tonight. Tonight, I take the long way around the bull-pen, skirting the crowd and out the lobby doors.

The police were just here. Call me!!

Those words hitting my phone before airtime almost gave me a heart attack. Today is the only afternoon of the week where I couldn't ditch this place, couldn't race out under the guise of some meeting-with-a-source bullshit. The best I could do was take the call in the privacy of my office, door closed, back to the glass. Heart clanging.

"I got your text. What's going on?" I asked.

"AC never showed today," Alex said, her voice wavering. "Not even to pick up her car. It's still parked out on the street."

The car she'd left when I poured her into an Uber at 12:07. The driver dropped her at her apartment at 12:31. I know, because Uber sent me the trip details.

"I'm sure she's passed out or something. She was just as plastered as you were."

Except she wasn't. I watched her walk out the door and slide into the Uber's back seat, and she didn't stumble or sway. Not once.

"That's what I said, but the detective didn't seem convinced."

The detective. I had to sit with that word for a moment before I could speak.

"What else did the detective say?"

A sigh. "I don't know. Today's been a literal beatdown, and I'm a hot mess. I don't remember half of it."

I would have asked more questions, but I was already late for hair and makeup when there was a frantic knock on the door—one of my best researchers, on the brink of tears. I had to let Alex go to put out my own fire, only to spend the rest of the day playing and replaying these snippets of conversation in my mind. The police are looking for AC. They came to my house, looking for her. It's a miracle I made it through my segment.

I zip through Buckhead traffic and am home in record time, ten minutes door to door. I drop my keys and wallet on the table by the stairs, listening to the sounds of a hushed house. The girls will be upstairs, finishing homework and getting ready for bed, and who knows where Alex could be. Once upon a time, she would have been waiting for me to walk through the door. She would have jumped me in the foyer—literally thrown herself into my arms and hooked her ankles behind my back. Now *that* was a greeting.

And then I hear a familiar sound, glass chinking against marble, and follow it into the kitchen.

Alex is seated at the island, on the very same barstool AC sat on not twenty-four hours ago, fingers twirling the stem of a half-empty wineglass. Alex's laptop stands open in front of her, lighting up her face with its glow. I take in her red and puffy eyes, her bare cheeks splotchy with emotion. The most beautiful creature I've ever seen.

"Hi."

Alex startles. "Oh my God, *finally*. Listen to this. 'What scandal-soaked influencer has been lying all this time about the father of her twins?'"

I pause, giving myself a couple of breaths to play catch-up. So, this meltdown isn't about the detective, or the mysterious AC's whereabouts. It's about some stupid clickbait. And honestly, it was bound to happen. All those gossip sites, all the online tabloids, make up shit like Alex is a genuine celebrity, which I suppose she is these days. As much as I love my wife, I really, really hate her job.

"Lying how?" I say. "About what?"

Alex doesn't like to talk about her first marriage. From the few things she's told me, I only know the basics. An on-again, off-again romance just out of college, him sweating bullets at their shotgun wedding only to bail soon after the kids' second birthday. He's never been supportive and after a few years completely vanished, leaving her to raise these magnificent girls all by herself, even though she never complains—at least not out loud. It's one of the things I love most about my wife, that she never says the first bad word about their deadbeat father.

"They don't say and they don't even have to, because everybody will draw their own awful conclusions about me now. And they used that meme, Patrick, the one that makes me look…" She looks at me, unable to finish. "Just in case anyone has any doubts which scandal-soaked influencer they're referring to."

Another pause, this time to think through my response. I've seen the meme and it's as bad as her tears imply, but this feels like one of those do-these-jeans-make-my-butt-look-fat conundrums. There's no good answer here.

"Back up a little," I say, coming around to her side of the island. "Did the detective have any news about AC?"

Alex's forehead creases in a frown. "No, but Shannon did. She said she saw you and AC arguing last week in the front yard."

Above our heads, a floorboard creaks. One of the girls, moving around in her room, and the tight knot between my shoulder blades releases just a tad. Everyone's here, safe and sound. All my girls are home.

"Who's Shannon?" I pull out a barstool and sit.

"The Westbrooks' nanny, and not that long ago, my intern. She was walking the dog, and whatever you and AC were fighting about was so distracting you didn't notice the fuss Wolf was making. Would you like to tell me what that was all about?"

"Is Wolf that annoying Chihuahua?"

"Stop stalling and answer the question. What were you and AC fighting about?"

"We weren't fighting, we were arguing, and it could have been about any one of a dozen things. The tire tracks she dug in the grass, or those olive pits she tossed in the garbage disposal that burned out the motor, or the bills she shoved to the back of a drawer that I didn't find until months later. With AC there's always something she's mucking up."

Alex watches me through narrowed eyes, and I can practically hear her mind whirr, the gears shifting into place. My wife is too smart. She knows when there's something I'm not telling her.

But she also knows how I feel about her personal assistant. There were enough accurate nuggets in my answer that, with any luck, she'll let it go.

"Shannon said you were pissed. She said you looked like you wanted to kill her."

"Then Shannon is exaggerating." I laugh, and Alex shakes her head. "Come on, Alex. I'm not going to kill your personal assistant for messing up the front lawn, that's ridiculous. Now tell me what I'm looking at here." I point at the screen, dragging her attention back to the laptop.

"DeuxMoi. They're a gossip page that publishes blind items. People can send them DMs or texts with tips about random celebrities, and then they publish them without checking to see if they're BS or not." She looks at her laptop screen, her cheeks turning hot pink. "The twins are going to see this. They're going to ask me what I've been lying about."

"So, tell them what you told me. Tell them it's just some stupid clickbait."

She looks over, and I see it then, the tiniest flicker of something I know all too well: guilt. There's more to this story, more my wife hasn't told me or the twins. I catch it, right before she buries her nose in her wineglass.

I shift the laptop to get a better look at the DeuxMoi page, a colorful feed of celebrity gifs and memes. I gesture to the words across the top. "It says here they publish rumors and conjecture, not facts. Why would the twins believe anything they say? Why would anybody?"

"Because ninety-nine percent of what they publish is actually *true*. The tipsters are assistants, friends of friends, publicists, nannies, flight attendants, drivers, sometimes even the celebrities themselves. They knew about Meghan's pregnancy weeks before she and Harry announced it. They hardly ever get anything wrong. And, Patrick, look." She clicks through the stories until she finds the one she's looking for, a picture of her and the twins with a heading in big, flashing, neon letters: *spill the secret @unapologeticallyalex the girls deserve to know daddy dearest.* "Now everybody's going to be digging. They're going to find him, Patrick, and they're going to shine a spotlight on everything the twins and I are trying really hard to forget."

My heart pinches for the girls, because she's right. They don't talk about their father, not ever. It's easier for them all to forget he even exists. The press digging up old pictures, plastering his name across websites and social media, tagging the twins…it's going to kill all three of them.

But one word echoes in my brain and bites down. *Assistant.*

"How much does AC know?"

"About Daniel? That he's not in our lives. That he lives on some hippie commune in Vermont. I don't talk about him unless I have to. You know that."

"But she would have known he was a sore spot." A familiar heat climbs in my chest. "I told you AC was bad news. I told you you were telling her too much."

"Can we please not have this conversation again? It doesn't change a thing. I'm still getting canceled, and AC is still holed up somewhere. Meanwhile, the police are asking *me* where the hell she is when I want her found as much as anybody. Because tell me I'm wrong, Patrick. Tell me this isn't her screwing with me."

A knot throbs in my stomach because I want to tell her. I want to tell Alex everything. The words are right there, piling up on my tongue, begging to bust out. I want to come clean, spill it all, but I can't.

And she's wrong about one thing.

This is not AC screwing with Alex.

This is AC screwing with Alex in order to get to me.

"You were here last night, too," she says. "Did I do something to piss her off? Did we… I don't know, have a fight?"

"Not that I saw, but I had a work call with a banker in Asia. I took it upstairs in my office."

"Okay, but when you came back down, were we acting any different? Was there, like, tension in the air?"

"No. When I came back down, you were getting ready for belly shots."

Alex winces like she's trying to shake off the memory. "When she first knocked on the door, I freaked out. The detective, I mean. I thought something happened to you or the girls. She spent the first few minutes calming me down. It never occurred to me she was here about AC."

I nod, shifting gears in my mind yet again. Conversations with Alex always go like this, ping-ponging from subject to subject. It's one of the many things I love about my wife, that she keeps me on my toes. "Okay."

"But then she started asking all sorts of questions. When I last saw AC, what time she left, if I knew where she was or had the phone number for any of her friends." She turns to me with big eyes, and something clamps down on my heart. She lowers her voice even though it's just the two of us in the kitchen. "Apparently her roommate told the police she never came home."

It's hard not to frown. I have to fight against it. "You didn't tell me that part."

"Which part?"

"The roommate part. When we talked on the phone earlier, you didn't mention her."

"Oh. I got the feeling she's the one who called the cops, something about the rent being overdue. Anyway, she wants to talk to you."

"Who, the roommate?"

"No, the detective. I told her AC's Uber was on your account, not mine, but I didn't mention it was because I was wasted. Oh, and she wants to see the feeds."

"The feeds," I say, going completely still even though I know exactly what feeds my wife is referring to. The cameras—four of them in all. A Ring video doorbell that picks up any motion on the front stoop and three cameras up near the roofline, covering the front yard and circular drive.

"Yeah, she wanted to know what they record, whether or not we can access the files, things like that. I told her security was your department. Her card is by the microwave."

I move from the stool, pulling a glass from the cabinet, filling it with water from the tap, taking my time. I pick up the card, sliding it into my pocket. "I'll have to check, but I don't think they're set to record. Actually, I'm pretty sure they're not."

A lie, and on both counts. The roofline cameras record on a constant stream, sending their feeds not to an app but to a computer in the basement, one with a hard drive big enough to hold five days' worth of video. Anything older than that gets recorded over.

The Ring, however, is a different story. That little asshole delivers top-of-the-line, high-definition, motion-activated clips to an app that saves them until the end of time. Like the argument Alex was asking about earlier, the one I had with AC on the front lawn.

"Leftovers are in the warming drawer." Alex's gaze is glued to her laptop again, her fingertips scrolling through whatever's on her screen.

I pull out the tray of lasagna and slap some on a plate, thinking for the millionth time what a ridiculous concept social media is. When we met, I didn't take Unapologetically Alex all that seriously, not until she started beaming out our most personal, private moments so strangers could discuss us in the comments. By the time I realized how exposed it made me feel, like walking down Peachtree in my tightest pair of underwear, Alex was

59

already closing in on a quarter of a million followers—and with an engagement rate of more than eight percent, a sponsor income of well into the six figures.

And now AC has disappeared as suddenly as she appeared, and there is a new goal, an urgent, shimmering need leapfrogging to the top of the pile. The camera feeds. The string of text messages my wife doesn't know about. The hundreds of lies, stacked on top of one another like a shaky Jenga tower. Yet another lie to smother all the others.

But I can't think of any of that now.

Because now there is just one thought *bang, bang, banging* away in my brain, a sharp order hounding me on repeat.

Find her—before she finds you.

> **@soulfedtracy** helloooooo @unapologeticallyalex this is not the time to be going silent. Apologize to that poor girl you miserable bully. What happened to open hearts and inner peace?

> **@ LALizzy** it's not like @unapologeticallyalex was saying anything that wasn't true. She's a mother too, and Krissie isn't exactly the best role model. If you had daughters you'd understand.

> **@soulfedtracy** I do have daughters three to be exact but thank you for illustrating my point that women shouldn't be tearing other women down. If Alex meant even half the crap she's said on her feed she would have apologized ages ago #unapologeticallyfullofshit

> **@TheRealKrissieKelly** so I'm a whore with fake boobs but at least I own my shit, unlike @unapologeticallyalex. Who's the real fraud here?

> **@misterfluffles** @LALizzy @soulfedtracy What have I been telling you? @unapologeticallyalex is a lying, opportunistic fraud who doesn't live by one word of the nonsense that comes

out of her mouth. Have you seen all her followers jumping ship? People are finally wising up. Just wait until they hear about her husband lol.

SEVEN

It's midmorning by the time I slide out of my car and onto the cracked sidewalk, studying the building for signs of life. Three stories of cement and crumbling stucco, with peeling paint and a wonky roof and single-paned windows dotted with rusty air-conditioning units. One of the last remaining seventies monstrosities in this part of town, a quiet corner tucked between Piedmont Park and Virginia Highlands.

The place hasn't changed much since the first time I saw it, now over four months ago. Same withered bushes on either side of the front doors, same run-down cars parked along the curb. Same wrinkled and grubby sheets covering the windows in apartment 203.

The door opens, and the woman rolls her eyes. "You again."

The woman's name is Little Kathi, and she's a stripper. Not the sexy kind of stripper, nor is she particularly little. Pushing six feet, with praying-mantis limbs and perky boobs despite her age, somewhere in her late sixties. When she climbs onto the bar at the Clermont Lounge, a basement dive known for its unconventional strippers, Little Kathi's wig brushes up against the tobacco-stained ceiling tiles. She's well past her prime, but she pulls in a crowd because her showstopper act entails lighting her boobs on fire. I've seen it, and it's as nuts as it sounds.

I greet her with a grin, holding up the three shopping bags I brought as a peace offering. "I come bearing gifts."

Unlike last time, she doesn't slam the door in my face. She just turns to stride down the dark hall, and I take it as an invitation. I follow behind with the bags—clinking jars of baby food, crackers, shampoo, soap, formula, diapers and wipes and whatever else I could find in the baby aisle at Publix. A couple hundred bucks' worth. Little Kathi has seven grandchildren, four of them under the age of three. Clermont tips only go so far.

At the end of the hall, she calls out over her shoulder, "I guess that means you got some more questions."

"Just a couple."

"Okay, but I already told you everything I know. Girlie found me on Craigslist. She paid the rent on time and in cash. She stayed in her room and didn't eat any of my food. Until she took off, she was the perfect roommate."

I drop the bags by a pile of shoes and coats and what looks to be a dented beer keg. "Is that what you think, that she took off?"

"Of course that's what I think. It's why I called the cops, because—" Little Kathi squints, her eyes flat, suspicious lines. "Hang on. You didn't have anything to do with that little girl going missing, did you? Because I'm stronger than I look, and there's enough mace in this place to take down ten of you."

I hold up both hands, giving her my friendliest on-air smile, the one Alex calls my prime-time panty dropper. "I've seen your act, Little Kathi. I know how quick you are on the draw."

I also know her creativity when it comes to hiding Bic lighters in her nearly naked body, though I really wish I was able to forget.

"I promise I'm not here for any sort of nefarious reasons. I'm only here for information."

My words seem to appease her. She rounds the corner through the living room, a dark, spare space with dirty walls and a futon, and into the kitchen.

"Anyway, as I was saying, rent was due last week, so when she took off, I figured she was stiffing me. That's why I called the cops, because I got a better chance of holding off my landlord with a police report. Except wherever she went, she didn't take nothing with her. Room's still full of all her crap. Closet, too."

Interesting. It means either AC had to get out of town fast, or someone helped her do it.

I lean a shoulder against the door frame, looking around the tiny apartment. On my last visit, I didn't make it farther than the front door, so I had no idea things were this bad. The place reeks of mold and garbage and an acrid smell coming from the toaster. Little Kathi pokes it with a plastic knife, digging out two black slices of bread.

"If you're wondering why I look so tired," I say, aiming my attention at Little Kathi, "it's because I live in a house with two twelve-year-old girls. Twins, and between the two of them, somebody's always getting into trouble. This past weekend it was Gigi, who came home an hour past curfew because she was at a friend's house watching *Fast and Furious*. She didn't remember which number."

Little Kathi makes a face. Without her heavy makeup and stripper gear, she looks like any other woman at her stage of life: wrinkles, crepey skin, thinning hair and age spots. She looks like my mother—a depressing thought I wipe lightning-quick from my mind.

"A waste of a perfectly good hour if you ask me. And I wasn't wondering."

I point a long finger at her nose, grinning. "See? That's exactly my point."

Little Kathi frowns. "What is?"

"No girl sneaks out to watch *Fast and Furious* with a friend unless that friend happens to be a boy. In this case, a friend's older brother, who's a punk. She swears her girlfriend was there the whole time, but we still grounded her for lying. That boy is *not* a good influence."

While I talk, Little Kathi lays out the ingredients for lunch on the countertop—a jar of generic peanut butter and some squirtable grape jelly, a paper plate she pulls from an industrial-sized bag on the counter. The toast is charred and rock hard, but she drops the slices on the plate, anyway. The bread bag lies empty and deflated in the sink.

"All this goes to say, my stepdaughter slipped up. She told her mother the truth, but the truth caught her in a lie."

Another roll of Little Kathi's eyes. "Can you just get to the point? I take it you didn't come here to share parenting advice."

"My point is that maybe something like that happened with AC. Maybe you're sitting on a valuable piece of information without even knowing it. Something that didn't seem all that significant at the time, but could make all the difference now. Something that could help me find her."

"Something like what?"

"Well, after all these months living under the same roof, she must have slipped up. She must have revealed things about herself without meaning to. Details can reveal a lot when you pay attention."

Little Kathi picks up the plastic knife, using it to smear a thick layer of jelly. "I pay attention, but I work nights. She worked during the day. We exchanged maybe a hundred words the whole time she lived here. I barely ever saw her."

"Okay, then. Things you saw. A sticker with the name of a

college, maybe, or a piece of mail with a different name and address."

Little Kathi makes a sound low in her throat. "Like a driver's license from Utah?"

My skin goes tingly. Exactly like that. "She had a Utah driver's license. Are you certain?"

"'Course I'm certain. I remember 'cause I asked if she was one of them sister wives. I was hoping for some drama like on that TV show, but she just mumbled that I must have seen it wrong. But I know what I saw. My eyes are working just fine."

"Do you remember the name?"

"Why, you think she's lying about hers?"

"Could be." I shrug, keeping my eyes on the sandwich and my expression neutral. "I'm guessing you didn't check references."

Little Kathi slaps the slice of toast to the sandwich and presses down, but the bread is like a board. Melted peanut butter and jam seeps out the sides. "What do you think this is, apartments. com? She pays me in cash, and up until this past month she's never once been late. What do I need references for?"

How about so she doesn't steal all your stuff, or sell meth she cooks in the bathtub, or leave you hanging the day rent is due?

I bite my tongue, not fussing at Little Kathi just like I didn't with Alex when she showed me the flaming pile AC called a résumé. The social security number she gave my wife doesn't belong to her, either—a federal crime that comes with up to fifteen years in jail, assuming Alex would ever catch it, which she won't. She pays AC through Venmo, for crap's sake. And there was no mention anywhere of the Utah driver's license.

Little Kathi takes a noisy bite, and a wad of jelly glops out the other side and lands on the linoleum by her toes. She ignores it, and so do I.

"Did she ever talk about where she was from? Did she mention the name of a town?"

"Somewhere in Michigan, I think? Which is weird 'cause her

accent is all over the place. One minute this exaggerated northern twang, the other like somebody straight out of *Deliverance*.
It's like she copied it from TV or something."

I make a mental note to give her accent another listen on the
videos Alex uploaded to her page, then move on. "What about
her room?"

"What about it?"

"Is there anything in there, pictures or some mail or an ID
card, for example?"

"Not that I saw, but then again, I respect my tenant's privacy
and the cops cleared out all the good stuff. Her laptop, a couple of iPhones, some fancy purses I was gonna sell on eBay to
make up for the hole in my rent money, all gone before I could
get to it."

A couple of phones. What kind of person has multiple iPhones?
Especially one who works for the peanuts Alex is paying her.

"Mind if I take a look?"

Little Kathi chews, loud and slow, staring at me with a blank
face. I peel a twenty from my wallet and drop it on the counter.

She smiles. "Second door on the left."

AC's room is as bare bones as the rest of the place: a mattress on a metal frame, a rickety nightstand with a lamp and a
couple of dog-eared novels, a chest of drawers with nothing on
top. Unlike our house, where every piece is curated and placed
just so, where there's more decor than flat surfaces to put it on.
Here there are no pictures, no decorations, not even a necklace
or a ring of keys. I tug on the top drawer, revealing a neat stack
of underwear, the basic cotton kind. I poke through it, checking underneath and in between, finding nothing.

The next drawer down is filled with clothes, and I shuffle
through the pile of jeans and T-shirts, looking for anything with
a logo or an identifying text. The closest I can get is a faded label
inside a shirt collar—*Property of Bush Creek*—in plain, embroi-
dered letters. I take a picture with my cell and keep going. I'm

not sure what I'm looking for, exactly, just anything the police might have missed.

Whatever it is, it's not in the chest of drawers, or under the bed or stuffed between the mattresses, or taped to the underside of the lamp. I flip through the paperbacks and wriggle them upside down, but the only thing that falls out is a travel-sized nail file, the metal kind. I feel around in every pocket of clothing, stick my hands in every sock and shoe. No forgotten receipts. No hidden papers or personal items. Nothing but lint and dust bunnies.

I'm on my way out the bedroom when I spot it wedged under a baseboard, a spark of something shiny between splintery wood and grungy carpet. I fall to my knees, but it's shoved too far back for me to shimmy it out with a finger. I grab the nail file from the novel, wriggle it under the baseboard, and it's a key, generic enough to open anything, tarnished enough to have been here for a dozen years. I slide it in my pocket, anyway, then head back into the hall.

Little Kathi is sprawled on the futon with a bag of barbecue potato chips and her phone.

I pull a business card from my wallet. "Please call me if you think of anything. Even if you think it's not relevant, I want to know it."

Little Kathi looks at the card, but she doesn't reach for it. She just shoves another handful of chips into her mouth, raining crumbs on her generous bosom. I try not to look at them. Every time I do, I see them bursting into flames.

"That number at the bottom is my cell. Text me a list, and I'll bring anything on it, no questions asked." I step closer, still holding out the card. "All I want is for you to think really, really hard."

"I wouldn't mind some of that fancy Pantene shampoo and a couple of boxes of Miss Clairol Born Blonde." She runs greasy fingers through her hair. "Which I was, I'll have you know, once upon a time."

"Remember something good and I'll buy you a lifetime supply. Just please, don't take too long."

My words do the trick. She plucks the card from my fingers. *Bingo.*

EIGHT

ANNA CLAIRE

They pulled into the Starlux Motor Lodge, and AC tried to see it like he would. A dingy L-shaped building that's seen too many years since its last paint job, a second-story catwalk overlooking a grubby parking lot. The Starlux was like every other cheap roadside motel. Seen one, seen them all. His fancy car looked like a luxury spaceship floating through a junkyard of beat-up sedans.

She snuck a glance as he rounded the last curve, but she couldn't read his face. Couldn't read anything about him, really, seeing as he'd gone silent the second she'd slid into his passenger's seat. It made her wonder if she was wrong about the way he'd looked at her before, if he'd even meant that offer to take her to dinner, or if he'd just been making small talk.

"You can just drop me over there," she said, pointing to the office at the far end of the lot. AC pictured the nosy day manager, Terri, just inside, her face pressed to the glass. "Thanks for the ride, by the way. I hope I didn't take you too far out of your way."

It was her way of asking where he was from, because it wasn't from here, that much was clear. His clothes, his confidence. Everything about this man screamed city.

He eased to a stop by the office door and leaned over the wheel, studying the building through the side window. "What kind of occupancy does this place have?"

It was such a strange question, so out of nowhere, that the only thing she could think of to say was, "What?"

"On a typical night, how many of these rooms are booked?"

"I know what occupancy means, I was just surprised, that's all. And it depends on the day and the season. Summers are a little busier, people on their way to and from Florida, but that's not saying much. Most customers are salesmen of some type, so weekdays tend to be busier. Still only about half the rooms have people in them. Things generally slow down on the weekend."

"What's the price per night?"

"A whopping thirty-nine dollars. Why, you need someplace to stay?"

He laughed, and she took it for a no. Still, she couldn't quite decide how to feel about it. On the one hand, she couldn't picture him sinking into a mattress teeming with bedbugs or padding across the moldy carpet for the bathroom with stains no amount of bleach would ever be able to scrub out.

But on the other hand, she wasn't ready for him to go. He still hadn't repeated that offer to take her to dinner, and she didn't want to ask. She searched for something to say that would bring them back there, to that flirtatious moment on the side of the road, but came up blank.

She was reaching for the handle when he shot off another question.

"Who owns it?"

Her hand fell back to her lap. "Some guy named Steve. He's a real pervert, as you can see from the uniforms, but he's not around much, thank God. I mostly deal with Terri inside." She looked over, and yep. Terri's face was in the glass, all right.

He nodded, staring out the window. She waited for him to say something more, another question or…well, anything, but he was quiet, obviously deep in thought.

She gave the handle a tug. "Okay, well… Bye."

He didn't even look over, so she climbed out and shut the door.

Disappointment bloomed hard and heavy in her belly, which was fine, really. Men like that want women like her for one thing and one thing only. And though she certainly wouldn't have minded seeing what was underneath that nice shirt of his, she didn't need him for a good time. There were plenty of willing guys in this town. Maybe not as handsome, maybe with a lot less money, but she didn't need a fancy stranger to buy her dinner. Probably for the best, anyway.

By the time she'd reached the office door, he was gone. With a sigh, she stepped inside.

Terri was back behind the desk, her mouth stuffed with breakfast biscuits. The front of her Starlux polo was littered with crumbs. "Who the hell was that? You're late, by the way."

AC knew she was late. She also knew she'd have to kill herself to get all her rooms cleaned and ready for check-in at two, and that she hated this damn job. She plucked her time card off the slot in the wall.

"Somebody you don't know and never will."

A television blared the weather in the corner.

"Well, whoever he is, he's got an awfully fancy car, that's for sure. You got yourself a sugar daddy?" Grinning, Terri crumpled the food wrapper into a greasy ball and tossed it in the trash, missing the wastebasket by a mile.

AC rolled her eyes, even though she wouldn't say no to a sugar daddy. Hell, just a little taste of sugar would do. "Just some random guy on his way out of town."

"So how come you were in his car?"

She didn't want to be reminded of his car, the way he smelled, that he'd thought better of his offer to take her to dinner sometime in the ten minutes it took him to drive her here. "Can we just forget about him? I'm certainly trying to."

With a huff, Terri shoved a grimy piece of paper across the desk, the list of rooms AC was to clean. Of the fifteen, eight were occupied, which meant they were likely disgusting, and she'd have to hurry. "You got the shittiest block, sorry. Shoulda been here earlier."

AC sighed, then headed for the workroom around back, a door halfway down a cinder-block wall looking out over a gravel lot littered with trash. The other maids had already been and gone, probably on their third or fourth room by now. She plucked a fresh uniform from the shelf and changed out of her wet one fast as a whip, one eye on the door in case her skeevy boss walked in to find her in her underwear, which he had the tendency to do. The Pepsi-stained dress went in the laundry pile, and then she grabbed a cart and stocked it with supplies, towels and toilet paper and cheap soaps wrapped in waxy paper, bottles of bleach and industrial cleaner.

At the first of her block of rooms, she tapped on the door with a key. "Housekeeping."

Silence.

She slid in the key and stepped inside, making a face at the mess. Overflowing ashtrays and empty liquor bottles and what looked like an entire bag of Doritos ground into the carpet. She grabbed her spray bottle and a rag and got to cleaning.

All day long she thought of him. She changed stained bedsheets and scrubbed toilets and thought of the handsome, charming man who'd flirted with her on the side of the road, then gone silent the second she got in his car. Did she say something wrong, *do* something wrong? What happened to make him go from hot to cold? The only thing she could figure is that she got in his car.

She'd just stripped the bed in room 205 when she heard animated voices coming down the catwalk. The other maids— a couple of them were friendly enough, though she wouldn't call them friends. She dumped the dirty sheets on the floor, right as Crystal appeared in the doorway.

"You little minx, you." She leaned a hip against the doorway, snapping her gum between her molars. The two other maids, Francine and Linda, stood behind her on the catwalk. "Come on. Spill."

Of the three, AC liked her the best. They were around the same age, same background, and Crystal had lost her mother, too, though her grief felt different, hot and angry. Crystal's mom was mean as a snake, apparently, and she didn't understand the hole losing a good mother could drill in a girl's heart.

"Spill what?"

She stabbed her fist into a hip. "Who did that to your car?"

AC pulled a fitted sheet from the cart and shook it out. "A pothole, I guess. My car is sitting on the side of Old Clyatteville Road with a busted tire, right past the Higgins farm." And then something occurred to her, and she clutched the sheet to her chest. "Shit, did somebody take it? Did some asshole ram it into a field with his tractor?"

Crystal's grin went even wider. "Nope. And the tire ain't busted no more."

AC stood quiet for a moment, trying to figure how these women would know such a thing. Impossible, unless—

She tossed the sheet on the bed and pushed past them out the door, where she stopped dead on the catwalk.

"What the..."

She clutched the railing with both hands because there it was, parked in the middle of the lot. Her piece-of-shit Honda with its missing back window and more rust than paint. Someone had towed her car from Old Clyatteville Road to here.

No—not to here. First to the tire store and *then* to here, because there were four brand-new Goodyears under all that rusty paint, glimmering like black diamonds in the sun. New tires were expensive, far more than she could ever dream of affording. And he bought her not one, but *four.*

Her skin tingled, and her gaze scanned the parking lot. She searched the shadows of the pines that lined the lot, the air between the cars parked across the road. Was he out there somewhere, watching for her reaction? AC made sure not to smile just in case he was.

"There's a note," Crystal said, stepping up to the railing beside her. "On the front seat, I mean. There's a note under the keys and a red rose."

"Is that so?" AC put just the right note of indifference in her tone, even though of course she cared. He picked her up on the side of the road and he bought her *tires.* Four of them. She cared a *lot.*

Crystal nudged her with an elbow. "Come on. Don't you want to know what it says?"

"As long as it's not a bill, I don't much care."

It wasn't true, of course, but darned if she was going to show it—not to these girls. Not to him if he was out there watching.

Crystal pulled the note from her pocket and passed it to AC, and her heart fluttered. Not at the heavy card stock with his initials embossed in navy letters at the top, but at the message just below it, in neat square caps.

SKOBY'S STEAKHOUSE—FRIDAY, 7 P.M.

NINE

ALEX

"I hate to be the bearer of bad news, Alex, but the auction is off." Jenny's upstate New York accent is extra sharp today, grating in my ear.

I slump in the chair at my desk, my bones going heavy like they did when I first saw my literary agent's name light up my cell phone screen. Jenny *never* calls, not even when we started getting nibbles on the book proposal I labored over for six months. That news came like all the others, with a concise, dry dispatch in my in-box. Going to auction next week FYI.

"What, why?"

"I'm pretty sure you know why, because I've been on your socials, and people are *rabid.* Have you seen what they're saying about you?"

Yes, Jenny. They're threatening me and my daughters. Innocent girls who can bleed and die. They're calling me a bitch and a filthy whore. They're sending me death threats.

Thirty-six hours, that's all it took for the trolls to gather into an angry, hysterical mob. My words about Krissie Kelly are long forgotten, and now the focus is squarely on me. My lips, my face, my house, my voice, my boobs, my clothes, my parenting skills, my skin, my flat forehead, my stupid laugh, my character, my husband and daughters, who must loathe me. My page is a writhing mess of mindless hatred and fury, and it's all aimed at me.

"Just ignore it," was Patrick's sweet but somewhat laughable advice, because he won't ever understand why I would spend an entire hour studying myself in the bathroom mirror, trying to determine what is so detestable about my face. People go to his socials for financial wizardry, not to debate his hairstyle. They comb his posts for how to get rich like him, not call him a bastard or a bad stepfather.

Also, men don't hate-follow. It wouldn't even occur to them to do such a thing. Following another man with the sole purpose of spewing ugliness and criticism, it does not seem to compute in their brains.

Women, however, they hate-follow in droves. Women screenshot my posts and pick them apart in Reddit threads and group chats. They trawl my Instagram only to nitpick me in the comments. Patrick's solution is to simply not look. To not read what they have to say. He will never understand how impossible that is, how their words dig deep into my cells and stick there.

"It's true the trolls have gotten ahold of the post, yes. They're blowing things way out of proportion but—"

"These aren't trolls. These are former fans who are now accusing you of hypocrisy. They feel duped by you, Unapologetically Alex, their fearless leader who preaches inner peace and self-love, and then goes off in the worst possible way on some poor, innocent girl. They're calling you mean and jealous and spiteful and a fraud, and a whole bunch of other things I don't want to repeat out loud. They're calling you a *Karen*."

Better than a cunt, I think but don't say. I've seen that one plenty, as well.

And here's some irony for you—I know how Krissie Kelly feels. How *my post* made her feel. Because celebrities like her and me, we are fair game. Everything we do and say, how we look and walk and talk—it's all fodder for people to pick apart in the comments section. Now that I'm on the receiving end, I know the criticism doesn't stick to the screen. It echoes in your head and rewires your brain. It fucks with your neurons.

"Look, I know things look bad right now, but it's only a matter of time before a Kardashian does something scandalous again. Makes a sex tape, maybe, or…or dry humps her boyfriend at a friend's wedding." It's what I keep telling myself, that trolls are lazy and unoriginal. They go wherever the collective spotlight is focused. "The trolls will move on soon enough."

"This is not the time to be living up to your handle, Alex. Where's your apology post? Are you planning to do that? Are you going to apologize?"

There's a beat of silence, just a tad too long, and I find myself rushing the answer. "Of course."

"When?"

"As soon as we hang up. I'm putting the final touches on the apology post now."

It's a lie, and not a particularly good one. Jenny *tsks* like she knows it, too.

The truth is, there's no apology post because I have no earthly idea what to say. All the promises of new and terrible ways to make me pay, all the death and rape threats and assurances of blood and violence. I am literally frozen in fear that one wrong word, one even slightly dodgy sentiment, will rile up the angry mob even further, stir up a whole new onslaught of abuse. It's easier to hide and say nothing at all.

"You need to apologize. Go all in on a groveling tour. Give interviews to magazines and radio. Get on some podcasts, or maybe launch one of your own with a long-winded and sincere expression of regret. Acknowledge what you said was wrong and talk about how you're going to fix yourself moving forward. Be vulnerable. Bawl and plead for forgiveness. Take accountability and promise people you'll learn and grow. That's the only way you're going to make this book a reality, by getting the trust back of your following."

I sit with her words for a minute. This isn't the first time she's told me that as eager as publishers are to sign me, what they're most eager for is my fan base. A built-in audience of a million enamored Alex Stans who will happily plunk down $28.99 plus tax for my book. Hate followers don't buy books, and neither do ex-fans.

But a groveling tour. A bunch of podcasts and interviews begging for forgiveness for a post I may not have even penned. Can I do that? Do I even want to? And would an apology placate the trolls? I can't unsee their nasty words, and I certainly can't forget them. Even if only a small percentage actually mean their threats, their words have taken a toll.

Jenny is still talking, her voice squawking in my ear. "Fix this and do it quick. Because the trolls might move on at some point, but the internet is forever."

At noon, the skies open up, pummeling the slate roof with a deafening roar as I sort through my in-box. An avalanche of ugliness, interspersed with emails from sponsors asking me to untag them. "For now," they all say, at the same time calling for immediate action. Kindly confirm at your soonest convenience quickly becomes Timely response requested becomes Confirm ASAP!!!

But their messages are clear. Posts that once garnered them thousands of clicks must now come down, no matter how much money I made them. Companies that courted me with long, gushing emails declaring their products the perfect match for my brand, that sent truckloads of products for giveaways and to share with all my friends and family, no longer want their organic lotions and serums anywhere near my toxic face.

It takes me hours to remove them all. I find myself wishing

AC were here to help me shoulder the work, right before new doubts niggle. Where is she? What if she had something to do with this?

At two, an email lands in my in-box from Target, a partnership I've been courting for almost a year, canceling our planned meeting with the most corporate gobbledygook ever.

We're going to have to table today's Zoom, as the social landscape seems a bit disrupted on your end. Let's touch base again when/if things settle as we don't want to boil the water here. In the meantime, best of luck.

Boil the water, what does that even mean? And that sign-off. *Best of luck*, as if burning some sage or plucking a four-leaf clover out of the grass would fix things.

Delete. Scream. Breathe.

And then the kicker comes just before three, when a message from LinkedIn pings my phone.

Account suspended.

LinkedIn, for Pete's sake! Arguably the least fun of the social media platforms, the water cooler nobody wants to hang around longer than absolutely necessary. What kind of loser gets banned from LinkedIn? Me, apparently.

I'm still staring at my screen when my phone lights up with a photo of Penelope. I swipe to pick up her call. "What happened?"

When one of my girls needs something, to borrow ten bucks or ask if I can drop her at a friend's house after practice, she texts. When she calls, it means she's having a meltdown.

"Oh my God, Mom, *you* did. *You* happened. Your stupid post is all anyone can talk about."

Her voice is amplified, as if she's cupping her hand over the phone. Loud despite all the background noise, kids laughing and squealing all around her. I picture her standing in the middle of a busy hall, and I am a like a sponge, soaking up her emotions as if they're my own. For the first time since this all began, my eyes fill with tears.

"Ignore them," I say, shaking my head because now I sound like Patrick. I know how fruitless that advice feels when you're on the receiving end. I backtrack with a sigh. "I realize that's not possible. But try, okay?"

"No, I need you to pick me up. You have to come pick me up."

"But what about soccer? Coach will bench you if you miss practice."

"Mom, there's no *way*. Please. I want to *die*." Even when she's not upset, Penelope tends to speak in superlatives. She lowers her voice, pressing her lips close to the phone. "Have you seen what they're saying about us? About…*him*?"

Him, as in her father. I wince, a pressure kicking up in my head like someone's squeezing me in the temples because of course the girls have seen. Kids that age are on their phones even more than I am. If one of the twins didn't spot the DeuxMoi post, one of their friends certainly would have.

"They're just looking for attention, so don't give them any. Actually, maybe stay offline until this all blows over."

"But when will that be? Cassie already canceled our sleepover for next weekend because her mom is crushed. That's what she said, that she's crushed, whatever that means. She says she always thought you were so nice."

I try not to be offended. I've always found Cassie's mom to be a bit of a suck-up, hovering by the door whenever I drop the twins at her house, inviting me in for a drink and a chat. I've learned to come armed with a list of vague excuses, somewhere pressing I need to be. Now Cassie's mom is crushed.

"I know it's hard, but go take your frustrations out on a soccer ball, okay?" And if Cassie's mom is there, maybe aim for her face. "We'll talk about it after practice."

But I'm talking to a dead phone. Penelope has already hung up.

I drop my cell to the desk with a groan, reaching for my laptop. And even though the idea of posting anything makes me want to curl up in a ball, I close everything down but Word and start typing.

I'm not going to do this perfectly, but these are words that come from my heart. I'm deeply sorry about the post berating a fellow influencer and the hurt I have caused Krissie, her followers and mine. I know I have disappointed so many of you, but no one is more disappointed than myself. I take full accountability and will work hard to do better, to *be* better. My heart is wide open, and I am so sorry.

I arrange the text in a plain white box, no frills or decoration, and post it to Instagram.

Almost immediately, the comments pile up faster than my screen can refresh.

Stop it. Just stop.

Tone deaf OMG

This is honestly just like so funny because she's not sorry for what she's said, she is sorry that there's backlash

Cry me a river. Your career is done. You're such a piece of shit person.

And maybe it's the call from Penelope, or maybe it's yet another new and terrible wave of trolls stoked by the vile Mister Fluffles, but I feel something building in my chest. It heats me from the inside out, slithering like a hot snake under my skin, along my shoulder blades and down my spine, erupting out the top of my head like lava.

Fury. I am positively feral with fury.

I snatch up my phone and pull up the text thread with AC. Dozens and dozens of texts from me, delivered but unread, a progression of emotions that is its own story. Are you okay? becomes WTF where are you? becomes Don't bother, you're fired. Pages and pages of blue bubbles without a single response.

I add one more to the pile—the final one, the last word—pounding out the ones that won't stop bouncing around my brain.

If you did this, I will kill you.

The bitch doesn't respond to that one, either.

TEN

On Saturday, at Patrick's insistence, I take a mental health day. That's the thing about being an influencer—the lines between real life and social media are pretty much nonexistent, and there's no real time off. But today I take his advice and leave my laptop sleeping on the carriage house desk, delete all the social apps from my phone and let him drag me and the girls to the crowded neighborhood pool. It's the first perfect summer day of the season, with the sun beating down from a cloudless blue sky. Kids are everywhere, yelling and splashing and racing by, parents shouting at them to slow down between sharp blasts of the lifeguard's whistle. So much noise and activity that I can barely hear myself think.

And yet nothing can drown out my anxiety.

It doesn't help that the pool is teeming with eyes. Mothers. Neighbors. Women I know from book club and the gym. They pretend to watch their kids, but really, they're watching me, and their Chanel shades can't disguise the pity smeared across their faces or worse—the satisfaction.

That's the thing about the country club set. The women here operate like a sorority, a tight clique looking for a common enemy. Apparently, after the shitstorm these past few days, I'm it.

They've probably seen the meme, the one Penelope informed me is making the rounds, a new one featuring Patrick and me on a beach—last year's spring break trip to the Dominican Republic. The two of us stand ankle-deep in the turquoise water, me beaming at the camera while Patrick looks the other way, distracted by Gigi in a perfect handstand on the beach.

Only Gigi's not there. Someone has Photoshopped her out and, in her place, a half-naked Krissie Kelly. Her come-hither eyes, her glistening skin. My husband's arm may be around me, but in this meme he's ogling an underage girl, the one I slut-shamed and called a whore.

It also doesn't help that Patrick is on the opposite side of the pool, holding court with Estelle Owens. Estelle, newly divorced and desperate to show her ex what he's missing. According to her Instagram, her life is one big party, girls' nights at Umi and the Garden Room, birthday trips to Tulum and Ibiza, shopping with friends in Buckhead, big orange bags dangling from their wrists. Her outfits are skimpy, skimpier, skimpiest, tiny strips of silky fabric to show off her banging body, just like all those busty Brazilians Patrick used to date.

She leans in close, draping a hand over his arm, and I wish she didn't look so perfect in that goddamn bikini. Not a stretch mark or belly roll in sight.

Shannon snorts from the lounger next to me. "If it helps any, last week that woman asked me if an egg was a fruit or a vegetable."

I sigh and flick a sweat bee from my thigh. "Well, I mean, who can blame her? The keto diet *is* complicated."

"What do you think they're talking about, anyway?" She shoves her glasses to the top of her head and stares across the water. "Because you and I both know it's not financial advice."

"Me, probably—or at least, that's what she was talking about earlier, before she and her friends noticed me standing behind them in the line for towels."

They were passing a phone around, giggling about that awful meme, and though I didn't hear all of it, I caught the general gist. That Patrick is such a hottie, and did you see that six-pack? Alex is clueless, pretentious, too big for her britches. It's about time I was getting canceled and Patrick set free.

I watch him across the busy pool, but mostly I watch Estelle. I watch her chiseled stomach and pert breasts, the way she bats her lashes at my husband, and she stirs up something inside, something intangible and slippery. Something a lot like jealousy.

Which is ridiculous. I'm not a jealous person, and Patrick has never given me any reason to think I should be. Not with Estelle, who he keeps trying to put some distance between, not with any of the other women here. Not even with AC, who was constantly looking for ways to be at the house whenever Patrick was around. Swinging by on the weekend to pick something up or staying long enough for him to get home, and everything about her changed when he walked through that door. She stood up a little straighter, talked a little louder, watching him with this weird, close-lipped smile. Patrick did his best to pretend he didn't notice, but I did. I noticed.

Another reason to hate those fucking trolls. They've planted their roots deep in my brain, sprouting doubts as relentless as kudzu. That Patrick has roaming eyes, that there's something wrong with me—my face and my voice and my ass, which apparently has been deemed droopy.

Shannon flips a page of her *People* magazine with a flick of her wrist. "Stop letting that bitch get in your head. She's so not worth it."

"Estelle Owens is *not* in my head."

Estelle Owens might be a *little* in my head, but Shannon is right. She shouldn't be.

"Not Estelle. That hooker who used to work for you. Stop letting—" Without warning, Shannon lurches upright, cupping both hands around her mouth. "Robbie! Push your sister in the pool one more time and we're going home. I mean it!" She falls back to the lounger with a sigh. "It's a good thing that kid's father is a lawyer. I swear he's headed for juvie one day. Anyway, I take it AC hasn't resurfaced?"

"Nope. Still radio silence, though that could be because I blocked her."

She nods. "Good call. And Krissie? Did you block her, too?"

"No, why?"

"You know she's the queen of clapbacks, right?" Shannon digs a bottle of SPF from her bag, slathering another layer on her shoulders and arms. "I'd just suggest staying off TikTok for a while, or maybe forever. Did I mention she has six and a half million followers?"

Six and a half million people, and they all hate me.

Her words have me reaching for my phone, my fingers itching to dig up all the awful things her fans are saying about me now, but I shove my hands under my thighs. All those Karens harping about how social media addiction is ruining an entire generation of kids are only partially right. It's ruining me, too.

On the other side of the pool, I spot Patrick crouched in front of Gigi, seated on her towel in the grass. Gigi has always been the more animated twin, the one hanging upside down from the monkey bars, hollering for everybody to look her way. It's why Patrick lovingly calls her Thing One, because she sucks up all the attention. Now she sits, knees pulled tight to her chest, arms wrapped around her legs, while her friends practice Tik-Tok dances ten feet away.

"What now?" I say, worry stabbing me between the ribs. "If

I were one of your case studies at school, what would your digital marketing professors say I should do?"

"That depends on the professor, and honestly, they're all ancient so I'm not convinced any of them have a freaking clue. Social media is volatile, and it moves at the speed of light. Oftentimes, when people latch on to something, they blow it so far out of proportion that ten minutes later they don't even remember *why* they're all riled up, only that they are. When that happens, it's really hard to turn the tide."

"Those are your words of wisdom? How much are you paying for that degree, anyway?"

"Hope Scholarship, remem—*Robbie!*" She pops off her chair, tossing her magazine to the ground and marches off, zigzagging through a sea of kids to the shallow end.

As soon as she's gone, Patrick returns, his hands full with two margaritas. He hands me one, icy cold and crusted with salt.

He sinks onto the lounger next to mine, tapping the liquid off his straw and dropping it onto the ground by his shoes. "Thing One is in one hell of a mood. Something about a got-me blog?"

I cringe. Gigi found the GOMIBLOG. I look at her sitting alone on the grass, and sure enough she's glaring at her cell.

"GOMI stands for Get Off My Internets, and it's not really a blog. More a message board for mean girls to rip people to shreds. Witch hunts, draggings, pile-ons. It's really, really ugly."

"And people actually read that shit?"

"Oh, yeah. Lots of people. Women, mostly, and they're mean as snakes. So much for female solidarity, I guess." My gaze crawls back to Gigi, tapping away on her phone. "Maybe we should take their phones away. At least until this thing blows over."

"And when will that be?"

I startle at the sharpness in his tone, then bury my hurt in a sip of margarita. So far Patrick hasn't said much about the furor online other than that I should just ignore it. He likes to act like the drama doesn't touch him, but I've seen the station's Facebook page. He's getting slammed, too, all because he's married to me.

"There's no one that wants this to die down more than me. It's killing me that the trolls are swarming around you and the girls. If I knew how to stop them, I would."

He sighs, draping a hand over my knee. "I know. I didn't mean it like that. I'm just wondering if this is worth it, you know? You, being an influencer. I know you like making your own money, but it's not like we need it. And as much as I support you having a career that you love...do you? Love it, I mean."

I think back to that very first viral post, a picture of me flaunting the stretch marks the girls carved into my stomach, with some silly caption about being unapologetically real. Within days, that post racked up more than ten million views and 325,000 likes. It prompted women everywhere to post their own body-baring photos. It sparked the hashtag that trended on every social platform: #purpleandproud. At the time, I loved every second.

I also loved the opportunity for a do-over. A second chance to capture the most Insta-worthy moments of my life, craft them into the scenes I wish I'd snapped the first time around. Me and my people, but staged to look a little more glamorous, more colorful, more picture-perfect than usual. Not fake, just...better.

But it was the weirdest thing, watching how quickly people went from talking *to* me to talking *about* me. One minute I'm posting a picture of my stretch marks, the next I'm fielding calls from *The Atlantic* and *Vulture*, journalists vying for an interview. Suddenly, my life—or at least the parts of it I uploaded to Instagram—stopped belonging to me. My pictures became content, my Instagram a lifestyle magazine of pretty squares and peppy captions.

I love the money, but do I love the job? Especially now that the trolls have zeroed in on not just me but my family. I pick my daughters out of the crowd—Penelope hurling herself backward into the pool, Gigi on her towel, her forehead crumpled in a perma-scowl. Adolescence is hard enough without all the attention online.

My cell buzzes under the towel.

Stop staring at me. It's weird.

I laugh and pass my phone to Patrick. "Emergency over. Gigi's fine."

And that's when it happens. My phone comes to life in his hand, ringing and buzzing between his fingers. He hands it back like a hot coal, and I try to make sense of the words rolling across my screen. Calls and texts, rolling in faster than I can swipe them away, faster than I can register the strings of numbers.

"What are these area codes—937, 216, 518. I don't... Do we know anyone there?"

"Your phone doesn't," he says, leaning across my lounger so he can see. "Otherwise it would have matched them up to a name in your contacts."

In other words, strangers. Calling and texting my phone—a nonstop avalanche. I silence the ring, but the phone still buzzes in my hand. A sensation that fills me with dread.

"They're leaving voice mails, too."

I flip to that screen, pages and pages of them. I scroll to the top and tap a message. A woman's voice, northern and nasal and nasty, fills my ear.

We found you, girlie. I mean, hey, sorry, sucks for you, but maybe next time don't be such a hypocritical skank. You can play the victim all you want, but you're about to get more attention than you ever bargained for. Lock the doors, bitch, because we know where you live.

I drop the phone like it's radioactive. "She says they know where I live."

"Who does?"

I think of the woman's words, and I feel it all over again, that icy sick spreading through my belly.

On the towel, my cell is still going off, more calls and texts and voice mails lighting up the screen.

"How did all these people get my number?" I say, even though I already know. "How did they find me?"

Gigi's shriek carries across the water. *"Mom."*

ELEVEN

The rest of the weekend passes in a blur.

We rush from the pool to hunker down at home, closing up the house like a bunker. Curtains shut, doors and windows locked, alarm armed and active. Patrick reports the doxing to the police and the neighborhood watch, both of whom set up extra patrols on our stretch of the street. None of us talk about the danger circling closer and closer to the house, and Gigi says nothing, period. She and her sister binge-watch Netflix in their respective rooms while I make hamburgers like a normal mother. The four of us eat in silence.

On Sunday morning, we wake to a frantic banging on the bedroom door. I lurch upright in bed, heart clanging.

Gigi's voice pushes through the wood. "*Mom*. They're here."

I frown at Patrick, already marching across the carpet to the window. "Who's here?"

"Cars. *Lots* of them."

A steady stream of them, slowing at the curb.

Patrick calls around until he can find someone to adjust the cameras on the roofline. He sets them to zoom in on the road, close enough to pick up an occasional license plate. While they tinker with the hardware, Patrick hammers a You Are Being Watched sign into the grass and pries the house numbers off the mailbox, but still, it's not enough. All day long, the cars keep floating by like some kind of macabre parade.

Fucking Mister Fluffles. That's who tweeted my cell phone and address into the world, and even though Twitter took the post down, there are still a million screenshots floating around the web. As soon as one is deleted, a dozen more pop up like poisonous mushrooms after a storm.

It's afternoon by the time it hits me, this danger that's suddenly becoming all too real. The online trolls, showing up here. Who knows what they're capable of?

And Mister Fluffles, my ass. Every time I close my eyes, I see AC behind a laptop somewhere, sending her snark into the world. I think of all the things she knows about me, all my wounds and sore spots, and my insides boil because I don't know what's coming next. Only that it will be bad.

The doorbell rings as I'm shoving the last of the dinner plates into the dishwasher. I stand there for a long moment, thinking of the trolls, of the anonymous drive-bys and Mister Fluffles promising bodily harm, of the darkness that by now has a firm hold on the sky. I look to Patrick, seated out on the patio with a glass of wine and his phone, fiddling with the camera feeds. He whirls around, and I see dread on his face.

The doorbell rings again as we're coming into the foyer, and when he opens the door, it's the detective on the stoop. I take in her suit, navy pants topped with a jacket and white blouse, the mirrored shades shoved atop her head even though the sun has long since dropped behind the trees, and my heart gives a hard kick. A detective doesn't stop by—after hours and on a Sunday evening—to bring good news.

"Did you find her?" I say at the same time Patrick reaches out a hand. "Hi, I'm—"

"Patrick Hutchinson, the financial freedom guy. I know. My husband and I took your 25 Ways to Cultivate Wealth workshop last month and, so far, we've netted over a thousand bucks."

The news lights up his face with a wide smile, like it does whenever he meets a fan. "That's fantastic. Stay tuned, I'm putting the finishing touches on part two of that series. It should be out next month."

She whips out a badge, holding it up just long enough for him to get a decent look. "My name is Detective Muriel Bennett, Atlanta PD. I'm sorry to disturb." She slaps it closed and shoves it back in her pocket. "Thanks for sending over those Uber specifics, by the way."

I look at my husband, frowning. Patrick didn't tell me he's been in touch with the detective. He'd slid the card into his pocket and hadn't said another word—about her, about the vanished AC. I tell myself it's because of all the other drama, the trolls and the doxing, but still. Something about his omission nags.

"Not a problem, Detective. I hope it was helpful." He flashes her another one of his smiles, and I've got to give it to him. His television persona comes in handy at times like these.

Brake lights flash up at the curb, a dark Mustang stopped at the mouth of the driveway, and my thoughts scatter to all the threats that have come to life today. I look back to the detective, wondering if she's got a weapon under all that fabric.

"Yes and no," she says. "The driver confirmed he dropped her in front of her apartment complex that night, but he didn't wait around for her to get inside, and unfortunately the complex doesn't have security cameras." The detective's gaze slides to me. "I take it you still haven't heard from your assistant?"

"She's no longer my assistant. I fired her." Not that she responded, but still. My message was loud and clear. "And she picked up her car over the weekend," I say, gesturing over the detective's head to the street beyond. One minute it was there, baking on the hot asphalt, the next it was gone. *Good riddance*, I thought as we drove past the spot—both AC and the car. "It happened yesterday while we were at the pool."

"That was me." The detective blinks at me with pretty green eyes, decorated with nothing but a swipe of mascara. "I had the vehicle impounded because it contained evidence."

"What kind of evidence?"

"Her cell phone, for one. DNA and prints. Things like that."

The iPhone 11 I gave her in January because the camera on her ancient Android was a piece of crap and taking Insta-worthy pictures is a big part of her job. *Was* a big part. A pressure builds in my head, a sharp ringing that puts me on edge.

"So what are you saying, that she's *missing* missing?"

Detective Bennett gives me a peculiar look. "No one has seen or heard from your former assistant for more than seventy-two hours, not since her Uber driver dropped her off. She never made it inside. Her neighbors reported another car, a dark SUV much like the ones you and your husband drive, pulling out of the lot around the time she was dropped off, but unfortunately nobody got a license plate. We're looking through the footage of other, nearby cameras, but these things take time."

"A car like ours," I say. "Is that some kind of accusation?"

"Not an accusation, a fact. A woman is missing. I'm trying to find her."

And just like that, I realize the greater implications of the detective's visit. Of her first visit last week, when I opened the door with a red face and bones jumping out of my skin. I didn't invite her inside. I barely even remember what I said, only that I was in the middle of a work disaster and couldn't talk long. I wasn't thinking straight, and I definitely wasn't taking AC being missing seriously.

Now I stand here, a fresh wave of dread expanding in my chest.

"She...she probably just went to visit her father or something. I can't remember where he lives, exactly. But close, definitely driving distance."

"With what car?" The detective flashes a closed-lipped smile, a tight, perfunctory one that feels like it doesn't come easy.

I fall silent. Stupid, *stupid*.

Thank God Patrick is his usual, charming self. He invites the detective inside, offering up something to drink along with a well-placed wisecrack about how she got saddled with the weekend shift. He fills three glasses with ice and water and the kitchen with chatter, while she takes in the view of the terrace with its giant pots of flowers, the pool lit up a dark blue.

Patrick hands me a water and slides another across the kitchen island to the detective. "What about credit cards? If she visited an ATM or made a charge, she'd leave a trail, right?"

She sinks onto a stool at the island, pulling a pad of paper and a pen from her inside pocket. "Her wallet and credit cards were in the console of her car, along with her phone. She hasn't used any of them since Wednesday afternoon."

The day I sent her to pick up my dry cleaning, and she'd grabbed lunch from the deli next door. Tuna fish on rye. The sandwich made the carriage house smell like pickles, which I spent my entire pregnancy avoiding since I'd throw up if I caught so much as a whiff. Even now, twelve years later, the scent still sends up a wave of sour. I asked her if she'd mind eating outside. I remember all this with a weird sinking feeling.

The detective flips to a fresh page in her notepad. "What happened last week to make you terminate Anna Claire?"

"AC," I say automatically, putting down my glass with a thwack. "Nobody calls her Anna Claire but her father, and I didn't *terminate* her. I fired her, and for good reason. A very of-fensive post was uploaded late Wednesday night to my Insta-gram feed, and I'm pretty sure she was the one who did it. Plus, in the days since, some gossip sites have published information that could have only come from her, and this weekend we were doxed. That's why I haven't been worried about her. She's not missing. She just doesn't want to be found."

"But why would she do that? Why would she want to sabo-tage your career?"

"It's the question I've been asking myself all weekend long. But she's the only person besides me who has access to my so-cials. *Had*, I mean. I changed all my passwords on Friday."

"Did she mention any plans she had for this past weekend? Any names of friends she might be staying with?"

I shake my head, frowning. The detective's sudden switch-ing of gears feels vaguely insulting, and she already asked me this question the first time she came by. My answer is the same.

"That's not the kind of stuff AC and I talked about. Our conversations were usually limited to me and the job, captions and Insta-content, things like that. She didn't talk about her-self much."

"Why do you think that is?"

"Because I was her boss. Because she's a private person, I don't know. She never mentioned any names or whether or not she had a boyfriend. She never talked about what she did in her free time. I know practically nothing about her."

I know that nobody calls her Anna Claire but her father. That her mother died when she was young. That there's a brother out west somewhere. I got the feeling there were issues there, long-simmering resentments and maybe some kind of addiction. She hardly ever talked about any of them.

But what about friends? Boyfriends? Hobbies or how she spends her time when she's not here? The truth is, I never even asked.

The detective scribbles something on her pad. "Don't you find that strange? That she knows all these things about you, private, personal things you don't want revealed on these gossip sites, and yet you know very little about her and her life."

I try not to be insulted by the detective's tone or what she's insinuating, that I'm too self-centered to have asked my personal assistant about herself. And then I wonder if her question is meant to be bait, a trick to make me respond. It puts me on guard, and so does Patrick's expression.

"It's not that I never asked, Detective. It's that AC told me very little. She'd always flip the subject back to work, so after a while I simply stopped asking. She made it obvious she didn't want to talk about her private life."

"What about someone she might be having issues with? Someone who could have been harassing her?"

Again, we've already been over this. I swallow down a sigh and rattle off the same answer I gave her on Thursday. "Nothing she ever said makes me think that might be true, but AC has been on my feed often enough that my fans know her as my assistant. And I've been receiving plenty of threats, which I'm guessing you've heard since we filed a police report. It's possible that someone might see her as a way to get to me. Have you looked into that?"

"Any chance you know the passcode?" she says without answering my question.

I frown. "The passcode to what?"

"Ms. Davis's iPhone, the one we found in her car. Do either of you know how to open it?"

Her gaze bounces from me to Patrick and there's a moment, just a breath, where I almost let the digits roll off in a tumble. The ones I've seen AC tap in a million times: 2-4-6-4-6-2.

And then I think of what the detective will find on the other side of the lock screen, and a loud clanging starts up in my head. Dozens and dozens of messages from me, my voice animal-hot with rage. Voice mails accusing her of sabotaging my business. Texts promising revenge.

If you did this, I will kill you.

Detective Bennett is still waiting, pen poised to the paper, and suddenly I want nothing more than for her to leave. I want to go upstairs and huddle under the covers until this somehow magically all disappears—vanished, like AC.

But the detective is still watching me, her eyes probing into mine like searchlights. Without thinking, I hear myself say, "Sorry, but I have no idea."

"Worth a try," she says with a shrug, then turns to Patrick. "I'd like to talk a little more about the cameras."

His body is still loose and relaxed where it's leaning against the counter, but his back goes a little straighter, a muscle flexing in his jaw. "Sure, but I already sent you everything I had."

"I thought they were set to automatically record."

"Yes, but only when they pick up some kind of motion, and then they record in a continuous loop, meaning new footage records over the oldest, at most only three or four days. And the technician just dumped the footage, unfortunately, when we installed the new cameras earlier this afternoon. If you've got the time, we can run downstairs and I'll show you the system."

She slaps her notebook closed and stands, and now it all makes perfect sense. The timing of this visit, the way she didn't look the least bit surprised to find both of us home. The detective didn't come here to speak to me, to ask me all those same questions. She came to talk to Patrick. To ask him about the camera footage, to get him to show it to her. Behind that disguise of the overly reserved, overworked cop, Detective Bennett is sharp as a scalpel.

Patrick leads her to the stairs, and suddenly I'm thinking of our conversation on Thursday night, when I mentioned the detective was asking about the camera footage. Which he just dumped, earlier today. A coincidence, surely.

As soon as they're gone, I pour my water in the sink and tug open the fridge door, reaching for the bottle of sauvignon blanc.

@ashleexoxo Hold up. So now her personal assistant has gone missing and we're supposed to feel *sorry* for her? I mean come on. There's something fishy going on here.

@suzieqknits I'm with you @ashleexoxo. Alex doesn't deserve our sympathy but the assistant sure does. I'm praying for her safety.

@morninggloria47 @unapologeticallyalex is a vicious whore I wish someone would make her disappear

@misterfluffles Whatever has happened to that poor personal assistant, you know what they say. It's always the husband.

TWELVE

ANNA CLAIRE

There was a jackalope on the bar at Skoby's Steakhouse. A stuffed rabbit with beady eyes and fluffy tail and antlers slapped on top of its head, just sitting there at the corner of the bar like it was about to hop off it. AC had heard about it, of course, but she'd never seen the stupid thing in person. And unlike the rest of the people in town, she didn't find it the least bit funny.

But she had to give it to Jim Skoby, this place was nice. Roomy booths with red leather couches, wood-paneled walls covered with art, crisp white tablecloths and candles every-where—on the tables, in big candelabras on the bar, hanging in glass bowls from the ceiling. And then there was the smell, but-ter and garlic and meat, and her stomach growled. She couldn't remember the last time she'd had a good steak.

She stepped up to the hostess stand. "Hi, I'm——"

"I know who you are, AC. We only went to school together for like ever."

AC stared at the girl, her mind a blank. The problem was, school was a while ago, and she'd dropped out two months into her junior year. Her mother had just died, which meant high school was a blur of flunked tests and crying jags in a bathroom stall. It was a time AC was trying really hard to forget.

The hostess rolled her eyes. "Heather. The name's Heather."

A cheerleader, one of the spunky ones who climbed over other girls' backs to the top of the pyramid. Now she brought people to their tables at Skoby's. AC didn't know which was worse, peaking in high school like Heather here, or never peaking at all.

"Hey, Heather. I haven't seen you in forever."

"I passed you last week in the dairy aisle at Ingles, and the week before that we were getting gas at the same pump. I waved but you looked the other way." She paused for AC's response, but when she didn't get one, Heather rolled her eyes. "Anyway, how's Adam?"

A dig, one AC didn't appreciate.

"Adam and I broke up." The *again* was silent but implied. Heather was likely well versed in their on-again, off-again dating drama. There'd been plenty of it. AC gestured to the reservation book, spread open on the hostess stand. "I'm meeting somebody for dinner. Can you maybe check if he's already here?"

With a sigh, Heather plucked two menus off the hostess stand. "He's not, but your table's ready."

AC slid into the corner booth, cursing herself for getting here first. After the weird ending to the car ride to the Starlux, after the tires and the red rose and the note ordering her to meet him here tonight, she'd debated the wisdom of coming at all, but the promise of a steak dinner wore her down.

But that didn't mean she was going to make this easy.

It's why she made sure to waltz in this place a full twenty

minutes late, why she didn't spend the entire afternoon in front of a mirror, fixing her makeup and hair, or run to the mall for a new dress she couldn't afford. She wore her favorite shirt over a miniskirt she'd found for a dollar at Goodwill, threw her hair in a side braid. She didn't want him to think he was worth all that much effort.

But she'd still beat him, dammit.

"Ma'am." The waiter appeared with a glass of bubbly yellow liquid, placing it on the table with a nod.

"I didn't order that."

"It's been taken care of," he said, and then disappeared.

She stared at the glass, watching the bubbles ping-pong up the inside. How much did a glass of champagne cost, anyway? A lot, that much she knew. Her cheeks flushed at the idea she was worth a glass of champagne.

She picked it up, took a sip. Then another, humming because champagne was freaking delicious. She never thought she'd ever be drinking it, and now she was. Now she was the kind of person who drank champagne.

One glass turned into three, and AC checked her watch. Thirty-eight minutes past seven, which…seeing as she'd arrived twenty minutes late, meant she'd been waiting only eighteen minutes. Eighteen minutes certainly sounded a lot more acceptable than thirty-eight.

But still. Was this some kind of trick? Was it a game? Why buy her tires and invite her to dinner—twice—only to not show? AC shook her head, hoping to shake out some of the booze, but she couldn't think straight. Her stomach was empty and her head was buzzy with champagne.

Suddenly, the waiter reappeared, his arms stacked with plates piled high with food. Her mouth watered at the smell.

"What's all that?"

"Filet mignon, veal martini, creamed spinach, three-cheese au gratin, black truffle gnocchi and a side salad, ma'am."

One by one, he settled the plates on the table. On her side of the table. Like she was eating alone, which by now she knew she was. She knew it by the way the waiter wouldn't quite meet her eyes.

"What am I supposed to do with this? I can't eat it all by myself."

She could. Probably. She was that hungry. Starving, really. Her everyday diet consisted mainly of pasta and tuna fish, American cheese and white bread. This was meat, *fine* meat, and enough of it to keep her stuffed for days.

She stared at the steak, perfectly browned meat still sizzling from the grill, at the black-flecked pillows of steaming potatoes smothered in creamy sauce, and her stomach roiled with hunger and something else, something that felt a lot more painful.

He pulled the champagne bottle from the ice bucket, wiped it with a white cloth and refilled her glass. "Is there anything else I can get for you?"

"No. I'm fine, thank you."

Except she wasn't fine. She was fucking humiliated.

She waited until he was gone, until Heather was clear on the opposite end of the restaurant, leading three men in dark suits to their table. And with one last, longing look at all that delicious food, she slipped out into the night.

THIRTEEN

PATRICK

My eyes pop open and I stare at the ceiling, breathing hard. My hands are tight fists, my muscles like concrete under the cool sheets. I roll to my side, check the time on my phone: 4:18 a.m. I've been asleep for all of forty minutes.

Not Alex. Alex passed out the second her eyes were closed, as usual. I've always admired that about her, how she can zonk out no matter how stressful her day. I used to be like that, too, used to getting a solid eight hours of effortless unconsciousness that left me rested and ready for the day. Now I can't remember the last time I slept through the night.

I watch her in the quiet dark, lips slightly parted, dark hair fanned across the pillow like a silky crown, and I feel it all over again, that tingling in my chest. The first time I saw this woman, running up to the valet stand with drenched hair and clothes,

I knew I wanted her here, in my bed, in my *life*. Even if that meant breaking some promises.

My eyes are drifting shut when it occurs to me: Why is the neighbor's dog barking?

I'm awake again in an instant, a tightening in my chest lurching me upright. I picture Ned Gibson creeping down the stairs in his overpriced briefs, aiming his shotgun out whatever window his golden retriever is trying to bust through. There's only one reason for a dog to lose its shit in the middle of the night. I peel back the covers and step out of bed.

I make a quick pit stop in the closet for a rumpled pair of sweats and some sneakers, shoving my feet in without bothering with the laces. I need my gun, dammit, but there's an empty spot in the back of my sock drawer, and I have no idea how long the gun's been missing. Two weeks? A month? Five? I dig out the Taser I'd shoved in its place, testing it to make sure it's got a charge. I'm taking a Taser to a gunfight.

I'm creeping down the hallway when a door pops open, and my response is instinctive. I spin toward the sound, and my arm lifts while my brain screams, *Hold fire*. My muscles obey just in time.

"*Penny*. You scared the *crap* out of me."

My pulse hammers hard in my ears, ramped up by the adrenaline my stepdaughter just dumped into my bloodstream.

Her nose wrinkles at the name. Penny hates it when people call her that, which I've done since the day we met because her hair demands it—copper colored, and as glossy as a new penny in the July sun. Now it's a wild mess around her head, fluffy curls rising up like tiny flames, ones she'll wrangle in a few hours with a flat-iron before school. A bedside lamp blazes in the room behind her, silhouetting her in golden light and illuminating her face, setting her hair on fire.

"I heard something," she whispers. "A thump."

I nod. A thump is what woke me up, too.

"Go back to bed," I whisper, shifting my body so the Taser is tucked behind a hip, but it's too late. The eagle-eyed Penny has already spotted it.

She steps into the shadowy hall, reaching for it with a skinny arm. "Since when do we have a Taser? Cool. Can I try?"

"Not a chance in hell."

The twins have no reason to be afraid of a thump or a Taser, and I'm fine with that. Alex tries very, very hard to protect them from the fact that there are real monsters in the world, a reality that runs like a black river underneath their country-club, private-school existence. If my wife has her way, these girls will stay innocent as long as possible, taping posters to their bedroom walls and spending weekends practicing back dives with their girlfriends.

But like every other privileged girl her age, Penelope is well versed in Snapchat and TikTok and Instagram. Alex and I know we are walking a fine line. We know the twins' passwords, we monitor their socials, we have the best parental controls money can buy.

But there's no way to shield them from the Unapologetically Alex shit show.

You see her daughters? I'd tap that.

Twins, double the fun. Might just pay them a visit now that I know where they live.

I also don't believe they're just words. I know that somewhere out there, in between the mindless hate and petty insults, lives a very real sociopath who can turn their threats into reality without a second's notice. It's why I'm standing in this hallway with a freaking Taser, because I know it could happen at any time. I know what the onrush of danger feels like, and this is fucking it.

"Get back in your room. Lock your door. Don't come out until I give you an all clear."

"But what—"

"Do it, Penny. *Now.*"

She rolls her eyes, but she obeys. She shuts her door, and I wait for the sharp click that tells me it's locked.

For a brief second, I consider reaching into Gigi's room to flip her lock, as well, but as long as I've known her, she's been a difficult sleeper. I'm surprised she isn't awake already.

On the stairs, I avoid the squeaky spots by sticking to the far edges, straining to hear anything over my pounding heart. The air is cooler down here, pushing chill bumps up like braille on the skin of my chest. I should have grabbed a shirt, dammit, and a dark one. My bare chest might as well be a reflector.

I jiggle the handle on the front door—locked.

On the wall, an alarm pad glows in the darkness—green, not red—and I stop to think. Up until this past week, Alex always treated the alarm as something of an afterthought, no matter how many times I stressed its importance. Something she'd turn on as she's running out the front door, something she used to protect the *house*, not herself in it. I've always been a stickler about turning it on, and after these past few days, Alex finally agrees. I can't believe she forgot to arm it before going upstairs.

I tick in the code to set the system to stay. The light flips from green to red, and three rapid-fire beeps pierce the silence. I wince, thinking of the sleeping people upstairs. With any luck, Alex slept right through it.

I creep into the dining room, peeling back the curtains and peering onto the front lawn, a rolling sea of blackish green under the glow of a far-off streetlamp. The moon has dropped behind the trees, tall pines jutting up from the neighboring yards. But even without its glow, any criminal would be crazy to come in from the front, where there's the threat of street traffic and the bushes are too short to provide much cover. The only place to lurk is behind the cars, two hulking black smudges parked side by side on a wider spot on the driveway. I stare into the darkness, watching and waiting, but there's nothing but that damn dog.

I move through the dark rooms to the back of the house.

The kitchen windows, the glass doors, the wall of steel and glass overlooking the covered patio—these are the spots any criminal worth his weight would choose to come through. Last month, an owl rammed one of those panes hard enough to crack the glass. I peer out the windows onto the patio floor, my gaze sweeping the couch and chairs, the stacked wood by the fireplace, but there's no owl. Nothing else, either.

And then I spot it through the glass, movement in my periphery. My gaze moves over the pool to the shadows beyond, and it's a body, slipping around the side of the carriage house. I blink, and they're gone.

With three giant strides, I lurch backward into the kitchen, reaching for the phone on the counter. I punch in 9-1-1 while mentally rehearsing my next moves. Grab a knife from the block. Rush him with the Taser. While he's down, slice the tendons at the ankles. Slash slash boom—bloody and incapacitated.

"Nine-one-one, what's your emergency?"

"This is Patrick Hutchinson at 111 Club Drive in Brookhaven. There's someone in my backyard, moving toward the house. They were at the carriage house at the back of the yard and now they're..." I edge closer to the window, my gaze scanning the shadows. "I don't see them now, but two seconds ago they were coming this way."

"Sir, are all the doors and windows locked?"

"Yes, and the alarm's on. I just set it."

"Okay, I'm sending an officer your way. Just sit tight, sir, and keep everyone inside."

On the far side of the pool, something dark and quick moves across the grass, disappearing into a cluster of shrubs. I picture the other side of all that greenery, where a path cuts from the carriage house alongside the pool to the far end of the patio. A few more seconds, and they'll be coming out the other side.

I grip the phone and the Taser—the *Taser*, for Christ's sake.

The only thing standing between this asshole and my family sleeping upstairs is a lousy Taser.

I press myself into the curtains by the kitchen window and whisper, "How much longer?"

"ETA four and a half minutes."

Four and a half minutes. A fucking eternity.

I'm so busy staring out the back window that I almost miss it, the dark smudge of movement on the patio. A body, long and thin. An arm, reaching for the door.

And the profile of a face, as familiar as my own.

I see it and lunge for the doorknob, the phone and Taser clattering to the kitchen floor, but I don't get there on time. Gigi reaches the handle first, and she's not expecting anyone to be on the other side of the door, least of all her stepfather. She gives the door a tug, and three things happen all at once.

A steady beeping erupts at the front of the house.

Gigi screams.

A siren splits the air.

"So let me get this straight. While you were sneaking through the backyard, you didn't see or hear anyone else?"

Officer Graham is in his forties, pale haired and thick necked, with a scowl to let us all know he's annoyed as hell to be working the night shift. Gigi glances at her mother, then to Penelope on her other side and me on a nearby chair, but she doesn't find much support.

She looks up from her spot on the couch, shaking her head, her eyes huge and dark. "I heard Bruno barking. That's it."

"Bruno is Ned Gibson's dog," I explain. By now I have on a shirt, a semiclean one I dug out of the basket in the laundry room as the first cop car was pulling into the driveway, and I keep getting whiffs of nervous sweat mixed with floral perfume. "Ned lives two doors down."

Outside on the driveway, more cops mill around, dusting for

prints and bagging evidence. I can hear them talking and moving around, and I hope our neighbors have somehow managed to sleep through all the commotion—though I can't imagine how. Somehow, in the midst of all the chaos of Gigi and the wailing sirens, someone else was outside, taking a sledgehammer to Alex's car. My car, parked only a few feet away, didn't get a scratch.

Alex drapes a hand over my shoulder. She's still too on edge to sit down, still breathing hard from her sprint around the house, flipping on every single light inside and out. The house is so bright a plane could land in the backyard. "I still don't understand. What were you doing in my office at two a.m.?"

"I already told you," Gigi says, her voice verging on defensive. "I wasn't in your office."

"Then what were you doing outside?"

Silence. Gigi sighs, staring at her lap. I've been around her long enough to know the gesture. It's a dead giveaway that she's guilty.

Alex tugs her robe tight around her chest, and her cheeks are like apples, red and shiny. She steps around the furniture to glare at her daughter. "Gigi. It is four a.m. on a school night. Your little stunt just shaved five years off my life. What the hell were you doing in the backyard?"

Another long, begrudging sigh before she mumbles, "I was coming back from Tara's."

Tara Blum, a friend and fellow sixth grader who goes to a private school down by the airport—which in Gigi's mind makes her hopelessly cosmopolitan because it means she takes MARTA to school. Tara's a decent kid, but it's her older brother I'm more concerned about, a pimply little shit who wraps a Koozie around his White Claw and thinks he's got everyone fooled.

And I've seen the way he looks at Gigi, who sometime while I wasn't watching has bloomed into a gorgeous miniwoman, breasts and curves and all. She's a beauty like her mother, the kind that lights up a room. Everywhere she goes, people stop to stare.

People like Tara's punk brother.

I stare at her, this beautiful, gorgeous preteen who was in some boy's house in the middle of the night, and I want to put my fist through a wall.

Alex looks similarly furious. She stuffs her hands in her robe pockets, taking a couple of noisy breaths through her nose. "Tara Blum. You were at Tara Blum's house." She pauses for Gigi's nod. "When you were supposed to be in your bed asleep. When Patrick and I had no clue you were even gone. You were coming home from Tara Blum's house in the middle of the night."

Another nod.

"Do you have any idea," she says, her voice going high and frantic in the quiet house, "*any* freaking idea how many murderers there are roaming this city? Tell her, Officer." She swings an arm in his direction, but she doesn't turn around. "Tell her how many."

Officer Graham opens his mouth, but he doesn't get a chance to answer.

"A million, at *least*, but you don't know this because I protect you from that kind of news. From the shootings and rapes and assaults. And don't even get me started about all the pretty girls your age who disappear while just walking down the street or through their own neighborhood. Only they don't really disappear, Gigi. They get taken. Sold into sex slavery or worse."

Penny frowns. "What's worse than sex slavery?"

"Death, Penelope. Death is worse."

"Than sex slavery?" She makes a face. "Not in my book, it's not."

Officer Graham shifts on his chair, the equipment on his belt chinking. "If y'all don't mind, I'd really love it if you'd hold off on this family discussion until I get through my questions. Because you have to understand how it looks from where I'm sitting, young lady. Your mother's car is vandalized at the same time you're caught sneaking out. Now I'm not saying you are the vandal, but you look like a smart kid so I'm guessing you know where I'm going with this. Especially because you claim not to have seen or heard anyone else out there."

Gigi catches his meaning instantly, and her face goes slack with shock, with fear. "But I didn't do that to her car. Mom, tell him I didn't touch it. I *wouldn't*."

"You were outside," Alex reminds her. "At four a.m. You went to a friend's house in the middle of the night. Without your stepfather's or my permission."

Gigi's eyes go wide, shiny with fresh tears. "But that doesn't mean I did that to your car. Patrick, *tell her*."

I reach for Alex's hand and give a gentle tug, pulling her to my chair. I've always been a sucker for tears from any of my girls, but especially Gigi. The twin who almost never cries.

I turn to Officer Graham. "Gigi is telling the truth. She was coming through the patio door on the opposite side of the house when the car alarm started up. I had eyes on her when Alex's car started wailing."

"And the cameras?"

The cameras. My pores open up, and my skin starts to sweat.

Seventy-two hours. That's how long the Ring website told me it would take for their servers to wipe the footage. They promise me once it is gone it can never be retrieved. I sure fucking hope they're right.

I pull up the Ring footage on my phone, then flip it around so Officer Graham can see.

The video starts at 3:48 a.m., when it picks up movement. A figure in dark pants and a dark hoodie pulled tight around their face, skirting the edge of the driveway. Female? Maybe, but impossible to tell for sure. A small man, a tall teenager. The clothes are baggy, the gait purposeful enough that it could be either. What I do know for sure is that whoever it is holds a sledgehammer in one hand and a bucket in the other—one filled with white paint, currently dripping from Alex's car.

At just before 3:50 a.m. they stop at the edge of the grass and raise a middle finger at the Ring.

"Probably just a bored kid," Officer Graham says, as if that makes it okay, as if that means we should just shrug off what was clearly a giant threat.

"I was doxed," Alex shrieks, popping off the chair. "I've been getting all sorts of threats. Death threats. Rape threats. I'd appreciate it if you'd take this seriously."

"I can assure you, Mrs. Hutchinson, I am taking this very seriously. That kind of damage to a car like yours is a felony. I will be filing a report, but your footage doesn't give us much to go on in terms of identifying the perpetrator. The image is too dark and grainy, and we don't get so much as a sliver of his or her face. What about the roofline cameras?"

I shake my head. "Those are even farther away and pointed up at the road. I had them adjusted because of all the drive-bys."

At the front of the house, a door opens, and multiple cops file into the foyer, a chorus of shuffling boots and low murmurs. One of them breaks away from the bunch, heavy footsteps coming across the slate tiles.

"Found this stabbed to the front seat, sir," a uniformed officer says from the doorway, a clear plastic bag in a hand. Alex spots the contents, and she sucks in a breath.

A kitchen knife, a long silver blade with a black handle, resting on a sheet of paper, one long edge tattered from where it was ripped from a spiral notebook. About halfway down is a neat slice the width of the blade, and just below it, two words, slashed across the paper in bright red marker.

DIE BITCH

"Do either of you recognize the handwriting?"

What am I supposed to say? *My wife's assistant, the one who's supposedly missing, the same woman Detective Bennett is trying to lo-*

cate. The one calling herself Anna Claire Davis. That's who destroyed my wife's car. The cop would ask me how I know, how I can be so sure—and that's a subject I'm trying especially hard to avoid.

Alex shakes her head. "No, but I recognize the knife. We own one just like it, a freebie from a kitchen-store sponsor."

"Are you saying this knife belongs to you?"

"It might. Let me take a look." She disappears around the corner into the kitchen, and we sit here for a minute in silence, listening to her root through drawers, clattering the utensils in the dishwasher. "I'm not finding it."

"Prints?" Officer Graham says to the cop behind him, who shakes her head. He turns back with an *oh-well* shrug. "Send me that footage, will you? I'll see if our tech department can't get a better look at the face."

I nod. "I'll send it to you first thing tomorrow morning."

Officer Graham slaps both hands to his knees and pushes to a stand. "All righty, then. Give me a few more minutes to make sure everything's been handled the way it should be outside, and then we'll be out of your hair."

I show him out, and when I shut the door behind him, it takes everything in me not to slam it.

The police demanding answers. My family being threatened.

And in the middle of it all, the missing AC.

FOURTEEN

After Officer Graham and his team leave, I'm too wired to go back to bed, and the thought of staring at the clock while it counts down the minutes until my alarm goes off rattles my nerves even further. I fire up the coffee machine.

"Want a cup?"

Alex nods, sinking onto a stool at the counter. Her eyes are bleary but alert, and her robe has loosened up around her torso, gaping at the neck to show off a slice of silky lace. "Do you think it was her?"

I don't have to ask who Alex is referring to. No, the Ring didn't pick up a clear shot of her face. No, I couldn't get enough context from the rest of the yard to guess the person's weight or height, but that doesn't mean I'm not certain.

I pass Alex the first cup, nodding. "It sure looked like her, didn't it?"

"But why? That's what I can't figure out, *why*. What did I ever do to make her hate me this much?" She holds the mug in both hands, her fingers looped through the handle. "Never mind what she did to my car, but *die bitch*? Stabbed through with a butcher knife."

I tap the button for a second cup and think about everything that's happened since the Krissie Kelly post. The attacks are escalating, that much is clear.

Even worse, I have no damn clue how to stop them.

Alex plunks her cup on the marble without taking a sip. "You know what the general consensus is, right? People are thinking, *That's what you get*. If you don't want that kind of hate, then don't be an influencer. Don't put yourself out there, or else you deserve every bit of criticism you get in return. It's what those cops were thinking. It's what my mother is thinking. People are saying that's the nature of the internet, and I only have myself to blame."

I nod, because I've thought it more than once myself. Why let all these strangers in on our private lives, our family? I asked this a lot in the beginning, back before there was money, *good* money, involved, back when it felt like she was sending out all that content purely for likes and shares and comments. Back when the feedback was almost exclusively positive.

"I refuse to subscribe to that," she says now, "the this-is-what-you-signed-up-for mentality, because you know what I signed up for? Less privacy. That's it. I signed up for strangers wanting a peek into my personal life. Not for them to destroy my property. Not for them to harass me and my kids. To wish us bodily harm."

And there it is, the crux of the problem. Alex is the one who signed up for this lack of privacy. Not me, not the twins, even though it involves us, too. Alex is the one putting the Hutchinson family in perfect, pretty squares—big smiles at dinnertime even though the girls are pinching each other under the table, or piling out of a shiny Mercedes for the thousandth time because the first 999 takes weren't good enough. Nobody would blame her for figuring out a way to turn those followers into cash— least of all me. I'm the money guy, for crap's sake.

But a million followers, all those viral posts. Alex is really, really out there.

"I have to ground her," she says, staring into her coffee cup. "Gigi, I mean. How long do you think is reasonable?"

I lean against the counter, crossing my arms. "I don't know. Lock her in the basement until she's thirty?"

"Seems about right." Alex smiles.

Above our heads, water runs through the pipes, footsteps creaking the hardwoods. One of the girls, getting into the shower. I check the back windows, and the sky is lightening around the edges. Almost time for the alarm.

"Seriously, though," she says. "Two weeks? A month?"

I wince. Gigi has always been the more social twin, the one always angling to be anywhere but here. For her there's no torture worse than a Saturday night spent at home, without a friend to keep her company.

"She's going to make our lives miserable, you know that, right?"

"Yeah, well, she should have thought of that before she snuck out." Alex stands, gesturing to my empty cup. "Want a refill?"

"No, thanks. I've got an early meeting at the station."

I drop the mug in the sink and a kiss on her cheek and head upstairs to the shower, my thoughts returning for the millionth time to the key I found in AC's room, now taped to the inside flap of my wallet. A fairly common key, according to the locksmith I showed it to, but one that belongs to a discus lock. The kind people hang on lockers and self-storage units. In this case the latter, I'm guessing.

Talk about a needle in a haystack, seeing as there are thousands of those facilities in this city alone, each with dozens and dozens of doors. It would take me years to get to all of them, but it's all I can think about, what's behind the door that this key unlocks. A pile of money? A mountain of cocaine?

Or maybe just a grinning AC with my gun, waiting for me to find her.

I'm still thinking about it forty minutes later, as I'm herding the girls out the door. By now the sun is good and up, shining like a spotlight on the bright white paint splattered in great blobs over Alex's car. The hood, the leather interior, what's left of the windshield. The back windows hang like broken spiderwebs, a network of pebbles scattered across the asphalt below.

Gigi stops on the top step, sucking in a breath. "Whoa."

"Are you sure it was only one person?" Penny says, her nose crinkling. "Like, how did one person do all this?"

It's a fair question. How did she do all this damage before the car alarm started wailing, before the neighbors spotted her, before any of us could run to the front windows and see her whaling on it through the glass? I take in the angry slashes she keyed into the paint, the dents she slammed in the doors and body, and there's no way that car's not totaled.

I give the girls a little nudge. "We're already late. Let's go."

They climb into my car without their usual morning squabble about whose turn it is to ride shotgun (Penny's), or to play Spotify DJ (Gigi's). They toss their backpacks to the floorboards like sacks of concrete and fasten their seat belts without a reminder, staring at their mother's car through the windows.

At the four-way stop, I mute the morning news on the radio. "So, do we need to talk about last night?"

"No," the twins answer in chorus. I've seen their crumpled brows, the way they're chewing their bottom lips, and Penny's freckles are practically glowing, a clear indication that she's stressed.

"I'm not referring to Gigi sneaking out, because your mother made herself plenty clear on that one, and you're grounded for a month." There's a gasp from the back seat, one I don't pause to acknowledge. "I'm talking about what happened to your mother's car. I can only imagine how that might feel for you, knowing someone got that close to our front door."

Too close. Twenty feet max.

"I've already adjusted the range of motion on the camera app," I continue, "and I'll be adding more cameras to cover the backyard."

Penny snorts and twists around on the front seat. "Too bad for you."

Gigi rolls her eyes. "Shut up."

"You can maybe climb out the window at the end of the hall, but it's awfully high. If you fall, you'll probably break your neck."

"I said, shut *up*."

"*Both* of you, quiet." My gaze flicks to Gigi in the rearview, glaring at the back of Penny's head. "What I'm trying to say is, I've got eyes on the yard and driveway now, better ones, and the police are upping their regular patrols. What happened to your mother's car, it won't happen again."

Gigi rolls her eyes. "Right. Because all those million other A-holes out there, waiting for their turn, are scared of a couple cameras. You know they can hack them, right? Or jam the Wi-Fi?"

I don't argue, not even about the crude language. I've seen the threats on Alex's page, and the missing AC is not the only danger I have to worry about.

"And besides," she says, "that's not even what's stressing us out. Mom's stupid Instagram is all anyone at school can talk about. It's just so humiliating."

I note the *we*, file it away for later, because of *course* the girls have been talking about this. They've starred on their mother's socials since they were seven, twin starlets in matching princess dresses and plastic crowns. All those strangers watching them grow into the lean, almost-women they are now, girls with smooth skin and long limbs and muscles not quite strong enough to fight back. Alex always says she'll worry when their braces come off, but she's kidding herself. She should be worried now.

"It's true your mother never asked if you wanted to be a part of her business," I say, taking the right toward school. "But you do have a choice, you know. You're old enough to decide for yourself."

"Omigod, on what planet?" Gigi lurches to the edge of the back seat, leaning into the space between them. Her seat belt tugs on a shoulder. "How many times have you told Mom you just wanted to have a nice, normal vacation without posing for a bunch of stupid pictures, or that you didn't feel like changing clothes but she made you, anyway, because the red shirt matched better with her dress? She's not going to stop just because we tell her to."

"Okay, but have you tried telling her how you feel? Your mother loves you, but more importantly than that, she respects you. Did you ask her not to include you in her posts?"

"Only a million times. She looks at us like we're crazy. She says something like 'Every kid wants to be Insta-famous. You're welcome.' But, like, I never asked for this. Why can't she have a *normal* job?"

Penny nods, turning to me with big and lovely eyes. "I thought we were supposed to be the ones obsessed with social media. Not Mom. I just want it to stop."

The truth is, I want it to stop, too. I wanted it to stop the first time all those strangers flocked to her page. Strangers who know where the girls practice soccer and where we go on vacation and our favorite family night restaurant. It never occurred to Alex that someone might use those posts against us.

But it occurred to me. Every day. A hundred times a day. All these years, the worry has been sitting there under my skin, itching. A million followers, a million people watching.

I swing into the school lot, and the girls are gathering up their bags when I veer into a parking place and hit the brakes.

Penny looks up with a frown, taking in the line of snaking cars backed up to the bottom of the hill. "We can't get out here. We'll get in tr—"

"Order your thoughts," I tell the girls, twisting around to look them both in the eye. My voice is loud and determined in the small, closed-up space. "Write your arguments down, make a list, do whatever it is you need to do, and I'll do the same. Just be ready."

"Ready for what?" Gigi says, and her expression of relief, of hope, kind of breaks my heart.

"We'll talk to your mother tonight."

FIFTEEN

I hear them as I jiggle my key into the front door lock, animated, angry words on the other side of the wood. Their voices tumble over one another, rising and falling in sharp peaks. I'm an only child. My mother worked fourteen-hour days, which meant whenever she was home, she was far too tired to fuss. As much as I love my girls, I really can't stand the female dramatics.

I flip the lock and push the door open to find Gigi, mid-screech.

"—exactly what we've been telling you all along was going to happen. Your stupid Instagram ruined my life!"

The foyer chandelier is bright, lighting up Gigi's shiniest spots—her eyes, her hair, the tear tracks on her cheeks. The tears are fresh, and they're still flowing.

Alex's face is pink, too, but her voice is trying hard to stay calm. "You think that picture came from me? I wouldn't do that, sweetheart. Never, *never*." She stands between the two girls like a referee, her cell clutched in a fist.

"Omigod, Mom, you took the photo!"

"I deleted it! Ages ago! You asked me to, so I deleted it. Here, look. I'll show you."

I dump my bag on the floor by the stairs. "What picture?"

All three of them start talking at the same time, and my head pounds. Rachel was on my ass the second I got to the station, and the guest I interviewed for an upcoming segment turned out to be a dud, a stuttering, sniveling mess as soon as the camera light flipped on. And now I'm coming home to another crisis.

"One at a time." I point to Gigi, mostly because she's crying the hardest. "You first."

"She posted that picture, Patrick. The one without my tooth. Now everybody knows I don't have one."

I wince, but I don't ask which tooth picture because there are so many. Thousands on my phone alone. Both the twins were born missing a lateral incisor, the flat tooth to the right of their top front two—a genetics slipup that fills every dentist with glee. Flippers. Retainers. Bridges. And eventually, once their skulls are declared mature enough, implants. By the time both twins are done, those two missing teeth will have financed a luxury car.

"I wouldn't do that, sweetheart. I *wouldn't*." Alex reaches for her, but Gigi wrenches her arm away.

"Right. You've posted every other humiliating picture you can think of so why not that one?"

As much as I hate seeing Thing One's tears, I've always found it adorable, these matching holes in their mouths, and I remember feeling real disappointment when the dentist first plugged them with a temporary bridge. Gone were the quirky gaps in the smiles I loved so much, and along with it, that last little slice of their childhood.

And then early last year, as their skirts got shorter and their curls were sacrificed to a straight iron, Gigi lost her bridge in a collision on the soccer field. The dentist wanted to make a new one, but the orthodontist said to wait until the braces are off. He put in a temporary denture instead, but Gigi keeps losing that one, too. And for a twelve-year old girl on the cusp of puberty, there can be no greater embarrassment.

"Show me," I say, holding out a hand.

Three cell phones are thrust in my direction, all flashing the same picture. A hot and sweaty Gigi after a hike to the top of Stone Mountain, the city shimmering in the distance behind her. She has both arms up in the air and a smile from ear to ear, big enough to show off the dark, gaping hole where a tooth should have been. I know whose face I'll spot if I zoom in on Gigi's mirrored shades. She's right that Alex is the one who took the picture.

"Where is this?"

"Stone Mountain," Penny says. "Duh. You were there."

"No, I mean where is it posted? What sites?"

"All of them," Gigi wails. "It's everywhere. And now everybody in the whole entire world has seen it and I want to *die*."

Penny, who's used to her sister's emotional hurricanes, sinks onto the steps with a smirk. Her thumbs punch at her cell phone screen with a speed only teenage girls can manage. Texting one of her friends, I'm guessing, a play-by-play update.

I look at my wife, and nod at my two beautiful stepdaughters. It's as good an opening as any.

"What is happening here? Is this…is this an *intervention*?"

Alex blinks at me from across the kitchen table, her eyes dark and stormy. Between us is a messy pile of cell phones—a necessary measure at family meetings, and a mandatory one. So far this conversation is going about as well as I expected.

"I can't believe this. Y'all really want me to shut down Unapologetically Alex? Like, completely shut her down. Make it look like I never existed."

The twins' nods are a bit too enthusiastic.

I soften mine with an apologetic smile. "That's what we're asking, yes."

"Okay, but I'd like to remind you how hard I've worked to get here. How much money Unapologetically Alex brings in, how many perks. Nobody complained when Neiman Marcus asked the twins to walk the runway in the celebrity kids fashion show, or when Six Flags gave us those season passes. And who do you think made that yachting trip down the coast of Croatia happen, or the first-class tickets to fly us there? Those were *my* sponsors. All that stops if I log off. No more freebie trips, no more shopping the boxes in the garage whenever you want something new to wear."

"We get it, Mom," Penelope says. "We don't care about that stuff."

Alex blinks in surprise. She wasn't expecting the twins not to care.

Her gaze bounces between them. "Look, I know these past few days have been hard on all of us. I know the drama has bled over to your private socials, to our private lives and our *home*, but I have sponsors and partnerships. Agreements I'm contractually bound to fulfill. I have people who expect to hear from me on a daily basis. A million of them."

"Not anymore," Penny says, flicking the top off her Gatorade bottle. "I just looked, and your follower count is down to 899K."

I flash her a look that says, *Not helping.* She turns up the bottle and chugs the rest.

"Okay, fine. I'll take your photos off my page, I'll untag you and make it look like you were never there, but I can't just shut down. Not when I can still turn this thing around."

No one responds because no one—not the twins, definitely not me—believes it's possible. Turn this thing around…how?

And even if Alex could somehow manage to reverse the tide, the trolls still know where we live. Any time one of her posts strikes a wrong chord, they'll come here to terrorize our family all over again. It's too late. We're already too exposed. There's nothing for her to turn around.

She digs her phone from the stack in the middle of the table, awakens her screen and plugs a search in Instagram. After a bit of poking, she flips it around so we can see. "Look at this woman's posts. Read her captions. Notice anything familiar?"

I'd have to be blind not to. Whoever this woman is, she's not a dead ringer for my wife, but she's pretty darn close. Same dark hair she wears smooth and parted down the middle, same beauty mark by her right eye, same filter she uses to smooth out her skin and turn the colors a little smoky.

But even more striking are the images, the poses and picture composition, clothing I recognize from Alex's closet. The red dress with the ruffles at the hem. The white blouse and faded jeans with the tears on both knees. The cat eyeglasses over big feather earrings. This woman is a copycat. She recreated some of Alex's most popular posts down to the very last detail.

"The captions aren't word for word, but they're close enough to qualify as plagiarism. And look at her follower numbers— more than 150K, and that's just in the past month."

I shake my head. "What does this have to do with anything?"

"It means Unapologetically Alex isn't a fluke. It means I'm putting out content that people find valuable and necessary. They like it enough to follow a copycat me, even if they don't realize she is one. Big picture, this means that once the trolls move on to the next scandal, I can win my followers back. I just have to wait until the dust settles."

I'm about to ask how—how will she win them back, how will the dust settle—when her cell chirrups in her hand. The other phones erupt, too, one right after the other, a clash of melodic beeps and buzzes coming from the pile.

Alex is the first to pull up the message on her screen. She looks up with a frown. "Get ready for what?"

"I don't know. Why are you asking me?"

She flips her phone around, the brand-new one I bought for her after her old number was doxed, with a number no one outside this room knows about. My name is at the top of her screen with two ominous words floating beneath.

Get ready.

"Get ready for what?" Penny says, looking up from her phone. "Why? What's going to happen?"

Gigi grimaces, dropping her phone to the table. "Better not be another picture."

With a flash of heat, I reach for the last phone in the pile, swiping to awaken the screen. The message didn't come from my fingers—*obviously*. It didn't even come from my phone. I open my messaging app and check all three strings. The *get ready* message is not there.

I'm staring at my phone when a message lands on my screen. A text from a number I don't recognize.

It's a little different than the ones my family received. A few more words. A lot more meaning. Not that I'll be sharing it with Alex or the twins anytime soon.

Is everybody ready? Because here I come.

SIXTEEN

ANNA CLAIRE

By the time AC saw him, waiting on the cracked front stoop of her crappy rental apartment, it was too late to keep driving. She'd already swung the Honda into the driveway, already locked eyes with him through the dirt-smeared glass. It was bad enough that he knew what she drove and where she worked, but now he had to see where she lived, too? She cursed the dead bushes under the living room window, her lazy-ass landlord who thought weeds qualified as grass that he let grow waist-high before coming over with a mower.

She killed the engine and climbed out, a sudden spurt of heat rising in her chest. "Are you married?"

"What?" He stood, brushing the dirt from his pants. "Why would you think that?"

"Because it's the only thing I can figure for why you ask me to dinner—twice, for the record—and then not show. Your wife got suspicious, didn't she? She wasn't buying whatever excuse you used for sneaking away on a Friday night. How many kids do y'all have?"

"Zero. No children, no wife."

Yeah, right. Handsome and charming and rich, and he smelled good. There was no way a woman hadn't snapped him up yet, and he looked even better than the last time she saw him, too, dammit. Not the tiniest wrinkle in his charcoal slacks and white shirt, not even the faintest of sweat stains. Even from here she could see the softness of the fabric, the pieces expensive and well-made. Nicer than anything she owned by a mile.

And she was a wreck, she hated how much. Hair in a wild tangle on top of her head, dress filthy from eight solid hours of scrubbing stains she was trying hard to forget. She was exhausted and grumpy and pissed, and all she could think about was a shower, followed by a solid eight to ten hours of sleep.

"I came to offer my apologies."

"What, no diamond necklace? Or how about a marching band? I thought you were a man of grand gestures."

One corner of his mouth twitched, but he didn't quite smile.

"Let me tell you something. You may not know the people in this town, but I sure do, and getting stood up in front of them is humiliating. All those pitying eyes every time they looked my way, all their whispers. And then the food came and there was so much of it, like I'm some...some... I don't know, hooker you can buy off with steak and champagne." The memory got her upset all over again, and she shook her head, stomping up the walkway. "I couldn't even make up some bullshit story for the girls at the motel. They'd already heard about what happened because everybody, and I mean *everybody*, has been talking about it all weekend."

"I am very sorry about that. I'd like to make it up to you, if you'll let me."

"Oh, no. *Hell*, no. I'm not falling for that trick again." At the bottom of the steps, she flicked him out of the way with a hand. The asshole didn't budge. "Move it, buster."

"I don't think anyone's ever called me buster before. Not even when I was a kid."

"Fine. Move it, asshole."

Now he did smile, a soft, lopsided grin that tugged at her like a magnet.

"Seriously, can you just get out of the way?"

"You're adorable. And not until you let me explain."

"Let me guess. Your dog got hit by a car or your mother has cancer or your car broke down without—" She stopped, taking in the way his face fell at her words, shuffling back through them for which one it could be. "Your dog?"

"My mother." He shook his head. "She didn't die, not yet, anyway, but she is very ill."

He sounded sincere enough, but no way she was falling for this. "Oh, come on. I may be a maid, but I wasn't born yesterday. Sure she is."

He shrugged. "ALS, which is an awful way to die. She was diagnosed last year. It's come on fast and unforgiving."

"Okay, then. Why didn't you call?"

A trio of wrinkles appeared on his forehead. "I *did* call. I called the restaurant and talked to the hostess. I asked her to tell you there was an emergency involving my mother and to pass on my sincerest apologies, and that I would make it up to you as soon as I could get back to town. She didn't tell you?"

Fucking Heather. She thought about that smirk she'd seen from the other side of the room, the way she'd for sure laughed her ass off when she saw AC bolting out the door. She hoped that uppity bitch choked on one of those big-ass olives they piled in silver bowls on the bar.

"Heather—that's the hostess—she didn't tell me shit."

He cursed under his breath, and his frown deepened. "I will have her fired for this. I will see to it that she apologizes, profusely, to your face. She won't get away with this, I want you to know that."

AC looked up at him, still standing on the top step, and he seemed so charming, so sincere, that suddenly she didn't want to talk about Friday night, or his sick mother, or that bitch who owed her an apology. She didn't want to think about what her neighbors would say about his car parked on the street, or how many of them might be watching right now.

"Let me make it up to you," he said, his voice warm, his eyes pleading. "Let me take you on a proper date."

"When?"

"Now. Anywhere you want to go."

She looked down at her dress, her dirty skin. "But I… I'm a mess. I need to shower and wash my hair and—"

"I'll wait. Take as long as you need."

Even if he weren't looking at her like that, even if his eyes weren't so big and brown and warm, even if she didn't remember the smell of fresh bread and sizzling steak, she would have said yes.

Champagne bubbles tickling the back of her throat.

The smell of new car, the seats covered in soft leather.

The tires and the red rose on the Honda's front seat.

Yes.

SEVENTEEN

ALEX

It's raining when my alarm pierces the silence on Wednesday, a slow, steady patter that any other morning would lull me right back to sleep. I hit Snooze and lie here in the semidark, feeling the warmth of Patrick's body next to mine, the rhythmic puffs of his breathing. Still passed out cold, thanks to one of my sleeping pills.

I close my eyes and listen to the drizzle outside, thinking about how much Patrick hates pharmaceuticals. He says they give him a headache, that they make him sluggish and grumpy. And yet that was *him* riffling through my drawers last night in search of the bottle, *him* sleeping through the alarm while I stare up at the ceiling.

I look at him and I feel it again, that pit at the bottom of my stomach.

Last night. The kitchen table. His face when that text pinged his phone.

We were talking about the cryptic text he sent the girls and me. *Get ready.* Ready for what? And how did he send it when all four phones—his, too—were in a pile on the table? Not possible, obviously.

And then his phone chirruped with an incoming message, and I watched the emotions color his face like strobe lights. Surprise. Confusion. Anger. Fear. It's that last one that really did me in, especially when he shoved the phone in his pocket before any of us could see. A work text, he claimed, and for the first time in my marriage I knew that Patrick lied to me, right to my face, as if it were nothing. And then he bolted upstairs, leaving me and the twins blinking at each other in confusion.

The front door slammed a few minutes later, and I looked out the front windows to see Patrick sprinting up the driveway in running gear, the beginning of what would turn out to be an hour-long run through dark streets. He came back red-faced and drenched with sweat, and *still* he needed a pill to fall asleep. Meanwhile, there's not enough pharmaceuticals in the world to stop the thoughts squirreling around in my brain, poke poke poking me every time he so much as sighed on the next pillow.

This is a man who lies. Who's keeping secrets.

I feel movement beside me and look over to find Patrick, awake and staring in my direction. He blinks, eyes dark against bright white cotton.

"You're awake." His voice is thick with sleep, and he wraps his arms around me and pulls me close. His skin is warm, safe. "What are you thinking about?"

"Nothing." I wait for him to call me out on the lie or at the very least ask me again, but he doesn't do either. My alarm sounds again, and I reach over to silence it. "Want me to make sure the girls are up?"

"That'd be great."

Normally, this is Patrick's job, as the girls have the tendency to sleep through multiple blaring alarms. Water pumps through the pipes in the room closest to ours—Gigi, getting in the shower. Penelope's room is farther away, with enough walls between us I won't hear her moving around. She's also the daughter who could sleep through a bomb.

He kisses my neck and heaves himself out of bed with a groan. "Jesus, my head is killing me."

I roll onto my back, listening to the sounds of him shuffling toward the bathroom. The shower flips on. The glass door whines, then shuts with a dull thud. Water splashing as he steps into the stream. I wait until he's good and soaked, and then I lean across his pillow and pluck his cell from the charger.

Never, in all our years together, have I ever gone snooping on his phone.

But also: never have I had a reason to.

With the shower still in full swing, I tick in his passcode. The screen shimmies and then…nothing. I try it two more times, careful to hit the numbers in the dead center. But the end result is still the same. I'm locked out. Patrick's passcode, the one we all share by design, the one he's used for as long as I can remember, doesn't work. He's changed it.

"Who died?" Gigi says from the kitchen doorway, eyeing the platters lined up on the island like a breakfast buffet. Some people stress eat. I stress cook. A spread like this one is a signal to my family that something is very, very wrong.

"Ha ha, very funny." I plunk a bottle of syrup next to the pile of pancakes, my stomach churning. "Juice?"

"Uhhh, sure."

I pour her a glass of orange juice while she loads up a plate. Scrambled eggs, a minimountain of bacon, giant piles of fluffy, golden pancakes, the works. I haven't cooked this elaborate of a breakfast spread since Easter Sunday.

"Is that bacon I smell?" Patrick says, coming into the room. He slides his palm along my lower back, dropping a kiss on my cheek. "Sorry, babe. But we appreciate all the food."

Penelope is right on his heels. She snags a pancake from the platter and falls into her chair with a sigh. "Can I go ahead and put in an order for dinner? I saw on TikTok where they turned the entire kitchen island into a giant serving of nachos."

"That sounds like a huge mess." Patrick drops his wallet and cell on the table in a neat stack, exchanging them for a plate. "Not to mention unsanitary."

He shoots me a look, his eyes loving, his lips parted in a grin, and there he is, the Patrick I know.

The one I thought I knew.

I pour the coffee and juice and cart everything over to the table, wondering how does he do it? How does he smile and crack jokes and act like nothing's wrong? Today is one week since AC vanished, and never has a missing person had such a loud presence—in my head, in my life, on the web. The latest rumor is that Patrick and AC were having an affair. That I killed her in a fit of jealousy. Rolled her in Saran Wrap and stuck her in my freezer, buried her under my rosebushes, locked her in a *You*-style cage in my basement. These are just a few of the theories that have been floating around the internet.

"Ridiculous," Patrick said when I showed him the Reddit thread, and his posture stayed loose and relaxed despite the muscle ticking in his jaw. That thread pissed him off, too, but for some reason he downplayed it, swallowed down his anger. It makes me wonder what else I've missed, how many times he's slapped on his television face when secretly he's worried or angry.

I think about all the other things that have happened this past week. The doxing. The sledgehammer to my car. The gossip sites and ugly threads. An army of tireless trolls, organized and on the attack, led by that awful Mister Fluffles.

And no one will ever convince me it's not AC behind the handle.

I watch my husband eat, his posture relaxed, and an affair would be the most logical explanation for the changed passcode on his phone. Patrick is attractive, successful, smart. And okay, so a money guru isn't exactly a rock star, but he's got enough charisma that people treat him that way. I see the way women look at him when we walk into a room, the begrudging looks they give me for hanging on his arm. Women look at Patrick, and they see dollar signs.

But AC? No way. I think of his face when I introduced them that first day, the way he always turned quiet and grumpy whenever she walked into a room. He's always kind of hated her.

Someone at the station, then. I think about the cast of glamorous anchors and the constant stream of temps, young and pretty women who act more like fangirls than assistants. He's never expressed interest in any of them, but isn't that how affairs go? The lies, the secrecy. The slapping on a grin and eating breakfast with the family when your heart and mind are somewhere else, with someone else. I sip my coffee and watch him eat, smiling when he catches my eye like my own heart isn't breaking.

The sugar surge has made the girls chatty. They tell us about a fellow student whose older brother got kicked out of Harvard for selling cocaine, another whose mother just won her sixth or seventh Grammy. Welcome to private school in Atlanta.

His phone buzzes on the table, and I pretend not to notice him digging it from under his wallet, or the way he swipes a thumb up the screen he points at his face. Boom, he's in, no passcode necessary. A couple of taps later and he's scrolling through a string of text messages. I lean across him for a slice of bacon, catching a glimpse of the name at the top: Rachel, his boss.

At the opposite end of the table, Penelope leaps to her feet. "Omigod, how is it seven thirty? Let's go let's go, we gotta go. Move it." Penelope has always been our timekeeper, the twin with the list and a schedule that must be followed without fail, even on vacations and weekends. She snatches the bacon from her sister's fingers and flings it to the table. "I'm not getting another demerit because of you."

Patrick balls up his napkin, drops it on his plate. "You heard the lady. Let's get moving." He starts stacking dishes, but I wave him off.

"You go. I've got it."

He drops a kiss on my cheek that feels a tad sticky, and they leave in a flurry of goodbyes, Penelope practically shoving them out the door. I listen to them drive away, staring at a table littered with breakfast wreckage, wondering how to break into a phone that uses facial ID.

Forty minutes later, I've run a brush through my hair and traded my pajamas for a navy sundress of soft and stretchy cotton. My feet are bare and so is my face, nothing but scrubbed skin and new determination.

The mysterious texts on all our phones. Patrick's strange behavior last night and again this morning. The way no one bothered to ask about my plans for the day. My family saw me in my grease-stained pajamas, hair piled high on my head, and they just assumed I'd happily stepped into the role of short-order cook and laundress, homework helper and chauffeur. They think that is the power of last night's intervention, that it made a difference in my today. They assumed, so they didn't even ask. Honestly, it pisses me off.

At the carriage house door, I jimmy my key into the lock and step into a space that feels stale and musty. The last time I was in here I melted down—that was Friday, the day the trolls declared me canceled—and the air still feels charged with their ugly energy.

I'm almost to the top of the interior stairs when my feet stick to the treads. I latch on to the banister and look around, a quiet curl of unease spreading under my skin.

My gaze clocks the valuables. The two laptops sleeping on the desk. The Marshall speaker Patrick bought me last year for my birthday, perched on a far shelf. The vintage silver tray I bought from an antique store, a splurge when I hit a half million followers. Everything is still here, right where I left it.

But that lampshade, was it crooked before? And that stack of magazines, is it rotated ninety degrees? Have those papers been moved to the other side of the desk?

I step to my laptop and peel it open, waking the screen with a finger. My files are all still here, the emails and the website and the to-do list that I haven't looked at in more than a week.

But I still feel it, that heaviness in my gut, telling me something is not right.

Slowly, I turn in a circle. I'm thinking about Gigi's middle-of-the-night trek across the yard, how after the conversation with Shannon I've started locking the carriage house door. About AC, who had a key to the office and the house.

Her *key*.

I slide my cell from my back pocket and call my brother, Tommy. His cell rings and rings, then flips me to voice mail. I hang up and try again, then again and again. Finally, on the third try, he answers.

"If you're calling me to bitch about Mom, don't bother. I'm currently not speaking to her, either." His voice pushes through construction noise—Latin music, male voices shouting back and forth, sharp whumps from a nail gun. Tommy is a builder, a one-man business with half a dozen fixer-uppers in varying states of completion.

"Why, what did she do?" The "now" is silent but understood. Our mother is flighty and demanding and probably chemically imbalanced, and you never know what kind of mother you're going to get until she walks through the door. Last time I talked to her was back in the fall, when she called me a money-hungry snob and in the same breath asked me for two hundred dollars.

"She sold the generator I bought her because she needed a vacation. She's in Myrtle Beach, apparently."

And Tommy didn't just buy her the generator. He hired someone to help him haul it over and then installed the thing because our mother insists on living in the boondocks, where the slightest breeze will take out her power for days. As much as she drives us crazy, neither of us liked the thought of her all alone in the dark woods without electricity. And now she's sold that sense of security for a trip to the beach.

"Can we talk about this when you come over? I need you to switch out my locks."

"Which ones?"

"All of them. House and carriage house." I open the cabinet on a far wall, scan the shelves filled with supplies. Shut it when I see there's nothing out of place.

"That's a big job. How many doors are we talking about here—seven? Eight?"

"Something like that."

"Okay, but even with free labor, it's gonna cost you. Locks don't come cheap."

"I don't care how much it costs, Tommy. AC still has a key."

He grunts, and I hear shuffling. "Well, I could probably get out there by the end of the afternoon. Think you can hold down the fort until then?"

I look around the empty room, and I feel it then. Hot breath on the back of my neck, the light graze of snapping teeth. There's a smudge on the hardwood, a dark streak where something's been dragged across the floor. Something heavy.

I step to the next door, the one leading to a full bath—a holdover from when the carriage house served as a guest room. I yank it open, and it takes me two full heartbeats to realize what I'm seeing.

My face in the mirror, but red. The sink, the walls, the tiles on the floor. All of it's red, shiny with dark and sticky liquid. My bare foot lands in a puddle, and I jerk it away with a shriek.

That's when I notice the other thing on the floor.

A woman, lying facedown.

I see her long legs, skintight denim smeared with blood, her bony back still as a stone. I see matted hair, a pale slice of cheek. One open, unseeing eye.

And then I hear screaming, and Tommy's voice shouting in my ear, demanding I tell him what's wrong. But my lungs are on fire and the room is spinning and my hands shaking so hard I lose grip on the phone. It slides from my fingers and bounces off the woman's sneaker, landing with a splat in all that blood, and there's still screaming, so much screaming, as I race down the stairs and out the door.

EIGHTEEN

Fifteen minutes later, the place is once again swarming with cops. Poking through the house, gathered in clumps around the yard, in the carriage house documenting the scene. I stand at the edge of the pool and wait for one to come clomping down the stairs. Two uniformed men stand just outside the door, waiting for the path to clear so they can haul in the stretcher and body bag.

"Coroner says she's been deceased for some time. Days, possibly."

I stand here for a long moment, peeling through the fear and shock, processing the news. Days. While my family and I have been fifty feet away, going about our business in the house, a dead woman has been in the carriage house for *days*.

I shiver when I think of all the blood covering the mirror and the walls, the sticky puddle I stepped in. The rush of adrenaline has left me shaky and freezing despite the hot sun beating down, sparkling off the pool water and broiling the pavers under my bare feet. It's barely ten, and already the temperature has topped eighty. It's going to be a brutal summer, but for now I'm thankful for the heat.

"But how can that be? The blood looked...fresh."

"That's because the blood wasn't hers. From a cow, I'm guessing. Probably the easiest to come by."

And in the back of my mind, a new question filters to the top: Where does one buy cow's blood?

The cop makes a face, wiping a line of sweat from his brow. "And you're sure you didn't recognize her?"

No, I'm not sure, and we've already gone over this, multiple times. I only saw the dead woman for a few seconds before I got the holy hell out of there, and I definitely didn't get a good look at her face. I picture the parts I could see—a partial of her temple, a slice of grayish cheek, a side view of her dead eye—and chill bumps sprout on my arms and legs.

"I don't think so. But I was panicked, and she was facedown. How—"

"House is clean," someone yells from behind me, one of his colleagues filing out the patio door. "No signs of attempted entry."

The cop gives him a thumbs-up, and I try again. "How did this woman get in my bathroom? How did she die?"

"I can't answer any of those questions, ma'am." His squint shifts, his gaze wandering over my right shoulder toward the house. He lifts his chin. "But she probably can."

I turn, and even in a yard crawling with cops, I spot her almost immediately. Same dark jacket over matching pants, same clunky shoes that look built for a man. Detective Bennett, and she must be roasting in that getup. I lift a hand in a wave, but she doesn't return the gesture. She doesn't speak, either, doesn't move at all. She just stands there, sunglasses shoved to the top of her head, and stares.

The look on her face makes my pulse jump.

★ ★ ★

Detective Bennett and I end up at the kitchen counter, right as Tommy comes busting through the front door. I hear his steel-toed work boots thudding on the foyer tiles, his big, booming voice hollering my name. Two seconds later, he appears in the doorway, breathing hard.

"Alex, what the hell? You can't…" He pauses to shove a hand through his hair. His shoulders hang on his big frame, his sun-kissed skin and denim still dusty from the work site. "You can't just scream bloody murder and then not call me back. Jesus. Do you have any idea what that did to me? I called you all the way over."

I think of my cell, lighting up in that puddle of cow's blood, and I shudder. "I'm sorry. My phone landed in the evidence, and then I ran in here to call 9-1-1 and forgot all about you. But as you can see, I'm fine. We're all fine."

"Then what's all this?" He swirls a finger in the air, referring to the police still swarming through the house and yard, the detective seated at the island next to me. "What's going on?"

I tell him about the woman in the carriage house, about the blood smeared across the mirror and walls, about Patrick who I've called a million times with no luck. His phone keeps rolling straight to voice mail, and I didn't want to panic him with too many details. I asked him to call me on the house line as soon as possible and left it at that.

When I'm finished, Tommy is pale. "Holy shit, Alex. That's seriously fucked up. Who is she?"

Detective Bennett answers for me. "Female, age approximately sixty to sixty-five, identity as yet unknown. She wasn't carrying any form of ID, and Mrs. Hutchinson wasn't able to identify her, either."

Tommy frowns, his gaze bouncing between us. "Okay. So how'd she get there?"

I shrug, turning to the detective.

Twin parentheses dig into either side of her mouth. "When is the last time you were in the carriage house? Before today, I mean."

"Friday. Wait—no, Saturday. I'd left my flip-flops up there and wanted to wear them to the pool."

"Did you go into the bathroom?"

"No, but the door was open. If she was there, if all that... blood was there, I definitely would have seen it."

She scribbles my answer on the notepad lying on the marble in front of her, then poses her next question without looking up. "And your husband?"

"And my husband, what?"

"When was the last time he was in the carriage house?"

I don't like the way the question lifts up one of her eyebrows, or the tone she uses to ask it in, like Patrick is a prime suspect. I scoot forward to the edge of my chair.

"Patrick never goes in there, not unless I ask him to change a lightbulb or lug up something heavy. The carriage house is *my* space. He has zero reason to be there when I'm not. He *never* goes there unless he's invited."

"So the victim's body appeared sometime between Saturday at..."

"After lunchtime. Probably around twelve thirty or so."

She makes a note of my answer. "That gives us a window of less than forty-eight hours. My colleagues tell me they didn't see any security cameras on the back of the house. Did they miss something?"

I shake my head, frustration stabbing me between the ribs. After the scare with Gigi, Patrick called the security company, but they were slammed. "We're having some installed, but home security is a booming business, apparently. We're on the books for next week."

"So if your husband *did* go into the carriage house sometime this past weekend... Without security cameras tracking who comes through your backyard, without any sort of system monitoring the door, how would you even know?"

For a moment I'm stunned speechless. My gaze tracks to Tommy, leaning against the fridge, and I read the same question on his expression. My brother wants the answer, too. Heat flares behind my chest bone as I turn back to the detective.

"What are you suggesting, that my husband killed that woman and then planted her body in my bathroom? For what reason—to scare my pants off? To frame me? That doesn't make any sense."

"I agree. Which is why I'd love to talk to him, as well. Do you have any idea where he is?"

"At work. I've left him a few messages, but he doesn't always answer when he's conducting interviews or taping a segment." Either way, I don't like where this conversation is going, and I grasp at the first straw I can come up with. "And by the way, where's AC? Have you been looking for her at all?"

"Believe it or not, your personal assistant is what brought me here in the first place. I was on the way when I got the call." She pauses, flips to a fresh page in her notebook. "Anna Claire Davis, the woman you call AC, doesn't exist."

An oppressive silence fills the room, one I have to struggle not to fill with laughter. "No offense to your investigative skills, Detective, but I can assure you she exists. It's why my brother drove all the way over here, because AC still has a key. I asked him to change out all the locks."

"Let me rephrase. *Your* Anna Claire Davis doesn't exist. Her name and social security numbers match up, but they don't belong to her. They belong to the real Anna Claire Davis, who died in 1994."

Died. Another dead woman. The word rings in my head like a church bell.

"So who is—" I can't make my mouth say the words *my AC*. After everything that's happened this past week, after all my suspicions as to her hand in my downfall, it feels wrong somehow, claiming her as mine. "Who is my former assistant?"

"I was hoping you could tell me. Anything you know about her could be helpful."

"I already told you she didn't share much. What about her car? It must have been registered to someone."

"Yes, to a man in Arkansas who reported it stolen six months ago. The license plate was fake."

I sit still for a long moment, palms sweaty against the cool marble. AC lied, and not just about her name. She lied about everything else, too.

"But why would she do that? Why steal a dead girl's story and sell it off as her own?"

"You can't get a job without a social security number, so people tend to choose ones that don't send up a red flag. Minors. Dead people. Real numbers, just unused. They get caught eventually, but it certainly slows things down."

And in AC's case, it worked.

"But wait a minute. I called her former boss. I talked to a person who knew her."

It was her top reference, whose endorsement of her was so glowing that I didn't bother with the rest. No calling the other references, no running an official background check—which I'm now seeing was a big mistake—because I was overwhelmed and in a hurry, and she seemed like the perfect candidate.

The detective gives me a stiff smile. "Could have been a friend, or it's possible she scammed her former boss, as well. Do you still have a copy of her résumé?"

I nod halfheartedly, suddenly consumed with all the other stuff she included on there, the social marketing degree from USC, the internships with NBC and Showtime. Too good to be true, too perfect for the position I hired her for. I'm an idiot for never digging deeper.

And it's not like the IRS would have flagged it. I hired her as a 1099 and left it up to AC to file her own taxes. For all I know she was planning to do it under her real name, or maybe not file them at all. The IRS is a slow-moving behemoth. It's a hustle she could have kept up for years.

The detective pulls a paper from her notebook, unfolds it and slides it across the table. "This is a picture you posted in late December, soon after you hired her."

I remember the post, though I'm a little taken aback by the image. Her hair was much lighter then, her highlights too brassy, makeup too everything—too colorful, too heavy, too much. The first time I met her, I remember thinking she looked like she got a free makeover at one of those kiosks at the mall. She looked like she was trying too hard.

But the longer she worked for me, the straighter and darker her hair got, the more subtle the makeup. She traded the short skirts for flirty tops over fitted jeans, her heels for sandals under a floral sundress. I never asked her to. The transformation just happened.

But I see it now.

The detective pulls out a second picture, a printout from one of my more recent posts—me next to a beaming AC on a shaded terrace. We'd just come from a meeting with a local chain of stores, and we were both pink-cheeked with success. I asked the waitress to take a picture of us, chinking our glasses of celebratory champagne. I look at this picture, and the breath tingles in my lungs.

"So, what are you saying? That this is some kind of… I don't know, single-white-female situation?"

It's a silly, self-absorbed thought that doesn't make any sense. Why would she go to all that trouble—seeking me out for a job, imitating my hair and style of clothes, changing her appearance to look a lot more like me than she did just a few months ago—only to blow it all up with that Krissie Kelly post? None of it makes any sense.

Detective Bennett lifts both hands from the table. "That's what I'm trying to figure out."

"I thought you were trying to locate her."

"That, too."

"And you don't think all these things are connected somehow? Someone destroyed my car. They broke into my office and left a woman's body lying in a bucket of cow's blood, and they most likely did it while my family and I were right here in this house, less than fifty feet away. I've been doxed. I've been dealing with drive-bys. I'm telling you, someone is targeting me, my family."

"And you think that someone is AC?"

"She can't be *every* troll, obviously. But these things can't be unconnected. They just *can't* be."

If the detective shares my suspicions, she doesn't show it. She just scribbles something on her notepad and moves on. "I've seen the footage your husband sent Officer Graham from a couple days ago. The trespasser is unidentifiable. We can't even confirm it's a female."

Trespasser. A watered-down version of what happened if ever I've heard one.

"Okay, so the car could have been anyone, but there are only so many people who could have gotten into the locked carriage house. Me, Patrick, the girls, my brother and AC. Those are the only people with a key."

"Maybe the door was open."

"It was locked. I unlocked it myself this morning, right before I found a dead body in my bathroom."

She blows out a breath, one that's trying very hard not to sound like a sigh. The detective is making it clear she's not here to talk about my car or the doxing. She's here to investigate a murder, and she's looking to me for answers.

"I understand your husband owns a firearm."

Suddenly, the noise in the house stops. No officers chattering in the foyer, no chinking of metal hanging from their belts. Only silence.

I shake my head. Patrick knows my stance on guns. He knows what I would say if he ever tried to bring one in the house. "No. No, he doesn't. Patrick doesn't own a gun."

And the idea is ridiculous. My husband is a finance guy, not a gun-toting vigilante. He spends his days staring at spreadsheets and fine-tuning investment strategies, not shooting up targets at the gun range. When a few months ago there was a rash of break-ins in the neighborhood, he went to Dick's for a Taser because he knows a gun is my hard line in the sand. I will not live under the same roof as a gun.

I catch motion in my periphery, and I look up to see Tommy, leaned against the wooden frame of the doorway. He has his arms folded across his big chest, watching with his chin tucked down, his listening face. He knows what a gun in the house would do to me. He doesn't want to miss a word.

"According to Fulton County, he does," the detective says. "They hold a record for the firearm registered in his name, along with his license to carry, which he's kept current since 1995."

Her words hit me like a fist to the sternum, and I sit here for a long moment, absorbing the shock. Patrick owns a gun, and for more than a quarter of a century. He owned a gun when we met, when I introduced him to my girls, when he dropped to a knee with not one but three rings in his pocket because he knew we were a package deal, when I trusted him enough to tell him about the time I was dragged into the bushes at gunpoint. I went to therapy for *years* because of that gun, and all that time Patrick looked in my eyes and *lied*. A lie of omission, but still. My husband owns a gun.

Actually, it's worse than that. A license to carry means the gun is not just tucked away somewhere in a box, which now that I think about it had better fucking be locked. I picture Gigi or Penelope pulling open the lid, and horror rushes over me.

What would have happened if they had gotten their hands on it? How many times have the three of us sat next to Patrick in his car, in a store or a restaurant, at *home*, clueless that there was a gun *right there* and he didn't tell us? My vision grays out, and I breathe through a wave of fury.

"I'm sensing you didn't know about the firearm."

I shake my head, not trusting my voice. I want to ask why she came to me with this line of questioning, and at a time of day when she knew Patrick wouldn't be home, but I also want her to leave so I can call him and demand an explanation. I slide my hands under my thighs, mostly to stop them from shaking.

"So you probably also don't know where he keeps it."

Another head shake, and I'm not about to go looking for it. It could be in one of a million places, for one, and second, because of what finding it would do to me. I picture myself pulling it from the back of a drawer or an old shoebox, and I shudder.

Her phone chirrups, and she unclips it from her belt. "Your husband," she says, her thumbs flying across the screen. "What time will he be getting home tonight?"

I try to recall what day it is when already today feels like a year. I clear my throat. "On Wednesdays usually by dinnertime."

She smiles, not unkindly, and gathers up her things. "If you think of anything that may be pertinent to the investigation, anything at all, please let me know." She pauses for my nod, then smiles again. "I'll be out back."

And then she's off before I can answer, her sensible shoes squeaking across the hardwoods, the patio door opening and closing.

As soon as she's gone, Tommy blows out a loaded breath. "Seems like you're gonna need a lot more than just some new locks."

While Tommy heads to Home Depot with my credit card, I cope with the day's events in the best way I know how, by reorganizing the pantry. I take everything out, every box and bag and can, checking expiration dates and chucking the stuff no one ever eats, arranging them on the floor by size and type, because I need to keep my hands busy. I need to take my mind off the officers stomping through my house and my husband who owns a gun. I need to stop thinking about that awful day.

Instead, I think about the time I *told* him about that day. The way his forehead crumpled not in pity but with sympathy, how he shoved our half-eaten plates out of the way to reach across the table for my hand. It was our third date, and the restaurant was loud and bustling and filled with his fans, people dropping by the table to say hi or watching us from theirs.

But all of that fell away when his fingers wrapped around mine. "Alex. I can't even begin to understand what that did to you."

I tried to choke up a laugh. "I'm okay now. I've had lots of therapy."

It was the standard spiel I used with the few people who knew—my mom and Tommy, my best friend, Lisette, from college, my therapist. It was a small group on purpose, and I didn't intend to tell Patrick, at least not yet. But that night in the restaurant there was wine and candlelight and him, so handsome and funny in his quiet way. The story was out before I realized I was saying it.

"But it does something to a person," I found myself saying, "having a gun pointed at your head. It's like nothing else exists. The entire world shrinks down to that opening in the barrel, and you don't think of anything else. Not what that man was about to do to me, not the branches and dirt digging into my skin. All I knew was that tiny little hole pressed up against my temple, and the deadly power of what was about to come out of it."

He gave my thumb a squeeze. "You must have been so terrified."

I nodded. "It's why I can't be around them. Guns, I mean. When I see one, I just kind of…lose it. I know it sounds crazy, and my therapist says the fear is misplaced. That it's not the gun

I should be afraid of but the bad guy holding it, but that sounds too much like an NRA talking point for me. And honestly, I'd rather have this somewhat irrational fear of guns than of every strange man I run into on the street. At least with guns, you can erect boundaries."

"Like?"

"Like refusing to be in a room with one. Like asking people before I step the first foot into their house if they have one there. And before you say anything, yes. I realize half the people in this place are gun owners, and half of those have a license to carry. But ignorance is bliss, and as long as you don't have one tucked in your waistband or stashed in a box in your coat closet, we're good."

He grinned. "Does that mean you'll be coming to my house?"

"I don't know. Does that mean I'm invited?"

The invitation was understood, just like he knew my answer. Three dates in, and already I was smitten. Patrick was so easy to be with, easier than anyone I'd ever been with before. No, not just easy—it was deeper than that. We understood each other in a way that went far beyond our three dates, where his look was just as loud as words. *I want to take you home, and not just for tonight.*

How do you know when you finally find that person, that he's the one you've been waiting for all along? You just do. I looked at Patrick that night, and I knew.

We skipped dessert, and then we hightailed it to his house.

This was in 2016, more than two decades after the license was registered in his name, and for a gun that's at least that old. Was it somewhere in the kitchen when he poured me a glass of champagne, or tucked under his bed while we made love?

I don't know which is more unforgiveable, that he owned a gun, or that all these years, he made me think he didn't.

NINETEEN

ANNA CLAIRE

They ended up at Bubba Jax Crab Shack, which was as working class as it sounded. A wooden shack pressed up tight against the road, on the other side a parking lot of mud and grass.

But after the shit show at Skoby's, after he'd seen the state of her car and her work and her rickety rental house, AC figured she had nothing to hide. This was a test, one that, so far, he was passing with flying colors.

He pointed to a table by the window. "You go get a seat, and I'll order."

The worst spot in the house, but the place was packed, and AC nabbed it before anyone else could, watching him charm the pants off a giggling Patsy at the register. She took in his gold watch and tailored shirt, the fifty he peeled off a thick stack in his wallet, and she gave him a look filled with so much longing that it made AC blush. Patsy was like her, a hard worker with rough hands and a thin wallet, and AC knew what she was thinking.

She was thinking, *How do I get me one of these?* A sugar daddy, Terri had called him. He wasn't, not yet, but if AC had anything to say about it, he would be very soon.

He sank onto the chair across from her, plunking down a red plastic tray piled high with food. She reached for the can of Budweiser and divided it over two plastic cups, handing one to him.

"It's not champagne, but it's yellow and it's fizzy, so cheers."

They chinked cups, then tucked into the food. A po'boy for him, a fluffy French roll stuffed with soft-shelled crabs smothered in creamy sauce, and crab cakes, for her. They were easier to eat without making a mess, and she didn't have to worry about a glob of mayonnaise falling onto her chin like the one stuck to his. She was dying to lean over the table and lick it away, and the thought made her smile.

"What's so funny?"

"Nothing. It's just..." She shoved the plastic fork through the wrapper, wriggling the utensil out by the tongs. "I hope you don't mind me bringing you here. I'm sure you're used to way fancier places."

"Are you kidding? When I was little, my parents used to take me to a place exactly like this one. Enrique's Sandwich Shop, jammed between a liquor store and pawn shop. The food was so good you didn't even notice the hookers working the sidewalk outside." He paused to take a bite, swallow. "Why do you look so surprised?"

"Because I am. The way you act and carry yourself, it's so different than the people around here. I guess I just figured you came from money."

He put down his sandwich, wiped his mouth with a paper napkin. "My father worked in a factory. My mother was a maid. We didn't go hungry, but we didn't have much."

A maid. His words on the side of the road whispered through

her mind, after she'd explained her slutty outfit. *A noble profession*, he'd said, and she thought he was humoring her.

"So what changed?"

"Me. I changed. That kind of struggle forms you as a person, and it taught me to work hard. Eighty hours a week, fifty-two weeks a year. I'm always working, and when I'm not, I'm thinking about work. It's an obsession that's served me well."

"Are you thinking about work right now?"

"No." He smiled. "At this particular moment, I am very much not thinking about work."

She grinned, poking at a crab cake with her fork. "So what is it you do? When you're not rescuing damsels from the side of the road, I mean. Who pays your salary?"

"Me. *I* pay me, in addition to paying my mother's mortgage and her care. But to answer your question, my business is managing things. Money and assets, mostly, though I also own some real estate and stocks, too. Basically, I make sure my money goes where it makes the most return."

She nodded, even though it all sounded awfully vague. He was a manager, like grumpy old Terri down at the motor lodge, except that couldn't be right. Managing money, what did that even mean?

"I still have no idea what you do all day."

He laughed. "It's not that complicated, actually. I invest my money and then I live off the profits."

"That must be a lot of profits."

"I get by." He picked up his sandwich, smiling a little. "Enough about me. I want to hear about you."

"Oh, I'm nowhere near as interesting as you." She leaned an elbow on the table, mimicking his posture. Elegant but relaxed. Back straight but not stiff. "I've been on my own since I was sixteen, after my mother died and my father kicked me out for being a sinner and a fornicator who's going to burn in hell. His God is a real asshole if you ask me."

His smile vanished, and he settled the po'boy on his plate. "First of all, I'm very sorry about your mother. I'm staring down that barrel myself, so I have an idea of what that was like for you. The bond with a mother is special. Irreplaceable."

To AC's horror, tears burned in the corners of her eyes. All these years later, her mother's loss was still that fresh. She put down her fork and reached for her beer, burying her tears in the cup.

He reached across the table for her hand. "But secondly, how is any of what you just told me not interesting? On your own since sixteen. That tells me you are strong and smart and determined. Despite the way things have turned out with your parents, despite whatever problems you have with your father, he got the most important thing right. He raised a survivor."

Her skin tingled from his words, from his earnest gaze and his fingers wrapped around hers, and the combination knocked something loose inside her chest. Before she could stop them, the words bubbled up.

"We used to come here all the time. Back before things got bad, I mean. My father and Bubba Jax share a fishing cabin down by the Florida border, and they used to let me toss the fish scraps to the gators. Anyway, Daddy and Bubba Jax would start by bickering about the market price of snow crabs until Bubba Jax knocked a few cents off every pound, and then Bubba Jax would send over a mountain of those things, more than we could ever eat, so we could knock the shit out of them with these little wooden hammers. To this day, I can't smell butter without thinking of this place."

It surprised her how easily the story poured out. Most of the time, she tried very hard not to think of her father. She'd gone so long hating everything about him that it was intoxicating, remembering the good parts, letting someone see them like she did. It was the most she'd talked about her past with anyone in years.

But what surprised her even more was the reaction it summoned in the man sitting across from her. He shoved aside the empty plates and greasy napkins and grabbed her with both hands, giving a hard squeeze that didn't feel like pity, not even a little bit.

"We're a lot alike, you and I," he said, and the thought made something catch in her chest. "We understand each other, don't we?"

She nodded, her voice barely loud enough to rise above all the noise. "Please tell me you're not one of those guys."

"What kind is that?"

"The kind who swoops in and saves the girl, only to lose interest as soon as they've caught her. The kind who thinks chasing the rainbow is more fun than finding the pot of gold."

"I just told you I manage money for a living, so you can be assured that there's not much I like better than finding a pot of gold. But is that what you think I'm doing here, trying to save you?" His eyes searched hers, and there was so much interest there, so much kindness, that she was having trouble breathing.

"You literally picked me up on the side of the road. You bought me tires. And a steak dinner."

"Which you didn't eat."

So, he knew she'd left without taking a bite. She wondered if Heather was the one who told him or the waiter. Either way, she liked that he knew. It felt like a kind of victory.

"I don't like to eat alone," she said, and he smiled.

"Noted. But have you stopped to consider that—" he stroked her hand with both thumbs, a touch she felt all the way down to her toes "—you're not the one who needs saving? Maybe I am."

She hadn't considered that, not even for a second. Not after seeing his fancy car, those expensive clothes and watch. What could she possibly do for him? She couldn't think of any reason why a guy like this would need saving.

Then again, it's easy to think that money solved every problem—especially when you didn't have any. But AC had been through enough in her short life to know there were some things money couldn't buy. Like a father who loves you more than an imaginary man in the sky, like a mother who's still breathing.

"There's something else you should know about me," he said. "The most important thing. For me, winning is everything. There is nothing better. Nothing. And you should also know that when I set my sights on something, I win for keeps."

She didn't doubt it. Granted, she hadn't known him very long, but she could already tell he was the kind of guy who, once he'd decided he wanted you, threw out all the stops. It was probably the only way he knew how to behave, because he was used to always winning.

"Just so long as you don't think of me as your trophy."

That made him smile, even though they both knew she was lying.

AC was the trophy.

One she'd already decided to let him win.

TWENTY

ALEX

The rest of the afternoon flies by in a flurry of activity.

I'm done with the pantry around the time the carriage house clears out of cops, two of them lugging that poor woman down the driveway in a black plastic bag. Somebody covers the door in crime scene tape, a clear and unnecessary barrier we are not to cross—as if I need the reminder. As far as I'm concerned, they can burn the place down when they're done with it. I'll never go in the carriage house again.

Tommy installs the locks in record time, finishing up long before the detective leaves, but lingering until she raps a knuckle on the patio door. In her arm are two silver laptops, and I recognize the stickers on the cover as mine. I motion her inside.

"I figured you might need these," she says, sliding them onto the kitchen table. "If there's anything else you want from the space, let me know. I can't have you or anyone else out there, disturbing the scene."

"For how long?"

"Until we identify the victim, this case remains complicated. It could be weeks or even months, so if there's anything you will need in the meantime, please tell me so I can get it."

I nod my understanding. "As long as I have my laptop, I'm good."

"Speaking of, you told one of the officers that as far as you could tell, nothing was missing, is that correct? The trespasser didn't take the laptops, obviously, but what about other valuables?"

I give her a slow shake of my head, because suddenly I'm thinking of the diamond stud I'd written off as lost, the ring I accused my housekeeper of taking. And just the other day I was looking for the necklace Patrick gave me for my birthday, a long chain of tiny seed pearls with a diamond sunburst pendant. I couldn't find it anywhere.

"Now that I think about it some of my jewelry has gone missing from the house."

When was the last time I wore that necklace, Valentine's Day? Or was it that weekend in early March, when Patrick and I snuck away for a couple nights in New York City? The ring was on my finger more recently, for a restaurant opening last month in West Midtown. I remember slipping it off before I washed my face, dropping it in a dish on the bathroom counter along with my bracelet. The bracelet I wore the next day, but not the ring. What else has vanished?

"Did you report the pieces as missing?"

"No. I didn't even realize it until now."

"Well, I'm happy to work up a report. You'll need it if the pieces are insured."

I thank her, then offer to walk her out. She's on the front stoop when she fires her parting shot.

"Have you managed to get ahold of your husband?"

I shake my head. "Not yet."

"Please ask him to contact me. As soon as possible. I have some questions for him, too."

After she's gone, I thank Tommy by shoving a giant shopping bag filled with leftovers in his hand, lasagna and roast beef and tortellini in pesto sauce, a Ziploc filled with leafy greens there's no way he'll ever eat. My brother is a meat and potatoes kind of guy and hasn't touched a vegetable in decades, at least not on purpose.

"Lock the doors behind me," he says, gesturing to the brand-new keys he dropped on the foyer table, "and turn on the alarm. And call me the second anything feels off. I mean it, sis. Even if it's the middle of the night. I'll be over here in ten minutes flat."

"You live thirty minutes away."

"You know what I mean."

I smile, trying not to let on I see the worry that's crept up his face, or the way his shoes stay parked on my foyer instead of heading for his truck up at the curb. He doesn't like that Patrick owns a gun any more than I do. "There's something fishy here," he's said more than once, and I don't disagree.

But I'm the one who worries about Tommy, not the other way around, and this role reversal is doing a number on both of us. I drop a kiss on his cheek and herd him out the door.

Patrick calls at the end of the afternoon, right before I leave to pick up the girls. He tells me about the interviews that kept him occupied all day, apologizes for the way it took him so long to get back to me, but that he had his cell on Do Not Disturb. In a calm, level voice, I tell him about the body and my phone lying in a puddle of cow's blood, how the carriage house is now a crime scene.

"If this is some kind of joke," he says when I'm finished, "it's not a very funny one."

"Oh, I'm serious. Deadly so. I'm surprised you didn't get wind of it already. The police have been here all day."

There's a sudden rustling on the line, his voice pushing through. "Jesus. I'm on my way. Be home in fifteen."

"No, don't bother. There's nothing you can do here, anyway, and I'm about to leave. Besides, I think Detective Bennett would prefer you talk to her first. She has some questions about your gun."

Silence. The kind that crawls over my skin like a million tiny spiders. I imagine him sitting behind the glass wall of his office, racking his brain for a new lie to beat back the one I just caught him in, but then I realize that's not what's happening. Patrick is not denying owning the gun, not searching for yet another bullshit excuse. The silence is his way of confessing.

"Is it here? In the house, I mean. Am I under the same roof as a gun?"

"No." He sighs, long and heavy into the phone. "It's gone."

"Good. We'll talk about it when you're home," I say, then drop the phone on the charger.

The skies open up five minutes into my drive to the soccer field, turning the battle through Buckhead traffic ugly. It takes twice as long as normal to get to the girls, huddled under the concession stand overhang, shivering and covered in mud, thick Georgia clay that sticks to their skin in orange streaks. They slide into the car, leaving clumps on the floorboards and leather seats. For once, I'm glad for the rental.

On the way home, I tell them about the dead woman and how Tommy spent the afternoon changing the locks. I'm hoping to assuage their fears, praying the day's events don't give them nightmares. But judging from Gigi on the front seat and my glances at Penelope in the rearview, the twins don't seem so much fearful as shocked, and maybe a little bit fascinated.

At home, they race to the backyard, but without a ladder to look through the carriage house windows, there's nothing to see but crime scene tape. They focus instead on their phones, snapping a few pictures and texting the news to all their friends.

After that it's a whirlwind of dinner and homework and laundry and waiting for the next shoe to drop. I clean the kitchen counter, shove glasses in the dishwasher, anything to keep my hands busy and my mind occupied while I wait for Patrick to come home. I'm beginning to get all too familiar with this feeling of icy dread, a sickening wave that breaks over me every time some new, ugly bit of information is revealed.

The dead body. Patrick's gun and the passcode on his phone. My missing personal assistant who is not named AC.

The girls disappear upstairs, and I dig my laptop from the couch cushions. I open the browser and type "Anna Claire Davis."

Within seconds, my screen fills with links to my own Instagram, pages and pages of mentions of her on my socials. I scroll through the hits featuring her smiling face, which sometime while I wasn't noticing became eerily similar to my own. I think of Shannon, walking up on AC reciting one of my Reels and in a voice that sounded just like mine. Yep, she was definitely copying me.

I try it again, adding the word "death" at the end.

The first hits are for an Anna Claire Davis who made news when her body was found burned beyond recognition. I click on an article from ABC News and scroll down, skimming the article for details, then back out when I spot the date: 2007. According to Detective Bennett, the real Anna Claire died in 1994.

I go back to my search criteria, add the date, hit Enter and voilà. I'm staring at the real Anna Claire's obituary, which is short and to the point.

Anna Claire "AC" Davis left this world unexpectedly on October 11, 1994. She is survived by her father, Keith, and brother, Matthew. Her burial will be private. Those who wish to honor AC are asked to make a contribution in her name to the Valdosta Police Department, attention Officer Aaron Childers.

The Valdosta Police Department. Detective Bennett didn't mention how this woman died, but I think about why her family would ask for donations for their local police department, and I don't think I like the answer.

The rest of the hits give me the gruesome details. Anna Claire was found, naked and brutally raped, in the basement of a warehouse west of Valdosta. Her limbs were bound and tied with a combination of zip ties and rope, her body covered with stab wounds—on the head and face, lacerations on all four limbs, blood over all her torso. She was missing four fingers and a good chunk of her scalp, as well as a five-centimeter segment of her skull. According to police she was tortured, and she was alive for most of it.

A few clicks later, I land on the crime scene photos. Awful, horrible images with gaping mouth, blank eyes, confused limbs. Grainy but with enough detail to churn the dinner in my stomach. The kind of pictures a person can't ever unsee.

"Ew." Penelope's breath is hot on my ear. "Who is that?"

I whirl around, so abruptly the laptop lurches off my thighs and onto the couch. "How long have you been standing there?"

"Long enough." She's fresh out of the shower, hair dripping like wet string over her lime green pajamas. She leans forward to get a better look at my laptop, clutching hers tight to her chest. Her face crinkles in disgust. "Do we know this person?"

I snap the computer closed. "She's a very unfortunate young woman who died long before you were born. I hope those pictures don't give you nightmares, like they for sure will me." I eye her over the back of the couch, my fingers itching to get back to my laptop keyboard, to dive back into Anna Claire. "Speaking of bed, isn't that where you should be?"

"Mom. It's not even nine." She peels the computer from her torso, holds it out in my direction with an overly toothy smile. "I was hoping you could read my English paper?"

Okay, now I *know* there's something going on. Penelope has

always been the smarter twin, the bookish one with grades that are both impeccable and effortless. She hasn't asked for help with her homework in years, not from me or Patrick. I slide my computer onto the coffee table and pat the cushion next to me. "Come sit. We'll look at it together."

She hands me her laptop and I awaken the screen with a fingertip. "'Nevertheless She Persisted'? You're such a budding feminist."

"Elizabeth Cady Stanton and Lucretia Mott are totally important, Mom. They organized the first women's rights convention in 1848." She wriggles into a more comfortable position, sinking deeper into the couch, swinging her bare feet onto the coffee table while I read.

I'm halfway down the page when she sighs. Fidgets. Jiggles her foot back and forth. "Mom? I'm really sorry." Her voice is not quite a whisper.

I look over in surprise. "What do you have to be sorry for?"

"That post. The trolls. They're being way harsh." She fiddles with a lock of her wet hair, twisting a corkscrew coil around a finger, and suddenly I get it, why she's down here, asking me for help she doesn't really need. "Like, did you ever think it would get this bad?"

I nod. "Yeah, Pen. I did."

"Well, I didn't. Are you really getting canceled?"

"Maybe, I don't know. Trolls are like hyenas, they're loud and they're nasty and they descend in packs. We just have to wait for them to pick the bones clean." I bounce a shoulder, nudge her with an elbow. "Either way, Unapologetically Alex had a good run. Don't you think?"

She blinks at me in surprise. "Seriously? You're just going to let them win? You're going to give up?"

"I thought you wanted me to shut it down."

"I did. I *do*." She wrinkles her nose. "But I want you to do it because you *want* to, not because of some awful trolls. It's not fair what they're doing. Especially when you weren't even the one who posted it."

And here's the thing about my Penny—she's always been too smart for her own good. I haven't mentioned my suspicions that the Krissie post came from AC, but Penelope understands way more than I give her credit for. Maybe she overheard me saying it to Patrick, or maybe she came to this conclusion on her own. Either way, this is what she's come down here for, to talk about this very thing, under the guise of asking for help with her homework.

It's why I decide to level with her. "The detective was here earlier today. The one looking for AC. She says her name isn't Anna Claire."

Penelope frowns. "Then who is she? Why hasn't the detective found her yet?"

"I don't know. That's why I was looking at those pictures before, because they are of the real Anna Claire. She died a long time ago."

"Really? That's so weird."

Penelope sinks back into the couch with an indifferent sigh, but it's an act. She tolerated my assistant the way she tolerates my job—with weighted silence and angry eye rolls when either of them takes up too much of my time, but mostly by pretending the other doesn't exist. Whenever AC wandered into the house, Penelope shoved her nose in a novel or disappeared upstairs. That's always been her coping mechanism, retreating into herself.

But this is not indifference. This is worry. Penelope chews her lower lip, her leg still jiggling.

"Look, sweetie, I'm not telling you any of this to scare you, but I do want you to be aware. AC was lying to us, and from the very start. And thanks to her, people know where we live now. They know your and your sister's names, what you look like. Most of them are harmless, but I'm afraid she's not, which means I need you to be extra careful. Keep the doors locked and the alarm on."

"But for how long?"

"I don't know. I've already started wiping the pictures of you and Gigi from my socials. It'll take me a little longer to delete all of them, but I want you to know that I'm working on it. Though you have to prepare for the possibility those pictures will never disappear completely."

It's something we're constantly preaching to both daughters, that one little ill-considered nude can live on the internet forever. Images don't just vanish. Just ask Janet Jackson.

She grins. "Like Gigi's tooth picture?"

"Like that." I wince.

"Last year Sophie Christianson posted a picture of her boobs, and her dad's lawyer sued everybody who reposted it. They shut down their Twitter accounts and everything, but that picture is still out there. You just have to know where to look." A rare, unfettered stream of information.

"Poor Sophie."

Penelope makes a sound deep in her throat. "Don't feel sorry for her, like, at *all*. She says she's on OnlyFans but I don't see how. You have to be eighteen."

Oh, God. OnlyFans, already? I am so not prepared for this next phase of childhood.

"Let's finish your English report, shall we? It's fantastic, by the way. You're quite the budding writer."

My words fall on deaf ears because her phone beeps from deep in the couch cushions. She digs it out, and I spot a boy's name on the screen, one that summons up a secret smile.

She tucks her laptop under an arm and edges off the couch, thumbs tapping away on her phone. "Thanks, Mom. I'm good."

TWENTY-ONE

It's after nine by the time Patrick arrives. I hear his engine gun up the driveway, see his headlights flash against the windows, and I tick in the alarm code at the pad by the front door. When I open the door, he's standing on the front stoop, keys clutched in a fist and frowning.

"Is there a reason my key doesn't fit?"

"Tommy changed the locks because I remembered AC still had a key."

He looks up with a frown. "I thought we agreed not to give her one."

A flash of heat burns in my chest. "Oh my God, are you for real right now? You do not get to be mad at me about the key."

And we didn't agree. Patrick told me not to, but I ignored him. *Don't tell Patrick, okay?* I'd said, pressing the key in her palm. *He's very peculiar about it for some reason.*

I turn and head deeper into the house. "There's leftovers in the fridge."

He dumps his things on the hall table and follows me into the kitchen. "I grabbed a sandwich on the way to the police station."

That stops me, and I turn to face him.

"Yes, I talked to Detective Bennett. I'll tell you everything, but first I want to say that I know I fucked up. I should have told you about the gun. I wish I had, you have no idea how much. But I swear to you, I *swear*, the gun was only for safety. To protect you and the girls."

"Oh, come on. You and I both know that guns don't keep anyone safe in a house where three-quarters of the people don't know the gun exists or how to use it. That's not safety, it's insanity. And it's definitely not protection."

"Okay, but *I* know how to use a gun. How to store it safely, how to use it to keep you and the twins safe. Remember that string of burglaries? It spooked the hell out of me. That's when I bought it. I didn't tell you about it because I didn't want you to worry."

"That's bullshit," I say, my voice teetering on the edge of a scream. "You've had a license since 1995. Your gun has been registered for more than two decades. Detective Bennett told me." And then, before he can spout off another sorry excuse, I realize the other thing he said. "What do you mean *was* for protection? Did you get rid of it?"

"No." He shakes his head. He looks tired, his face pale and drawn. "At least not technically."

"Where's the gun, Patrick?"

"I don't know. I had it in a safety box under the seat in my car, but I must have left it unlocked because the next time I looked, it was gone. That's part of what I was doing at the police station, reporting the gun as stolen."

I sit with that for a minute. All those times I sat next to him, all those times I used his car to run to the store, the gun was in a box under the seat. All I had to do was reach out, and I could have touched it.

And also, this excuse feels too convenient, too neat. The gun he forgot to tell me about, the gun the detective came asking me for, is gone, vanished just like AC. Just like my jewelry. Why do so many things around here go missing?

"Why didn't you report it as soon as you noticed it was missing?" Great, now I sound like the detective.

"Because I don't know when it happened, exactly, and things have been so busy..." His words trail into a groan. "You don't have to tell me how stupid it was. The detective already reamed my ass enough. Christ, Alex, I'm so sorry. I should have told you about the gun. I *know* that. I just... I'm just so fucking sorry."

I cross my arms, tucking my hands around my sides before he can reach for them.

"Guns are part of living in the South, and as much as you try not to think about it, part of living in a city like Atlanta. Every house on this street has a gun in it, likely more than one. Your brother owns three. You know that, right?"

I *do* know this. I know that every time I walk through Target or Whole Foods or my favorite restaurant, half the people in the place have a gun strapped to their waist or tucked in a side pocket of their Gucci purse. It's why I tend toward online shopping, why I don't spend weekend afternoons wandering Lenox Mall. It's why, like my trauma, I try really hard not to think of it.

"But why was the detective asking about yours? She doesn't think..."

I can't finish that sentence. I can't have those words hanging in the air between us. It hasn't been that long since Detective Bennett showed up in the middle of the day, and while I still haven't filled him in on the rest of her visit, I'm guessing she did, in those however many hours he spent at the station.

"She doesn't think what, that my gun has anything to do with the body in the carriage house?" He pulls a glass from the cabinet, filling it with three fingers of his favorite whiskey. "No. I got the sense she was looking to me for answers, not as a suspect. She still has no idea where AC is, *who* she is. That's what took so long, because the detective wanted me to help her fill in some blanks."

I nod, telling myself this is good. Telling myself I believe my husband, but it's also ten o'clock. I think of him sitting at the detective's desk for all that time, answering her questions about the dead woman and AC and his stolen gun, and I wonder why it took so long.

"What about the passcode to your phone?"

His head jerks back slightly, and he narrows his eyes. "You were trying to get into my phone? Why?"

"Because you've been acting so weird. Because of that text the girls and I received when you hadn't touched your phone. I thought..." My words trail, and I shake my head.

"You thought I changed it because I had something to hide." I don't respond, and he puts his drink down. "I changed it for the IT guys at the station. They were installing some new apps and needed access, and I didn't want to give them mine."

For the past few days, I've thought about every single reason a man would change his phone's passcode. I've agonized about it for hours, staring into space, chewing the inside of my lip raw. And I'm not stupid. He still hasn't told me what the new passcode is.

It takes him a moment, but then he slides his phone from his pocket onto the counter. "It's 888888."

And then he takes his drink and disappears upstairs.

But either Patrick has already deleted anything even remotely incriminating, or there's nothing for me to find. I check his emails, his texts, his WhatsApp and LinkedIn, and I find nothing out of the ordinary. Money and sports and work emails. I leave his phone on the island and return to the couch, digging my laptop from the cushions.

I pull up Anna Claire's obituary again, focusing on the names at the bottom. Brother Matthew is a black hole. Too many Matthew Davises, and the geography "out west" is too broad. I plug in "Keith Davis Anna Claire Valdosta" into the search bar, only to find her father died last year.

Officer Aaron Childers is another story, thanks to a recent retirement party that floats him to the tippy-top of Google's results page. I click on the Facebook invitation, then scroll through the photographs, the well-wishes, the recaps from the packed room of partygoers. One comment stands out, ringing in my head like a church bell.

Don't forget about us up there in Conyers.

TWENTY-TWO

ANNA CLAIRE

The evening ended in AC's bed, of course it did. They'd been dancing around each other long enough. On the side of the road. Behind the tinted glass of his car. Over beer and fried fish at Bubba Jax.

After he'd reached across the table for her hands in the middle of the busy dining room, after his thumbs had stroked chill bumps on her skin despite the heaters and the noise of a hundred squealing kids, he'd tucked her in the leather front seat of his car and driven her home, his palm inching higher and higher up her thigh. By the time he'd pulled up behind her piece-of-shit Honda, she wanted him so bad she was practically levitating.

She took him inside, where he took his time. His hands explored her body slowly, his fingertips and tongue tracing every curve while she writhed and moaned on the bed. The more AC tried to hurry him along, the longer he took. When finally, after a million years they got to the good part, she came three times in a quick row—*boom boom boom*. The fourth orgasm took her by surprise, and that's when she knew she was in trouble. This guy was a drug, and she was hooked.

The strangest part of it all, something she'd never experienced before, was how he stayed so laser focused. It was like he didn't even hear the phone ringing in the other room, or the neighbors fighting in the house next door. For those however many minutes he was busy with her body, the outside world didn't exist, only *her*. It made her feel special, cherished.

And she wasn't used to that.

Afterward, he wrapped her in his arms and tucked her head in his chest, and she was glad the sun had long set so he couldn't see her smile. Right then, for that very moment at least, she was happy.

It was the last thing she remembered thinking before she fell asleep.

She awoke alone, in an empty bed. She lay there for a moment, blinking into the dark room. Did he leave? Go searching for the bathroom? She stretched out an arm, one hand splayed over the spot where his body should be. The sheets were still marked with the imprint of his torso, the fabric rumpled but cool. The clock on the nightstand shone the time: 2:08 a.m.

She sat up, her heart heavy in her chest. This was why she didn't bring guys home, because either they saw it as an invitation to stay indefinitely, hogging her covers and scarfing down all her food, or they snuck out in the middle of the night, never to be heard from again. Apparently, he was one of the latter. Maybe she was right, when she thought the chase was more fun than the win. She should have known he was too good to be true.

Or maybe he really *was* married. A wife would explain why a man up and disappeared in the middle of the night, running home to her and a couple of kids, the ones he swore he didn't have. Married men don't always wear rings, and even when they do, a ring isn't some magical kind of shield. If a man wanted to cheat, he was going to cheat. It was as simple as that.

She was cursing herself for falling for it when she heard his voice, a low murmur coming from deeper in the house. She slid out of bed, snagging his shirt from the floor. The fabric was soft as silk where it touched her skin, and it smelled like him, Italian leather and spicy cologne. She left it unbuttoned on purpose, padding into the hallway with the fabric hanging open.

There were only so many places he could be in a house this tiny. The bathroom across the hall, the square space to her right that was living room and dining room in one or the galley kitchen at the far end.

The last one was where she found him, in bare feet and slacks by the window. His back was to her, and a neighbor's porch light spilled a warm golden glow through the glass, silhouetting his broad shoulders. His phone was pressed to an ear, his voice low but firm.

"…need another day or two to finalize the details, but go ahead and tell our Atlanta contact that it's handled. I'll have things up and running by early next week."

Tonight at Bubba Jax, when she'd asked him what his job was, his answer was so vague. Managing money, he'd said, followed by a bunch of mumbo jumbo about stocks and other stuff she didn't really understand. And now this, a contact in Atlanta. Things that would be up and running next week. She stood there in the shadows of the hallway, listening.

"Tell them as soon as I've got the logistics nailed down, I'll drive up there and brief them myself. Tell them I'll be on the ground to manage the first few transactions myself. Assure them things will go smoothly. Make them understand that I will see to it."

A long pause. She watched the muscles on his back tense

around a lungful of air, his shoulders tight as he listened to whatever the person on the other end had to say. His voice might
have sounded relaxed and confident just now, but it was in sharp
contrast to his body. His skin was stretched shiny, his muscles
like rocks under his skin. Whatever logistics he was referring
to, whatever transactions he would be managing, he wasn't at
all convinced they would go smoothly.

"Look, we've already been over this a million times. We know
where we messed up the last time, but I took care of that. I need
you to trust me on this."

She wouldn't be lying if she said this conversation was turning her on. Even when he was arguing his case—to his boss?
A business partner?—he was so domineering, so in control, so
completely sexy in his skin. She stepped onto the cool kitchen
vinyl, leaning a shoulder against the fridge.

"Give me another few days to get everything lined up here,
and then when this deal is done, I'll stop by so I can say *I told
you so* to your face. In the meantime, stop worrying so much,
okay? You're going to give yourself a heart attack, and your wife
doesn't like you enough to bother with CPR."

His voice took on a jokey tone, but something told her what
he said about the wife was the truth. Whoever that woman was,
she wasn't all that fond of her husband, and neither was the man
standing in her kitchen. He didn't like the man on the other
end of the line.

His big body shifted, and he turned around, pausing when he
spotted her in the doorway. His gaze slid down her body, and
here, too, he took his time. His dress shirt, hanging half open.
Her bare thighs, tingling from the attention. He took it all in,
and the look on his face filled her with desire.

"I'll call you in the morning," he said into the phone, then
clicked it off and tossed it on the drying rack stacked with yesterday's dishes.

Only three steps between them in the small galley kitchen,

and they met in the middle. His palms slid onto her hips, spreading open his shirt. Her arms wrapped around his neck, fingers threading in his hair.

"Who was that?"

"Someone I work for."

"I thought you worked for yourself."

"I guess you could say he's a business partner."

She ran a hand over a muscular shoulder. Her other hand dipped lower. "Managing money."

He nodded. His hands grabbed her behind, pulling her hard into him, letting her know he was hard and ready.

She pushed up on her toes, teeth nipping at his earlobe. "And what kind of money needs managing at two a.m.?"

His answer wasn't much more than a growl, which was perfectly fine because she was pretty sure she wouldn't have liked the answer, anyway. She preferred to concentrate instead on the other words she'd heard him say.

A few more days. He'd be here for a few more days.

AC took him by the hand and led him back to her bedroom. She intended to enjoy every second.

TWENTY-THREE

PATRICK

Something has to give.

It's the one thought spiraling through my head on Thursday as I sit in my idling car, staring at the Atlanta Police Department headquarters across the street—my second visit in as many days. I watch the cops mingle in clumps on this stretch of sidewalk, while three men in plainclothes file past on their way to the MARTA station with, just beyond, a shabby strip mall crammed with bail bondsmen. They do a brisk business, long lines threading out the doors.

And still I sit, gathering up my courage to go inside.

I wonder if they're in there, Detective Bennett and Officer Graham and whoever else has been working our case, if they're talking about me right now. Discussing my bullshit story about the gun and the camera feeds, whether or not they should haul me in for questioning. I think this, and I try not to throw up.

So far I've been lucky, I can't believe how goddamn lucky. The gun. The feeds. The passcode thing, Jesus fucking Christ. Giving Alex the new one seemed to settle her down some, but I'm not sure she bought my reason for changing it. She's too smart, and she knows me too well. She knows there's something I'm not saying.

Something has to fucking give.

I think about what it would be like to march through that gleaming lobby across the street and just…tell the truth. To finally say the words I've been carrying around like a block of concrete, to lay down that heavy burden. My fingers are reaching for the door handle when Owen's name flashes on the screen. Of course it's Owen. Pretty much the last person on the planet I want to talk to right now, and yet also the only other person who knows what I'm going through. On the fourth ring, right before the call can go to voice mail, I tap to pick up.

"Where the hell are you? You were supposed to be here ten minutes ago."

Owen is a Fulton County judge, and he doesn't like to be kept waiting any more than I like to be late. Except for today, apparently, because I'm having trouble justifying it all.

"Pretty sure you know exactly where I am. I'm assuming that's why you called."

His sigh trills in the car's speakers. "You promised you wouldn't do anything before we talked, so let's talk. This isn't only about you, you know."

"Oh, yeah? Explain to me again how your life is falling apart. Tell me how some lunatic is coming after you. After your *family.*" I say the words, and I have to remind myself to breathe. Alex and the twins. They may not be my blood, but these past six years they've become my entire world. Not that this is about me. I'm sitting here, sweating though my starched shirt, because of my fear for *them.*

"I already told you, we're not going to discuss this over the phone. Just get your ass up here, will you, and we'll figure something out. I swear to you, man. We'll find a solution."

I don't respond, because I've already given this a lot of thought. I've made endless lists. Brainstormed possible tactics. Stared at the ceiling for nights and nights on end while I racked my considerable brain, but as far as I can tell, there *is* no solution. I don't know what to do, how to fix this. Marching across the street and getting everything out into the open might make *me* feel better, but would it help Alex and the girls? That's the whole problem, I just don't know.

"I need to hear you say it, Pat. Tell me you're coming, tell me we'll figure it out together. At the very least you owe me a conversation."

And there it is, the other reason I've been in this car for the past twenty minutes. Owen is a manipulative little shit, but he's right. I owe him.

I end the call and shove the car in Reverse.

I spot Owen as soon as I come around the curve of Wetlands Trail, lit up in a ray of sunshine. It turns his cheeks and hair orange like he's on fire, a cloud of mosquitoes whirling above his head like smoke.

"I have shit to do, too, you know." His voice is clipped and edgy.

I jam my hands into the pockets of my khakis. "Then maybe next time choose an easier place to get to. I had to park all the way on the other side of Monroe."

A hike of more than half a mile to the crappiest spot in all of Piedmont Park, a rickety boardwalk squashed between the dog park and the park proper, a looping path through a swampy, wooded marshland. Last night's rain has dried up everywhere but here, a stinky, soupy humidity that sticks my clothes to my skin. It's going to be a brutal summer.

He leans a hip against the handrail, glaring from behind a ridiculous pair of sunglasses that cover the entire top half of his face. "I was worried about you, man."

"About me? Or about where my little blue dot was on the app?"

An app Owen originally installed on both our phones, meant as a safety precaution. A way for us to keep an eye on each other by tracking our whereabouts in real time. "Just in case," he said at the time, and it made us feel safe—or at least, safer.

But the app was created for helicopter moms, for paranoid, hypervigilant parents looking to micromanage their kids. My phone beeped any time he drove too fast or went somewhere outside his regular routes. And just last month, when I was rear-ended merging onto the ramp for Roswell Road, Owen beat the cops there, screeching to a stop alongside my wrecked bumper. Far as I can tell, the app has only made us paranoid.

And it's how he knew I was sitting outside Atlanta PD.

"You can stop looking at me like that. I didn't talk to anyone. I didn't even go inside."

Owen grunts. "That may be so, but I bet you've got that detective's cell memorized."

It's not really a question. Owen has known me long enough to know I only have to hear a number once to remember it. It's the curse of my mathematical brain, assigning a meaning to every string of numbers, noticing a pattern within the digits that will stamp them onto my memory without even trying. Phone numbers, addresses, pins, license plates, long lists of data. I never have to write any of them down.

Owen crosses his long arms in front of his chest. "Any word from the stripper?"

"Not a peep." The sun is beating down, setting my scalp and the tops of my shoulders on fire, and I shift into a slice of shade. "Hard to talk when you're dead."

"Who's dead?"

"The stripper, Owen. Little Kathi is dead."

My chest goes tight around the words, my lungs as useless as a suction cup, just like they were yesterday when Detective Bennett slid that picture across her desk. Little Kathi lying on my carriage house floor, one cheek smashed into a pool of shiny black. I only saw one side of her face, but it was plenty. It was everything I could do not to puke right on top of that photo.

"I parked my car in front of her complex, Owen. I knocked on her door in broad daylight. I gave her my fucking card! It's in her apartment somewhere, which means as soon as they figure out who she is, they're going to find out I was there, which is exactly what that bitch wanted when she planted her in my carriage house."

"Whoa, whoa, whoa. What bitch planted *who* in your carriage house?"

Owen and I met in college, back when I was dirt poor and stupid. I was too enamored by his shiny new BMW, his closet filled with polo shirts in every conceivable color, his signet ring with a real family crest. Owen had everything I wanted at the time, the wealth and the confidence and the name. It made it easy to ignore the fact he was an entitled dick. If not for our shared history, I would have outgrown him ages ago.

"Little Kathi. Jesus, would you keep up? Somebody dumped her body in my carriage house bathroom, along with a couple gallons of cow's blood. And that somebody has got to be AC. I don't know who else it could be."

"But why?"

"To punish Little Kathi for giving me information. To make me look guilty of murder. To scare the pants off Alex and the twins. Probably all of the above."

He frowns, considering my words. "What information did she give you?"

"She told me AC's license was from Utah, which matches up with—"

"Hang on. I thought AC was from Valdosta."

"Oh my God, would you just let me finish?"

"So finish, then," Owen says, and I have to try very hard not to punch him.

I shove a hand through my hair, damp with sweat. "The license matches up with the T-shirt I found in her room, one with a label that said Property of Bush Creek Ranch. I found a couple places in the US with that name, but none in the South. There is, however, one in Utah. That particular Bush Creek Ranch is a wilderness therapy camp for troubled teens. Abuse, depression, eating disorders, addictions, trauma—you name it, they treat it. The kids build fences and drive cattle and do chores to keep them in line, teach them life skills. It's the sort of place you send your kids when nothing else works, kind of a Hail Mary pass for delinquents."

Owen shrugs. "She would have been a minor at the time, which means the ranch won't give out any personal information."

"Not to us," I say, feeling a familiar lurch in my stomach at the words that come next. "But they would to the police."

"Nope," Owen says, shaking his head so hard his hair slaps against his sweaty forehead. "No fucking way. I'm up for re-election again next year, and Advocacy for Action already has a target on my back. They're putting out calls for Black women to run against me, doesn't matter whether they're qualified or not. They want to unseat me in the name of diversity."

I breathe through a fiery flash of anger. Owen likes to pretend he won a seat on the Fulton County Superior Court on his own merits, and not because his father strong-armed all his wealthy friends to step up as donors, or because Owen was the only white male on the ballot.

"Do you hear how ignorant you sound? Next year's election won't matter if you're dead."

The blood drains from his ruddy cheeks, from pink to white in an instant. "We don't know that. Nobody's dead."

As usual, Owen is kidding himself. "That woman was in my *home*, Owen. With my wife and stepdaughters. She took my *gun*. I have no reason to believe she wouldn't use it."

"Okay, fine. *Fine.* Can we just slow down and think this through?" He holds up both hands, exhaling so sharply it sounds like a whistle. "Let me play the judge card on the folks at that Utah camp. I'll see if I can wrangle a name out of them, point us in the right direction. In the meantime, just...sit tight, will you? Don't make any moves until we know more. And no talking to the cops."

"How am I supposed to do that? That detective keeps showing up at my house. She keeps coming to me with more questions."

"Play stupid. Hold her off. I just need a couple of days."

"How many?"

"I don't know. Three."

I think about what those three days will be like. Seventy-two hours of waiting for the next bomb to drop from the sky. My blood thickens, and my heart feels like it's about to explode.

"This is my *family*, Owen."

"I realize that. And look, I get that you're freaked out, but you and I made a pact. We swore that if anything like this ever happened, we'd stay a team. No making a move without consulting the other first. Brothers for life, remember?"

My lungs empty out because I made a lot of promises that night and sticking together was one of them. I don't know what I hate Owen for more—being a douche or playing the guilt card.

I check my watch.

"Seventy-two hours. Starting now. But after that, you and I are even. I don't owe you anything, and you don't owe me. After Sunday at five, it's every man for himself."

TWENTY-FOUR

Rachel is standing in the hall, deep in conversation with one of the morning anchors, when I come into the station, still rumpled and sweaty from my hike through the park. She doesn't mention the team meeting I just bailed on or ask what kind of lunch lasts three hours when I should be here, preparing for my segment. She just gives her watch a pointed look as I sail by.

My assistant bombards me with a long list of appointments that have to be rescheduled, people that have to be called back, emails that have to be answered immediately or else. I tell her to prioritize the list and hold everybody off for thirty minutes. That's all I ask, thirty minutes to get my shit together.

I step into my office and shut the door.

The T-shirt, the Utah driver's license, my business card, the missing gun. Damned if I know where it is or how long it's been gone, but I do know one thing: that gun is going to show up again at some point, and a million bucks says it'll be pointed at my head.

What else?

I've already tried tracing the post—the Krissie Kelly one that started this whole shit show. I thought if I could trace it to the originating IP, I could pinpoint a location and maybe even cough up a name, but I'm a mathematician not a magician, and my computer skills only got me so far. Providers don't just hand out those kinds of details, not without a warrant. A hacker, then? I shoot a text to Simon in IT, asking if his offer still stands. The guy who knows a guy—the sketchier, the better.

I've just hit Send when my cell rings, the VP of one of the big day-trading firms I gave a crappy review on air. I swipe the screen to pick up.

"I know why you're calling, Sam, and I'll tell you the same thing I said on air, that your company caters to a bunch of inexperienced bozos who treat your platform like some kind of electronic casino. You don't offer phone or live chat support, which means when they end up with a big, fat negative balance, there's nowhere they can turn for help. Nobody's home."

"There's a contact form right there on the website. On the app, too. One click and they're in touch with a customer service representative."

The VP yammers on, his voice blaring in my ear, and that's when I notice that it's much louder than it should be. The office is quiet. Too quiet. The constant buzz coming from the bullpen is gone, like a needle ripped from a record. I look up, frowning through the wall of glass.

People stand around the bullpen in clumps, but they're not talking or shouting. Not moving, either. I take in their bent heads, the way their backs are hunched around a computer screen or their phones, and my skin prickles with dread. A terrorist attack, some kind of natural disaster, another school shooting. There are very few things that can turn a bullpen pin-drop quiet.

I look to my assistant stationed behind her desk, a phone pressed to her ear. Our eyes meet through the glass, and I don't like the blush that blooms on her cheeks, or how quickly she looks away. She's embarrassed, for *me*. I hang up on the VP, letting my phone clatter to the table.

I jiggle the mouse on my laptop, pulling up CNN, but the only breaking news is a sudden stock market plunge. Ditto for *Reuters* and the *New York Times*. I surf to a couple more news outlets, then turn to the source every reporter worth their byline knows dishes out news before it breaks: Twitter.

I begin with trending topics. A new Covid variant, an executive order, a Beverly Hills Housewife in legal trouble.

And then I see it, my own name.

Once, only once, has my name ever trended on Twitter, and that was after I skewered a popular investment platform as having servers full of holes on the same day CNN announced they'd had a massive data breach. Millions of emails and personal data exposed, and I was the first to call out their shabby security. The timing couldn't have been more perfect.

Now, though, my blood runs cold, and I know before I click my name that this isn't about a security breach, or even one of my more recent segments. I think about that mysterious text. *Is everybody ready? Because here I come.*

With an unsteady finger, I tap the link. The tweets line up in a neat column.

So it turns out @patrickhutch is a major creep. Who knew?

Alex I don't know you but run run run as fast as you can from this asshat @patrickhutch

@patrickhutch is as vile as his bitchy bully of a wife. What are those two going to do when no sponsor wants to touch their nasty asses?

If you think your day is crap, just imagine @patrickhutch trying to explain that voice recording to his shrew of a wife #awkward

A voice recording, Jesus.

At the top of the browser, I type my name + *voice recording* into the search bar and hit Enter. YouTube has the top hit, which is both good news and bad. Good because that means it hasn't spread to the major networks yet, but bad because whatever's in the two-minute-and-fifty-three-second clip has already racked up fifty thousand views.

Dread grips my gut, a vise squeezing my insides at the number. Fifty thousand is a *lot*, and in what—less than twelve hours? Shit. I brace myself and hit Play.

It takes me a second or two to place the party noise that fills the silence in my office, laughter and chatter cutting through some song. And then I hear the jingle bells, Bing Crosby's crooning voice. The station's holiday party?

No—not the station's party, the one Alex and I threw at the club. At the last minute, Alex had invited her new hire, her personal assistant, who I hadn't met yet.

I still see it when I close my eyes sometimes, that triumphant closed-lipped smile when she'd cornered me by the dessert table. Her voice pushes up through the music, a high-pitched giggle I recognize immediately, and it makes me want to punch my fist through a wall.

That bitch recorded our conversation.

I turn up the volume on my laptop, and then I sit very, very still.

AC: *I just want to say how excited I am to be working for your wife. You have such a lovely home, and your girls are just stunning. You must be so proud.*

Patrick: *Yeah, sure. Whatever.*

That's not what I said. It's not anywhere close. I was two drinks in by then, but still, I'm certain. My reply was more along the lines of, *What is that, a threat?*

AC: *Do you have any tips? Some helpful information you can share about how your wife likes to work? I really want to nail this job.*

Patrick [sharp laughter]: *Social media isn't a job, and Alex's followers are a bunch of stupid cows who drink her ridiculous Kool-Aid. I don't know if that makes her smart or vapid. Maybe both.*

Oh, for fuck's sake. I might have thought that about Alex's followers, but there's no way in hell I said *that*. I tap the space bar, and the recording stops.

Think, Patrick, think. What did *you say?*

I drop my head in my hands and press down hard on my temples, but the stress has short-circuited my brain and this was months ago. I come up blank.

I breathe through a wave of nausea, checking the numbers at the bottom of the YouTube file. Another two and a half minutes of this shit.

I steel myself and press Play.

AC: *You can't really mean that. Your wife is a rock star. Creating a profitable business out of pictures and good vibes. I mean, how brilliant is that?*

Patrick: *Can we please stop talking about Alex now?*

AC: *Um, okay. What would you like to talk about?*

Patrick: *That dress. [long pause] I'd like it a lot better if you weren't wearing any underwear.*

I stab the space bar, because I *definitely* didn't say that. Fuck. *Fuck.* My office turns hot and swampy.

I stare at my phone, considering my next move where my

wife is concerned. Call Alex and protest my innocence? Blow the whole thing off as a ridiculous fabrication? I can't decide if it's best to get out in front of the recording or dismiss it as a silly nuisance.

The door swings open on a half-assed knock, three quick raps that are more form than function. Rachel in her navy power suit, her hair slicked back making her look extra tough, and I wonder if today is my turn, if this is the day she makes me cry.

She shuts the door, but she doesn't come any farther. "I don't know if you're aware, but there's——"

"A voice recording, I know. But it's not me. I didn't say those things."

"I heard it, Patrick. There's no question it's your voice."

"It's my voice, yes, but I happen to remember that conversation. Maybe not word for word, but I don't talk that way about my wife, and I definitely don't hit on her employees. That woman recorded our conversation, and then she manipulated my words somehow."

Rachel looks dubious. One of her top prime-time personalities, caught up in yet another scandal. I try not to think about the station's Facebook page, how it must be getting bombarded right now. With fifty thousand views and counting, the trolls won't be far behind.

"I just came from HR, Patrick, and they are concerned. They say it's only a matter of time before the clip gets picked up by the mainstream media, and I agree. It's already all over YouTube and Twitter."

"But it's not me. I mean, it's my voice, but I didn't say those words. Not in that order, at least. Not even during that conversation."

"Can you prove it?"

My nod is immediate, even though I'm not one hundred percent certain. A pop or a skip in the audio would be easy to conceal under all the music and chatter, but there's got to be a way to isolate my voice. Bumps in frequency or amplitude, for example, anything that would indicate tampering. But audio isn't exactly my department. I wouldn't even begin to know how to go about proving it, but that doesn't mean someone else can't.

"Talk to Simon in IT," Rachel says, reading my mind. "Tell him I gave this top priority. But in the meantime, Patrick, I can't have you on the air."

"You can't be serious. My segment's in three hours! I've got the guests lined up and promos running on all the socials. I can't bail now. You know what people will think, right?"

She dips her chin, but she doesn't say the awful words out loud. She doesn't have to. We both know what they'll think—that I'm guilty.

AC's face shimmers through my mind, her mouth twisted in that ugly smirk, and it's like a surprise punch. The air leaves my lungs in a loud whoosh.

Rachel tugs on the hem of her jacket with both hands, straightening the nonexistent wrinkles. "Go home, Patrick. Let me know when you've got some answers."

TWENTY-FIVE

ANNA CLAIRE

On Tuesday, at five on the dot, AC pushed through the door to the office, flipping through the rack on the wall for her time card.

Terri dragged her gaze from the blaring TV, where a tornado was ripping through some trailer park in Wisconsin, a preview of doom and destruction coming up on the evening news. She hit Mute, and the room plunged into silence. "Uh-oh. What's wrong?"

AC dropped her card back in the slot, smiling. "Not one thing. Why're you asking?"

"Because you never finish your shift on time, no matter how many times I tell you that laziness don't get you any overtime. But yesterday you clocked out at five, and the day before at ten 'til. You got another job or something?"

"No, but I do have a date." AC couldn't help it, she beamed. These past three days, they'd managed to not go anywhere but her bed. Three days of his naked body under her sheets. This morning when he dropped her here, he told her to hurry. She fancied herself...well, not in love, exactly, but she was definitely deep in like.

She liked the way his big hands curved around the stitched leather steering wheel, how when the sun hit the crystal of his watch just right, it turned the windshield into a sparkly rainbow. She liked how his shirt felt against her skin when she slipped her hands underneath, silky soft like a cat's fur. She liked the soft swoosh his pants made as the fabric slid down his legs, the heavy thwump of his silver belt buckle hitting the floor.

But hands down, what she liked most was that he didn't sneak off every time that fancy phone of his rang. After that first time in the kitchen, when she'd caught him smack in the middle of a late-night business call with a mysterious man, he didn't wander off to talk in private. He picked up whenever a call came in— and his phone rang a *lot*. In the car, in her bed, at all hours of the day and night. He didn't mind that AC was always listening in.

And his calls were highly educational. Even though she only ever heard half of it, they were like sitting in on a class at business school. She'd learned things about supply and demand, about outsmarting your competition and the importance of having the right people in the right positions, about how reducing costs meant more money on the back end. And she heard numbers that made her eyes bulge.

He was managing money, all right. Big, huge piles of it.

Once, only once, she'd asked why he didn't just put all that money in a bank. The look he'd given her shut her right up, and that's when she knew. Whatever these "logistics" were, whatever these transactions he kept talking about, they weren't exactly the kind he wanted Uncle Sam knowing about.

But back in the tiny motel office, Terri was losing interest fast. Her beloved *Wheel of Fortune* was about to come on, and she reached for the remote, swiveling back to the television screen.

"As long as the rooms are clean, I guess. Just don't be late for your shift tomorrow."

AC tossed her a wave and ran out the door.

His car was right where he said it would be, idling at the edge of the gravel lot out back. She slid into the passenger's seat and kissed him, long and thorough. "Hi, honey. I'm home."

His laughter warmed her lips. "Pretty sure that's my line."

"I cleaned sixteen rooms today. What did you do?"

"I netted over seventy thousand dollars."

AC sat back in her seat, stunned. "In one day?"

He shoved the car in gear, flashing her a cocky smile. "And it wasn't even my best day."

More than seventy thousand dollars in one day? She couldn't even fathom a job that paid that much, and he earned it all in the eight hours since she'd seen him last. She was crap at math, but that was, what—five, six times more than what she earned in a whole entire year? Holy shit.

She thought about it all the way home. As he steered his car down the winding road to her house, she watched the familiar scenery flit by, the fields and the farms and the factories, hills and pastures she'd stared at all her life, and the truth hit her like a baseball bat to the head.

She wanted out. Out of this town, out of her job, out of this sad, sorry life she was living. Unskilled. Uneducated. Unmoneyed. What if this man next to her was temporary? What if when he left she'd go back to being the same old Anna Claire Davis she'd always been? The idea made her hot and itchy.

Especially now that she'd gotten a whiff of what life could be like when money made your worries evaporate like a puddle in the August sun. When there was food in the fridge and decent tires under her car. When clothing was made of the finest silk and cotton and shoes didn't have holes in the soles. Amazing how different the world looked from the fine leather seat of an expensive car.

She twisted to face him. "I was thinking maybe I could work for you."

He glanced over, eyebrows raised in surprise. "Don't you have a job?"

"Yeah, a really shitty one. I don't need seventy grand a day, but a couple hundred would be nice."

She was careful to put just the right note of detachment in her tone, and she didn't look over to read his reaction. She kept her eyes on the passing fields like she didn't much care what he thought about her idea. She'd been on this green earth long enough to know how to hedge her bets.

"Work for me doing what?" he said, and his tone told her he wasn't opposed to the idea, though he wasn't totally convinced, either. "Though honestly, I'd hire you for the blow jobs alone. Is that on your résumé? Because if you'd like, I could give you a reference."

She slapped his arm, pretending to be mock-insulted. "Keep it up, mister, and you won't be getting any more. And I'll have you know I have plenty of skills beyond mopping floors and blow jobs. And don't ask me if I know how to file, because I'm looking for a job that's a lot more fun than stuffing some papers in a cabinet."

He pointed a finger to the sunroof, waved it around. "Do you see a filing cabinet? Because this car you're sitting in, it's basically my office, and the type of work I do doesn't exactly come with paperwork." He put his hand back on the wheel, using it to negotiate another turn.

Interesting. No paper trail, no banks. She still didn't entirely understand where all that money came from, but she knew what that meant.

Still, it didn't much bother her. She was tired of seeing big chunks of her paycheck get sucked out for taxes, tired of having to make do with minimum wage. What the government didn't know wouldn't hurt them, and it would definitely improve the sad situation in her wallet. She wanted a cut.

"Okay, but who's going to watch things here when you take your mom to the specialist next week? What's going to happen then?"

"I have people working for me. They know what's expected of them."

"Yes, but these people." She leaned over the console, slid a hand up his thigh. "Do you trust them the way you trust me?"

He sucked in a breath. "Keep going."

She didn't know what he was referring to, exactly, her proposition or the fingers creeping up his thigh, but she did as he said and kept going.

"Because what if something goes wrong while you're out of town? What if these people of yours get lazy and slack off while the boss is away? Who's going to make sure something like that doesn't happen?"

"So what are you suggesting, that you be my spy? My personal assistant?"

Personal assistant. She liked the sound of that. She wouldn't mind personally assisting this man.

Her hand slid higher and higher still, until it was right where he liked it. He went instantly hard. She had that effect on him, she held that power, and the knowledge gave her a thrill.

"Personal assistant, but with benefits." She rubbed him with the heel of her palm. "Give me a job, baby. Let me work for you. I promise you won't regret it."

He groaned and gripped the steering wheel. "If nothing else, your negotiating skills are fierce."

With her other hand, she reached for his belt buckle. "I'm more than fierce. I'm strong and determined and a hard worker. You said so yourself." She unhooked his belt, worked the button open on his pants. "You said I was impressive. Remember?"

"I remember."

"And you know you can trust me. You know I aim to please."

He nodded, swallowing.

"So use me for something other than sex, baby." She tugged on the zipper, skimmed a finger along the waistband of his boxers, dipping it under but not quite getting there. "Give me a piece of your pie, and I'll give you one of mine whenever you want it."

"Jesussss." The word came out on the tail end of a moan. "You're hired."

She smiled and gave him his reward.

TWENTY-SIX

ALEX

I slide the rental to the curb in front of a house that's pretty if not a little cookie-cutter, two stories of red brick and sunny yellow shutters. A walkway slices through a neat yard, ending at a front door framed with fat green balls of buxus and rhododendron. I make my way up it and ring the bell, praying the address I dug up from the White Pages is right.

Don't forget about us up there in Conyers.

The man who opens the door is in fishing gear, a khaki vest and floppy hat with dozens of dangling lures in bright colors. I smile as I take in his pink cheeks and fluffy gray mustache, the generous paunch around the middle.

"Hello, Officer Childers?" I ask, even though there's no question this is him, the man I saw in the Facebook pictures.

He matches my smile with one of his own, one that's easy and friendly, if not a smidge reserved. He smiles the way you'd smile at a political canvasser or a Jehovah's Witness, right before you shut the door in their face.

"Just Aaron these days. I retired last year. What can I do for you?"

"My name is Alex Hutchinson. Sorry to just show up here out of the blue, but I come bearing gifts." I jiggle the box in my hand, a dozen Krispy Kremes, iced, glazed and filled. "Hopefully they're still warm."

"That's an urban legend, FYI. Not all cops eat donuts."

"Do you?"

He glances over his shoulder, in the direction of someone banging around in the kitchen, then turns back with a wink. "I eat the hell out of a donut, but only when my wife's not looking."

I laugh and flip open the box, and he surveys the contents, selecting a chocolate-glazed with rainbow sprinkles. He hooks a paw around the door and takes a massive bite, waiting.

"I understand you once worked a case involving the murder of Anna Claire Davis."

His smile doesn't lose elevation, but the way it sticks to his cheeks while he chews tells me the answer.

Yes, he worked the case. No, he hasn't been able to let it go.

"This is going to sound crazy, but for the past five months, I've employed a woman with the same name. She used the real Anna Claire's social security number, same birth date, same backstory. She told me her mother died when she was sixteen of lung cancer. That her father and she had a falling-out soon thereafter. She talked about a brother who was somewhere on the west coast. She said everybody called her AC but her father."

He stuffs the last of the donut in his mouth, licks the icing from his fingers. "Okay, Alex. You have my attention."

"I don't really have much to add, except that a week ago, she up and disappeared. She left my house last Wednesday night, and no one has seen or heard from her since. Atlanta police seem to suspect some kind of foul play, and they're looking to me and my husband for answers, but I think it's more likely she's gone underground. I think she's… I don't know, enacting some kind of revenge. On me."

"Why's that?"

"Because of all the stuff that has happened since. I was doxed, my car and office vandalized. I'm getting all kinds of threats, real ones. Scary ones. These people online, they've crossed all sorts of lines especially when it comes to my twelve-year-old daughters, and—"

"No, I mean, why would she want revenge?"

"I don't know. But if I'm to believe the stuff this handle Mister Fluffles is putting out there—"

"Hang on. Mister Fluffles?" I nod, and his bushy brows disappear under his hat. "That's one hell of a coincidence, and I've been a cop long enough to know there's no such thing. Mister Fluffles was the name of AC's childhood cat."

I don't quite know what to say to that, and Officer Childers doesn't say anything more, either. He just swings the door wide. "Get in here. And if my wife asks about that donut, tell her you ate it."

I step into a foyer that's bright and sunny, the walls painted an egg-yolk yellow against bright white trim. A Persian rug is stretched across the floor, with rose and peach swirls with a table perched in the middle, its surface smothered with porcelain knickknacks and photographs in pretty silver frames. Through an arched doorway I spot twin leather couches, oversized enough to stretch out on and then some, but softened with a dozen throw pillows, feminine florals with fringe and a karate chop pleat.

We follow the banging into the kitchen, where a birdlike woman is loading the dishwasher. Across her apron, in bright red letters, is written No Bitchin' in Nana's Kitchen. She gives me a bright smile.

"Well, hey there, darlin', you got here just in time. I just pulled a fresh batch of zucchini bread out of the oven, and unlike those donuts in your hand it's gluten free and healthy. I bet my Aaron has already scarfed down at least one, hasn't he?" Her voice is slow and syrupy, heavy with a south Georgian accent. "Sit down and I'll cut you a slice."

Aaron shows me to the kitchen table, an oval chunk of light-stained wood overlooking a landscaped backyard, and we sit. I slide the donut box to the far end.

"Tell me again," he says. "Start from the beginning."

And so I do. While Aaron's wife arranges the zucchini bread on a platter she coats with a dusting of powdered sugar, I tell him about my job and the post that blew it to smithereens, the trashed car and the knife-stabbed note and the dead body lying on my bathroom floor. I tell him about the online pile-on led by Mister Fluffles that includes death and rape threats, and I repeat my sneaking suspicion that the woman I knew as AC is behind all of it. His wife plunks two plates and the platter on the table between us, and he doesn't even notice. Not for a second does Aaron take his eyes off my face.

When I'm done, he gives a slow shake of his head. "The dead woman. Who is she?"

"As far as I know, the police haven't identified her."

"And how'd she get in your bathroom?"

"No idea. I didn't always lock that door, but it was locked all this past weekend when this woman appeared. AC is the only person besides my husband and me who has a key. We've since changed the locks."

"And have you thought about going to a hotel?"

"Do you think we should?"

He lifts both hands from the table. "That's not a decision I can make for you. You're the only one who knows what's good for you and your family. But whoever put that woman there did it as a warning or a promise or a threat, and whichever it is, if I were you, I would be taking it very seriously. Make sure the local police are taking it seriously, too."

I nod, my stomach giving a hard lurch.

"But," he says, softening his next words with a kind smile, "what I still haven't heard is your personal assistant's connection to Anna Claire, or either of their connections to you."

"That's why I'm here, actually, because I was hoping you could help me fill in some of the blanks. From the obituary, it seemed like you had a relationship with the family."

"That's putting it mildly, dear," his wife says, settling two cups of freshly brewed coffee onto the table. "Aaron was haunted by what happened to that poor girl. Our daughter was about the same age at the time, so it was all too easy to picture something like that happening to her. It gave both of us nightmares for years." She gestures to the cup nearest to me. "Cream or sugar?"

"This is perfect, thank you." Aaron hands me a plate, and I shimmy a slice of zucchini bread onto it, breaking off a corner. "Maybe you could tell me what you remember about the case?"

"I remember everything. If you've read anything about her murder, which it seems like you have, then you know she died a long and painful death."

"She was tortured."

Aaron nods. "All those injuries, from the stab wounds to the missing fingers to the five-centimeter hole in her head, those were inflicted while she was still alive. She was raped, multiple times, with all sorts of objects that didn't belong inside a human. But make no mistake. This wasn't just some maniac looking to torture her. This was an execution. Cause of death was a bullet through the brain."

I sit there for a long moment absorbing the news, peeling through my shock and fear. To live through such an excruciating torture, to be stabbed and cut and raped and who knows what else. Death must have felt like a relief.

But an execution?

"That wasn't in the papers," I say, the cake and coffee forming a sour lump in my stomach.

"We left a couple of tidbits out on purpose. Helps to weed out the crazies from the tip line. At the time, everybody figured it was her ex-boyfriend, a kid named Adam Holmes. He and Anna Claire had an on-again, off-again relationship since she was fifteen, despite her father forbidding her to see him. After his wife died, he'd gotten caught up in a church, a culty one that prohibits, well, pretty much everything. He didn't approve of his daughter having premarital sex. Between you and me, he didn't approve of much. But he was right to worry about Adam. That kid was bad news. He beat her up a bunch of times. Broke a couple bones."

"So... Anna Claire's death was a crime of passion?"

"Not passion. An execution, remember? And for the record, it wasn't Adam. He had an airtight alibi for that night, and abuse is a whole different ballpark than torture. All those injuries—the missing fingers, the stab wounds, the hole in her head—it didn't fit. Adam was a knucklehead, but he wasn't that evil."

"You speak of him in the past tense."

"He died a couple years later. Got drunk and behind the wheel of a car. Killed two people on his way out, a couple coming home from dinner. Keith blamed him for taking his daughter's innocence. He called it God's justice. But like I said, Adam had an alibi."

"So who do you think killed her, then?" My voice is quiet in the kitchen. It's such a gruesome question, such gruesome pictures Aaron planted in my brain. I try not to see her, poor, dead Anna Claire, but the image still seeps into my mind. So ugly I have to shake my head to clear it.

Aaron lifts his shoulders up to his ears. "Rumor had it she was pretty serious about someone, but none of her friends had ever met him. Her boss and neighbors gave us a vague description of him and a dark BMW, but Anna Claire did a good job of keeping him a mystery. What I do know is that a killing like hers happens for one of two reasons—either to extract information or as revenge. And before you ask me which one, beats me. That's the part that drove me nuts about this case, we could never figure out a motive."

I pick at the bread on my plate, thinking through his words. Information or revenge, they both point to something Anna Claire did while she was alive. Did she stumble into something that got her killed? There's so much here that doesn't make sense.

"Okay, but going back to the woman who worked for me," I say. "The fake AC. Why would anyone want to impersonate someone whose death was so awful?"

"Why does anyone do anything? Money's always a good motivator. So is revenge. Sex. Addiction. Control. Psychological issues. Problems at home. The thrill of getting away with doing something bad. Poor self-esteem." He brushes his hands together, raining crumbs onto his plate. "Want me to keep going? Because I can."

I believe it. You don't make it forty-plus years on the police force without hearing every possible reason for committing every possible crime. I reflect on Aaron's list, shaking my head.

"Well, it's not money, that much is for sure. I am a one-woman company. I paid her peanuts compared to what she could have earned at pretty much any other job, and she's never once asked for more. She didn't even negotiate salary, just took the one I offered without argument."

"Did she have access to your accounts?"

"She had access to everything. My socials, my email, my business bank account. My home and my family. She could have walked off with everything, but she didn't, though there were a couple of things from the house that went missing—jewelry, maybe some other stuff. I don't know, I haven't really had time to do inventory."

Honestly, though. Money would be the least offensive answer. All those other motivations Aaron just rattled off, the revenge and the sex and the control issues, feel so much scarier because they point to something personal.

"Maybe she was looking to hijack my platform somehow," I say, thinking out loud. "To… I don't know, announce something about the real Anna Claire's death. I have a million followers, and even my least popular posts get a good deal of traction."

"Seems like a lot of trouble when she could just announce it to the media or one of those gossip magazines, or even a true-crime podcast. There's a reason she came to you, why she chose to work for you when she could have gone anywhere else." He says the words slowly, and I can hear the gears whirring in his head, see the spark light up his eyes. Aaron misses this, the solving of the puzzle. "And the dead body in your bathroom was a message. Even if she's not the one behind it, you need to beef up your security."

"We are, believe me. But I didn't know the real Anna Claire existed until last night."

"I assume you're not the only person in the house," he says with a kind smile, and there it is, the something I was missing. The connection doesn't have to be with me. I think about what Patrick's connection could be with the real Anna Claire, but I come up blank.

"My husband grew up in Marietta, which is, what—a good three hundred miles north of Valdosta?"

"Something like that."

"He went to school in Athens, both undergrad and masters. How would they have even met? Didn't I read somewhere that she dropped out of high school?"

"Her junior year, not that she wasn't smart enough to graduate, but she had to find a way to support herself after Keith kicked her out of the house. There were not a lot of opportunities for an uneducated teenager, but she worked hard and did what she could to get by. All that goes to say no, your husband

and she wouldn't have met at school. What about vacations? You drive straight through Valdosta on the way to Florida."

"Yeah, but Patrick *hates* Florida. He says it's a sauna filled with tourists and little old ladies from Ohio who can't drive. Our girls can't even get him to go to Seaside, no matter how much they cry and beg. We vacation pretty much anywhere but Florida."

Aaron watches me over the table with kind eyes, and it doesn't take me long to figure out why. He's waiting for me to come up with the answer myself.

That maybe it's because Patrick has been *avoiding* Florida.

I shove my plate away, not liking how my thoughts keep veering back to Patrick. The gun, the new passcode on his phone. If this was the big secret, that he knew the real Anna Claire somehow, if when AC showed up at our front door he recognized the name and the appropriated history, why not just tell me?

I don't like that answer, either.

"I can see you've got some things to think about, and it could very well be I've sent you hunting under the wrong bushes, but the answer lies in the connection. The thread that ties this woman to Anna Claire to you." Aaron drains the last of his coffee, settles the mug lightly on the table. "Because it's for sure there. All you have to do is find it."

TWENTY-SEVEN

On the way home, I get sucked into traffic thick as soup, wall-to-wall brake lights across all eight lanes of the downtown connector. The buildings rise up on either side of the Grady curve, casting long shadows over the highway. I drum my fingers against the wheel, ride the bumper in front of me and check the time: 2:42. A traffic jam in the middle of the afternoon. This is why I work from home. How do people sit through this every day?

I'm thumbing through the stations on the satellite radio when my cell phone rings, yet another new one I picked up just this morning, and the name on the screen revs my heart. Because here's the thing about your children's school: they only call when something's wrong.

I tap Connect on the hands-free system. "Alex Hutchinson speaking."

"Hi, Alex, this is Iris Sheffield, the school counselor at Lake Forrest Academy. Is this a good time for a chat?"

My heart settles, just a tad. The school counselor, not the nurse or the girls' soccer coach calling to report a fall or broken bone. Not a recorded message calling to announce a gunman on the loose and a school lockdown. No sirens in the background, no panicked screams or gunshots. Just the school counselor, asking for a little chat.

"Of course. I hope they're not in trouble."

As much as the twins' preteen attitudes can fire up my temper, they're actually good girls. Respectful. Honest. Excellent students, especially Penelope. The only complaint I've ever heard from teachers is that they're too chatty (Gigi) or too hard on themselves (Penelope). But this past week has been a nightmare. I wouldn't be surprised to hear they've acted out.

"I'm afraid we've had an incident come up that involves the twins," she says, her voice kind but professional. "Apparently, there was a party a couple weeks ago at Jenni Weaver's house, one that both your daughters attended."

The girls are at an age where there are parties or sleepovers practically every weekend, so it takes me a minute to recall the details. "I think you're referring to the slumber party for Jenni's birthday. The girls went rock climbing and to dinner, then back to Jenni's for the rest of the night. Her mother's house, that is."

I don't mention that dinner was at the St. Regis, or that the girls got back to Jenni's to discover her basement had been converted into a nightclub complete with LED light show and a DJ. Jenni's parents are in the midst of a very noisy, very nasty divorce, and they're going a little overboard in the indulging department. Concerts, limo rides, spa parties in the penthouse of the Waldorf Astoria. Nothing is too lavish for their precious Jenni, no event too over-the-top for one parent to stick it to the other.

Iris clears her throat. "Yes, well, some photographs from that night have been making the rounds among the student body. In them, your daughters are holding an alcoholic beverage and smoking an e-cigarette. Now I realize this behavior didn't occur on campus, but as I'm sure you're aware—"

The Jeep in front of me hits the brakes, and I slam mine just in time, screeching my tires and missing their bumper by a hair. I shake my head, but I can't make her words make sense. The girls are *twelve*.

"Hang on. There was *alcohol* at this party?"

"Evidently so, though according to the photos I've seen and the students I've talked to, Gigi and Penelope were the only two who were drinking it. As I'm sure you know, school policy prohibits the use of alcohol or drugs both on and off campus, not just because such use is illegal, but because it also jeopardizes the health of the student and the safety of all students and seriously impairs learning. Simply stated, we strongly believe it is impossible to learn well, or to make a positive contribution to our community, while under the influence of drugs or alcohol."

"I one hundred percent agree. What I'm *not* buying is that my girls would be stupid enough to sneak a drink in front of all their friends at a party when there are cell phone cameras and a parent right upstairs. I mean…give them some credit. And even if they *were* drinking, which I'm not saying they were, they certainly wouldn't have been the only ones doing it."

"That may be so, but your daughters are the only ones doing it in the photographs I've seen. Everyone else is holding a water or a soft drink. They are also the only ones smoking. Because it's an e-cigarette and impossible to know what's in the pod, I'm going to give them the benefit of the doubt that it's nicotine, and not something more…narcotic."

Weed. She thinks the contents might be weed.

"Have you talked to the other students? Did you talk to Jenni?"

"Of course. Both Jenni and her mother claim no one was

drinking or smoking. Including Penelope and Gigi, who both deny it. Vehemently."

"See? There must be some kind of explanation like…like… an empty can. Maybe they were joking around for the pictures or something, because I know my daughters, and…they…" I'm fumbling for words, grasping at straws, when she stops me.

"Look, I know no parent ever wants to believe their child is capable of something this egregious and believe me when I say you are no more shocked than any of the teachers and coaches I've spoken to. They have only good things to say about your daughters. They find this way out of character, too. But I also know there have been certain stressors in their lives lately."

I ignore that last bit, focusing on the part that came right before. "You talked to Coach Kiersten?"

There goes this weekend's soccer tournament and the rest of the season. They'll be kicked off the team. I think of Gigi, their top scorer, of her teammates who will miss her on the field, and my stomach drops with dread.

"Like I said, Lake Forrest Academy policy is very clear as to what Coach Kiersten's next steps will have to be. We take drugs and alcohol very seriously, as I know you do, especially considering the girls' age. I expect you'll be hearing from her next."

I stare into the sea of flashing brake lights while she goes on and on, only half listening. Something about violations on a case-by-case basis following the procedure outlined in the student manual, which she refers to as if I might know the text by rote. The rest of her words fall into the car like a deadly smoke bomb. Suspension. Expulsion. Academic consequences.

"I'd like to plan a meeting with your family and the head of school, and for as soon as possible. I've already taken a peek at Headmaster Rawlings's schedule and will email you his availability as soon as we hang up. For now, I'd like to ask you to come get the girls."

Her words sit there, itching under my skin. I sag in the leather seat. "Are you…are the girls suspended?"

"No, not yet. I've lobbied for a couple of days of cooling-down time to let things settle before we come up with a game plan. We're not making any decisions until after the meeting with Headmaster Rawlings." She sighs, and her tone softens. "For what it's worth, I agree with the girls' teachers, that this seems highly out of character for the twins. It's worrisome, which is why I'd like to get this meeting on the books as soon as possible. In the meantime, their teachers have given them enough work to take them through Friday."

"Where are they now?"

"They're here. Waiting in my office."

"Tell them I'm on my way, but traffic is a beast. I'll get there as soon as I can."

We're signing off when I think of one more thing.

"Could you maybe text me the pictures? I'd like to see them."

"Of course." There's a long pause, long enough I check the screen to make sure the call is still connected. "I'm just a little surprised you haven't already seen them."

My heart gives a warning beat, one heavy thud against my ribs. "What do you mean?"

"These photographs…they're already all over the internet."

The girls are seated on the bucket chairs that line a wall in Iris's office, and I stop in the doorway to search their faces, not that I can see much of them. Their heads are down, their hair shiny curtains over their eyes, but their body language provides a clue as to their emotional state. Arms crossed, shoulders hunched.

And then they look up, and I take in their dark pink cheeks, their squinty eyes. Gigi and Penelope are not scared, or guilty looking, or sad. They are furious. Literally purple with rage.

Gigi opens her mouth, but I hold up a hand and turn to Iris, a tiny little thing except for her belly, as big as mine when it was filled with twins. She keeps one hand draped over the top as we exchange greetings, then settle on a date for the meeting.

"I'll have to confirm it with my husband. He's their stepfather, and I'm certain he'll want to be included. Can I let you know?"

"Of course." She darts a glance at the girls, then gives me a small smile. "Good luck, and please keep me posted."

I nod. "Come on, girls. We'll talk about this at home."

They're silent on their march down the long hallway, still crowded with students digging through their lockers, the occasional teacher, but the second we are alone behind the thick steel and tinted glass of the rental car, the girls lose every last bit of their shit. Their words tumble over top of each other, delivered in desperate screeches all with the same general theme.

It wasn't me. I didn't do it.

"Then explain the photographs," I say, throwing the car in Reverse. Three of them, to be exact.

Gigi and Penelope clutching a White Claw, their heads thrown back in laughter.

Gigi and Penelope sharing a vape pen, faces hazy behind a white cloud of smoke.

Gigi taking a can from Penelope's fingers, both of them grinning up at some boy who couldn't be a day under sixteen.

"Who was that boy, by the way? I thought this was a sleepover." I shift into Drive and try not to peel out of the lot, but it's difficult. I didn't miss the looks we got from students and teachers alike on our way out the double doors. Iris wasn't kidding when she said the photographs have been making the rounds. I saw it on their faces. They all know. Everyone knows.

"Just some neighbor," Gigi says from the back seat. "I don't know. Scott or something. He lives behind Jenni."

"You're *twelve*! What the hell are you doing with a high-school boy at a party? Drinking! There are *pictures* of you with a vodka drink and an e-cigarette! Where did you even get them?"

"That's what we're trying to tell you, Mom. We *didn't*. There was no White Claw. There was no vape pen. Ask Jenni's mom."

"I already did. I called her as soon as I got off the phone with your counselor."

"And? What did she say?"

"She said Jenni's going to be taking a little break from her friendship with you both until further notice."

Actually, I'm sugarcoating. What she said is she never would have allowed my daughters in her house if she'd known they were smuggling in contraband. She said the twins are mini Krissie Kellys in the making, and that people in glass houses shouldn't throw stones. She said she doesn't want her precious Jenni anywhere near the twins, and that she's praying for all of us.

"What? That's so not fair! Oh my God. Mom! We didn't *do* anything."

My gaze flits to the rearview and the girls in the back seat, both of them red-faced and glaring. Gigi leans her head against the window as if she can't hold it up anymore, and a prickle of something—understanding? Vicarious misery?—stabs me in the chest.

"I want to believe you, I really do, but I saw those pictures, as did everybody else on the planet including Headmaster Rawlings. And for him, *we didn't do it* isn't going to cut it. You're going to have to come up a better defense than that, as well as some genuine regret and remorse and a guarantee that this will never, ever happen again. I'm going to need both of you to think long and hard about what you're going to say. Because you're in grave danger of getting tossed out of school."

My words shut them right up, like I knew they would. For both my girls, getting suspended or, worse, *expelled* from Lake Forrest is pretty much the worst thing that could happen. It would mean losing their friends, their soccer team, their entire social sphere. And Atlanta is a big city but a small town. The other private schools will likely snub them, no matter how many strings Patrick and I manage to pull. Even if we did get them in somewhere, they'll forever be known as the hell-raising, White Claw–chugging twins who got kicked out of Lake Forrest.

We drive the rest of the way home in silence, the only noise a low growl of the engine and some breathy sobs coming from the back seat. I pull into my spot by the front door, sliding to a stop on asphalt still spattered with white paint, and they tumble out before I've come to a complete stop. By the time I've gathered up my things and climb out of the car, they're already on the front stoop, waiting.

I come up the front steps, holding out a hand. "Cell phones."

The girls exchange a look. "Why?"

"Because Jenni's mother told me about your finstas." Fake Instagram accounts, ones I didn't know about. Apparently, all the kids at school have them. Not surprising, and I probably should have suspected as much. These are the daughters of a woman whose job revolves around social media—getting likes, being visible. Of *course* they have a finsta.

Gigi stands perfectly still as the words sink in. "For how long?"

"Undecided. And let's not forget that, technically, those phones belong to me. They were always on loan, and now I want them back so hand them over."

My words elicit a fresh wave of furious glares, but the girls comply. They dig the phones out of their backpacks and slap them in my hand.

Penelope gives me a look of scorching contempt, the kind only a preteen daughter can deliver. "I told you this would happen."

"How is you getting caught with a White Claw my fault?"

"Not that. Your stupid Instagram. This is all happening because of you."

I wag their phones in the air between us. "Would you like to see the pictures? Because I'm not in them, FYI. Those photos have nothing to do with me."

"Because they're fake!" She's shouting now, but the tears are gone and, in their place, a feral fury. "And so are you, FYI. You are the queen of fake." Her words land with a breathless sting.

I glance at her sister for backup, but Gigi stares me down with a straight face, her arms folded tight across her chest. Thing One doesn't disagree.

"No. Unapologetically Alex is a job. She is a persona. And while she might not be entirely truthful all the time, she's not me. I'm not her, and I'm not fake."

"Oh my God, Mom, really? Fake lashes. Fake lips. Fake boobs. Fake smile as soon as the cameras are on. Fake dye in your hair and fake paint on your nails and fake bleach on your teeth, and newsflash: everybody knows that a deviated septum is code for nose job. There's literally nothing about you that's real."

It's one thing to get schooled by a bunch of anonymous trolls, another thing entirely to hear this kind of criticism from your own daughter. And it's obvious Penelope has given this some thought. From the way the words rolled off her tongue, she's obviously been holding them in for a while.

"Like it or not, I work in an industry that revolves around appearance. Where every patch of cellulite gets discussed to death in the comments, where every zit or fat roll gets blown up and slapped on a meme. And I know you don't want to acknowledge that influencing is a real job, but it is, and it pays for your clothes and your school and this roof above your heads. I have to look the part."

Penelope rolls her eyes. "AKA fake."

"You're grounded. Both of you." I open the front door, and the girls fly upstairs.

In the kitchen, I drop all three cells onto the island and pace the floors for a bit, walking off the heat in my bones. Yes, my job is a performance of fakery. Yes, I present myself in ways that make me look prettier, thinner, better, more joyful than I am, but there's a reason those filters are so popular. It's so the asshole trolls don't point out every imperfection.

And as much as I analyze the size of my thighs or critique the perkiness of my ass in the mirror, I've always been very careful not to put my own body issues on the girls.

And okay, maybe I *do* spend too much time and energy on my appearance, but the rest of me is real. I love my husband, my family, my life. I want the best for my daughters. I tell myself they're twelve, too young to understand, but I can't quite shake off Penelope's comments. Is this really what she thinks of me, that I am as fake as Unapologetically Alex?

I pour myself a glass of wine from the fridge, then distract myself with their phones.

Their finstas are mostly harmless, silly pictures uploaded for a couple dozen followers apiece, all names I recognize. Girls from school, a few from the country club, their soccer friends. I check the other apps, Snapchat and TikTok and Tumblr, but they're just as innocuous. The DMs are filled with the typical preteen nonsense, gossip about who likes who and which teachers give the most homework, a flurry of messages with a shocking number of typos. But if I'm looking for dirt, I don't find any.

Not until I scroll through their texts.

I know where you live, and which bedroom you sleep in.

You and your sister will be killed very slowly.

The words hit me so forcefully that I have a hard time breathing. The baying pack of trolls have found my daughters. They've crawled from my cell phone onto theirs. Worse—my daughters didn't tell me about them. I don't want to think they carried this burden around because they knew I would freak out, and yet I know that's exactly why.

I compare the phone numbers at the top of the texts, and they match up. It's the same few assholes who are harassing me that are taking their ire out on Penelope and Gigi. I take screenshots of anything even remotely threatening and Airdrop the images to my laptop. Officer Graham wanted detailed documentation, so that's what he'll get. I'm attaching everything to an email when a new text hits Penelope's cell.

Hi, P, just checking in to see how tonight's talk went, and interested to hear how your mother reacted. If you haven't told her yet, be strong, you can do this!

I check the name at the top, Mrs. Sheffield. Iris, the counselor at Lake Forrest. Penelope has been confiding in the school counselor.

And this talk Iris is referring to, is it the scolding I received on the way through the door, Penelope's hurled accusations that I'm fake? I scroll up, looking for more context, but if there were any texts before this one, they've been deleted.

By now it's almost seven, and I can't even contemplate dinner. I order a couple of pizzas from Mellow Mushroom and pour myself another glass of wine—my third and probably a mistake, but what the hell.

I'm picking up my phone to text Patrick when a message pings the screen, a Google alert for a blind item, and all I can think is, *That was fast.* I tap the link in the email.

Busted for booze! What scandalized momfluencer who flushed her career down the toilet has passed on her flair for bad behavior to her preteen twin daughters?

I scroll down, and there they are, the pictures Iris told me were floating around the internet on a national gossip site, one of the biggest ones. All three photographs in high-definition full color. The twins in all their vaping, White Claw–chugging glory, next to a nude of me.

TWENTY-EIGHT

"For the record," Patrick says, "that audio file making the rounds is fake. I didn't say those things."

The two of us are sitting on the far end of the terrace at the neighborhood Starbucks, our chairs pushed into a slice of shade, and I'm all too aware of the steady stream of cars and people milling all around. Still, it's better than sneaking down to the unfinished part of the basement to have this conversation—one that's been looming over our heads for days now—or doing it in heated whispers behind a locked door upstairs. With the girls suspended from school and the carriage house still a crime scene, it's impossible to find any privacy at home.

"I know." I nod because I do know. Patrick would never have said those awful words. Not about me, not at a public party and definitely not to AC. I knew the instant I heard it that the recording's fake, and now I'm having second thoughts about grounding the girls. Yes, they were disrespectful, and yes, they both had unauthorized finstas, but I should have believed them when they told me those pictures were doctored.

"And the ones of the girls...the nude. Those are all fake, too, aren't they?"

All night long, I watched that damn nude photo crawl across the internet while people picked it apart in the comments. They're calling me a porn star, a harlot, an insecure hussy desperate to stay relevant. They're blasting me for using my body in the exact same way I skewered Krissie Kelly for, while in the same breath they critique the size of my breasts, the roundness of my stomach, the scope of my bikini wax. The men slap Patrick on the virtual back while the women advise him to divorce me.

But it's not me. That's not my body. Those are definitely not my nipples.

Patrick smiles across the table. "Like I had any doubt."

I smile back, even though okay, yes, *fine*. I've been known to snap the occasional sexy selfie for my husband, especially back when we were dating. Over the years he's accumulated dozens of pictures of me draped across a bed, or posing in the bathroom mirror, and last year for our fifth anniversary I gave him a flash drive filled with seminudes a local boudoir photographer took, a potential local sponsor.

But those pictures are tasteful. Seductive and erotic.

This picture is not. This nude looks like it belongs on the centerfold of *Penthouse*.

I stab my latte with the straw, taking out my frustrations on the ice cubes. "Anyway, it doesn't matter what you and I say. We can deny it until we run out of breath, people will believe what they see and hear."

"Our friends will believe us."

"No, our friends will *want* to believe us. Only a few actually will. Perception is reality, Patrick. No one understands this better than an influencer."

"So influence them into understanding that the pictures and audio are fakes."

"It doesn't work that way. Scandals go viral while explanations fizzle. By the time you and I found out those files were making the rounds, people had already made their own assumptions. The girls are delinquents. You're a sleaze. I'm a hussy. It's too late, and even if it wasn't, proof wouldn't vindicate us in the public eye. I can't just Instagram us out of this problem."

He makes a face. "So...what? We just sit back and let people believe what they want to believe?"

"Pretty much, and things will die down as soon as some other scandal comes along. People will forget about it soon enough. But honestly, at this point the only thing I care about are the twins. Clearing them with Lake Forrest. If we can present evidence that their pictures were doctored, we can make a case to keep them in school."

"What about that girl's mother?"

I plunk my drink onto the metal table, rolling my eyes. "Forget about Jenni's mom, she's not going to back us up, but technology might. Not every Photoshop job is the same, if you know what I mean. There's got to be a way to tell the files have been faked."

He nods, leaning back in his chair. "I'm guessing things like shadows, pixelation, hard edges would be dead giveaways. I'll take a look, see what I can come up with."

"Thank you."

Patrick gets quiet. Silent, actually, for a good, long moment. "Alex. You don't have to thank me. You know that, right?"

I don't nod, because the truth is, I know this and I *don't* know. The twins' father left me when they were two. He hasn't paid them a penny or a lick of attention since. By the time Patrick came along, the girls and I had been plowing our way through the world, just us three, for years. His offers of financial and emotional support, his eagerness to step into a fatherly role... It's not that I don't trust these things coming from Patrick, it's that I don't trust myself enough to know, unequivocally and completely, when an offer like his is genuine. I've been so wrong before.

He leans forward for my hand, locking his fingers through mine. "I know that I'm not the twins' father, not biologically or even legally, but that doesn't change how I feel about them. I love Penny and Gigi like they're my own blood. They are the reason for everything." He goes serious and still, watching me from behind those dark shades. "And so are you. Everything I do, it's all for you."

Now I do nod, because this I believe. That my husband loves me more than anything. That it's a love big enough he'll do right by the twins. He'll love on them and keep them safe because of his love for me.

I think about Aaron's words, his question cloaked in a warning. "Do you think we'd be safer in a hotel?"

Patrick looks over in surprise. "Do you?"

"I don't know. Maybe. Just until things calm down."

"Okay, but after that audio file, I'm going to be working from home for the foreseeable future, and I'm already talking to the alarm company about updating the system. More cameras, some well-placed panic buttons, maybe even a panic room. But if you and the girls would feel more comfortable in a hotel, we can do that, too."

A panic room. The notion stuns me as much as it provides some weird kind of comfort. After these past few weeks, a panic room is not an awful idea.

"Let me talk to the girls, okay? This involves them, too."

"Of course." His phone buzzes against the metal table, a text message from a 404 number not saved in his phone. He taps out a quick reply, then slides his cell in his pocket. "Let's talk to them about it this weekend, okay? We'll come up with a plan."

I nod, and he leans over to kiss me, his lips lingering on mine.

I wrap an arm around his neck and kiss him back, holding on not just to him but this perfect, private moment. Despite the traffic whizzing by on Peachtree. Despite the chatter all around us on the busy terrace. From that very first soggy afternoon at the valet stand, Patrick and I have always been good at this—at shutting out the world, at becoming our own little island. The cars, the people, the noise. It all falls away and it's just us two.

"I love you." He presses his forehead to mine, smiling at me over the rim of his shades. "I love you, and I'm going to make this right."

TWENTY-NINE

ANNA CLAIRE

AC was a quick learner. It was what her teachers all said when she'd dropped out of high school halfway through her junior year: "But you're such a quick learner!" As if quick learning would have put a roof over her head or food in her belly. They didn't seem to understand that she couldn't eat their books, and she definitely didn't have time to read them, not when she was working forty, fifty, sixty hours a week. All that, and still barely getting by.

Now, though, she was earning five times that as a personal assistant, even if part of the deal was that she keep her job at the motel. That condition was a real bummer, but then he'd followed it up with a number so astronomical there was no way in hell she was saying no. But thankfully, she didn't do much cleaning these days.

At room 204, she tapped a key to the metal door. "House-keeping."

When there was no answer, she stuck in the key and stepped inside, making sure to slide the chain into place behind her. She was alone in the room, but she needed to make sure it stayed that way.

The bedspread was rumpled like someone had sat on it, but she was glad to see it was still made. Another room where she didn't have to scrub somebody else's shit from the toilet bowl. She straightened the bedspread, then moved to the bathroom, still pristine, and climbed up on the toilet seat. There, just at the edge of the middle ceiling tile, she found it. A grocery bag stuffed with cash.

"Rule number one," he'd said on her first day. "Never keep all the money in one place."

There was a lot to remember. Rule number three, never write anything down. Rule four, don't trust anyone but him. Rule six, don't talk about business unless they were alone in his car or behind the closed doors of her house. Rule number eight, and the most important of all: loyalty was not an option.

Loyalty. She rolled her eyes every time she thought of it, because by now she'd figured it out. That day when he'd rescued her from the side of the road and gave her a ride here, all those questions about occupancy rates and prices... He was making plans. He was grooming her for exactly this.

And he'd done one hell of a job. Taking her to dinner, luring her into bed, letting her dangle the promise of a blow job in exchange for a job as his personal assistant. He'd let her believe it was her idea, when all this time, what he'd really been courting was access to the motel. He needed it, needed *her*, to run his business. The idea thrilled her as much as it ticked her off.

She spread the cash on the bed, counted it, then counted it again. And then she wrapped it in a towel and dropped it in the laundry bag on her cart.

AC did five more of these transactions before her shift was through, five more rooms where she didn't have to scrub a single toilet. The first time she'd run the numbers, she'd been quietly stunned. She was moving tens of thousands of dollars a day, almost a million a year. Alone. All by herself. And she'd caught enough of those one-sided phone conversations to know there were others like her out there, doing the same job. He wasn't kidding when he said he managed money. He was positively rolling in it.

His dark BMW was parked on the street when she got home, and she checked her face in the mirror. Months ago, after they'd hammered out her job description and agreed on the pay, she'd given him a key. Tied it with a pink bow and slid it into his pocket, both a reward and an invitation. Told him to use it anytime, which lately was less and less often.

Last time it was ten days ago, and before that, almost three whole weeks. It's why she hasn't yet told him the news, but she can't put it off any longer. As soon as he got her out of her uniform, he'd see it, his baby pushing out a noticeable bump.

She found him in the bedroom, standing by the chest of drawers—except he didn't look happy to see her. He didn't look happy at all. His expression made her feel dizzy, drunk.

"What's wrong?"

"My mother…" He shook his head, his gaze going to the window. "It's not looking good."

First was relief—it wasn't her, she wasn't losing this man, her job, her future—then sympathy. She rushed across the bedroom floor, wrapping her arms around his waist. "Oh, baby. I'm so sorry."

His arms snaked around her, pulling her close.

"Can I do anything?" She pushed her nose into the open spot at his collar, and his skin smelled…different. Like spice mixed with rose and vanilla perfume. Her body went tense against his.

If he noticed a change in her, he didn't show it. He just

squeezed her tighter, his fingers combing through her hair. "That's why I'm here. I need you to do me a favor."

She pulled back to look him in the eye. "What kind of favor?"

It was then she saw the bag on the bed. A Nike bag, the kind an athlete would take to a gym. Big and bulging. She untangled herself and gave the zipper a tug, and she wasn't all that surprised at what was inside.

Cash. Piles and piles of it. More cash than she'd ever seen in one place. Enough to live on for a year, if she was careful.

"I need you to hold on to that for me until I get back."

She pulled the zipper closed, trying not to let on that her skin was tingling. "And how long will that be?"

"Soon. A week at the most. I just need to take care of a few things at home, and then I'll be back. I was thinking we could go to the beach. I could use a vacation."

She grinned. "That sounds amazing."

He tipped her head up, kissed her slow on the lips. "I can trust you, right?"

"Of course you can. But I don't like it when you leave me for so long. I don't like being that girl, the kind just sitting around waiting for her man to show up."

She wasn't trying to be needy, but she could feel him slipping away, and she hadn't even told him about the baby yet. And now there was that damn perfume on him, and she wondered if he'd found another rainbow to chase. She reached for his belt, gave it a little tug.

His hands wrapped around hers, stilling her fingers. "Sweetheart, I can't stay. If anything happens, if anybody shows up at the Starlux who rubs you the wrong way, play dumb. Tell them you're just the maid."

Just the maid. The words poked like a sharp knife between her ribs.

"Okay, but what do I do with all that money I'm collecting?" She gestured to the bag on the bed. "And I can't just leave that thing lying around the house, not with my neighbors. Most of them are either wanted or on parole."

"Hide it somewhere safe. Remember the rules."

"Where?"

"You're a smart girl." He leaned in for a lightning-quick kiss, then brushed by her for the door. "You'll think of something."

By the time his car pulled away from the curb, she knew exactly where.

Like her teachers said, she was a quick learner.

THIRTY

ALEX

I'm shoving a cart up the dairy aisle at Trader Joe's when my
phone buzzes in my bag. LAKE FORREST comes up on the
caller ID, and my heart takes off until I remember the girls are
at home, and I'm waiting for their counselor to return my call.
I park the cart by the milk fridge and pick up.

"Hi, Alex, this is Iris Sheffield, how are you?"

The *fine* I spout off is automatic, then I pause to shake my
head. "Actually, I'm a hot mess right now, but that's not why I
called. I wanted to talk to you about Penelope. After I learned
about those pictures, I confiscated both the girls' phones. I was
looking through Penelope's when your text came in, asking if
she'd talked to me."

"I see."

"And before you say anything more, I promise I'm not going
to be weird about it. I've done enough therapy of my own to

know you can't tell me what you and my daughter talked about, and honestly, I'm glad Pen's found someone to talk to. She's not always all that forthcoming with me, so it makes me feel better to know she's talking to someone she trusts. You're obviously very supportive, so thank you."

"I'd say you're welcome, but no offense, I'm not doing it for you." Her voice is pleasant but firm, pushing through the noise and activity all around me. "Does Penelope know that we're talking?"

"No. She also doesn't know I saw your text."

"Well, if you hadn't confiscated her phone that would be my next call, to tell her that you and I had this conversation. You said it yourself, Penelope trusts me, and I've worked hard to build a healthy rapport with her. I can't risk going backward by talking to you without Penelope present."

Someone bumps into me from behind, another reaches past me for a container of coconut milk. As usual, Trader Joe's is packed. People all around, watching and listening. I slide my cart a few inches to the right.

"I understand. And I'm not calling you to pry, but I was hoping you could give me some direction on how I can best prepare for whatever it is Penelope wants to talk to me about."

"I'm afraid I can't do that, not without saying something that would break confidentiality."

"Can you at least tell me if it involves her father? Her birth father, that is. His name has come up in the tabloids, and if this talk is going to be about him, I need to mentally prepare."

It's not an exaggeration. Just thinking about that conversation sends my heart skittering, makes my lungs lock up. I stare into the milk cooler and think, *Please let this conversation not be about her father.*

At the same time, after that blind item on DeuxMoi, I know it's one that's coming. One I've been dancing around for years, ever since Daniel vanished into thin air. Because when I tell them about their father, they will want answers, explanations. And neither will be what they want to hear.

Iris launches a response packed with lovely words cloaked in therapy-speak, a long and convoluted answer that is a polite but hard no. She's not going to tell me a thing. Frustration wells, hot in my chest, at the same time I respect the hell out of her.

I thank her, and I'm hanging up when my cell starts back up again, bleating Patrick's ringtone, followed by the other two, Gigi's and Penelope's confiscated cells, in my bag. My heart flips over as I dig them out, because three phones don't ring at once unless something is very, very wrong.

I line them up on the shopping cart and do triage. A neighbor, an unrecognized number, Patrick. Of course I choose Patrick.

"What's wrong?"

His voice cuts through car sounds, hissing air and gunning motors. "The girls are at Kelly's, they're okay. Everybody's okay. Where are you?"

Kelly is the neighbor across the street.

"I'm at the grocery store. Why, what happened?"

"Meet me at home. The police are there now, searching for the bomb."

The first police cruiser sits, empty and a half dozen houses down, blocking traffic. No siren, but its lights swirl red and blue against the overhanging trees, silent shrieks of caution, danger, emergency. A dozen more cruisers line the street just beyond, a parade of cars parked every which way that ends in a fire truck.

I drive as far as I can, then yank on the wheel, lurching the SUV over the curb and mutilating the Romeros' perfect lawn. People see me coming and dart out of the way, curious neighbors and dog walkers, folks hoping to get a closer look at the drama. I scan their faces for Patrick's, but I don't see him, and I don't have time to wait. There's a dark, anxious knot in my chest that won't ease up until I find the girls, see with my own eyes they're okay.

I slam the brakes, throw open the door and hit the ground running, soles clacking against the hot asphalt. My heart bangs in my throat as I dodge the cruisers and uniformed men yelling at me to stop. My dress, a floral wrap I threw on this morning, flaps in the wind as I sprint up the pavement.

A big man in fire gear intercepts me by hooking a beefy arm around my waist. It's like hitting a wall, and I stop so abruptly my feet fly up, tipping me backward into his chest. His arm tightens, holding me steady. In his other fist, he holds a leash attached to a panting German shepherd.

"Ma'am, you can't be here. It isn't safe."

I try to peel his arm off my skin, but it's like a steel hook. The flesh doesn't budge. "My daughters! I need to find them."

"You're Mrs. Hutchinson?" I give him a frantic nod, and he releases me and the leash at the same time, ordering the dog to stay. "Your daughters are with a neighbor. Come with me, I'll take you."

"I know where Kelly lives."

"I understand you want to get there quickly, but we need to stay outside of the blast zone. We're going to have to take the long way."

The blast zone. Three little words that are like a spear through the heart. "So it's true? There really is a bomb?"

"The dogs are in there now. Come on. I'll take you to your kids."

I barely have time to process his words because up ahead, high up on a hill, I spot two small figures hunched on Kelly's front steps. I see the shock of auburn curls, the long limbs and narrow shoulders, the bright colors on the shirts they pulled on this morning.

The relief is immediate and overwhelming, flushing my skin

and softening my bones. I sway, and the fireman catches me with solid arms, two giant paws holding me upright.

"I'm fine, I'm *fine*." The last word comes out too screechy, and I make sure to soften the rest. "Just please, take me to them."

He does, leading me up the first driveway we come to, then at the top of the hill taking a sharp right to the neighboring lot. My heels sink like golf cleats into the hard dirt, so I pause to slide them off and then hurry to catch up on my bare feet, pushing through shrubs and stomping on flowers. We do this three more times, crossing over three more yards until finally we squeeze through a line of yew trees into Kelly's.

"Mom!" Gigi yells.

The girls pop off the steps and race across the driveway, and for a minute I forget they're twelve and ninety pounds of solid muscle apiece. They leap into my arms and my shoes go flying from my fingers. I throw my arms around them and press my daughters close until there's not a pocket of air between us, skin against muscle and bone.

"Oh, babies. Oh, God. You're okay." I drop kisses to the tops of their heads as they bury their faces in my chest. "I'm here and you're okay."

We spend a couple of seconds like this, all of us breathing hard.

Gigi is the first to recover. "Oh my God, Mom, it was so *scary*."

Penelope nods, fast and frantic. "The police busted in the front door. They said there was a *bomb*."

I flinch at the word, even though I already knew this, of course, and my gaze tugs to the house. A lot of it's tucked behind the neighboring trees, but through the branches I spot a flash of copper rain pipe, a slice of slate rooftop. I think about all the things inside, the pictures and portraits, the baby footprints I framed for myself on my first Mother's Day, the box of the girls' artwork I've been meaning to sort through. Irreplaceable items I'll never get back. I stare at the slices of my house through the branches, and my muscles go tight with waiting.

Without letting the girls go, I untangle us enough to take their hands and lead them to Kelly's front steps. I spot movement in one of the front windows—Kelly, who waves.

"Stay here until we give the all clear," the fireman says. "Good?"

I'd forgotten all about him. I nod, taking in my shoes that he dug from the bushes and laid in a neat row on the edge of the driveway. "Good."

He turns and jogs back down the hill, running straight into the blast zone.

As soon as he's gone, the girls start back up.

Gigi stares at me with eyes big and wide. "We were just sitting there, watching a movie in the den, when suddenly there were sirens, like, *everywhere*. We couldn't even hear what the people were saying on the TV. I think they had megaphones or something. It was *so loud*."

"And then they busted in the front door," Penelope says, "and started screaming 'Evacuate, evacuate!' so Gigi and I just took off. We ran out the back door and that's where the cops found us. They grabbed us by the arms and dragged us through a bunch of yards and then to here. Miss Kelly tried to get us to go inside, but, like, what if the house blows up?"

"What about Patrick, have you talked to him?"

Twin heads shake.

"Miss Kelly called him, though," Gigi says. "She said he was on the way, but that was forever ago."

I think about my phone, sitting in the cup holder of the monster rental, and I wonder how many times he's tried to call. Also, did I leave the engine running? Possibly. Probably. The keys are definitely still where I dropped them in the console, the door still yawning open because I didn't take the time to shut it. The rhythmic ding-ding-dinging will be like a flashing neon sign to any passersby—*take me, I'm free.* Or maybe they'd just reach in for my bag, sitting open on the passenger's seat. They can have the rental, the bag. Really, the only thing I care about at this point is my phone, because it connects me to Patrick.

I'm about to suggest we go inside to borrow Kelly's when there's a surge of activity on our front lawn. A swarm of bodies spill out the front door, both human and canine, all of them moving fast. I watch them sprint across the grass to the line of police cars at the curb, and it's like the streets of Pamplona, a mad dash to safety.

They found something.

I'm scanning the moving people when I spot a familiar tall frame, talking to a cluster of uniformed men. Or maybe he's yelling, because his spine is stiff, his arms flailing around. One of them must tell him where we are, because his head whips in our direction. I can't see his face from here, but I can tell he's spotted us by the way he takes off running.

Patrick.

Gigi and Penelope get to him first. They race down Kelly's hill and leap into his arms, and Patrick catches them, pulling them both tight to his chest. His gaze finds mine over their heads. "Two explosives. Both of them upstairs."

"Where upstairs?"

He shakes his head, and in his face I see the answer.

In one of the girls' rooms. In ours.

Something cold and reptilian slithers down my spine, and I stand there, Kelly's grass tickling my toes, trying to sort through my emotions. Fear, certainly, along with fury someone would plant bombs in my home, in our *rooms,* horror at how close we came to losing the girls. If that person hadn't made that warning call, if my daughters had still been in the house when—

I stop the thought before it can go further. I can't go there. That's a thought that will make me go crazy.

But also, a not-so-tiny part of me feels relief. My bones go slushy with it, my skin hot. *Finally* the police will understand that something real and terrible is happening here. Finally they'll believe me when I say the threats are more than just words.

Patrick shifts the twins under each arm, then motions for me to step in the middle—a Hutchinson huddle, he likes to call it—and my heart gives a squeeze. Radio silence from their own father on birthdays and holidays, but Patrick races home in an emergency. He's the one who takes them to school, dries their tears, makes sure they're fed and safe. He loves them, and they love him right back. A better father than their own will ever be.

I think of all the things that have happened this week, that Krissie Kelly post that set off the virtual bomb. The online threats and harassment, the blind leads on the gossip sites, the drive-bys and manipulated photographs of me and the girls, the audio file of Patrick, the dead body in the carriage house. These things are terrifying when they're happening in real time, and when they're aimed at you certainly feel catastrophic, but they're nothing like this. Two bombs upstairs where we sleep. Where the girls shower and do their homework. This feels like we've entered a whole new universe, a deadly and dangerous one.

It was so easy to put the blame on AC for the Krissie Kelly post, so easy to picture her lurking behind the vile Mister Fluffles handle every time she stoked the trolls, but dead bodies and bombs are so much bigger than threats and harassment. It doesn't fit with the girl that I knew, the one who seemed so eager to please. And okay, fine. Say it *was* some kind of single-white-female situation like the detective implied, the assistant looking to become the boss. If that's the case, why blow it all up? My career and reputation, my house, my family. What does she stand to gain?

It makes me wonder if my suspicions have maybe been off base. If maybe while I've been looking the one way, pointing the finger at my former assistant, someone else, someone much more threatening, has been circling ever closer.

"What if I was wrong?" I say, my voice muffled in Patrick's chest. My head is spinning and my stomach is lurching and I can't make it make any sense. "All this time I thought it was AC, but now I'm not so sure."

Patrick puffs out a sharp breath, his big body going hard against mine. "This is my fault."

I crane my neck to look up at my husband, taking in his pale face, his skin the color of wet paper. "How is any of this your fault?"

The destroyed car and dead woman in the bathroom, the threats on my page, that ridiculous nude and the pictures of the girls—those definitely feel aimed at me.

"All this...it has nothing to do with you. I can't—"

"All clear." The voice comes from behind him.

I lean to my left, and there she is, Detective Muriel Bennett, her face crimped in a squint that's supposed to look like a smile, her sensible shoes sinking into the grass. I have no idea how long she's been standing there, how much of our conversation she's heard. The sight of her sends adrenaline zinging through my veins.

"The bomb detection squad inspected the objects and found they didn't contain any explosives."

I untangle myself from Patrick and the girls. "I don't understand."

"Basically, they were dummy devices. Wiring and other elements were found to be similar to an IED, an improvised explosive device, hidden in what looked like books, but they weren't real."

"So let me get this straight. Someone broke into our house and planted two dummy bombs, then called 9-1-1 to report the bomb threat?" She nods, and I shake my head. "But why?"

It's the one word that keeps screaming through my mind,

the question I keep coming back to, the heart of the issue that makes zero sense.

Why why *why*?

The detective lifts a padded shoulder. "Could be a trial run, or it could be somebody looking for attention, yours or theirs. The caller basically led us straight to them."

"This caller," Patrick says, "was it male or female?"

"Undetermined. The voice sounded male, but it was highly manipulated so we don't know for sure just yet. Our tech department will be able to tell us more soon."

"How did they get in?" I'm thinking, of course, of the key AC still has, the locks Tommy replaced only a few days ago. How long have the dummy devices been in there? How many nights have we slept in the same room as a dummy bomb?

"Officers found footprints and a crowbar in the shrubs on the back side of the house, near the open window to the laundry room. They're taking molds, dusting for prints. They'll take a while."

"Tell them to take all the time they need," I say at the same time Patrick asks, "Could you trace the call?"

"The caller used Google Voice and a virtual proxy, which is basically like putting a mask on your computer. We're working with Google to get access to their account, but these things take time and a lot of paperwork."

Frustration rises in my chest where it mingles with fear and dread. The detective just called this a trial run, which means it could happen again. And next time, the bombs will be real.

The world tilts, and I dig my toes into the grass for balance because a panic room won't help when there's a bomb. Even locked behind stone and steel, we wouldn't survive a blast.

I hate this feeling, like I live inside a ticking clock, that it's only a matter of time before it explodes. My daughters could have been blown to bits because of me, because of something I started. All this is because of me.

The detective's gaze wanders to Patrick, then back to me. "I have an update on Anna Claire."

THIRTY-ONE

"Her name is Nina Morris," Detective Bennett says, and I'm still so focused on the possibility the police dogs might have missed something during the search, still so busy fighting the panic that this place could suddenly rip apart, that it takes me a couple of seconds to process her words. Their meaning.

I sit up straighter in my chair. "You're referring to my former personal assistant. The woman claiming to be Anna Claire Davis. Her name is really Nina Morris?"

Not that that tells me much of anything. A name, but not who or where she is, what her connection is to me.

"That's correct. Born on or around October 13, 1994, in Orlando, Florida. Not in a hospital, as far as we can tell. That's just where she was surrendered, to South Seminole Hospital. These days, the place falls under Orlando Regional Medical Center."

The three of us are seated on the back patio—the detective on an overstuffed chair across from Patrick and me, side by side on the couch. I sit here on the edge of the cushion, tension threading through me like a trip wire, listening to the sounds of the girls moving around in their rooms overhead. I am quite literally waiting for the bomb to go off.

"Orlando," Patrick says, almost like a question, but my brain is snagged on another detail.

Baby Nina was surrendered in 1994, the year the real Anna Claire died. Officer Childers's words ring through my mind, complete with his thick Southern twang. *That's one hell of a co-incidence, and I was a cop long enough to know there's no such thing.*

Patrick shifts closer on the couch, reaching across the cushion for my hand. "Surrendered as in abandoned?"

"Surrendered to the hospital, yes," Detective Bennett says, brushing a speck of lint off the knee of her navy pants, which she's got to be regretting right about now. It's still sweltering out, a steamy eighty-four degrees according to the thermometer hanging from the brick wall, and she's wearing a jacket. Underneath, her white cotton blouse is spotted with sweat.

"So she was adopted," I say.

The detective nods. "Yes. Nina Morris is her adopted name."

"But that's allowed, right?" Patrick says. "There are laws that allow a mother to do that. Surrender her baby to a hospital."

"Safe Haven laws allow a mother to leave her newborn in designated places like a police station or a hospital, yes, but there are some stipulations the mother must follow to avoid facing criminal charges. The big ones are that she'd have to leave the baby with a person, an employee or volunteer, a janitor even. She'd also have to provide her full name and address upon surrendering the baby. Nina's mother did neither of those things."

There's a thump directly above our heads, and I think of the girls upstairs. I think about how loved they are, how cherished and wanted—by me, by Patrick, but not by their father, who's been out of their lives for so long they wouldn't recognize him if they passed him on the street. I think of Nina, surrendered to strangers by an anonymous mother, and my heart squeezes with understanding, with sympathy. She knows how it feels to be abandoned, too.

"What kind of mother leaves their baby in a stairwell?" I say. "Who would do such a thing?"

"Actually, other than handing her to an employee, the stairwell was the safest spot for Nina. It was cool and dry and sheltered from the weather, which I understand was pretty bad the night she was found. She was clean and well fed and wrapped in sheets and a pillowcase. The trash can she was in had been emptied out beforehand, then lined with pillows and blankets to make sure the baby was comfortable. Whoever left her there called the hospital to make sure she was found quickly. The doctor who checked her out reported not a single thing wrong. Baby Nina was perfectly healthy."

Still. A baby tossed in the trash like garbage. I think about what kind of person would leave a newborn in a trash can, even a clean one, but I can't wrap my head around it. Whoever Nina's mother is, in her mind she must have had very few options.

"Okay but you have a name now," I say. "You know who this person is. You know her history from the moment she landed at the hospital, the family she ended up with, her friends. Have you asked any of them where she might be?"

"Her adopted mother died four years ago. Nina has an aunt, but this woman has never met Nina, and she didn't even know her sister had died before we told her. From what I've been able to gather, the mother had some mental health issues, and she left Nina alone much of the time. Her upbringing wasn't exactly stable."

So we're back to square one, with a name but otherwise no idea who this person is.

Officer Childers's parting words echo through my head for what must be the millionth time—*What you have to figure out is the connection. The common thread that ties her to Anna Claire to you*—and automatically my gaze wanders to Patrick. Who was arguing with her on the front lawn only days before she disappeared. Who disliked her the second she walked through the door.

He throws up his hands with an impatient sigh. "So what now? Where do you look for her now?"

The silence stretches, heavy and thick like tar, and I find myself aware of everything, the dishwasher whirring through the open door to the kitchen, a fly caught in a web in a corner of the patio, the blood pulsing hard through my head. The detective looks at me, then Patrick, and in her silence I read the answer.

Here. She's looking for Nina here.

And why wouldn't she? Detective Bennett is a detective, just like Aaron Childers once was. She will be working under the same parameters: *find the connection*. Nina Morris worked for me. My husband was the last person she saw before she disappeared. These two coincidences put us squarely in the center of this investigation. The detective thinks that Patrick and I are the connection.

She pulls a folded stack of papers from a notebook wedged between the cushion and the armrest, flips them open and runs a palm across the crease, flattening them on her lap. Text messages, spread across two columns, pages and pages of them.

"The good news is, our tech department managed to unlock Nina's phone."

The couch shifts as Patrick sits up straighter.

"There are some messages from the two of you I'd like to go over if you don't mind."

She doesn't give us a chance to respond or even process the implications, just passes us each a stapled packet of paper. The top page belongs to me, the series of unanswered texts I sent in those first awful days, accusations that ultimately escalated in a threat I fired off without thinking. I cringe at the awful words, ones that look way worse on paper.

If you did this I'll kill you.

"For the record, I sent that the day after the viral post. I'd woken up to a shitstorm and things only escalated from there. And as you can see from all the texts above it, she wasn't responding to me at all. I took her silence as confirmation she was behind the post."

"You threatened to kill her." The detective's words cut through a sudden roaring in my ears. "Around the same time she disappeared without a trace."

"Yes, but I didn't *mean* it. Obviously. I'm not *that* stupid." I let out a ragged breath that I hope sounds like a laugh. "And even if I did mean the threat, which I didn't, I wouldn't have put it in something as easy to crack as a text."

Patrick drapes a hand over my knee, a not-so-subtle gesture for me to *stop talking.* "Emotions were high that day, Detective, and my wife was angry, but she's not a violent person. So she said some unkind things. They're just words."

"Kind of like the trolls' words?"

It's a shitty comparison, and my brain whirs into motion, searching for something to explain it away, but I come up blank, and so does Patrick. We stare at our laps for a minute, a *long* minute, the quip hanging between us like an angry storm cloud.

The detective flips to the next page, and I follow suit, scanning texts that go back months. It doesn't take me long to figure out what I'm staring at, a long string of back and forth between my husband and my personal assistant. Patrick and AC had entire conversations via text. I scan the words, and my skin goes hot.

"What does this mean?" I point to a blue bubble halfway down the second page. "*Who do you work for?* She worked for me. She even says so right here. *I work for your wife, remember?*"

Patrick's throat moves, but he doesn't say anything. One by one, the hackles rise on the back of my neck. When he flips his packet to the next page, I don't miss it, his fingers shaking the paper.

I look back to the packet on my lap, speed-reading through the messages.

AC: *Just give me what I came for and I'll go. I'll leave and you'll never have to see me again.*

Patrick: *I already told you. We're not having this discussion over text.*

AC: *That's something only a guilty person would say.*

AC: *What are you guilty of, Patrick?*

AC: *Your wife is sitting across from me right now. What do you think she'd say if she knew you were a fraud? What do you think the twins would say?*

AC: *ANSWER THE QUESTION OR I'M TELLING.*

"Why does she call you a fraud?" I say to Patrick. "Why would she say that?"

And his response—*Leaving now, home in 20*—makes perfect sense when I check the time stamp on the text. Friday at just past two in the afternoon. The day Shannon saw them arguing on the front lawn.

Patrick doesn't answer. He doesn't look up, either, just continues flipping through the pages on his lap, breathing hard.

"You said that argument was about…about tire tracks in the lawn. You brushed it off as stupid and insignificant. You made me think I was crazy!"

"Alex—"

He stops before he says anything more, and the way he looks

at me makes something inside of me deflate because it's not confusion or anger or denial in his eyes. It's fear. Whatever he was
going to tell me, he's afraid of my reaction.

"Patrick, what did AC come here for? What did she want
from you?"

Across from me, the detective lifts an interested brow, and I
realize I'm stepping into her shoes, interrogating my own husband while she listens in, but I can't seem to stop myself. She
crosses her legs, leaning back into her chair. Waiting.

He twists to face me on the couch. "AC has been lying to you,
to us, since the second she started working for you. The detective just told you that, and you know I've never liked her. From
the very beginning I've been saying there was something off
about her, but now we know it's worse than that. AC, or Nina
or whatever the hell her name is, is toxic. Manipulative. And
she's a thief. She's the one who took my gun from upstairs—"

The detective's attention prickles at this admission. "I thought
it was stolen from your car."

Patrick scrubs a hand down his face. "Or it was upstairs. Honestly, I don't know for sure. But, Alex, you have to agree that
things started disappearing after you hired her."

I nod, saying to the detective, "Jewelry mostly, but a bunch of
other stuff, too. Random things. A pair of sterling salad tongs.
The scented candle on my nightstand. Books and one of my
bras. At first I thought I was misplacing things, but Patrick's
right. I just recently put the two together."

"She's unhinged. You get that now, right? She wanted all
this—" he waves a hand through the air, indicating the patio,
the house "—at the same time she hated us for having it. Her
life was shitty and so she wanted ours. The entire time she was
here, she wanted what we have."

Talking about her is getting him worked up, his tone rising
in a fit of frustration like we're arguing about the dishes. Still,

it's difficult not to notice how Patrick is trying very hard not to answer the question at hand. What were they arguing about?

Aaron's words whisper through my head. *Find the connection.*

"Did you know her?" I say, changing tactics. "When you met her that first time, I mean. When I told you the name of the girl I'd hired. Did you know who she was?"

"No. *No.*" He shakes his head, firm and steady. "When I first met this woman, I'd never seen her before in my life. I swear to you, I *swear.* I didn't know her."

He holds my gaze as he says it, and he looks like he's in physical pain, like those words he's trying to swallow are sharp as rocks, but I know when my husband is telling me the truth. I stare at his face, gaze into those familiar eyes, and I'm certain. He's not lying. Patrick hadn't seen her before.

"But?" I say, because I'm also certain there's more.

"But." His voice cracks on the word, and he pauses, taking a second to run a hand through his hair. "But that audio file was a message. She'd been threatening it for a while, to plant those kinds of doubts in your head, to claim that I said or did things that crossed a line, even though I didn't. That audio file was her, making good on that threat."

It's so much information coming at me all at once I barely know how to process it. I sit here for a long moment, trying to wrap my head around what he's saying.

"Are you…are you saying she accused you of…something sexual?"

"No, I'm saying she was *threatening* to accuse me, even though I hadn't touched her. You *know* me, Alex. From the second you and I met, there's been only you. You know that, right? Right?"

I sit very still, thinking about my answer. The unexplained argument on the front lawn. The changed passcode on his phone. The texts and the detective with her questions and suspicious eyes, watching from the chair across from us. She knows it, and so do I. There's more my husband is not telling. I look at him, and I don't nod. I can't, because the truth is I *used* to know it was only me, but I don't anymore. I want to believe him, but I can't, not fully, because there's so much still I don't understand.

"Alex," he whispers, and my eyes fill with tears. I'm trying to ignore the pleading in his voice, the little quaver that makes him sound desperate, like he might cry. He reaches across the cushion for my hand, wrapping his fingers around mine. "What you and I have, I could never find that with anyone else. I wouldn't even *want* to. It's always been you, only you."

I want to believe him. I want to believe him so fucking much. But all those little nudges I gave him this past week, all my dodged questions. I can't help but feel angry when I think of what he made me believe, the way he made me feel. My face flushes with blood.

"I wanted to tell you. You have no idea how many times I almost came out and said it. But I was afraid of..." He lifts his hands, lets them fall back to his legs with a slap. "This. Shit, I was afraid of this."

He's telling the truth about the fear, at least. I see it in the way his lips are a thin, white line, the way his muscles are gathered up tight. I see it in the shadows under his eyes, the hollows in his cheeks. My husband is definitely afraid of something, but there's more he's still holding back.

Maybe it's whatever's driving the other emotion pushing down on his brow, setting his lips in a hard line. Fury. Patrick is furious—at this Nina person, at this confession having to happen in front of the detective, a stranger, or maybe just that it's happening at all. I wonder if the detective can see it, this anger he's trying very hard to hide.

"I also realize this doesn't help my case any," he says to her now, "admitting the missing woman was manipulating me, but I swear to you, Detective, it's the truth. I didn't touch her in any sort of inappropriate or harmful way. That audio file circulating around the web is a fake. I didn't say any of those things, not in that order and definitely not to her."

Detective Bennett drops her head, reading aloud. "*This is a dangerous game you're playing. If you know what's good for you, you'll disappear back into whatever hole you crawled out from.* What did you mean by that?"

Patrick puffs a laugh. "You're taking that text completely out of context. Look at the one above it, where she's threatening to follow us to Serenbe. The four of us spent a weekend there back in March, and AC thought she could tag along like she was part of the family."

Something nags at the back of my mind, like a song you can almost hear the tune to but can't come up with the lyrics. The memory resurfaces on a gasp. "Omigod, she *did* follow us, didn't she? We ran into her at the café. She was coming out of a yoga class."

Patrick's shoulders slump in relief, and he nods. "Like I said, Detective. Obsessed."

"So basically, what I'm hearing is you both had reasons to want this woman gone."

"Yes, but not like that," Patrick says, in a tone that says *ridiculous.* "We're not violent people. We wouldn't do whatever it is you're suggesting."

I back my husband up with an enthusiastic nod—at this point mostly to protect myself, or at least the me I'd like to believe I am. Loving mother, supportive wife, charismatic business-woman. One with an enviable, Instagrammable life.

As Penelope would say, fake.

"I fired her," I say to the detective. "*That's* how I got rid of her. And let's not forget why you're here, why a bunch of your colleagues are out there right now, making molds of the foot-prints in our yard, because a dead body and two dummy bombs were found in our home."

I shudder as hard as the first time around. A dead woman on

my bathroom floor. Two dummy bombs tucked in what looked like a book, one for each daughter's room. On the table next to their beds, only feet away from their heads. I can't stop picturing them there, imagining all the bloody what-ifs. Homes are supposed to feel safe, a shelter protecting us from harm, and lately ours feels like anything but.

"My wife and stepdaughters are in danger, Detective. Someone killed a woman and dumped her in the carriage house. Someone planted two bombs. My family is being threatened and harassed in our own home."

"Funny you should mention the body," she says, her gaze bouncing between me and Patrick. Something buzzes at her hip. She silences it, but the sound starts right back up again. "The victim's name was Kathleen Letitia Wallace, known around town and at her work at the Clermont Lounge as Little Kathi. She and Nina were roommates."

I gasp, but Patrick remains still. His chin is concrete, his gaze superglued to the detective.

She reaches for her notebook, wedging it out from between the cushions, looking him straight in the eye. "Perhaps you can tell me why your business card was found on Ms. Wallace's nightstand."

THIRTY-TWO

ANNA CLAIRE

Grief was the weirdest thing.

Most days, Anna Claire could go long chunks of time without thinking about the ditch her mother's death carved into her life. Oh, sure, she thought about her mama plenty. She'd be going about her day, changing sheets or wheeling a cart up the cereal aisle, and she'd catch a whiff of vanilla or hear a snippet of conversation that sounded just like something Mama would say. But those were happy memories, ones that made Anna Claire smile. They didn't wallop her upside the head with missing her, didn't make her want to curl up in a ball and weep.

Like now. Maybe it was the pregnancy hormones, but now that Anna Claire was carting around a belly out to there, she really missed her mama.

She wanted to show off her swollen fingers and ankles and hear her mama's laugh.

She wanted to press her mama's hands to her belly and watch her face while her grandbaby tumbled and rolled.

But mostly, she wanted to ask her mama what to do about the man who lately, whenever she talked to him, seemed a million miles away.

Today marked a whole twenty-nine days since she'd last seen him. The longest stretch they'd gone, by far. And this morning, he hadn't even picked up when she called him to say hi.

Actually, she knew what her mama would say. She'd say men who were too good to be true usually were. A depressing thought because she really needed this particular man, really needed this job. Especially now that there was a baby on the way.

She tapped her key to the door at room 215. "Housekeeping."

When the only reply was silence, she stuck the key in the knob and opened the door.

Most of the rooms she was assigned to these days didn't need cleaning, but she had to keep up appearances of being a maid. That was part of the deal when she became his personal assistant, and he offered so much money she'd readily agreed.

But rooms like 215 made her think she should have pushed back.

The smell was the first thing to hit her, fast food and vomit. She covered her nose and flipped on the light, and Jesus Christ, she hated this job. She took in the pizza lying upside down next to an overflowing trash can, the stained bedding in a grimy heap on the floor, the brown liquid seeping through a pile of towels in the corner, the trail of something slimy across the rug. Any other hotel would toss the linens and rip out the carpet, replace them both with fresh and new. Here at the Starlux Motor Lodge, they just scrubbed up what they could, poured some extra bleach in with the laundry and hoped for the best.

Anna Claire cursed under her breath. She was too pregnant for this shit.

Seven months ago, she would have marched down to Terri's

office and told her where to stuff it. There were plenty of other jobs, other places that needed cleaning, but now she had a baby to think about, and a man who was putting on the brakes. For the millionth time today, Anna Claire thought of her mama. She sure could use some advice.

She stepped over a McDonald's bag to the phone, then dialed the number she knew by heart.

He picked up on the third ring. "Hello."

Not a question. A demand. It's how he always answered the phone. He might as well have shouted, *Speak!*

"Hey, baby, it's me." She tried to coo the words, but they came out sounding a little funny. She was trying real hard not to breathe through her nose. "Sorry to bother you, but—"

"Is something wrong?"

She looked around the filthy room. Where to start? With this dreadful job? With the baby he didn't seem all that happy about? At the thought, the little peanut did a somersault—or maybe that was her heart, nosediving behind her ribs.

"The baby and I just really miss you, that's all. How's your mama?"

In the past few months, the woman had made a miraculous recovery. It was part of what had been keeping him close to home, first when she was sick, then when she was on her deathbed. She was out of the danger zone now, but things were still touch and go, and he didn't dare leave her for too long. Anna Claire understood—she'd do the same for her own mother if given the chance—but deep down she was really starting to resent the old bat. God how she missed having him around.

"She had a fall last week. I don't think anything's broken, but she's banged up pretty good. I'm taking her to the doctor this afternoon. Can I call you back after?"

Her heart gave a disappointed pinch. "When will that be? I'm at the Starlux and—"

"This afternoon sometime. I'm waiting on a business call, and I need to keep this line open."

These days, Anna Claire had a much better idea of what this business entailed. He wasn't just moving money, he was moving drugs. A whole shit ton of them. Managing a web of mules spread out over three states, trading pills for cash that they left for her to collect at the Starlux. That bag he'd asked her to hold on to? She'd stockpiled five times that by now, all of it hidden under a pile of dirt in the McGillicuddys' abandoned barn.

But she couldn't very well keep it there forever, now could she? What if someone saw her coming and going? What if someone followed her, or the barn caught fire? She shuddered at the thought of all that cash going up in smoke.

"Okay, but it's business I need to talk to you about, actually. I need you to come pick up the latest batch of money. I'm running out of room to stash it."

"I'll send somebody."

"I don't want you to send somebody. I want you. It's been so long. Aren't you curious about how big my belly's gotten?" She draped a hand over it and tried to picture his face when he saw it, that cocky smile she liked so much climbing up his cheeks, but she couldn't quite get there. It'd been so long, and he'd been so distant, and that promised trip to the beach had never happened. "One night, that's all I'm asking. I'll make it worth your while."

Once upon a time, this would have been enough. Her voice purring in his ear, the promise of a sexy weekend, and the man would have come running.

But now? Now he was quiet so long that she wasn't sure.

"Maybe Sunday," he said finally, and she squealed. "I said maybe. I promise I'll do my very best, okay? But for now, I really do have to go."

Anna Claire said her goodbyes, feeling a million pounds lighter. A million times more hopeful. Her man was coming on Sunday. She had so much to do. She hung up the phone and whirled around, barely even grimacing at the mess. She just rolled up her sleeves and got busy.

She was still riding the high hours later, when she shoved through the office door at the end of her shift. The television was blaring as usual, the tail end of some society show. Terri waved a distracted hand, but she didn't bother looking over. Something about a fancy restaurant party in the city.

Anna Claire plucked her time card from the rack on the wall. "Whoever was in 215 needs to be blacklisted, FYI. I'm pretty sure that was shit I cleaned off the walls."

Terri rolled her eyes, and she didn't bother lowering the volume. She just shouted right over the noise. "Girl, if I blacklisted everybody whose ass missed the toilet, we wouldn't have any customers left."

"Well, one of those carpet-cleaning machines wouldn't be too much to ask for, would it?" Anna Claire stamped her time card and dropped it back in the slot. "Toss some perfume in that bad boy and—"

She shut up at the sound of a voice.

His voice. Coming from the television on the wall.

She turned, and there he was. Wearing that cocky smile over a suit, dark and perfectly pressed, on top of a crisp white shirt. Those slick shades, the ones he'd tossed on the dashboard that first day on the side of the road like they didn't cost a thing, were freshly polished and sitting on his nose, catching the evening's sun. He looked handsome and glamorous, and her heart tugged.

But not because of him.

Because of the woman on his arm.

She was young. Classically pretty. No, not pretty. A knockout, dammit, all long limbs and dark shiny hair, generous curves draped in expensive, colorful silk.

A reporter thrust a microphone in her face, and the woman yammered on about the food at the chef's table. Anna Claire's stomach cramped so hard she wrapped both arms around it and doubled over with a groan.

Terri eyed her over a desk piled high with keys and food wrappers. "Better not be about to drop that baby on my clean carpet."

Anna Claire didn't answer. She couldn't. She couldn't do anything but stare at the television screen.

At the way his arm was slung around that woman.

At the gold band catching the light on his ring finger.

At *her*, his beautiful wife.

Anna Claire straightened, both hands still wrapped around her belly. "That fucking motherfucker."

Like her mama would say, too good to be true.

THIRTY-THREE

PATRICK

I stare the detective down, and it's not all that hard to hold her gaze. She wants to know why my business card was on Little Kathi's nightstand. I sink back into the cushions of the couch, putting some distance between us. This is the easy part.

"There are piles of my business cards lying all over the house. I have boxes and boxes of them upstairs. Nina could have dropped one in every building she visited and I'd have no idea there were some missing."

Next to me, Alex nods, but she doesn't speak.

We're still seated on the patio out back, and the air is both muggy and cooler, the sun long disappeared behind the trees. I'm keenly aware of the pool lights flipping on, the music coming from a neighboring yard, a bead of sweat slipping down my neck. My brain struggles to stay focused on the detective's questions when my mind is stuck on Alex, sitting stiffly beside me on the couch.

"Cause of death was a gunshot wound to the back of her head, according to the coroner sometime between the hours of two and eight p.m. on Sunday."

Sunday. One day after Alex went inside the carriage house to get her shoes, the day we went to the pool.

"So she was dead before she appeared in our bathroom." I pause for the detective's nod. "Which means she was moved. Her body was planted there."

"That's correct. Scuff marks on the stairs and wall seem to confirm it, and only traces of the blood on the floor came from her. By the time she was put there, the bleeding from her head wound had stopped. A perforating wound, which means the bullet passed through the brain. Thus far, we haven't been able to recover it."

I sit with that for a minute, hearing the words she didn't say. That they're looking for the bullet, to see if it came from a Smith & Wesson like mine. From *my* Smith & Wesson.

I think back to late Sunday, to the thump that woke me in the middle of the night. I just assumed the sound had come from Gigi, but now I'm wondering if it was something else. Something like Nina hauling a heavy body through the backyard and up the stairs to the carriage house.

And while we're on the subject, how? Little Kathi was scrawny, but she was tall. Did Nina drag her in a tarp? A wheelbarrow? Or maybe she had help, which would explain the extent of the damage to Alex's car.

I glance at Alex, and I'm pretty sure she's thinking the same.

Detective Bennett shifts on her chair. "Let's back up a little, shall we? I'd like to know where you both were in the days following Nina's disappearance. Start with Wednesday evening, when you put her in the Uber."

"I already sent you the details, Detective. As I recall, you confirmed receiving them."

"Yes, but what happened *after* you put her in the Uber?"

"It was past midnight. I locked up and went to bed."

The God's honest truth. But if I've learned anything since marrying Alex, it's that the truth can be a slippery concept.

Detective Bennett scribbles something on her pad. When she looks up, her gaze is on Alex. "And where were you in the hours after midnight?"

"Passed out in bed. I'd had a lot to drink that night. I slept straight through until the morning."

So much for not revealing the part about the booze. I reach across the cushions for my wife's hand, giving it a squeeze. There are a million things I'd go back and fix if given the chance, but Alex isn't one of them. In fact, I've spent much of these past six years telling myself she was my reward, the universe throwing me a bone in the form of this perfect, gorgeous woman. Falling in love with her and the twins has been the easiest thing in the world.

"So," the detective says, "if for example your husband hadn't come upstairs, if he hadn't been in the bed next to you until much later, you wouldn't have known because you were sound asleep?"

Alex wouldn't have had a clue, but you'd never know it by the way her eyes narrow into straight lines.

"I would have known," she says, her voice firm. "And I don't like what you're suggesting."

"I'm not suggesting anything. I'm just trying to understand, because there's no camera footage to back up your story. Those new cameras up on the front roofline, they came with a brand-new hard drive. The old one has disappeared. Your husband claims the installers took it when they left Sunday, though they say they left it here for him to trash. Either way, I'm guessing that hard drive went someplace we'll never find."

I don't answer, mostly because I don't have one—not a good one, anyway. My brain stutters into gear, trying to explain, to fix this, but what the hell am I supposed to say? *Yes, the hard drive is gone. No, you will never find it.* I stare at the detective, and my skin goes hot, my pores opening up.

She leans forward, her gaze steady. "I checked with Ring. They were very helpful, by the way."

Fucking Ring. Those fucking cameras.

Alex sucks in a breath, and her fingers go stiff in mine.

"They sent me three files, three videos that had been deleted from your account. They said there may be others. That these were just the ones they were able to easily recover from their system."

Three files. That's it, just three, and I wait for Detective Bennett to tick them off even though deep down I always knew it would come to this. I knew this conversation was only a matter of time. Alex's fingers go slippery in my hand, and I don't know if the sweat is hers or mine.

"The first is of Nina leaving," the detective says. "We see her get into the Uber at 12:07. She waves to someone as the car is pulling away. I'm guessing that was you."

I nod, the skin of my scalp tingling. "I was standing in the doorway, yes, but that wasn't a wave. She flipped me a bird."

Middle finger wagging in front of a toothy smile, but it was dark and the video only showed movement through the glass. Why wouldn't the detective think it was a wave?

"The other two videos are from the Friday prior, and they were recorded back-to-back. The first starts at 2:18 p.m. when you pull into the driveway. You park your car and get out, but you don't go inside the house. You just stand there, waiting. Nina comes out two minutes later."

And this is where I know I'm screwed.

Because Nina came outside, all right, and then she parked her shoes on the top step. She didn't come any farther, but I sure did.

I marched right up to the edge of the driveway, a mere fifteen feet from the fish-eye lens pointed at my face, and I didn't hold back. The Ring doesn't have a microphone, but that doesn't mean the cops won't know what I said. My mouth was flapping plenty. And the police will have definitely consulted a—

"The lip reader I talked to says you used the word *money* at least five times. *Murder* was also a common refrain, used at least three times, maybe four, as was the word *kill* followed by *you* twice. Same thing if you ask me, but perhaps you'd care to offer up a different explanation?"

No, actually, I wouldn't. I wouldn't care to explain at all.

Detective Bennett slaps her pen to the paper with a sigh. "If there are more deleted videos, you might as well just tell me. We're going to find them eventually."

"I already told you this Nina person was threatening me. She wanted money, a car, for me to pay for a nicer apartment. She said if I didn't give her those things, she'd tell Alex I was inappropriate with her, that I was harassing her."

"Kind of like you did in that audio file making the rounds on YouTube?"

"That audio was fake. And I intend to prove it."

More for Alex than to save my weekly money segment, which I already know is toast. I've made peace with that, and it's fine. My face on the nightly news only inflated my ego, anyway. It never had anything to do with the salary. I've got more than enough socked away, lots more than Alex knows about. If nothing else, I've seen to that.

"And your threats to Nina's life?"

"People say all kinds of things in the heat of the moment."

Except I meant every word. I told her I wasn't giving her a motherfucking cent. That if she didn't stop messing with me and my family, I'd dump her body someplace no one would ever find it. I stare down the detective and wonder what else she's holding back. If the lip reader picked up on the other stuff.

"I have to be honest," she says, a sudden breeze stirring up a whiff of jasmine from the neighbor's yard. "I'm getting the feeling there's more you're not telling me."

Rein it in, big guy, I think, breathing through a surge of nausea. *Pull yourself together.* But my thoughts are thick and sticky, like sludge.

"Like what?" I say.

"Like how do I know you didn't follow Nina home? How do I know you didn't harm her roommate?"

"Because I didn't do either."

"You deleted three incriminating videos from the Ring servers. How do I know there isn't more footage of you driving off after her?"

"Because I'm telling you, Detective, there isn't. The people at Ring can search their servers until the end of time, but that video doesn't exist. And okay, sure. I get that I haven't exactly proven myself trustworthy in this respect, but what I also know is that you can't prove something that didn't happen. I didn't touch Nina. I haven't seen her since she got into the Uber I ordered for her, the one that the driver confirmed dropped her at her apartment. So maybe instead of sitting here, interrogating my wife and me, you should be out there hunting for Nina. Because she's obviously still alive and dangerous."

"Are you referring to Ms. Wallace's murder?"

"Her murder, the bomb threat, my wife's car and office bathroom, the missing gun. You realize that's all Nina, right? There's no one else it could have been. No one else has that kind of access to our home."

Next to me, my wife makes a humming sound. Purple splotches wind up her neck like poison ivy, a clear indication she's pissed. It happens every time we have a fight.

"What about your house cleaner?" the detective says. "Other employees, maybe. A babysitter?"

"The girls are too old for a sitter, and our house cleaner has

been with me for a million years. There are no other employees, at least not ones that are here regularly."

"You're sure."

"Yes." I nod. "I'm certain."

Detective Bennett stares me down for a long moment, and I
hold her gaze and think about all I've done to get here, to this
moment in time. All the sacrifices I've made, all the lies I've
told to protect Alex and the girls, to keep them alive and safe.
I'm not afraid of Detective Bennett. I've survived a hell of a lot
worse than her.

She flips her notebook closed, gathers her things and stands.
"We're not done here. Both of you, stay easy to find."

Alex nods, but I don't move. Neither one of us shows the detective out. We don't even say goodbye. We just sit there, listening to the sounds of a neighbor's kids, playing in a backyard
nearby, and the detective moving through the house. Her fading
footsteps, the front door opening and closing. The double chimes
of the alarm followed by silence, letting us know we're alone.

Alex wrenches her hand out of mine. "You deleted the security videos?"

At this point, there's no denying it. I just stare at this woman I
love so much, her skin pale, her eyes huge in her face, and I nod.

A shock wave ripples across her expression, and she winces.
"And that story you told about the sexual harassment?"

"That was true. Nina really did make all those threats, but I
swear to you, I *swear*, there was nothing going on between us. I
wouldn't do that." I reach for her hand, but she snatches it away
before I can get there, her body leaning backward on the couch.
"Please, Alex. You have to believe me."

"No, actually. I don't have to believe a single word you say.
Did you…did you *do* something to Nina or her roommate?"

"Are you asking me if I killed them?" She doesn't respond,
doesn't shake her head or nod, but she also doesn't have to. That's
what she thinks. Alex thinks I killed Nina and Little Kathi. "I

swear to you, Alex, on my life, on the girls' lives. I didn't touch a hair on either woman's head. I know at this point you have no reason to believe me, but it's the God's honest truth."

She stares at me, searching my face like she's looking for something. For someone. When she can't find it, she sighs, looking away. "Tell me how. How do I believe anything that comes out of your mouth? So far you've done nothing but lie."

"I've never lied about loving you and the girls."

She shakes her head, disappointed in my answer, and hell, who wouldn't be? I can see the words lodged in her throat, the accusation she can't quite bring herself to say. Two little words ring clear as a bell in my head, and not for the first time. For the millionth, at least.

Tell her.

"Shannon has access," she says. "She drops by a lot. She knows all the passwords to the laptop."

It takes me a second or two to switch gears, then another to place the name. Shannon, the neighbor's nanny. The one who saw me arguing with Nina on the front yard. The one with the annoying Chihuahua.

"Okay. Why didn't you tell the detective?"

"Because I'm not throwing an innocent girl under the bus just to provide cover for you." She wipes her palms on her skirt and pushes to a stand, her gaze working hard to avoid mine. "The girls and I are going to a hotel. And before you ask, no. You're not invited."

THIRTY-FOUR

I don't sleep. After Alex drags the twins out the door with an overnight bag, I spend the rest of the night behind the computer, chugging coffee and combing through the audio file. I transcribe every word, highlighting the parts I'm sure I didn't say, dredging memories of that conversation from the darkest corners of my brain and plugging in the ones I did. I click on every video and audio file I can find of myself online, and there are a *lot*, searching for the worst of the words—words like *cult* and *underwear* and *stupid cows*—and then I import the files into a database, noting the exact second where my words were pilfered from one audio file and pasted into another. I end up with an Excel sheet ten pages long.

I copy it to a thumb drive and head to the shower, scrubbing the sweat and desperation from my skin until it's an angry pink. Last night's talk with the detective, the way her words made

Alex deflate like a birthday balloon. All night while I worked on the file, compiling the evidence and arranging it in neat, color-coded columns, I kept seeing her face. The disappointment. The suspicion and fear. I turn the water up to scalding, and it still doesn't wash the stink away.

I towel off and throw on some clothes before heading outside to my car, thinking it's a good thing she and the girls left when they did, before the others started to arrive. Up at the road, new faces mingle with the parade of trolls and rubberneckers—reporters spilling out of news vans and lingering at the edge of the lawn, neighbors watching from their windows and porches.

I plow through the crowd, ignoring their stares and shouted questions.

What happened to Anna Claire Davis, Patrick?

Were the two of you having an affair?

Are you the reason she went missing?

I clutch the wheel and steer through traffic far too thick for a Saturday morning. I take the long way down Peachtree, clocking the hotels rising up on either side. Marriott, Westin, Grand Hyatt, Waldorf Astoria. Wherever Alex is, she used her own card, which means there's no way for me to find her.

In the Atlanta Tech Village deck, I check my phone for a message, but there's not one. I think about shooting off one of my own, but to say what? I'm sorry? Come home? I flip off the screen, grab my keys and hustle inside.

The elevator dumps me into a cluster of kids on the fifth floor—or at least that's how they look to me. ATV males have a type, and this is it: scrawny limbs, dark-rimmed glasses, jeans and a rumpled T-shirt, full heads of hair that haven't even thought about receding. Not that long ago I would have felt right at home. Now I push through the bodies, feeling every one of my forty-six years.

A harried girl in overalls and complicated braids points me to Brandon's desk, a shiny piece of black steel at the edge of a communal workspace, busy even on the weekend. People talking into their phones, banging on their keyboards, playing Ping-Pong and holding animated huddles on overstuffed beanbags. How people get any work done here is anybody's guess.

Brandon sees me coming and pops out his AirPods, sliding them into the case. "Hey, man, you're the Channel 10 money guy. I knew I recognized your voice. Cool." He swipes his laptop and phone from the desk, motions for me to follow. "Let's snag the conference room until somebody kicks us out."

And Brandon's not the only person here who recognizes me. I don't miss the double takes as we move through the bright space, and I wonder if they know me because of the news, or from the gossip currently blanketing their socials. Both, most likely.

He leads me into a glass-walled room with a table for ten and every high-tech gadget imaginable. Video conferencing system, digital projector, high-def video cameras and interactive whiteboards. One of them flickers to life after a few taps on Brandon's laptop. Automatically, I glance behind me, out the wall of glass overlooking the workspace, but no one on the other side seems to be paying us much attention, and even if they were, they probably wouldn't know what to make of the complicated Excel sheet taking up almost an entire wall. Numbers, text, spectral analysis charts. I scan the whiteboard, trying to make sense of it myself.

He sinks onto the chair at the head of the table. "Okay, so I compared the audio recording circulating online to the exemplar you sent with identical wording, and the two match up in terms of things like pitch, pronunciation, voice tone and inflection, vowel and consonant formations, accent, dialect."

I nod, because I figured as much. The exemplar Brandon is referring to was me, reading my parts of the conversation word for word, even though by then I didn't need a script. The words were imprinted on my brain.

And as infuriating as it was to say those disgusting words out loud—*I'd like your dress better without underwear*—it was even harder to make my voice seem natural while doing it. I ended up sounding angry and forced, like a soap opera actor the writers kill off after only a few episodes because he's so godawful.

But in both cases, they were still my words, still my voice. Makes sense that the recordings would match up.

"Please tell me there's a but."

"But." Brandon stabs a finger into the air, lets it hover there for a second or two. "While the voice on both recordings is undeniably yours, there are some significant differences when it comes to delivery. Where you build in a pause for breath, which words you place the accent on, things like that. That could possibly be because you were trying, either consciously or subconsciously, to sound different than the voice on the recording, but it could also be that the original recording wasn't original at all, but spliced together from various source files."

"And was it?"

"Yes." Brandon flips to the next slide, another table with long lines of numbers and what looks like date stamps. "Yes, it was."

I pound both fists onto the table. It's what I told Rachel, what I swore over and over to Alex, what I told the detective before she'd even demanded an explanation. Only now, thanks to Brandon and my spreadsheet, I have proof.

He navigates with the mouse, pointing the arrow at a dozen or so rows of text along the left side of the screen. "Okay, so this is the metadata embedded in the audio file, which reveals that the recording was captured with an iPhone 11. It's why I asked you to record the sample on your iPhone. Not the exact same model, but same or similar technology. It's easier to compare the two that way."

I nod. So far, so good.

Brandon's phone buzzes on the desk, and he picks it up, his thumbs flying over the screen as he talks. "The splicing was pretty clumsy, honestly. It's probably why they chose to use party noise as a backdrop. Easier to hide the stops and starts under the music and chatter."

"What about the source of the doctored file?" My eyes sting from the harsh lights, the lack of sleep. From everything. "Can you see the owner, or the computer it was created on?"

Brandon's thumbs are still typing away, and he doesn't look up from his phone. "Metadata is rarely useful in pinning those things down. I've never come across anything in an audio file that identifies the source that specifically, unless it was something the creator chose to add. Which in this case, they didn't."

I shove the thumb drive across the table. "I put together an Excel sheet with the original audio. I bet if you put the two files next to each other, the time stamps will line up. What about the JPEGs I sent? Can you see the source on those?"

And yes—it felt creepy as fuck to hit Send on a pornographic image of my wife, of my two very underage stepdaughters chugging booze, but it had to be done. Those files can be traced, as well.

"Potentially. I'd have to do a little more digging to know for sure, but I could probably find you an IP address, assuming you don't mind paying extra for somewhat questionable methods."

Questionable, as in illegal.

"I'll pay whatever it takes. How long do you need?"

"I can probably have something for you by the end of the day. But in the meantime…" Brandon gives a demonstrative tap to the laptop, and the image of the twins, the one where they're sharing a can of White Claw with some neighbor's asshole kid, lights up the screen. He taps another key, and the image shifts. The White Claw becomes a Sprite. He taps it again, and it's a can of Coke. "I had to do a little guesswork, but I figured one of these was probably in the vicinity. Certainly looks a lot more legit."

I sit silent, watching while Brandon cycles through the other two images. The vape pen morphs into a Popsicle, then a candy bar, then a tube of lip gloss, and with another click the vape smoke vanishes from the screen. Except for the teenage boy crashing a party of twelve-year-old girls, the pictures look completely innocent.

"I can't be a hundred percent sure without the source material, which makes it hard to conclusively prove what was in your stepdaughters' hands. But these images do demonstrate how easy the files were to manipulate. However." Brandon serves up a smarmy grin. "I saved the best for last."

I brace, because I know what's next. The photograph of Alex splayed out on the bed. I think of the nerds on the other side of the glass behind me, dicks hard at the sight of my wife in all her naked glory, and I wince.

Only it's not really Alex. I've known that all along. The breasts are too big, the ribs are too sharp, and that soft swell of skin I love so much under her navel, the one marked with stripes her daughters put there, is smooth and flat as a board. This body is beautiful, yes, but it isn't anywhere near as perfect as my wife's.

Brandon taps a key, and Alex's face morphs into that of another woman, a pretty blonde. "Meet Amber Foxxxx, with not triple but quadruple Xs. Former stripper turned hard-core porn star with a particular talent for taking on multiple men at the same time. This is an image I nabbed from her website. A simple search took me straight to the source material."

I lean back in my chair, blowing out a sigh. "Holy shit."

"People are visual creatures. It's gonna be easier for them to understand how a photograph has been altered as opposed to an audio file, because they can see it with their own eyes."

On the one hand, Brandon is right. People *are* visual creatures, and it's hard to dispute evidence as solid as the picture of Amber's body, plucked from her own website, with Alex's face slapped on top.

On the other, Alex was right, too. The doctored files are already plastered on every social media wall. People are already having full-on debates about the state of our marriage on Alex's Instagram, on the station's Facebook page. Brandon's files might get the girls back into school, but they're not going to change the public's opinion.

I look up, and Brandon is watching. "How come you don't look happier? I'm telling you the pictures and recordings are fake. I'm giving you undeniable evidence that you didn't say those things."

"Because as my brilliant wife told me, scandals go viral, while explanations fizzle. There's so much noise that nobody sticks around to hear the acquittal."

Brandon frowns, settling his phone facedown on the table. "So why are you here, then? Why did I do all this work?"

"Because I'm not looking for vindication. I'm looking for the source. The asshole who doctored all these files and uploaded them onto the internet, because I think it's the same person. I think she's hiding out somewhere, and I want to find her."

"So you want revenge." He gives me a halfhearted shrug. "Look, man. I'm not here to judge. I'm just the tech nerd here to point you the way. Give me a couple hours to dig into things. I'll let you know as soon as I've got a lead."

"The sooner, the better." I reach down the table to pump Brandon's hand.

In the elevator, a text pings my phone, and I dig it out of my pocket, hoping it's from Alex. I wince when I see it's from Owen.

Nina Morris. Camp was court mandated, address on file a dead end.

I roll my eyes, then pound out a reply.

Old news and deal still stands.
You and I are even now.

I'm almost to my car when another message hits my phone, an email with a file I requested the morning after Nina didn't show—the call logs from her cell phone. Technically, the phone wasn't ever hers; it belongs to Unapologetically Alex, LLC, of which I am a registered agent. I start at the top and work my way down, punching the numbers into the car's hands-free system.

It takes me almost an hour, but finally, on my thirty-sixth try, I hit pay dirt.

"Thank you for calling ATL Storage Center. Please listen carefully, as our menu options have changed."

THIRTY-FIVE

I don't think about much on the way to ATL Storage Center, a forty-minute drive to the crappiest corner of East Atlanta. I just follow the direction from the nav system until it alerts me I'm here, slowing to eye the row of cars behind a rusty chain-link fence. Beater, clunker, hooptie, shitbox, banger and, at the far end, a boxy and dented heap that could do double duty as a kidnapper's van, newspapered windows and all.

When I started at the news station, WXBA made a big deal about how I came from nothing. Rachel called it the essence of my brand, how I went from a bag of pennies to a million bucks all by myself, despite the shitty cards I'd been dealt. They called me scrappy, and I let them because they weren't wrong. These cars, this neighborhood, they're not all that different than the ones I grew up around.

I park on a side street, not because I'm worried about someone taking a swipe at my Mercedes, but in case I need to make a quick getaway. The plan is to get in and get out—quickly and without being noticed.

The building is basically one big box, split in half by a long internal hallway. Doors line it on each side, dark metal and hinged so they roll up like the kind you hang in a garage. I clock them as I pass, keeping my head down because I know how things work in this place. I know not to smile at the people lugging boxes to and fro, but to look them in the eye just long enough they'll feel noticed but not provoked. I know to keep my mouth shut and my face turned down from the cameras screwed to either end of the hallway ceiling. And I know to check every door for a Brink's discus lock, the kind the locksmith told me will fit the key taped to the inside of my wallet.

I find it on unit 22. The key slips in without a hitch, and I remove the padlock and roll the door just high enough for me to slip under, then flip the light switch before I let it fall shut again. It's probably a risk, especially if anybody's manning those security cameras in the hall, but then again I won't be here long. Unit 22 is small, a four-by-four space of cinder-block walls and dusty concrete, and there's only one item here to search through.

A forty-eight-gallon Rubbermaid tub, smack in the center of the room.

I flip the lid, and it's like looking into a moving box—one filled with my things, from my house. A wedding photo of me and Alex in a sterling frame. A pair of salad prongs engraved with a curly *H*. A scented candle and one of Alex's paperbacks, the pages wrinkled and dog-eared. A crystal candlestick, heavy enough to bash in a person's skull. A red silk blouse, a bra of black lace and creamy satin. Penelope's diary. Her *diary*. A surge of something red-hot erupts up my chest, and I breathe through an urge to scream.

All those months that bitch has been in our house, wandering our rooms, poking through our drawers and searching our closets, slipping our things into her pockets and walking off with them as if they were hers. *Valuable* things. Like one of the diamond earring studs I bought for Alex when she hit 500K, a pearl necklace and gold charm bracelet she thought she'd lost, the band of diamonds I gave her for an anniversary.

That bitch. That fucking bitch.

There's more—random, useless things she plucked from dressers and bathroom counters and nightstands, odds and ends we've never missed and have long forgotten. I dig through them, searching for my old Smith & Wesson, but it's not here.

I check the time—4:48—then close the box and lug it into the hall. I don't bother rolling down the door, and I leave the lock where I'd tossed it on the floor, in a pile of swept-up lint and dirt. I'm almost to the glass door at the end of the hall when a voice calls out from behind me.

"Hey. *Hey.* Who the hell are you?"

A man, and a large one. Six feet and then some, with broad shoulders and a belly that hangs low over his waistband. I don't think he's an employee, though. No polo with ATL Storage Center logo, no name tag. Just beat-up jeans over a ratty T-shirt, the kind you pick up at a concert.

"I'm a customer, same as you."

I clock the distance to the door—five feet, maybe six. Even with the box in my hand, it's good odds. This guy must be pushing three hundred pounds. I could outrun him easily.

"Then how come I've never seen you here before? I saw you come out of that girl's unit."

"She gave me the key. She asked me to pick up her shit."

He thinks about this for a few seconds, taking in the empty unit, the key sticking out of the lock on the floor. His sun-weathered face scrunches into a scowl. "Yeah, well, she asked *me* to give her a call if anybody came snooping around."

"So call her, then." I back up a step, then another. Close enough to feel the last of the afternoon sun beating down on the glass door, the heat coming from outside. "Better yet, send her a picture."

And maybe it's the lack of sleep or the steady diet of caffeine and little else, but the idea thrills me, and more than a little. The man pats his pockets for his phone, then aims the camera at my face. I hold the box high and picture her face when it hits her burner phone, the frustration and fury when she realizes I'm on her tail, and it's a dark and beautiful thing.

"Hang on, hang on," he says, poking around at the screen. "Lemme make sure she's cool with this before you go."

Screw that.

Two more steps and I'm at the door. I don't break stride, just give it a shove with a toe hard enough to swing it wide. It slams against the cinder-block wall with a loud thwack. "Tell her she can come over and grab it anytime," I say over my shoulder, and then I break into an easy jog.

This thing is ending soon, one way or another.

THIRTY-SIX

ANNA CLAIRE

Sunday came and went, and he didn't show. He didn't call to explain, either, and even if he *had* called, Anna Claire wouldn't have picked up the phone. He might not have figured it out just yet, but Anna Claire wasn't speaking to him.

The asshole was married. Of *course* he was. He probably had a couple of babies running around the yard, too, didn't he? And how many others were out there just like her? How many other pregnant fools? She was an idiot to believe him.

At the thought, she yanked the fitted sheet off the bed so hard that it ripped right down the middle.

"Hey, AC? You better come downstairs," Terri said, standing in the doorway. The woman rarely left her office except to climb in her truck and motor off for home. She certainly didn't abandon her afternoon soaps to haul her body up three flights of stairs when she could have called AC's block of rooms until she got her on the room phone.

Anna Claire frowned. "What's wrong?"

"There's someone in the office to see you." Terri poked a thumb back out on the catwalk, aiming it in the direction of the stairs. "A man. A big one."

Ten whole days after his supposed Sunday visit, though Anna Claire was a little surprised to hear he actually came inside. He was funny about being seen at the Starlux, and he knew her work schedule. It was more his style to show up at the end of her shift, rolling up just in time for her to drop into the passenger's seat of his idling car.

Anna Claire dropped the torn sheet to the carpet. She pulled a fresh one from the cart and shook it out, taking her time. "Tell him I'm busy."

"*You* tell him. I ain't going back down there." Terri shrugged, jiggling her generous belly. "He's kinda scary."

Which explained why Terri let him chase her out of her office, but still. *Scary* was not a word Anna Claire would use to describe the father of her baby. Striking, yes. Intimidating, sure. But scary?

She'd show him scary.

Anna Claire pushed past her boss and stomped down the catwalk for the stairs. At the office, she jerked the door open.

And then she stopped.

He was standing at the edge of Terri's desk, using a letter opener to dig the dirt from under his nails, and he was big, all right, with shoulders broad enough to be a linebacker. His dark shirt was stretched tight over a barrel chest, gaping open at the neck over a thick gold chain. He looked like a bouncer from one of those nightclubs down in Panama City, the ones wearing dark shades and angry expressions.

"Who the hell are you?"

He dropped the letter opener back into the penholder, his

gaze taking its time on the skin of her bare legs, her stupid Starlux dress, the way it stretched tight over her swollen breasts and belly. Her cheeks lit up with a dull throbbing, heat creeping up her neck. By the time his eyes landed on hers, she felt violated.

He shook his head, sank onto the edge of Terri's desk. Behind him, the television blared a Doritos commercial. "When are you due?"

"None of your business."

"If that baby belongs to who I think it does, then damn straight it's my business."

She wrapped both hands around her belly, almost knocked sideways by the sudden surge of emotion for her unborn child. "This baby belongs to *me*. It's *mine*. And since I still don't know who you are or what you're doing here, I'm not telling you squat."

He stood and crossed the room, a giant hand outstretched. "Name's Gary. And I guess you could say we're colleagues. We both work for the same boss."

Anna Claire crossed her arms, liking this guy even less. She wasn't just some employee. She ran things here at the Starlux. All that talk about being a personal assistant was a joke, one they usually laughed about while naked in bed. He trusted her with his body and his business. She was so much more than just an employee.

"So you work for the Starlux, too, huh? Tell Steve I want a raise."

Gary dropped his hand to his side with a slap, his eyes narrowing. "So that's the way we're going to play it, huh? Okay. You were right before. You don't know me, but if you did, you'd know I'm employee of the motherfucking year. When my boss tells me to not come back without the money he sent me here to collect, I don't come back without the money."

"What money?"

"Very funny." He smiled, and he was missing a tooth, a gaping black hole between his front tooth and canine. It made the gesture feel the exact opposite of friendly.

"It wasn't a joke. I'm a maid, as you can tell from my outfit, and this place pays for shit. I have about six dollars in my purse, and most of it's spare change."

It was a lie, of course. She had the money—loads of it. While the father of her baby played house with his wife and kids, she'd been collecting it from behind toilet tanks and ceiling tiles, adding it to the growing pile. It might not be all that much to him, but it was enough for her. Enough to raise this baby all by herself, to clothe and feed it, to live a comfortable and simple life without ever having to wonder where their next meal would come from.

"Just give it to me, will you, and I'll forget you were ever rude." When she didn't respond, Gary stepped even closer. "Please don't make me have to rough up a pregnant lady."

He was looming over her now, and though he still hadn't touched her, everything in his expression spoke of violence. He didn't want to rough up a pregnant lady, but he would if he had to. The idea her so-called boss had sent this thug on an errand he'd promised to do himself—*ten days ago*—sparked a fire inside her chest.

"You can ask me nice, or you can threaten me. Hell, you can toss me through that plate-glass window if you want to, but it's not gonna do you any good. I'm only following the rules."

Rule number four, don't trust anybody but him. Rule number six, don't talk business unless they were alone in his car or her house. Gary frowned, but he didn't argue, which told her he knew the rules, too.

Anna Claire lifted a brow.

And all those other rules, she'd followed them, too. She'd moved the money to five separate locations, ones nobody would ever find and nobody but her knew about. She committed everything to memory, every hiding spot and how much she'd stashed where, so she didn't have to write anything down. And that rule about loyalty… Loyalty, her ass. Anna Claire didn't trust anyone, not even him.

Especially not him.

She whirled around, calling over her shoulder on the way out the door. "Tell him whatever he wants from me he'll have to come and get it himself."

As far as Anna Claire was concerned, that money was hers now.

THIRTY-SEVEN

ALEX

Patrick is home when I pull into the driveway, golden light spilling from an upstairs window. By now it's good and dark, a full twenty-four hours that I've stayed away from this house. From Patrick.

If Tommy or my girlfriends saw me right now, jogging up the steps to the front door, they'd call me an idiot. They'd ask if I've lost my mind, tell me to cut my losses and run run run from this man, from his lies, but I can't.

All day long, I've thought about the detective's visit, her tone when she confronted him with the deleted camera feeds, the look on his face. I ran errands with the girls, to Target and Starbucks and the nail salon for an impromptu mani-pedi, fielding their incessant questions about where Patrick was, why he wasn't with us, and if he was at home, then why we couldn't be, and my mind wouldn't be still. I drove all over town, sat on pedicure chairs and stared into space, the darkness of my thoughts regurgitating every detail.

The pages and pages of text messages. Those three deleted Ring files. Patrick's mouth carving out those awful words. *Money. Murder. Kill.* He threatened to kill that girl, and now she's missing. What am I supposed to do with that?

I step into the foyer to complete silence. No comforting chimes from the alarm, no banging around in the kitchen, only a stillness that amplifies the sound of my breath, my heartbeat loud in my ears. Either Patrick didn't hear me come inside, or he's not here. On a run, maybe.

I dump my things on the foyer table. "Patrick?"

For the life of me, I can't square these past ten days with the man I know. The stepfather and the husband. The provider. The sweet stranger who fronted the valet tip when I was out of cash, who wrapped his cashmere scarf around my neck just because I was cold. I think about how quickly I fell for him, how exciting things felt and at the same time so familiar, like I'd been waiting for this man all my life. The joy and relief when he finally said those words—*I love you*—a sentiment I hadn't heard from a man for *years*, one I didn't realize until then I'd been starved of.

And then there's how he is with the girls. Patient. Affectionate. More levelheaded than I am most of the time, and definitely more available than I've been since Unapologetically Alex took off. It's been almost miraculous, how he slid into a fatherly role without ever stepping on their own father's toes, not that Daniel had much of a say about it. But Patrick has never pushed, never asked they call him anything other than Patrick. The girls love him, and he loves them back. I trust him intrinsically—or at least I did, up until these past ten days.

Six years versus ten days. That's why I'm here, because of those six amazing years.

I'm about to check the patio when there's a noise from upstairs, something thumping above my head.

Because it's possible, isn't it, that this whole thing is being orchestrated somehow. The fake pictures and recording. That mysterious text that landed on all our phones: *Get ready.* Maybe this Nina person has decided to take a wrecking ball to our lives because her own life was so shitty. Because she's jealous of what we have. Because we are a normal, happy family when she was abandoned and neglected. Aaron's ominous warning plays through my head for the millionth time. Maybe *that's* the connection.

I find Patrick in his study, deep in concentration behind his computer. The hall lights are on, but he hasn't bothered in here, no overhead light or a desk lamp to illuminate the room, only his screen. It silhouettes his head with bright, high-definition images of skin. Legs. Breasts. None of them mine.

"Why is there a naked body on your computer screen?"

He jumps at the sound of my voice, whirling around on his chair. "Alex. Hey."

He wasn't expecting me, that much is clear from his jumpy eyes, the guilt that flashed across his features at the body taking up his screen. "I got the proof we talked about. The pictures. The audio. I was putting it in an email to you. This is Amber Foxxxx, by the way, with four Xs. She's a porn star."

Of course she is. Someone slapped my face on the body of a porn star. Alex vs. Amber Foxxxx.

"I'm sending you the girls' pictures, too. Fakes, obviously." He tips up the open bottle of bourbon on the desk, pouring three fingers in a glass already sticky with amber dregs. "Where are they, by the way?"

"At Kim's. They're spending the night."

"Aren't they grounded?"

I give him a look. "Seriously? Stop trying to change the subject."

"Okay." He swipes his glass from the desk, swiveling all the way around to face me. "What *is* the subject?"

"Hell if I know. I guess I was just hoping you could...explain things." I sink onto the orange couch with a crushing fatigue, like someone pulled the plug on my energy supply. "I just want to understand."

"Is this about the deleted camera feeds? Because—"

"It's about the feeds, the changed passcode on your phone, that bullshit story about the argument with AC on the lawn. Aaron said to look for the connection, the common thread that tied Nina to Anna Claire to us, and you know what I think? I think the connection is you. Because all those things I just mentioned, they all point to you knowing something about AC that the rest of us don't. Some secret the two of you shared. Tell me it isn't true."

I watch a shock wave ripple across his face before he pulls himself together, and I don't miss the way his body stiffens, how his tone sounds weird and flat when he repeats one word.

"Aaron."

"Aaron Childers, yes. The police officer who investigated Anna Claire's death. He lives in Conyers now. He said that AC— that *Nina* chose us for a reason, and I think that reason is you."

His skin is paler now, too, the blood literally drained from his cheeks, which hang in an expression I've seen plenty on the twins, all those times I've caught them in a lie. Mouth twisted in a mixture of guilt and fear. And now, here it is, on the face of my husband.

"You talked to Officer Childers."

Again, not a question, but I nod, anyway.

"What else did he tell you?"

"He said that the real Anna Claire was tortured, a long and painful process that she was alive for most of, but that cause of death was a bullet through her brain. An execution, he called it, though he never figured out why because he never caught the killer. Oh, and she had a cat named Mister Fluffles."

He's quiet for a long time. No sound, no movement but his

big chest, rising and falling with air. Then, finally: "You know I love you, right?"

Ten days ago, my nod would have been immediate. But not after these last ten days. That's what makes this all so baffling. And I heard that wistfulness in his tone just now. He loves me *but*.

"Is it an affair? Did you sleep with this Nina person?"

"*No*. There's no affair. There's no one else. I swear."

The words shoot out of him so loud and forceful that I wonder, just for a second, if maybe I'm imagining things, seeing things that aren't there, conflating my past with my present. Any explanation is better than none. I learned that much from Daniel.

"And that story you told the detective about the sexual harassment…"

"That was true. She did make all those threats, but I didn't touch her, not that way or any other way."

"But you did know her somehow. When she came here the very first time, when I told you about the girl I hired. You heard her name, and it wasn't the first time you'd heard it."

It's the only way I know to explain his behavior these past ten days. I think back to the day I told him, sometime during the chaotic weeks before Christmas. Patrick had been pushing me to hire an assistant for ages. Someone to do the grunt work, he said, someone to share in the day-to-day burden. When he got home from work I told him about the smart, driven young girl who emailed me out of the blue, the one with a résumé so perfect it was almost too good to be true. Patrick popped the champagne, then peppered me with a million questions—about her background, her résumé, her references and experience.

But when I said her name, he didn't even blink. He's that good.

And that look on his face now, his silent stare across the dim room—it's answer enough.

"Six months, Patrick! She's been here for six months. And

all that time, you let her waltz around our house. She ate at our table. She spent time with my children. She drove them around town, to soccer and to friends' houses, picked them up from school for five fucking months. And all that time, you knew her. You knew something that gave you reason to hate her. And now I want to know what."

I think of all the secret texts—*tell me what you want, this is a dangerous game, disappear back into the hole you crawled here from*—of her following us to Serenbe. I think about the missing gun, the threats and break-ins and the dead body, the dummy bombs planted in my daughters' rooms. He knew this woman was dangerous, and he let her into our lives, anyway.

Now, looking back, I feel like a fool. It hadn't been a happy coincidence that her résumé landed in my in-box when it did. Nina sought me out. She played me like a fiddle, and this was never about me. The job, her constant presence in our home—it was all about getting close to *him*.

"Our *house*, Patrick, my *daughters*. I think of everything you've done, that one's the most unforgivable. You knowingly put me and the girls in danger."

"No. I was trying to *keep* you from danger. Everything I've done these past five months, hell, these past twenty-five years, has been for you, for *our* future."

He's so earnest, his voice so sure and confident, I want to believe him. Despite all the lies, despite the way he's still holding something back, I want to believe my husband, desperately.

And yet I have absolutely no idea what he's talking about.

"Twenty-five years? You're not making any sense. I've only known you for six and a half years. I swear to you, Patrick, if you don't—"

He grabs my wrist out of the air, his fist clamping down tight on my skin. "Shh. I think I heard something."

I hold my breath, and I hear it, too. Glass breaking somewhere downstairs. Not the light tinkling of a wineglass tipping over, but a big sheet of it, heavy pieces raining to the floor. The sound is an electric current, zinging through my bones.

"Is that her?"

I don't give Patrick a name. Nina, AC, Anna Claire. We both know that it's her downstairs.

The look on his face terrifies me, and so does his answer. "I sure as hell hope so."

THIRTY-EIGHT

I stare at Patrick in horror, my gaze darting to the open doorway. From up here, in the study at the end of the second-story hall, there's only one way out, and that's down the stairs. Where someone has just broken in.

Patrick whirls around on the chair, yanking open the bottom drawer on the big oak desk. "Stay here."

He pulls an object from the bottom, and my body flies backward, a jolt of adrenaline and fear that presses my back against the wall.

It's a gun, a dark silver thing that takes up his entire palm.

"Wh-where did you get that?"

He stands, searching out my gaze. "Alex, did you hear me? Lock the door, push something heavy in front of it. The cabinet if you can manage. Otherwise, the couch and chairs."

I shake my head, the protests warring in my brain. I don't

want to go downstairs. I don't want to stay up here alone. I'm terrified of both scenarios.

He steps closer, nudging me out of the way. "Alex, did you hear me? I can't protect you and myself at the same time."

"Protect me from what? What do you think she's going to do?"

He doesn't answer that question, either, just shoves past me into the hall.

I hurry after him, heart pounding against my ribs. "Patrick, wait!"

He whirls around, his lips set in a hard line of determination. "Go back."

I stare at him, this stranger wearing the body of my husband. Muscles hard as rocks under his skin. A gun clutched in his fist, one I have zero doubts he'll use. He'll kill with his bare hands if he has to. "The p–police. Shouldn't we be calling the police?"

"No. That's the last thing we should do." He gestures with the gun behind me, to the door we just came through. "Get in the study and lock the door."

"No. Not until you tell me what you're going to do."

"Alex, I am begging you. Go back in there and barricade the door. We don't have time to argue."

He grabs my arm, and he's not so gentle about it this time, his fingers squeezing like a clamp on my bicep as he steers me back up the hall. Patrick is a big man, over six feet, and I've always loved that about him. His size, his strength. He's never turned either on me, but still. I can see how some women might find him dangerous.

There's more noise from downstairs, the dull thud of a door closing followed by footfalls, almost as loud as my heart pounding in my ears.

"Please don't leave me up here."

Patrick lets go of my arm, his chest heaving in frustration. "Listen up, because you have to do exactly as I say." He holds the gun between us, his voice fast and low. "This is the safety. See? When it's on, like this, the trigger doesn't move. You have to flip it before the gun will shoot. Got it?" He shows me how, moving it back and forth with his thumb, then stops when the safety is on. "You only get one chance, Alex. Make sure to point it somewhere deadly."

"What? Why me?"

"Because she'll never suspect it of you. Just make sure not to give her your back."

He slides the gun into the back of my waistband, covering it with my shirt, and he's not wrong. I've never been shy about my aversion to guns, a fact that is well documented on my Insta-feed, lots of mentions of how I can't be in the same room with one, how they turn me into a shaking, sniveling mess. Nina even asked me about it once, and I brushed it off with a laugh, some silly joke about being killed by one in a past life. Nothing about my own personal trauma, even though I've thought about it plenty.

Now there's a gun pressed against the skin of my back. There's a bullet aimed at my ass.

And what am I supposed to do with the thing, whip it out duel-style? I'll be dead before my shaking finger can find the trigger.

"Wait—"

"There's no time." Patrick turns for the stairs, leaving me no choice but to follow closely behind. I wince at a floorboard creaking beneath my feet, the groan of the stairs as we come down them. In the foyer, the alarm pad by the front door is lit up green, which means I didn't arm it when I came inside. I pause, taking in the three tiny buttons that line the left side.

Fire. Medical. Police.

I glance behind me, where Patrick is already stepping into the living room shadows, and I don't think. I just do it. I stab the button for the police, counting the seconds in my head. The installer said for the silent alarm to work I had to hold it in for three, but I give it five, then hurry in the wake of my husband.

A familiar voice floats around the corner. "I want my shit back."

I hustle across the living room carpet as Patrick says, "It's in the car. Take it, including the car. Key's on the foyer table."

And even though I know it's her, it's still a shock to step into the doorway to find Nina, seated at the island in the same stool she sat on over a week ago, the night I whipped out the tequila. I take her in—the hair that's dark and flat-ironed just like mine, the makeup blended to perfection. A younger, shinier version of Unapologetically Alex, all the way down to the bright silk scarf wrapped around her neck.

An oversized Hermès I never wear, but still. "That's my scarf."

So is the blouse underneath, the Tiffany locket on a golden chain, the diamond hoops Patrick gave me last Christmas, the ones I didn't even know I'd lost. It's all mine, all the way down to my Chanel ring on her pointer finger. I spot it, and that's when I notice the gun.

She hops off the chair, stabbing it across the island at Patrick. "Turn around. Lift your shirt. Empty your pockets. Show me your ankles."

He steps to the end of the island so she can see, doing as she orders. When she's satisfied he's not concealing a weapon of his own, she turns to me. The gun throbs against the skin of my back, my heart beating so hard I'm surprised she can't hear it, but I make sure to hold my breath under her gaze. If she gets her hand on the gun, we're as good as dead.

"I should have killed you when I had the chance," Patrick says, and his words do the trick. Her gaze flits away from me and lands on him.

"That's hilarious. I want my money."

"This again?" Patrick lifts his arms in frustration, then lets them fall to his sides with a slap. "I don't have your money."

She rolls her eyes, and I see it now, the animosity fueling every gesture. So obvious that I wonder how I didn't notice it before, the way she's completely unhinged. Her muscles are jumping under her skin, her eyes big and bulging.

"I may not be educated, you asshole, but I'm not stupid, and I did the math. Two million dollars in 1994 is $3,760,000 and some change today. Tell you what, give me four and we'll call it even."

I frown, my gaze bouncing between them. "Why does she think you owe her four million dollars? For what?"

She keeps her eyes and the gun trained on Patrick. "Yeah, Patrick, for what?"

"What is it you don't understand?" Patrick is shouting now, his face turning red. "I didn't take the money!"

Without warning, she lunges, lifting the gun from his chest to his face, pointing it directly between his eyes. "Next time you say it, there's a bullet in your skull. Are we clear?"

I think about the gun pressed to the small of my back, and my fingers twitch, my skin tingling. I stare at Patrick, trying to catch his eye, trying to decide. What if I can't get there fast enough? What if it gets tangled in my pants, or my fingers fumble on the safety, the trigger? She'll shoot me the second she sees me pulling it out.

Patrick holds up his hands, showing her his empty palms. "Let Alex go. She has nothing to do with this."

"Are you kidding me?" Nina laughs, the sound loud and mocking. "Alex has *everything* to do with this. She and her two little brats have been living off my money for *years*. She lives in *my house*."

I shake my head, not in answer but in confusion. "This is Patrick's house. He's lived here since long before you and I came around."

She looks at Patrick, one brow rising in ridicule. "Would you like to fill her in, or shall I?"

I don't know what she's talking about, but I don't press the point, either. Not with that gun pointed at Patrick's head.

Whatever Nina says next gets sucked up in the sound of my own panting, the blood roaring in my ears. He's all the way across the kitchen now, the distance between us widening. Too far for him to grab the gun from my waistband and shoot this maniac dead, which means I'm going to have to do it myself. My only options are to stall or fight.

And where the hell are the police? I glance at the microwave clock, noting the time. It's been, what—four, five minutes since I sent up the silent alarm?

"Hello, Alex. Are you listening?"

"What?"

"I said sit down. It's high time the three of us had a little chat." She turns to Patrick with a grin. "Pour up, Patty. We all know how much Alex loves her booze."

THIRTY-NINE

PATRICK

Then

"What a dump," Owen said, sitting in the driver's seat next to Patrick, squinting through the windshield at the hotel parked at the edge of I-75. Two stories of cinder blocks and concrete, with metal doors and what was once a neon sign, now dark with dirt and cracked bulbs.

The Starlux Motor Lodge wasn't exactly Owen's style, but it's not like they had much choice. It was getting dark, and black clouds swirled overhead. Though it hadn't yet started to rain, the wind was bad enough to almost blow them off the road, multiple times. While northbound traffic filed past in the opposite lanes, Owen had been steering them straight into the eye of the storm.

He cut the engine and pocketed the keys.

"It's only for one night," Patrick said, reaching onto the back seat for his duffel. He was trying to stay positive, but honestly, this hurricane was going to be a big one. Category four, projected to hit land just south of them. "By this time tomorrow, we'll be ass in the sand."

He opened the door, and the wind almost ripped it out of his hand.

In the cramped hotel office, Owen plunked down his father's credit card for the stay, and like every time he covered Patrick's half of the costs, he swallowed his pride. Patrick was decent at stretching a dollar, but he wasn't a magician. His student loans didn't cover his room and board at the University of Georgia, didn't cover books or transportation or food. He worked full-time to pay for those things, while Owen here skated though life on his father's money and his family name. It was a silent trade-off, one they'd never discussed. Patrick's friendship for Owen's occasional funding. As far as Patrick could tell, he was Owen's only friend.

Up in the room, Owen grimaced at the grubby carpet, the scratchy bedspread, the television he flipped on and deemed the screen grainy and too small. He did inventory, counting the towels and punching the pillows and opening the minifridge—moldy. He slammed it shut with a sneer.

A gust of wind rattled the milky glass in the room's only window, high on the wall above the shower, and the lights above their heads flickered and dimmed. Patrick braced for darkness, but at the last second the lights swelled again. The electricity was holding, for now.

He poked a finger toward the TV. "Mind if I change the channel? I want to see how long we're going to be holed up here."

"Dude, I don't give a shit." Owen picked up the phone and stabbed zero. "Yeah, we're gonna need some more towels, and while you're at it, these pillows are garbage. Can you bring up some that are down-filled?" He paused, rolling his eyes at Patrick. "Okay, well, how about a couple *without* lumps? Do you think you can manage that?" Another pause. "Oh, and send up some ice." He dropped the phone back on its cradle without a thank-you or goodbye.

Patrick tossed the remote on the bed. "Why do you always have to be such an asshole?"

"What? The pillows *are* garbage. I'm going to have to be completely wasted to fall asleep."

And Patrick was going to have to be wasted to spend all night trapped in this room with Owen. When he fished a giant bottle of vodka from his bag, Patrick took a grateful slug.

They sprawled on the beds, watching the storm roll up the television screen and passing the bottle back and forth. Ten-foot swells, one-hundred-and-fifty-mile-an-hour winds. Hunker down and haul your pets inside, the weatherman warned, and Patrick prepared to sit through eight more hours of this shit. By the time the knock came, he was well on his way to good and drunk.

A female voice pushed through the television chatter. "Housekeeping."

He opened the door, and the first thing he saw was her stomach. Big and round and low, like the baby could drop out of her at any second. It bulged through the cheap fabric of her dress, hiking the hem up in the front, giving him a long stretch of leg so bare it was almost indecent. She had a stack of towels balanced on an arm, and with her other, she pressed three pillows into her side.

He gave her a friendly smile, holding out his hands for the linens. "Thanks."

On the far bed, Owen lurched to a sit. "Whoa. I don't remember asking for the naughty maid, but okay. Night's looking up." He flashed a grin at Patrick, who winced.

The maid didn't even flinch. Without a word, she pushed into the room and dumped the pillows on Patrick's bed. The towels she carried into the bathroom, where she shoved them one by one on top of the others, in a metal holder hung on the wall.

Owen flopped back onto the bed. "What about the ice?"

"There's a machine at the top of the stairs." Her voice was high and feminine, thick with a country twang. When she was done with the towels, she tugged at the hem of her dress where it had ridden up, shimmying the fabric back down her hips before she stepped back into the room. "Bucket's on the dresser."

"I'll get it." Patrick grabbed the bucket and met her at the door. He gave her a smile on her way out, one she didn't return, and Patrick didn't blame her. What was it his mother always said? *You are the company you keep.* The maid probably thought he was just as bad as his friend, and hell, why wouldn't she?

Outside on the catwalk, the noise of the storm filled his ears, a wild roaring as loud as an oncoming train, whipping at his clothes and her hair. He had to shout over it. "I'm really sorry about my friend. Does it help to know he's really miserable?"

It was how Patrick had always justified the friendship, by telling himself that anyone that offensive had to be deeply unhappy inside. And Patrick wasn't the only one who thought so. Everyone on campus hated the guy, from the professors to the RAs to the students and janitors. It was a friendship built on convenience and pity.

But tonight, stuck in a cramped hotel room while they sat out the storm, Patrick had officially had it. This friendship had reached its limit. As soon as they got back to Athens, he was going to put some distance between them. Honestly, he should have done it ages ago.

The maid bounced an impartial shoulder. "I'm used to it. Like I said, top of the stairs." She pointed down the long catwalk behind him, then turned to go.

"Hang on." She paused, and Patrick dug three crumpled dollars out of his pocket and pressed them into her hand. "Thank you. For bringing up the towels and pillows, but mostly for not punching him."

Now, finally, she smiled. "Y'all have a good night."

He was about to say goodbye when her gaze flicked over his shoulder, and everything about her changed. He noticed how the smile dropped off her cheeks and her spine went suddenly straight, the way her hands curled into tight balls.

But it was her panicked expression that made him turn and look.

It was a man, tall and dominating, owning the far end of the catwalk. In the middle of a hurricane, the air hot and sticky with wind and the coming rain, he wore a suit and dark sunglasses like he was some kind of gangster, which Patrick was pretty sure he was. The sight of him sobered Patrick up instantly.

"Oh, shit," the maid said from behind him, and that's when he saw it, too. The gun dangling from a fist.

After that, it was like everything happened at once. The man, lifting his arm. The maid, lunging for the door they'd just come through. Both of them yelling as she fumbled for her keys, something about babies and wives and money. She gave the door a shove and sprang inside, and even in his vodka haze, Patrick was fast enough to follow, right before she slammed the door behind them.

She locked it and pressed both hands to her belly, panting slightly. "I'm gonna need y'all's help."

FORTY

NINA

Alex chooses a chair at the kitchen table, as far away as possible from me and the gun. It's pointed at her husband, but still. This is one thing about Unapologetically Alex that seems to be true. She really is terrified of the thing. I wonder if she knows it came from Patrick's T-shirt drawer.

"Red wine," I tell him. "The good kind. Don't try to pass off a bottle of crap, because I'll know."

Not that the Hutchinsons would have a bottle of crap in the house, but still. Châteauneuf-du-Pape. That's the one Alex would open. More than a hundred bucks a pop.

While Patrick selects a bottle from the wine fridge, I circle around the island to the barstools, sinking onto the one at the end.

"You know, at first I thought it was all an act," I say to Alex, perched like a coil on the edge of her chair. Tight limbs, straight back, muscles ready to run. She looks like a windup toy, one flip of a switch and she'll spring. "The cluelessness, I mean. The whole I-don't-know-anything-about-anything schtick. I thought it was as fake as the shit you spew on your feed."

"I may only show the most pleasant parts of me on Unapologetically Alex, but I've never pretended to be someone I'm not. Unlike you."

I glance at Patrick, loose and relaxed as he uncorks the wine, but it's an act. He's got one eye on Alex, his big body angling closer and closer. His phone buzzes in his pocket, starting and stopping again and again, but he ignores it, and so do I.

I keep my gun trained on him but pivot my gaze to Alex. "I'm not pretending."

"Of course you are. Your hair. The way you talk and move your body. Shannon even caught you pantomiming me in the backyard. You're literally wearing my clothes."

I look down at her blouse, her jewelry and shoes. Even the OPI polish on my toes is hers, a shiny hot pink I snagged from her bathroom drawer. "So? That's nothing compared to what your husband took from me. You owe me a lot more."

"*I* owe you?" Her cheeks sprout pink, and so does her neck, a splotchy pattern climbing up it. "For what? I gave you a job. And I get that the salary wasn't all that great, but up until that Krissie Kelly post you were the perfect personal assistant. You were on time, you were smart and a quick learner. I actually liked having you around."

"Okay, first of all, as much as I'd love to take credit for getting your ridiculous ass canceled, that's all on you. I didn't have anything to do with that Krissie Kelly post. Though I certainly get why you'd prefer to blame me. So much easier than thinking your precious self is capable of blowing up your own life. And second of all, this place belongs to me." I wave the gun around, indicating the kitchen, the house. Everything. "Seeing as the money Patrick used to pay for it is mine. He stole it."

"No, I didn't," he says. "I didn't steal anyone's money."

Alex ignores him. "I treated you like family. I fed you. I took you to nice restaurants, let you have your choice of freebies in the garage. What did I ever do to make you hate me so much?"

And there it is again, that burning rage that bubbled up every time I sat across from her at the carriage house desk. I didn't expect it when I first came here, looking for a way into Patrick's world. It was a nice little surprise, this volcanic thing I kept having to shove down. A constant reminder of why I was here.

"Seriously? I have a gun trained at your husband's head, and that's your question, why I hate *you*?" She nods, and I can't believe she's so clueless. Marrying this man. A liar and a thief. A murderer. "Not everything is about you, you self-centered bitch. Who cares what brand of face cream you use or that you're a Pisces sun and Scorpio rising? Social media isn't a personality. It's a giant, fucking waste of time."

Alex doesn't flinch at the *bitch* comment, doesn't so much as blink. Just looks away with a breathy laugh. "You really are Mister Fluffles, aren't you? Though the rape threats were a bit much, especially the ones aimed at the girls. Honestly, those were uncalled for."

Trolls are so easy to whip into a frenzy, gladly going wherever I pointed them with a few sufficiently nasty words. Last night one of my tweets hit a reach of more than ten million. Mister Fluffles was some of my best work.

"All the other stuff," she says. "The dummy bombs and the fake pictures and the body in the carriage house. That was you, too?"

I shrug. "It wasn't my original plan. But you make it so easy for people to hate you."

All those stupid affirmations she was always spouting off. *Small steps are big steps! You've already survived one hundred percent of your worst days! You're bigger than your fears! Good things are coming to you!* All those virtual high fives, like she's everybody's personal cheerleader, speaking in clichés and gushing platitudes.

It's ridiculous and completely unrealistic for the vast majority of her followers.

All to fill this desperate need for a million strangers to love on her because half a million wasn't enough. Three-quarters of a million wasn't enough. This house, this family, this *life*, isn't enough to feed the bottomless pit of need inside. Alex Hutchinson is one of *those* women, the kind who's always hungry for more, more, more. Nothing is ever enough.

I hate her. Unapologetically Alex sucking up all the air in every room, turning every subject back to her, hijacking every conversation. This woman and her Insta-perfect life, treating every moment like it's a colorful little window into her vacuous life. Even more than Patrick, I fucking hate her so much.

"And the blind item about my ex-husband?" she says. "Did you tip off DeuxMoi? Did you tell them where he is?"

"Ah. The mysterious ex." I smile, raise a brow at Patrick. "Looks like you're not the only one around here keeping secrets. You should probably delete all those files off your hard drive, by the way. Somebody's bound to find out."

"Whatever this vendetta you have for me is… Just leave the twins out of it."

"Oh my God, can we stop talking about you and your precious brats now? How much did Patrick tell you about why I'm here?"

Her gaze wanders to Patrick, filling three wineglasses with generous pours.

"Very little. Because none of this involves Alex," he says, picking one up from the counter. His voice is calm but his grip tight enough to snap the stem. "Let her go. I'll give you what you came here for."

He plunks the glass in front of me, and I don't miss the way he gauges the distance between his fingers and the gun in my hand. His old Smith & Wesson, too far for him to reach, too much marble in the way of a lunge. I'd see him coming from a mile away.

"Don't even think about it." I smile at the way his expression goes dark, the way his lips flicker. I look at Alex, still seated at the table. She's quiet, but I can see her thinking, her mind trying to wade through the maze.

"Anna Claire is your mother." At my impressed look, she shrugs. "Aaron didn't say anything about a pregnancy, but he did mention holding some things back, or maybe the autopsy missed it, I don't know. But she was murdered around the same time you were abandoned at the hospital. I would have been an idiot to miss it."

"Bravo. And Patrick killed her."

"That's a lie." Patrick swipes the two remaining glasses from the counter and carries them over to the table, handing one to Alex. She takes it and puts it right down, the foot chinking on the table. "Anna Claire was alive when I left. I saved her ass. Yours, too. I did, however, shoot your father. Cheers." He raises his glass in my direction, then tosses it back, chugging down half the liquid.

Alex twists on her chair. "You shot him? You actually killed a man?"

Patrick's answer is more for her than for me. His tone goes softer, and so does his expression. "Nina's father was a bad, bad man. A monster who managed to get a knife in Owen's side even though he was tied to a radiator. I killed him before he could do it to Anna Claire or me or anybody else that night."

He steps closer, but Alex holds him off with a hand. She stares up at her killer husband, leaning back as if to put more distance between them, and her forehead is wrinkled with doubt, with disgust. A thrill travels through me, because I did that. I put that look there.

"Owen was there? He knows about all this, too." She picks up her glass, shaking her head in disgust. "I always hated that guy."

I laugh. Finally something we can agree on. "Owen Chamberlain is an entitled prick, but he's not the one who pulled the trigger. That was your darling husband."

"For the last time, I didn't kill your mother. I was *helping* her, and I didn't take anything, her life or her money or anything else. I realize that you didn't exactly win the adoption lottery, and I'm truly sorry about that, but that's not on me. I did what Anna Claire asked me to. I saved your life."

Heat rises in my chest. "You *ruined* it. You killed my parents, you took their money, you left me in a trash can for some adoption agency to hand over to a pathetic woman who thought a baby was the way to stop her loser boyfriend from leaving. My life went to shit because of you."

"You actually killed a man," Alex says. "Murdered him."

"Not murder. Self-defense. Nina's father was a—"

"A monster who deserved to die, so you've said." I roll my eyes, the fury rising in me again. These people and their ridiculous masks, not one thing about them is real. The friendly finance guy is a cold-blooded killer. It's too absurd for words. I hold out my free hand, wriggling my fingers. "Alex, get over here."

Next to her, Patrick's spine goes straight. He clutches the glass in a white fist. "What for?"

"Just come here." When Alex doesn't move, I sigh, summoning a tone I've heard her use on the twins. "Don't make me ask you again."

But she does, that condescending bitch. She just sits there on her chair, watching me with those ridiculously blue eyes, so I pinch off a shot that misses her head by a foot. A dish in the cabinet behind her explodes, shooting splinters and shards at her back, raining them down on the table and floor. Alex screams and covers her ears, but it does the trick. She pops out of her chair and runs across the floor, not stopping until she reaches the island.

"I'll give you the money." Patrick glares at me over his wife's head. He steps closer, coming up at her back. "I'll give you whatever you want."

"I want the truth. Tell Alex what you did to my parents. Tell her what you stole from me."

It's not like I haven't asked him before. Hundreds of times. Thousands. But all those threats to blow up his high-profile career, his marriage, his *life*, haven't made him budge. Like every other time, Patrick lies, denies, deflects.

"Okay, and then what? What's the plan here?" he says instead, moving close enough to plunk his glass onto the island. "Because a detective has been looking for you. She seems pretty determined."

I shrug. "Not as determined as I am."

"And you told Alex your name was Anna Claire Davis. You used her social security number, which I then gave the IRS when I filed her taxes. Pretending to be another person is a crime, you know."

"Yeah, well so is murder and theft. Now tell her."

His teeth clamp down, his pallor the color of spoiled milk. Alex stands a few feet away, her arms stiff by her sides.

I roll my eyes. "Fine, I'll tell her. Patrick was in the room the day I was born, which, coincidentally enough, was also the day he murdered my parents and took off with their money, two million dollars in cash. All those stories about him sleeping in his car, all that bullshit about his first investment being a Ziploc bag of pennies he'd managed to save, it's complete bullshit. Patrick Hutchinson isn't a self-made man, not even close. He got a head start with two million dollars of stolen money. He's a thief and murderer and a fraud."

"Not true." His voice is loud, cutting through mine. "I didn't steal anything. She's lying."

"It's true," I say to Alex. "He stole it, and I have proof."

"No, you don't," he says, but now his voice doesn't sound so sure. He shakes his head, and a muscle clenches in his cheek. "There's no proof because it didn't happen."

"Yes, there is, because what Patrick doesn't know is that I took one of those DNA tests, you know where you spit in the tube? It led me to Matthew Davis of Bend, Oregon, a DNA match of 26.74 percent. Uncle Matt died last year, but his widow was awfully helpful. She told me that my mother wrote letters, long, detailed accounts of her life that she mailed off to her brother all the way on the other end of the country. I'll spare you the first fifty-six and jump straight to the last one. She wrote it the day I was born."

Behind me, Alex turns to Patrick. "Did you know about the letters?"

No, he didn't know about the letters. Isn't it obvious from the way his lungs have locked up? From the way his mouth is open but his chest is concrete, no air going in or out.

With my free hand, I pull an envelope from my bag. The paper is old, torn at the edges and along the crease, and I'm careful unfolding it, spreading it gently onto the marble.

I wink at Patrick. "Only a couple of pages. How bad can it be?"

I pick up the letter and begin to read.

FORTY-ONE

ANNA CLAIRE

October 13, 1994

Dear Matty,

That asshole came back. After all these months of me screaming into my pillow, Ricky showed up at the Star-lux like it was any other day, waving a gun around and shouting about his money. Not for me. Not for our baby. For the money. You'd think that would have made me furious, but the only thing I felt was tired.

Tired of cleaning other people's shit, tired of lugging this big belly around. Tired of yet another man tossing me to the curb like a hunk of trash, yet another generation of discarded Davis women. You can't raise a baby on a maid's salary, that's just a fact.

I told him I was keeping it—the baby and the money— which as far as I was concerned was our daughter's reward for him being such a miserable asshole. I told him he'd have to kill me for it, that he could kill both of us and still he'd never see one dollar, because no way in hell would he ever find where I hid it.

He was going to do it, too. That sweet man who stopped on the side of the road to change my busted tire was suddenly long gone, and the next thing I knew he was busting down the door. He shoved me so hard I saw stars, and the whole world turned upside down. And then one of those college boys whacked him upside the head with a vodka bottle. If not for them, I'd be dead.

We put Ricky in his car and took him to the fishing cabin, you know the one Daddy and Bubba Jax used to take us to. I talked them into carrying Ricky inside, and after that, things started happening really fast.

The baby came in the middle of a hurricane, in a cabin in the middle of a swamp, in a room filled with two million dollars, two college boys and her dead father's body. Before you get all freaked out, I should probably tell you I wasn't the one to pull the trigger. It was one of those college boys, the nerdy one, though you'd never know it from the way he handled Ricky. Just walked right up to him, pressed the gun to his pretty forehead and shot him boom dead. Just like that, like it was nothing. Didn't even flinch when blood spattered all over his face and clothes. And the irony of it is, a killing that cold would have made Ricky proud.

The boys tossed him in with the gators and then they took my baby and all that money and they ran, even though it won't do them a lick of good. Ricky's people will be looking for him soon, and they always get their man.

I know you're not the praying kind, but say a little one

for that baby girl, will you? I was crazy before, to think our lives could have ever been different.

xo,
Anna Claire

FORTY-TWO

PATRICK

For the longest time, no one says a word. Nina watches Alex with this weird smile, while Alex stares at me, her jaw slack, her cheeks fever bright. "You threw his body in the *swamp*?"

Her words put me right back there, in that rickety hunting cabin. The howling wind, the smell of blood and standing water. My own vomit splashing on my shoes.

"You fed a dead man to the alligators." Alex's voice is sharp in the quiet kitchen.

I find it a little strange that this is the part she's fixated on, not the part where I killed a man without even blinking, not the part where I took a woman's baby and a bag stuffed with cash—Nina was wrong about that part, it was more than three million dollars—but on the alligators in the swamp. I see them swarming, their big tails whipping up the murky water, and my stomach flips upside down, just like it did that night.

I groan, scrubbing a hand down my face. "What else was I supposed to do with him? I didn't exactly have experience hiding a body. I puked for months if it makes you feel any better."

"It doesn't." Alex picks up her wine, then puts it right back down. She's pissed, that purple pattern climbing up her neck again. "It doesn't help even a little bit."

As much as I love my wife, she doesn't get it. Alex has known about Nina's father for all of five minutes, while I've lived under his shadow for decades. I may have killed Ricky that night, but AC was right. His brother would have been all too eager to hunt me down, to do to me and Owen what he did to AC. Especially me, since I'm the one who pulled the trigger.

My gaze whips to Anna Claire's letter on the counter, on Nina's bag hanging open on the chair. I wonder if they're in there, the other fifty-six, and my fingers itch to toss them, bag and all, in the fireplace outside, then flip on the gas starter. Watch whatever else is in there go *poof*, up in flames.

Nina laughs, a deep, guttural sound that's not from amusement. An outburst of pent-up, poisonous emotion. "You're just as bad as your ridiculous wife, you know. Not one single thing about you is real. You claim to be this brilliant money guru, you brag about how broke you were when you invested that stupid bag of pennies. You tell everybody about how you grew pocket change into a million dollars by the time you were twenty-two, but it's a lie. Your entire career has been a lie."

"What Anna Claire wrote in that letter wasn't what happened, not even close. She left a lot of stuff out, the biggest being that the money wasn't hers. It belonged to your father. That's what they were fighting about, and he was about to kill her for it. Do you see now what we were up against? I killed him because otherwise it would have been *us* in that swamp. I'm the reason you're still alive."

Nina rolls her eyes dramatically. "Oh, come on. He wouldn't have killed his own daughter."

"You don't know what he was like."

"You keep saying that—*what he was like*—as if he was some kind of psycho."

Dark custom suit despite the heat. Sunglasses despite the storm clouds swirling overhead. I still see him sometimes when I close my eyes, raising that gun with a face twisted with fury. This was not a man to be fucked with.

Yet that's exactly what that pregnant maid did, got right up in his face and called him all sorts of awful names. While Owen and I watched, he backhanded her across her cheek. Just… whacked her hard enough to chip a tooth. He shoved her and she went sprawling.

It's also true what people say about time slowing down. Every second of what happened next is imprinted on my brain, playing across my memory in slow motion. One second I was standing against the wall, watching him aim a gun at her head, the next I was swinging a vodka bottle. I didn't think. I just did it.

And here's something else I think about a lot: What if Owen and I had kept on driving all those years ago? What if we'd never taken that exit to wait out the storm, what if we'd gone right instead of left? It's like that movie I once saw, where a butterfly flapping its wings whips up a hurricane on the opposite side of the planet. I've spent the past two and a half decades running from that hurricane, hoping it would never find me.

And now here she is, sitting on a barstool in my fucking kitchen.

"If he's so awful, then why didn't you call the cops?"

"Because I busted his head in with a vodka bottle. I thought I killed him. And that was before I knew that he was a sadist who got off on torturing people before he put them out of their misery. Who in his short, despicable lifetime killed hundreds of people just for looking at him the wrong way. He would have fed you to the gators piece by bloody piece, and he would have laughed while doing it."

And while Nina might not know her father's last name, I do, and a simple Google search will detail every one of his heinous crimes. The turf wars, the victims, innocent people gunned down in the street for being at the wrong place at the wrong time, the loved ones he dismembered and mailed to his enemies piece by piece. Women, children. Each body part serving as a promise: *you're next.*

All this time Nina has been in my house, pestering me for what she thinks I took from her, she used Alex and the twins like a carrot. Holding them over my head, threatening to tell, when really, my family finding out was the least of my worries. All this time, it's Ricky's family I've been worried about.

But whether she knows it or not, Nina is her father's daughter. It's why I've always believed her threats, her promises, that at some point she'd get even. She doesn't get her evil from a stranger.

"You're just saying that because otherwise it's murder. The nerdy clue wasn't much of a help, by the way. It could have been either of you two losers. But Owen confirmed it. He told me you're the one who pulled the trigger."

"He meant I pulled the trigger on your *father.*" I throw up my hands in frustration because fucking Owen. I can't believe we were ever friends. He has only ever been out for himself. I can't believe I was such an idiot.

I step to the island for the bottle of wine, refilling first Nina's glass, then my own, buying time to think. I don't need another drink. What I need is to get a grip on this conversation. Time to show a card or two.

"Look," I say, softening my tone. "For what it's worth, your mother was inconsolable when I left with you. She wanted nothing more than to keep you there with her."

"Then why didn't she?"

I carry the bottle over to Alex, topping off her glass, too. "Be-

315

cause she knew your father's people would be coming for her, and that's exactly what happened."

"No, she said those people would be coming for *you*."

I reach behind me, settling the bottle on the table, putting me directly behind Alex. "She meant they would be coming for all of us. She did the only thing she could think of to keep you safe. She told me where to take you, which hospital in Orlando, where to stash the money so she could find you both later. But I swear to you when I tell you I didn't keep a dollar of that money. Owen and I left it exactly where she told us to, in a self-storage unit west of Kissimmee."

"And the key?"

"I dropped it in an envelope and mailed it to her at the Starlux, just like we agreed. No note, just an envelope containing the key. She was supposed to call me for the address and unit number, but she never did."

Nina is silent for a long time, long enough I think she might believe me. Then she frowns and shakes her head. "That's not what Owen told me."

"Then Owen was lying."

"Owen says you never mailed the key. He says he never saw you do it, and who becomes a self-made millionaire at twenty-two? Not without some kind of a head start."

"Again. Owen is *lying*. He's a self-serving prick who will say anything to save his own ass."

I step up behind Alex, three feet between me and the gun. If I stretched out my arm, my fingertips would brush the lump under her shirt. I take another step, flexing my fingers so they're ready.

"I'm getting tired of this." Nina swings the gun to Alex, pointing it at her head. It's what her father would have done, what his brother would do if he were here. Nina's instinct is to go for Alex because she knows *her* life, the threat of *her* death, is a much better motivator. "This is your last chance to tell me where's the money. I want my goddamn money."

I look at Nina over my wife's head, and the world slows down, just like it did that stormy night on the second-story catwalk. My adrenaline recedes like an ebbing tide. Suddenly, I see myself as Nina sees me, as Alex certainly will after tonight. Standing in a house bought with stolen money. Clutching a glass of pretentious, hundred-dollar wine. The thief with the trailer park past, the cold-blooded killer who lied to survive.

The legal system may disagree, but there are things so much worse than killing a man, and that's watching the people you love most in the world go first.

"I already told you where. A self-storage unit west of Kissimmee—5135 Broadway Boulevard, Polk City, Florida. Unit 13."

And then my fingers find the hem of Alex's shirt.

FORTY-THREE

NINA

Your mother wanted you.

I sit here at Alex's spotless kitchen island, and Patrick's words hit me harder than they should considering he's a liar. A damn good one, too, good enough to fool Alex for all these years. That sound she made when I read the part about him throwing my father in the swamp, a breathy cross between a gag and a gasp. She didn't know of her husband's sordid past until tonight. That much was clear.

"I know you don't believe him," Alex says now, "but Anna Claire asked her brother to pray for you in her letters. That's got to mean something."

She smiles, and fuck me because this is her power, this ability to know exactly what people want to hear, this magical pull that draws people into her spell. I can't deny I'd enjoy putting a bullet in her brain. It wasn't the plan when I came here five months ago, but plans change.

First her, then Patrick.

He stands there, pressed up against his wife's back, and the look on his face makes me smile. The helpless fury, the undisguised terror—just like my father must have felt before the bullet tore through his skull, just like my mother would have felt when Patrick came back and did it to her. I want him to watch Alex die, too. I want him to feel all of it.

He steps around her, his gaze moving from the gun in my hand. "I promise you, Nina, you do not want to do this. This is madness."

"Give me the fucking money," I say with a stab of the gun. "It's mine."

And just to make myself clear, I slide off the barstool and step down the island until there is nothing but air between me and his insufferable wife, no marble or barstools—only a few feet between the gun and Alex's forehead, a clear shot.

She gives me a soft smile. "Unapologetically Alex would say you don't need your father's approval to find peace in your own heart. She'd say knowing either one of your parents isn't a prerequisite to finding gratitude for the bond you share. She'd tell you to pick yourself up, dust yourself off and hold your head high because you own your own magic. She'd say that's your superpower, you just don't see it yet."

I frown. Is she serious, or is this all part of her act? With Alex, it's hard to tell.

"But that's a load of crap, isn't it? Because life is messy, and no one person is an island. We get fired, we get divorced, we get addicted, a loved one gets cancer and dies. Shitty things happen, and where's the bright side then? A walk in the woods won't bring you peace. Being kind won't solve anxiety or grief. When someone is hurting, hitting them over the head with positivity doesn't help. In fact, it does the opposite—it invalidates what that person is going through, and oh my God, Mister Fluffles was right. Unapologetically Alex was full of shit."

Patrick's hand presses at the base of her spine. *Stop talking.*

I roll my eyes, cough up a disgusted sound. "You're not exactly helping your case, you know."

But Alex is getting herself worked up, and she doesn't even notice. "It's even worse than that. All these years I positioned myself as this…this ever-positive, ever-encouraging ideal, spouting off affirmations with authority when what the hell do I know? I am just as stupid and scared and insecure as everybody else. I certainly don't live by any of those things I preach, because when the tides turned and people started hating on Unapologetically Alex, my inner peace went to shit. My self-worth is based on what other people think, just like yours is, just like everybody's is. It's *normal* to want approval from the people around us. It's *human.* I just have a talent for telling people what they want to hear."

"So tell the truth, then. Say your husband is guilty. Say you'll give me my money."

"I'm standing here with a gun aimed at my face, and I just admitted I'm full of shit. Why would you believe anything I say?" Another smile.

"Then he needs to say it." I flick the barrel to Patrick, then back to Alex.

Next to her, Patrick is silent. His chest rises and falls, hot puffs of air as he stares me down.

"And then what?" she says. "The police will find you before you can spend a cent of your money."

I'm so focused on her that I see it too late, the way Patrick leaps forward, quick as a snake. One arm swings in my direction, and the other gives Alex a hard shove. She goes flying backward, limbs windmilling in a fight to stay upright, but it's a losing battle. Her shoes lose their grip on the polished hardwood, and she tumbles into the table. Chairs scatter, her legs tangling in theirs, and I don't hesitate.

I pull the trigger.

FORTY-FOUR

ALEX

Fear is the strangest thing. You're so busy obsessing about this perceived danger, dreading it, avoiding it, running from it, spiraling in it, that it becomes a living, breathing thing. That thing you were afraid of, it grows vague and slippery, and you lose sight of what it was that scared you in the first place. Like Patrick for all these years, bracing for a visit from Ricky's brother. Like me all those years ago, dragged by gunpoint into the bushes. I focused all my fears on the actual gun and not the person who was holding it.

Patrick's shot took Nina down, a direct hit to the shoulder. Her body dropped to the floor like a cinder block, sending the gun she was holding spinning across the hardwood.

Somehow, Patrick managed to keep a grip on his, the one he'd whipped out of my waistband while shoving me out of the way with his other hand. The gun was still clutched in his fist as he bled out on the kitchen floor.

It wasn't until I had snatched up both guns, one for each hand, that I had a taste of what it felt like to conquer my fears, to take control. I wasn't scared by all that firepower, not even a little bit. I called 9-1-1 and then I pointed both those guns at Nina's head without the slightest trepidation or tremor, holding steady until the windows lit up in swirling lights.

Now, though, the buzz of adrenaline has ebbed, leaving me cold and shaking on the living room sofa. I pull the throw someone draped over my shoulders tighter and watch two paramedics wheel a stretcher out the front door. Detective Bennett sits across from me, her gaze intense.

"Will she be okay?"

The detective nods. "Nina will live to see the trial. I'm very sorry about your husband."

Her sympathy prickles in the corners of my eyes, though I'm still in too much shock to produce tears just yet. I can hear them in there, a team of cops collecting evidence and taking pictures, though they were quick to cart his body out. I just hope they clean up the blood, that they don't leave behind a taped-up outline of his body on the floor. I don't know if I could bear it.

I lean back on the couch, far enough to block most of my view of the kitchen. If I turn my head to the left, I'll see it, Patrick's shoe, the laces that sometime in the struggle came undone. I make sure to stare straight ahead, gaze locked on the detective, who as of tonight is looking at me with a lot more compassion.

"What took you so long to get here? I pushed the button for the silent alarm when we came downstairs, more than thirty minutes ago."

"I don't know anything about an alarm. The first officer arrived two and a half minutes after your call to 9-1-1." She pauses to let that sink in, then switches gears. "Do you know the name Richard Cirillo?"

The name sounds oddly familiar. *Cirillo.*

"Isn't that the guy who was arrested last year?"

I struggle to recall the details but can only come up with the big picture. A shootout just outside of Tampa, multiple cops mowed down before they reeled in the big fish, a drug lord with tentacles in a bunch of southern states, including Georgia. For weeks, the news was plastered on every newspaper front page. WXBA even diverted Patrick's segment to make room for all the coverage. When I teased him about it, he said, "That asshole is the reason we will never live in Florida."

But the detective shakes her head. "That was Doug Cirillo, the younger brother. At one time second in command to Richard, who ran the family business until late 1994, when he suddenly vanished."

And just like that I understand. Richard, as in Ricky. Disappeared because two college kids tossed him in a swamp.

She lifts a notebook from the table next to her, reading. "'You're going to get us killed. Not just me and Alex and the girls. When he finds you, you're good as dead, too.'" Detective Bennett lifts her head, finding my gaze over the coffee table. "That's according to the lip reader, anyway. But it makes sense, considering. Back in the nineties, the Cirillos ruled the opioid trade up I-75, otherwise known as the Oxy Express. They had mules stationed all up and down Florida and Georgia, running pills into Tennessee, Kentucky, a big stretch of the Appalachians. Pillbillies, their customers were called. Until his arrest last year, Doug Cirillo ruled the drug trade in the southeast. He was a conduit for a whole slew of drug cartels, mostly from Mexico and South America. He's powerful and he's ruthless."

A drug lord. Patrick killed a drug lord and threw him in a swamp.

I clear my throat. "Nina says Patrick took two million dollars that belonged to Richard."

"Nina has been telling every officer at the station the same thing. Either way, your husband was protecting you. That's not to say his methods were okay or even legal, but he was right to fear the Cirillos. Even from prison, Doug has plenty of henchmen doing his business, all of whom would be eager to prove their loyalty by going after the man who killed his brother and stole two million dollars of his money. Doug is not the type of man to let someone walk away with either unscathed."

"How do you know all this? I was under the impression that Nina didn't know much about her father."

"I learned it from your husband, the day he came to report the stolen gun. He didn't mention the Cirillos by name, but he asked me about witness protection, and he dropped enough clues about the brothers that I put two and two together. But one of the requirements of WITSEC is that he be an actual witness, meaning he'd have to provide testimony of a crime. Your husband seemed to indicate that plenty of crimes were committed that night, but none that would qualify to provide him protection."

"Do you really think he stole the money?"

She shrugs. "We'll have someone look into his finances, but Judge Chamberlain backs up Nina's story. He says it's highly possible Patrick went back to retrieve the cash at some point."

A flash of heat hits me in the solar plexus. Owen Chamberlain is an arrogant ass who burns through money without a single thought as to where it came from. Country club dues, private school tuition, big house on one of the swankiest streets in Buckhead. There's no way he can pay for all that on a judge's salary and it can't all be family money.

What was it Nina called it? A head start. Two million dollars in cash, and Patrick officially a millionaire only a couple years later. And what about Owen's explanation whenever anyone questions his finances, which the media often does? I hear his jokey laugh, the arrogance in his tone as he brags on his brilliant financial adviser who just happens to be an old college buddy.

A money magician, he's always calling Patrick. The money guy from the nightly news.

Stupid, *stupid*.

I look around me, at the marble foyer and wooden floors and hand-carved crown molding I was so impressed by the first time Patrick walked me through this house, at the artwork and furniture we picked out together because Patrick wanted it to feel like my home, too. The diamonds on my fingers and the jewelry in a safe upstairs. Nina was right. None of this is mine.

"So now what?" I say, thinking of the broker I'll have to call in the morning, all the experts I'll have to hire to help me unwind Patrick's finances. The idea makes me exhausted.

The detective sighs. "Well, you're too visible for witness protection, and unless you know something that can tie Doug Cirillo to Anna Claire's murder, I'm not certain you'd even qualify. Atlanta PD can provide protection for a few days, around-the-clock security, until you can arrange a permanent solution. I can suggest a couple of local security companies, if you'd like."

For a moment, I'm struck dumb. "Hold on. You think we need bodyguards?"

"Doug Cirillo does not play around. He's going to catch wind of this if he hasn't already, and then he's going to send someone. And he won't be coming just for the money."

I think of the thirty-six terrifying minutes between me pushing the silent alarm and the sirens on the front lawn, and then I think of Anna Claire, and my heart beats faster in visceral terror. Poor, tortured Anna Claire, who endured all those hours of agony only to end up murdered. This house has a starring role on my Instagram page, the photos of every room hashtagged and geotagged and uploaded often enough I might as well put the address in my bio. And all those other defining details from the livestream, the fishing cabin and the baby and his big brother's name. How long until one of Doug's men show up at my front door?

I gasp. "The girls—"

"The girls are safe. They're currently in a patrol car headed here." She glances toward the kitchen, where a half dozen of her colleagues are still traipsing around. "I told them to take the long way, and not to come inside until I give the signal."

My heart settles, but only a little. I think about what their futures look like, going to school with bodyguards parked outside the classroom door, patrolling the sidelines of the soccer field, tagging along on their first dates. That's not a life I want for them, not an existence that's sustainable for any of us. The constant worry, always looking over our shoulders. I think about it, and I know it will make me crazy.

And there they are, finally, the tears. My eyes fill so fast that they spill over in a steady stream, not from fear or sorrow or grief, but from anger. It starts in the center of me and explodes outward, heating my skin and shaking my bones. I am seething, literally boiling over with rage, at Patrick for putting us in this position.

"Tell whoever's driving the girls they can come now. This involves them, too."

The girls arrive in a flurry of wails and tears. I gather them up by the front door, my breath hitching at the scene behind them on the front lawn. The cordoned-off area by the bushes, the crowd gathered on just the other side, neighbors standing around in sweats and pajamas with folded arms and worried faces. I slam the door, but it'll be ages before I can scrub the image from my mind.

I take my daughters by the hands and lead them straight up the stairs, leaving the kitchen for another time. The police are still in there, gathering up their things, but I can't face it now, not yet. Right now my only concern is for the girls.

We end up in the bedroom, seated in the middle of my bed, and I hold them close while they cry and cry. For Patrick, for the stepfather they loved and lost, for yet another fatherless future. There's no way to spin that, no positive affirmation that can change that hard truth. The only thing I can do is let them sob.

When finally they're quiet, I tell them the rest. What the detective told me downstairs about the Cirillos, that Ricky is dead and Nina is talking, which means Doug will find out soon enough. That even if what I suspect about Patrick isn't true, even if he didn't take the money, that won't matter to a man like Doug. He'll want it back, every single cent, plus interest.

"Do we even have that kind of money?" Penelope says, her eyes wide. She and her sister are sitting across from me, red-faced and clutching hands. "What'll we do? He's going to find us, right?"

Before I can answer, Gigi shakes her head. "Maybe he'll never know. Maybe we're getting all worked up for nothing."

"The whole entire world knows you don't have a tooth, and you don't think Doug is going to find out what happened here tonight? You heard Mom. This Nina chick is talking, and Doug is a drug lord. Drug lords don't take IOUs."

I don't push back on any of it, because Penelope is right. Doug will find us at some point in the not-too-distant future, and he'll send someone to demand we pay for what Patrick took from him. It doesn't matter that Patrick is dead, or that I didn't know about any of this until tonight, or that the twins and I don't share his blood. We are connected to Patrick. He loved us, and now we will have to pay for his choices.

I watch my daughters' expressions as they process this news, their faces shiny and fish-belly white. I take in their wet cheeks, their eyes swollen from crying, and I'm slammed with a wave of motherly love so fierce it almost knocks me backward. These are my babies, two little girls who right now want nothing more than for me to tell them they're safe. That we all are.

"Listen to me. I will not let anything happen to either of you." I take their hands, one in each of mine, and squeeze them hard. "We are going to get through this. I promise and swear to you we will."

"This is all my fault." Penelope moans, quick and guttural, pitching her body forward on the bed. "I did this. I'm the reason all of this is happening."

"Oh my God, Pen, self-centered much? Not everything is about you, FYI."

"But this is!" She shrieks the words, hard enough that Gigi flinches at her sister's outburst. The rest comes out in a rapid-fire spurt. "I'm the one who posted that video, Mom. The one of Krissie Kelly. You were passed out, and I got on your phone and wrote those awful words about her on your page. I never would have done it if I thought that anybody would get hurt. I only wanted Unapologetically Alex to shut up and go away. I hate her so much."

I don't defend my online persona, or try to explain once again that she is only a role, that I am not Unapologetically Alex, because that would be making this moment about me when it's not. My daughter lit the fuse that ended in the death of her stepfather, and now she feels responsible. I keep the focus where it belongs, on this confession she's been trying to unburden herself from for days now.

Because suddenly I'm thinking about her unexpected apology that night on the couch, when she'd caught me Googling the real Anna Claire. I'm thinking about the text message I found on her phone from her counselor, asking if she'd talked to me, about my conversation with Iris a few days later. Now, suddenly, it all makes sense.

"Penelope, the only thing you are guilty of is penning that post. No, it was not your Instagram, and yes, it was the wrong thing to do, but that post is the *only* thing you are guilty of. None of the stuff that happened afterward is your fault. Not the trolls, not the threats, not Patrick—" My voice catches on his name, but I hold her gaze, moving in close so she can't miss my next message. "This is superimportant. I need you to understand that the blame does not belong on you. It belongs on Nina. On Patrick. They are the guilty ones here. Not you."

She looks at me, and her eyes shine, fierce and firm. She doesn't believe me, not yet, but I won't let my daughter feel guilty for something she is not responsible for. If it's the last thing I do, I'll make sure she doesn't carry that weight.

"And listen. I'm just as guilty as you are when it comes to Unapologetically Alex. I knew you two weren't crazy about the way my job put the spotlight on you, on our family, but I didn't let that slow me down. I pretended not to see your discomfort, pretended not to notice all the signs you were throwing off that you didn't want to be a part of my page. It wasn't fair to either of you, and if I could erase us from the web, I would in a second. All that goes to say, I'm sorry, too."

The tears start up all over again, and I hold them close while the three of us cry it out. When they're done, when their sobs have died into occasional sniffles, I take both of their hands in mine. I didn't give them a choice before. The least I can do is give them one now.

"I need to tell you something. About your father. About the story I told you about him living on that commune in Vermont." I pause to haul a bracing breath. "It's not true. Daniel... your father is in prison."

I watch their faces as they process this news—that I've lied to them, that their father didn't just disappear, that he is a criminal and locked away like Doug. The drug lord who will be coming after us soon.

They exchange a look, but Gigi is the first to speak. "What did he do?"

"Grand theft auto, which...and I wish it was as innocent as the video game. Unfortunately, he stole a bunch of really expensive cars, which made him a repeat offender. He has another ten years before he's up for parole."

"Okay," Gigi says. "But you're allowed to write letters from prison, aren't you?"

And this right here is why I've never told them the truth. How after Daniel vanished, after the PI I hired to find him led me to the Ohio State Penitentiary, I was on the next flight to Akron. It didn't take much prodding to get Daniel to sign over his parental rights. I only had to offer to pay for the attorney. I couldn't afford it, could barely afford to keep a roof above our heads, but I paid every penny of that bill, anyway.

I nod. "Yes, baby. You are."

"So he could have. He could have written to us if he wanted to."

Yes, he could have written to them. I don't know what I would have done had I found that letter in the mailbox—burned it, ripped it to shreds, placed it on their pillow at bedtime. The point is, he could have written, but he chose not to. For four years now, he hasn't reached out to them at all, and I will never forgive him for it. But maybe the twins will.

"You two are old enough to decide for yourselves what kind of relationship you want to have with him. If you want to reach out to him, I'll support that. If you want to visit, I'll take you there. No questions asked."

They weigh this, but not for long, their expressions settling into the usual fierce anger whenever his name comes up. A defense mechanism, I know, a hard and lonely shield so they don't have to grapple with the terrible, impossible hurt of being abandoned by a parent. Because how do you grapple with that?

Only twelve years old, and already they've given up on their father. It's part of why I loved Patrick so fiercely, because he showed them how a father was supposed to be. He opened up their hearts to that kind of love. And now it's just me, the sole parent again. With time, we'll find our way, but my heart breaks for all three of us.

"You don't have to decide now. You can decide tomorrow,

or next month, or ten years from now, or never. It's up to you, and there's no hurry. And whatever you do or don't decide, I will support that, I promise. But we do have a decision we need to make tonight, one that doesn't involve him but your stepfather. After what happened here tonight, Detective Bennett suggested personal security."

Gigi grimaces. "You mean, like, bodyguards?"

"I'll get us the very best. Our very own personal secret service."

"What, like we're the president's daughters or something?" Penelope's nose wrinkles. "No thanks."

"That sounds awful," Gigi says.

I nod, because I agree. It sounds awful, but so does death.

"I know this is a lot for you to take in. You're both still so young, and it's unfair of me to weigh you down with these kinds of decisions, but we can't wait until you're ready. We have to think about this now. We have to decide how we want to live our lives."

In the end, it's their idea, not mine.

FORTY-FIVE

Four months later

I stand at the edge of the soccer field, watching Gigi blow past a thick line of fullbacks and stoppers. She fakes left, then sprints right, kicking the ball through a defender's legs and skirting around her to pick it back up, barreling toward a slightly pan-icked-looking goalie.

The coach cups his hands around his mouth and shouts, "Shoot it!"

I pull out my cell, snap a few pictures, then slide it into my back pocket. Later, I'll drop them onto Gigi's phone, so she will always remember this moment. Pictures that won't get filtered or cropped or uploaded, not unless she chooses to. These shots are for Gigi and me and no one else.

She rears back, kicking the ball in the upper corner of the

net without breaking her stride. Her team goes wild, but my eyes are not on them, they're on the junior Olympics scouts on the opposite side of the field. They press their heads together, and I don't have to wonder what they're saying. They want my daughter, that much is clear, and Gigi would love nothing more than to be a part of their team.

Automatically, my gaze slides up the sideline to her twin, seated on a folding chair, her nose in a novel. In the days following that awful night in the kitchen, Penelope came to me with another confession, that she wanted to quit soccer. All these years I've been plunking down a small fortune to enroll her in traveling teams, all those lessons and uniforms and cleats she outgrew faster than I could reorder a new pair, and Penelope detested the game. She told me this with a crumpled brow and worried eyes, and I laughed and kissed her on the forehead. "No more soccer for you, then," I said, and that was that.

We're a team, the three of us, and we're navigating our new world together.

A new world that includes honesty, but also constant risk—one the girls are all too aware of, thanks to Nina. For months now, she's been making waves from her prison cell where she awaits trial—for the murder of Patrick and Little Kathi, for armed burglary, for criminal impersonation and a whole host of other charges. There she tells anyone who will listen about the tragic Anna Claire and her missing money. About Ricky, whose body ended up in an alligator's belly. About her uncle Doug, who knows everything. I learned this from Aaron, who visited him in a South Florida prison.

The judge has since put a gag on Nina, but by then it was too late. *People* magazine had already published the last letter from Anna Claire, and for months now the other fifty-six have been crawling across the internet. Her story is way out there, which means ours is, too.

The clues Aaron and Detective Bennett managed to track

down back up a lot of Anna Claire's story. Ricky's BMW, dragged from the same swamp where Bubba Jax once owned a cabin, pages and pages of transcribed interviews with former neighbors and fellow maids at the now defunct Starlux Motor Lodge, all of them with a common refrain—a mystery man, one with money and a fast car. One they all assumed was the father of the baby growing in AC's belly. When she first disappeared, that's where people thought she'd run off to, with him for her happily-ever-after.

I can see it now, so clearly. A violent fight in a hotel room, the younger Patrick caught in the crosshairs. Of course he'd rush to defend a pregnant girl. That's just the kind of man he was, one who'd let a soaked woman skip the line at the valet stand, who dished financial advice to help people grow their bank accounts. Patrick couldn't have known what he was getting himself into that night, couldn't have had any idea the kind of storm he'd summon by stepping into that fight, but he was not the type of man to have turned away.

But was he the type to steal her money?

Not immediately, no. Of this I am certain.

But when weeks turned into months turned into years and she still hadn't called, did he go back to empty out that unit? It would have killed Patrick to know the money was just sitting there, gaining dust and no interest.

So far, though, no one has been able to cough up any evidence that one cent of his wealth didn't belong to him. Not Detective Bennett, not any one of the forensic accountants I hired to do a deep dive, not Doug Cirillo, who denies knowing anything about anything, which of course he would. But just because he can't claim the drug money doesn't mean he's willing to let it go.

And this all happened twenty-five years ago, with a pile of unmarked cash. Patrick would have known how to cover his tracks, how to spread the money so as not to get noticed, how to make it look like his so no one would ever know. I'd like to think he was telling the truth when he said he left the money in a storage unit west of Kissimmee, but I've also been there, to Polk City, Florida. I drove up and down Broadway Boulevard a dozen times, but 5135 doesn't exist, and there's no self-storage facility at all on that street.

Which makes me wonder, because there's no way Patrick made a mistake. No way he was so panicked he accidentally fudged the address. If there's one thing I know about my husband, it's that he never forgot a number.

Owen, the last living witness, wasn't much help. In his tearful resignation as Fulton County judge, Owen confirmed most of the story—the fight he and Patrick landed in the middle of, the pregnant maid they saved, the baby they delivered in a swamp and dropped at an Orlando hospital. In Patrick's absence, Owen took credit for saving Anna Claire, though he denied all the crimes. The money. The murder. He put the blame for those firmly on Patrick.

"This team is a much better place for Gigi," the man next to me says, his eyes on the game. On my daughter, sprinting up the field with the ball. "She's really thriving under this new coach."

It's not the first time I've spoken to him, and I'm sure it won't be the last. When I first noticed him, in the checkout line at Kroger, he fit the image of an upscale Buckhead male—designer jeans, good hair, eyes sparkling with interest. The face of a man who zeroes in from the other side of the bar, watching me like I was the only woman in the room. I thought he was there to hit on me.

Now, I see him everywhere. At the Starbucks. In the carpool line at school. At the four-way stop and jogging past the house. Every time our eyes meet, I think of Patrick, of the terror he must have felt all those years, looking over his shoulder for the men hiding in the shadows. If nothing else, it's provided me with an understanding of his plight, given me a fresh, new perspective. The fears that kept my husband awake at night are mine now. I live with them every day.

"You can tell him the house sold." I keep my gaze on the field, but the heat coming off me is palpable. I can't see it, but I know it's there, the redness creeping over my skin, up my neck and face. "I don't have an exact closing date yet, but it'll be sometime next month."

It's the last big chunk of what I owe his boss. What *Patrick* owed. In the past few months, I've cleaned out his savings, sold off his stocks, cashed in his retirement fund, hammered a for-sale sign in the front yard to cough up the ungodly amount Aaron agreed to with Doug. It's a *lot*, way more than Nina demanded, but I'll gladly pay every dollar if it means my daughters get to live without fear.

That they get to live, period.

"Mr. Cirillo will be glad to hear it, though I'll admit, I'm going to miss this." He pulls out a pack of Juicy Fruit, offers me some. "The soccer, I mean. I'm a big fan."

I slide a stick of gum from the pack, peeling open the wrapper. "Does that mean you'll be leaving us alone?"

He laughs. "You offend me, but yes. Once you've met your end of the bargain, so will Mr. Cirillo."

I don't believe him, not for a second. Not for one second will I ever let my guard down, or trust that a man who'd done such horrific things to Anna Claire wouldn't go back on the bargain he and Aaron struck and send someone to do the same to me or the twins. For the rest of my life, I will operate as if they're watching, because they always will be.

The ref calls the game with a sharp whistle, and the players file off the field. I fold the gum into my mouth, toss the wrapper in the trash and meet the twins at the car.

Gigi slides onto the backseat, still breathing hard. "What's for dinner? I'm starved. Omigod I have so much homework."

The old Unapologetically Alex would have pointed out the

glorious day, or told her to be grateful for the sunshine and her strong, capable legs. To not dwell on what we've lost but to be thankful for what we have, to cherish the memories we hold of their stepfather.

But I meant all those words I said to Nina that awful night: that kind of positivity is toxic. There's no way to put a happy spin on a loss like ours, no way to pick the positives out of a steaming heap of shit. The girls would hate me for even trying, and so would my followers.

Two million at last count, thanks to all the press. Unapologetically Alex, the Instagram influencer turned tragic widow paying for her husband's mistakes, is everybody's favorite influencer again. The internet is a fickle, fickle place.

It was the girls' idea to reinvent my public persona, to shake off some of her dust and make her relevant again. If I could do it once, they said that night on the bed, I could do it again, and as much as they hated the old her, they couldn't deny I have a talent for knowing what people want to hear.

"Do you understand what you're saying?" I asked them more than once. "I'm going to have to address what happened here tonight. People are going to want to know how we're doing. How you two are coping." Keeping Unapologetically Alex alive meant putting us out there all over again, and I wanted to make sure they understood the consequences.

"Yes, Mom," Penelope said. "Be her, but better. G and I will help."

Gigi nodded. "How else are we going to pay back the money?" *We.* A team.

And so Unapologetically Alex is going stronger than ever, a new and improved version of my online persona—one that uses her story to empathize rather than impress. Content as a kind of confessional, and I encourage my followers to share their own stories in the comments, where they mention my name in the same breath as Brené and Glennon and Martha. An Instavangelist, some critics call me, but I'm not trying to be anybody's moral authority. I just happen to know there are millions of women out there just like me, eager to unload their own traumas, desperate for others to hear and understand their pain.

Unapologetically Alex hears, and she definitely understands.

And like the girls said, we can certainly use the paycheck.

I shove the car in Reverse and back out of the lot. "I haven't even thought about dinner. What are you in the mood for?"

"Mexican," Gigi says. "No, pizza."

I glance at Penny, who shrugs. Pizza, it is. I point the car to our favorite, Mellow Mushroom.

There are still so many unknowns, a million lingering questions. What happens when people tire of my story, when Unapologetically Alex grows old and stale all over again, or people migrate to a new social media platform? Can I stay in demand, keep all those new followers engaged? Will I ever stop feeling so angry?

"Anger is a secondary emotion," my therapist keeps telling me. "Dig deeper and find the emotion fueling it."

But I'm not ready to dig deeper yet, not when rage carries such a comforting weight. It's why I've let it plant roots under my skin, where it grows uncontrolled like a weed. For months I've tried to reconcile the Patrick I knew with the one who dragged me into his drama, who dragged my daughters, but I can't. I adore him for leaping to the defense of a pregnant stranger, and I'm furious that he put us in this position. I hate him and I love him for what he did.

But mostly I miss him, and for that I won't apologize.

I pull into the lot, squeezing Patrick's old SUV into an open spot, when suddenly Gigi lurches forward on a gasp. She presses her upper body between us and her face into the windshield, and my heart stops. My lungs lock up. I'm scanning the lot for him, for a weapon, when my gaze lands on the same thing Gigi sees.

Two women on the terrace, causing a scene. The shorter one

sinks to a knee, holding up something sparkly between two pinched fingers, the other stands in front of her, nodding and crying. The women embrace and the crowd cheers, including Penelope next to me, Gigi on the back seat.

"For the Insta," Penelope says, handing me my phone. "Just make sure to give me photo cred."

I look down at the snapshot of the two women, caught in the exact moment of *yes*, and I don't want to think my daughter is better at this than I am, but she's certainly faster on the draw. While I was spiraling in fear and regret, Penelope reached for the camera and captured the perfect shot. Already I can see the caption, something snappy about letting go and new beginnings.

And maybe that's the lesson here, that even in the midst of the messiest, scariest lives, there are moments of beauty, and you have to be relentless in snatching them up. In holding them up to the world as proof that, despite everything, you can still feel joy. Even if you're not quite there yourself.

The things we say. The things we believe. Perception is reality, nobody knows this better than me.

I follow the girls into the restaurant, where we place our order and find a corner booth in the back. I watch them across the table, their long, copper curls trailing halfway down their backs, their matching faces lit up by their cell phone screens, and this little slice of normalcy cools me out, centers me.

Some days, I think he must have known what he was doing when he called me up, as I was dropping an envelope with the valet's tip money into the mailbox. Dragging me into his drama, smearing my life, the twins' lives, with his peril. Sometimes I think if he loved me as much as he said he did, if he truly wanted the best for me and the girls, he wouldn't have taken that risk.

Other days, I understand.

Because I felt it, too, that day at the valet stand, an attraction that was too strong to shake. By then Patrick had spent two decades waiting for somebody to show up at his front door—the police, a Cirillo—and all that time, nobody came. Maybe all those years weakened his resolve and made him reckless. Made him think that when real love came along, it was worth the risk. Maybe one day, I'll think it, too.

What I do know is that he should be here right now, sliding into the booth next to me, swiping the pepperoni from my slices and joking about how he should buy stock in this place as much as the twins want to eat here. There will never come a day when I don't miss that man, when his lies or his loss feels acceptable.

But now, sitting here across from the girls, I think of him, and I smile.

Patrick was right. The twins are the reason for everything.

"Let's turn off our phones," I say, dropping mine into my bag on the bench next to me. "I'd much rather live in the moment."

HELP WANTED

Atlanta-based influencer seeks smart, upbeat, supercompetent, do-it-all, right-hand-human who can comfortably bridge the roles of personal assistant, executive aide and unwavering secret keeper. Experience in social media marketing is appreciated but not necessary, much more important you be trustworthy, discreet and able to maintain confidentiality at all times, always, in every single situation. Salary is negotiable, but the NDA you will sign (airtight) and background check you will submit to (comprehensive) are not, and you better believe I will be checking references. Sorry, but also really not sorry.

★ ★ ★ ★ ★

ACKNOWLEDGMENTS

I wrote this story in 2021, well into the second year of the pandemic. Yes, we'd stopped washing our groceries by then, but life still felt so much smaller than before. No travel. No parties. No fun. Where my first pandemic book was a welcome distraction from the world's woes, with this one I had to fight for every word. A story about an Instagram influencer, no less. As the pandemic raged on outside my office windows, I wondered if anyone would care about follower counts when the real world was a dumpster fire.

And then I realized that was the whole point of my story, and the lesson Alex needed to learn. When your world turns into a dumpster fire, it forces you to stop and adjust. To reassess your priorities and drill down to the very essence of what's essential in life. People. Family. As Alex learned in her story—as we learned in ours—the rest is just noise and fluff.

Laura Brown, your insightful edits were spot-on, and your guidance throughout led me to the story I was hoping to tell. Thank you for your belief in me and my writing, and for elevating this story in every way. This book is so much better because of you.

Mega thanks, too, to my agent, Nikki Terpilowski, for the many (many!) reads and suggestions. You've been with me since the beginning—day one, book one. Thank you for always having my back and wanting the very best for me. We make an excellent team.

Endless gratitude goes to my publicity gurus, Emer Flounders and Emi Battaglia, to copy editor extraordinaire Gina MacDonald and all the other editors who saved me from myself, to all the tireless folks working behind the scenes at Park Row. It's true what they say, it really does take a village. I'm so thankful to have found a home at Park Row.

Big, squishy hugs to Kris and Shannon Tuttle, whose winning bid got Shannon the dubious honor of having a character named after her. Shannon, I hope I did you proud.

To all the readers out there, to the book groups and book sellers and book lovers everywhere, thank you for spending your time and hard-earned cash on Alex and AC's story. I have the best job in the world, and I owe it all to you.

And finally: my people. Ewoud and Evan and Isabella. I couldn't be prouder of you three, and I could not possibly love you more. It didn't take a pandemic for me to know you are the very essence of everything.